Tribes of the Orange Sun

Tribes of the Orange Sun

Gene Shiles

Writer's Showcase

San Jose   New York   Lincoln   Shanghai

Tribes of the Orange Sun

Writer's Showcase
an imprint of iUniverse, Inc.

For information address:
iUniverse, Inc.
5220 S. 16th St., Suite 200
Lincoln, NE 68512
www.iuniverse.com

ISBN: 0-595-20319-1

Printed in the United States of America

To the memory of my dad.

Chapter 1

Adam

The engines hummed contentedly. Passenger Adam Hampton, his head back in the headrest, dozed in his seat. He stirred when a voice over the cabin speaker intruded. "We're passing the city of Louisville," the crew manager announced, "on the left."

Adam opened his eyes and straightened up. Seated next to a left-side window, he raised a hand to block the morning sun and glanced down at what he guessed to be the city center far below. He rubbed his eyes, and then looked around the cabin. Not one of the three hundred or so other passengers would show much interest, he told himself. He could see only a few of them, but he knew. Just about everyone had forgotten—or simply disregarded—the Louisville incident, even though nearly a hundred people had died in the panic and riots two years ago.

He looked out the window again. It hadn't been a true supply problem, he thought. A data error had delayed the city's weekly food deliveries. The government's claim, to this day, was that it "can't happen again." The private news services had called the incident a "one-in-a-billion chance event." Adam shook his head. He had often wondered if he was the only one on Earth who understood the real meaning behind the Louisville incident.

The city fell back behind the wing, but Adam believed he had been able to pick out the city center from its surroundings while it was in sight. He glanced at his watch, and then tried to put Louisville out of his thoughts. The craft would set down at Earth City in about thirty minutes, and he could use a little more sleep before he reported in for his new job. He had boarded before dawn. He leaned back, closed his eyes and listened to the hum of the engines.

*   *   *

The waiting line in the air terminal was long and Adam was last, but the line moved swiftly. He smiled when he reached the end, and rested his datacase on the table between himself and a uniformed guard.

"How long do you plan to stay in the city, Sir?" the terminal guard asked.

"I guess I'll be here a while," Adam said. "I have a new job."

"Then I'll have to see your permit." The guard stepped to his left, toward the computer display screen and hand analyzer at one end of the table.

Adam opened his datacase, took out several documents and handed them to the guard. He watched while the man checked the documents against information brought up on the *photronic* display screen, and complied when asked to place his hand on the analyzer.

"Everything looks proper, Dr. Hampton," the guard said. He handed the documents back to Adam. "I apologize for the delay. We've had to make some new rules."

"That's all right. I understand the problem." Adam had to look up at the guard, who was considerably taller than his own 185-centimeter frame. He wasn't used to that.

"It's over sixty million." The guard smiled. "That's just the city proper."

"And still growing," Adam said. He shook his head and added, aloud but mostly to himself, "How are we feeding them all?"

Adam saw the guard glance at a half-wrapped and half-eaten *barquille*, a popular kind of machine-produced sandwich, on the table next to the analyzer. "I've never gone without, Dr. Hampton."

Adam winced. An hour or so earlier he had flown over Louisville. He expected only a blank stare if he mentioned the two-year-old incident, so he simply grumbled, under his breath, "I'm talking about the whole world."

The guard shrugged. "But I could use a little more elbow room," he said. "I see you'll be working for Administrator Avery's office."

"I don't yet know just what I'll be doing." Adam stuffed the documents back into his datacase. "They have a new plan to handle this situation."

The guard looked at him. "A new plan?"

"I already told you everything they told me. Sorry." Adam heard shuffling behind him. He glanced back and saw that other travelers, from another flight, were getting in line.

"They're a busy bunch," the guard said. "I won't delay you any longer." He smiled. "Welcome to Earth City, Dr. Hampton."

*   *   *

Adam departed the city shuttle, or *chute*, that had carried him from the air terminal, climbed a flight of stairs and stepped out onto the pavement. He consulted his pocket locator for directions and proceeded, on foot with datacase in hand, toward his destination. A brisk wind blew between the surrounding tall buildings, but it was at his back and pleasantly warm.

While he walked, he remembered his only previous visit to Earth City and smiled. His father, who had referred to the city by its historic name of Atlanta, had taken him to the Great Earth Zoo on his seventh birthday.

How he had loved the great cats and other large animals at the zoo! He recalled how fascinated he had been when his father told him that such animals had once roamed freely, without support and control from people.

Wild animals? Large animals running free, just like the small ones? His father had explained such things.

He thought of the ten years that had passed since the accident that had taken his father from him, and the more than eighteen years since that zoo trip. Now Earth City, the seat of Earth Government, was nearly the biggest on the planet. It didn't look at all like he remembered. Even though the city had grown in those eighteen years, the buildings had looked bigger back then.

Those memories were from the perspective of a child, he told himself. He dodged and weaved past others on foot in the crowded streets. They must be government workers, he thought, since most of the surrounding buildings housed government agencies. He sidestepped another hurrying pedestrian, turned a corner and reached the building described by his locator.

A pair of lion statues guarded the entrance to the white marble building. He hesitated and gently patted the head of one of the lions. He then climbed a short stone staircase. He hesitated again, and then entered the building and approached the reception desk. He brushed back his hair with his hand, grinned and said, "It's good to see a real live receptionist. I'm Adam Hampton."

"Hello, Dr. Hampton." The receptionist smiled. "And welcome! We've been expecting you. Oh, Dr. Avery wanted to see you as soon as you arrived. I'll have someone show you to his office." She turned to her voice-visual terminal and said a few words.

A man soon appeared, and Adam recognized him from a recent conference. The two exchanged greetings, thanked the receptionist and took a short ride on the jet lift. On the building's top floor, Adam followed through a maze of hallways to a pleasantly furnished waiting room.

His companion pointed to a large double door. "That's Bill's office. I have to get back to work, so I can't go in to introduce you. But no need. Oh, don't get lost in there."

"Lost in there?" Adam asked.

"You'll see."

"Thanks, Stan. Good seeing you again." Adam smiled.

Stan returned Adam's smile. "You too, Adam. We'll get together later this week. You'll be working with us on the planning."

Adam hoped to clear up some of the mystery before meeting Avery. "Stan, I haven't been told anything."

"Yeah. Better ask Bill. But you may have to wait for the meeting. See you then." Stan turned and headed back down the hall.

Adam didn't pursue it. He nodded, and then turned and faced Avery's office entrance. A sign by the door read: ADMINISTRATOR, EARTH POPULATION ADMINISTRATION. A photronic receptionist terminal stood next to the door.

He hesitated a moment. He had just graduated from Earth University with a doctoral degree in population science. The administration had offered him the job a few months earlier; completion of the doctoral program had been the only requirement. *Why did they choose me?* he asked himself. Many others were more qualified for such a high level position, he thought, even though he didn't yet know what he would be doing. Now the administrator wanted to see him even before he had a chance to relax after his long trip. Avery had been administrator for nearly thirty years; he likely would remain so for the foreseeable future. Adam knew he had better be able to get along, even though he opposed Avery's most basic policies on population growth.

Adam looked at the photronic receptionist, and told himself to stop daydreaming. It was time to meet the administrator. Stan had called him "Bill," he assured himself. That didn't sound like an autocrat. He quickly straightened his tunic with his right hand, and then glanced at the datacase in his left. He placed his right hand on the horizontal screen of the receptionist.

"Come in, Dr. Hampton. I've been expecting you," said a voice from the receptionist.

Adam stepped up to the metallic door. It buzzed as it parted in two before him and slid into the side walls. He entered the large office, and the leaves and branches of a potpourri of potted plants appeared to jump out at him. Some displayed brilliantly colored flowers. Green ferns reached almost to the ceiling, and the reds and whites of coleus accented the lower levels.

He stopped just inside, and noticed a flowery fragrance while he glanced around. The plants lined much of the wall space, and a few even graced the middle of the floor. Data cabinets created a small maze in one corner and several desks and chairs lay here and there, but the greenery and floral colors took command.

Through the few windows not blocked by leaves and branches, he saw only the tall buildings of Earth City.

He jumped when the voice sounded again, this time not from a machine. "You're admiring my jungle."

Adam peered past the greenery. He tried to find the source of the voice.

The voice went on. "The experts insisted that most of this stuff wouldn't grow well in here. But I simply applied the best of our technology."

Adam spotted the administrator seated behind a large desk at the far end of the room. Several potted geraniums adorned the desk, and a shaft of late morning sunlight illuminated the man's full head of white hair. The now embodied voice continued, "This is an elixir for my mind, Dr. Hampton."

Adam nodded.

He knew that Avery was just over ninety-one years of age, but the man appeared fit and strong. Although average life spanned more than a hundred years, he thought, most people retired from active work by age eighty. The man at the desk looked like he could handle whatever came his way, and do so for a long time to come. Adam knew that much came the way of this office.

"Well, speak up, young man!" The man at the desk stood up and leaned over the desk toward Adam. "At least say 'hello' or 'pleased to meet you.'"

"I apologize, Sir," Adam said. He grinned. "I'm happy and proud to meet you, Sir. And I like your jungle."

"Come in. All the way, that is." Avery pointed to a fat couch next to his desk. "Sit down here under the impatiens." He smiled. "By the way, call me Bill. And may I call you Adam?"

Adam stepped up to the desk. "Yes, please do, Sir—Bill." He shook hands with Avery, put his datacase on the floor and sat on the couch.

"Let's talk a while. Then I'll show you around." Avery sat down and leaned back in his chair. "I understand that in your dissertation you explained how the advance of technology allowed our human population to grow to its present level—and still produce enough of life's necessities to go around."

Here it comes, Adam thought. He responded hastily. "Just the past two hundred years. Since the very late twentieth century."

"I'm curious," Avery said. "Why did you pick that particular starting point?"

"That was the beginning of the era called the information age. I guess I figured it'd be easier to research the data after that time." Adam leaned back in the couch. He had been sitting on its edge. He craved a cup of coffee, but Avery hadn't offered any. He didn't ask.

"Sounds logical. It could've taken years longer." Avery smiled.

"Yes. But that wasn't my motivation," Adam said. "I mostly wanted a way to be sure I had all the relevant data." He looked around for the cup of coffee that wasn't there.

"You did all that very well," Avery said. He picked up a small photronic disk from his desk, and then put it back down.

Adam believed that the disk contained his dissertation. Avery had prepared for this encounter, he thought.

"But your basic conclusion," Avery asked, "was that technology had just barely kept up with needs?"

"Yes, Sir. Bill. I believe that we're reaching a crisis. More than twenty-four billion people! Science and resources just can't keep up indefinitely." Adam, on the edge of the couch again, hesitated.

Avery smiled, and Adam understood this to mean "Go ahead, I'm listening." He went on. "We're holding on to technology by a thread. I firmly believe that the voluntary rules of the past century and a half cannot work. In the long term. These barely slowed growth."

"But the rate has slowed," Avery said. "I would say considerably."

Adam had the growth numbers memorized. On average, Earth's population had more than doubled in the twenty-first century and nearly doubled again in the nearly completed twenty-second. The time for the population to double had been much shorter during the twentieth century, and that greater rate had continued only into the very early twenty-first. He conceded to himself that Avery was technically correct. The "rate" had decreased. But when one looked at absolute numbers, he thought, growth remained a problem. He could argue that numerical point with Avery some other time, he told himself. "We must have zero growth," he said, "or even a reversal." He added, hastily, "By natural attrition, of course."

Avery nodded.

Adam raised his voice. "I believe we've reached a point where Earth Government must impose involuntary measures. Scientific measures. There are effective methods." He stopped abruptly.

"Take it easy, Adam." Avery smiled and pointed to the small disk on his desk. "You've done a fine job, and you'll have plenty of opportunity to express yourself."

"I apologize." Adam relaxed back in the couch. "I guess I just have strong feelings about it."

"I will agree that Earth has had the benefit of what could be called a best case scenario," Avery said. "Since the middle of the twenty-first century things have fallen into place very fortuitously." He added, "But you must give technology some credit, too."

Since the middle of the twenty-first century indeed! Adam thought. The first half of that century hadn't been fortuitous. More than two billion people had died from causes directly tied to human numbers.

He hadn't found that number listed in the records. Instead he had determined it by painstaking addition from thousands of individual sets of records. He had published his findings, but they had been generally ignored.

Since the middle twenty-first century science and technology had attacked that death rate, with vigor and very successfully. They had never, he told himself, seriously assaulted the birth rate. *The problem? Those disasters had been spread out in time, fifty years; and in space, at scattered locations earthwide.* To many they must have looked like isolated incidents rather than symptoms of a global and more sinister problem.

Adam's diffidence won out. "Yes," he said, "I guess I do give credit."

"Rest assured that you'll be heard," Avery said. He nodded. "But you'll have to convince many people in addition to myself."

Adam shrugged. "I expect that."

"I suggest that you not push it too hard until you have better arguments than those you've presented and published so far." Avery pointed again to the disk. "While they're good arguments, they aren't proof."

"I don't know how to prove it." Adam sighed.

"Of course we all examined your ideas before we agreed to make you part of our team." Avery smiled, and glanced toward the disk rack at the edge of his desk. "All of us here believe that we can use our rapidly advancing technology to provide for our growing needs, and it's what our elected officials demand. They control the resources."

"Of course. I understand." Adam added in a small voice, "But I don't know how to argue with politicians." A smooth-talking young Earth

Senator, he recalled, had made a fool of him nine years earlier. He frowned. An audience of billions had witnessed that debate.

"Perhaps you'll have to learn," Avery said.

Adam nodded.

"As you know," Avery said, "we're planning the next major project. You'll be a big part of this grand plan."

Adam perked up. "Tell me about it."

"We call it Population Accommodation-Next Step," Avery said. "We've talked about it here for a few years, and now have the know-how to begin. I can't tell you anything today, but we'll go over everything at our first official meeting in a few days." He put his hands on his desk.

Adam didn't pressure Avery for the information, and he tried not to show his disappointment. *It's apparently accommodation*, he thought, *not control.* He wondered if he was in the right job; maybe he had been too hasty in his acceptance of this position. He would, he quickly decided, stay around long enough to find out the details. He could resign later, he told himself. Since Avery appeared to be preparing to get up, Adam slid to edge of the couch. "Will I be able to help, Bill?" he asked.

"Adam, we need a devil's advocate," Avery said. "We expect a lot from you." He got up from his chair. "Come, I'll introduce you to the other members of the team."

Adam stood up as Avery stepped out from behind the desk. He noted that Avery was five or six centimeters shorter than himself, but was well proportioned. The man's ninety-plus years, he thought, showed only in his white hair and the wrinkles around his eyes.

He picked up his datacase and followed Avery. As they left the greenery-filled office and entered the hallway, he asked, "Is Hugh Bruce on the team?"

"Oh, I expected you to ask that," Avery said. "Yes, he is."

Adam watched Avery stop by his photronic receptionist and press a few keys. "I understand you and Hugh had a little dispute recently,"

Avery said. He turned and motioned Adam to follow. "At a conference, I think."

Adam followed Avery down the hallway. "He disagreed with something I said," he said. "I usually don't mind criticism, Bill."

Avery interrupted. "Hugh's notorious for his lack of tact. He's a young hothead, but he's a brilliant and valued member of the group. I expect to have my hands full keeping you two working together."

"I won't start any fights," Adam said. He took a deep breath through his nose. He missed the flowery fragrance of Avery's office.

"You'll meet eight of the team members this morning," Avery said. "The rest are away right now. Seven more. I believe you already know a few."

Adam followed Avery around a turn and down another long hallway. "The team will be the decision-making body for our project," Avery said. "We'll organize other groups—many other scientists and engineers—to work out the details. But we'll run the show. We're responsible only to the people. We'll report directly to their elected officials."

"I'm curious, Bill." Adam said. "I hope I can be of help."

"You'll earn your keep. I know you'll do a great job." Avery motioned Adam to get in the jet lift. "But please keep an open mind." He smiled. "We're about to begin mankind's greatest endeavor."

That's not much of a clue, Adam thought.

He followed Avery from office to office on several floors and visited briefly with seven of his new teammates. The eighth, Hugh Bruce, was not in his office, but Adam spotted him in the hallway.

He glanced at Avery, and then approached Bruce and said, "I'm Adam Hampton. We talked briefly a few weeks ago." He extended his hand.

"Hello, Hampton," Bruce said. "I'm Hugh Bruce, but I'm sure you know that. Yes, I remember your outmoded ideas."

Adam noted that Bruce had a firm handshake. "I use the word 'realistic,'" Adam said.

"Welcome to the team anyway," Bruce responded.

Adam amused himself with his thoughts while Avery greeted Bruce. He had tried to grow a moustache, but, the color of his dark blond hair, it had looked like just a dirty face. Bruce's moustache was dark and full, matching his black hair.

After Bruce had gone on his way, Avery said to Adam, "You handled that brusquely. Both of you." He smiled. "But I'm optimistic. By the way, Hugh approved of your joining the team."

Adam decided that he was going to like Avery. That smile certainly put him at ease. He again followed Avery down the hallway, until the two reached the open door of a small but cozy-looking office. "This's your new home," Avery said.

Adam entered the office, while Avery stood just outside. "Nice," Adam said as he glanced around. A desk, smaller than Avery's, stood near a relatively large window. Several empty disk racks adorned the desk. A combination computer and voice-visual terminal, on a wheeled cart, sat on the hard tile floor next to the desk.

"Talk to Jim Croner. I'll ask him to v-v you. He'll see that you get what you need." Avery smiled. "I'm going to abandon you right now."

"All right." Adam returned Avery's smile.

"If you haven't anything planned for dinner," Avery said, "why don't you join Brenda and myself at our home. I don't want you to be alone on your first evening in the city." He turned to leave. "I'll give you directions later."

"I'd be delighted," Adam said. "I'll look forward to meeting Brenda." He watched Avery walk away, and added quietly, "And to finding out about that new project."

Chapter 2

Earth's Problem

Adam put his datacase on the floor and sat in the chair behind his new desk. He was alone for the first time since he had entered the building a few hours earlier. He glanced around, but didn't see what he wanted. He got up and stepped into the hallway. He could get a coffee decanter for himself later, but now he would have to borrow. A new teammate had an office nearby.

He returned to his office a few minutes later with a cup of steaming black coffee in his hand. He raised the cup to his nose and inhaled deeply. *They drink the good stuff here,* he thought. He sat down behind the desk again, and pulled the terminal closer. He glanced at his watch and noted that it was still morning at Earth University's faraway main campus. He took a careful sip of coffee, and then put the cup down on the desktop.

He switched the terminal to voice-visual and hit a few keys on the keyboard. He hesitated a moment, and then hit the last key. A few seconds later he heard a familiar voice. "Adam, old buddy." A familiar face, in three-dimensional colored lights, appeared in the space above the terminal screen.

Adam understood that his own image had materialized above another terminal, over two thousand kilometers away. "Hello, Pete," he said. "Haven't seen you since last week."

"You just missed Linda," Pete MacDonald said. "She went over to the institute to finish those forms."

Adam relaxed. He would rather not see or speak to Linda, at least not for a while. He had to forget. Pete and lovely Linda Donner were engaged to be married, and Adam wished only the best for his two good friends. "I spent most of the morning with Bill Avery," he said. "Something big's going on here."

"Bill?" Pete asked.

"He asked me to call him Bill." Adam smiled, and took another sip of coffee. It was still quite hot.

"And what's the big project?" Pete's face grew larger. "You didn't know anything last week."

Adam also moved closer to his terminal. "I don't know anything now," he said, "except that everyone's excited about it."

"Avery's directly involved?" Pete asked. "Anything to do with *food factories?*"

"If so, I'll let you know." Adam picked up the cup and took another quick sip. "Maybe you can give me some help."

"Sure."

"I'll contact you again when I know more. But now I'd better get to work." Adam put the cup down on the desk. "I have to order some supplies, and get this office in working shape."

"All right," Pete said. "Later, old buddy."

Adam hit a key. Pete's image disappeared.

*   *   *

In the late afternoon Adam checked into the new apartment that the administration had prearranged for him; it was not far from the population administration building. He looked over the few trunks and suitcases stacked inside near the entrance and saw that all had been delivered intact. He unpacked a number of items and settled in.

In the evening he donned his tunic and walked the kilometer or so through the crowded city streets to the Averys' home. He entered the building and rode the jet lift to an apartment on the top floor, the eighty-fifth.

After Avery introduced Adam to his wife, Brenda, Adam noted that their apartment, while more luxuriously furnished, was not much larger than his own new place. Individual living space had to be limited even for those of high rank, he thought, in a city of sixty million.

A hint of jasmine hung in the air. It was quite different from the aroma of Avery's office.

He endured Brenda's lighthearted teasing as the three stood in the living room. "I'm surprised you came here alone," she said. "A tall good-looking young man like yourself must have young women beating down his door." She laughed, and her graying brown hair brushed her shoulders.

"I'm new to the city," Adam said. "I don't know anyone." He had never thought himself good-looking. Agreeable-looking was a better description. He returned Brenda's compliment. "I hope I'll be fortunate enough to meet someone as charming as you are, Brenda."

He smiled when Brenda turned to her husband. "You didn't tell me what a gentleman our young guest is," she said.

Such small talk, over glasses of wine, filled most of the evening during and after dinner. Adam noticed that Avery avoided any talk about the new project; instead Adam learned about his hosts. Brenda was eighteen years younger than Bill, and they had been married for over fifty years. They had no children.

Later, when Adam prepared to leave, Avery handed him a photronic disk. "Scan this when you get a chance. I'll give you more tomorrow. You'll need the background."

Adam read the words "Virtual Mass Drive" on the disk container. He frowned slightly, and then said, "All right. Goodnight, Brenda. Bill. And thanks for a great meal." He put the disk in his belt pocket, walked out the door and rode the jet lift back down to street level.

Nightfall had not cleared the crowded city streets. Adam had to weave his way just like earlier. The main campus, where he had spent the past eight years, had had its crowds. *It was never like this*, he thought. He carried his tunic over his shoulder. He hadn't expected this mid-autumn evening to be so warm.

He thought about the disk in his belt pocket. He knew a little about virtual mass drive. While this source of power was almost routine now, at least in certain very large applications, it had been new and exciting some thirty years earlier. His father, an engineer, had worked on early projects.

Virtual mass drive, or vm-drive, "borrowed" energy from empty space. Adam never did understand the scientific explanation. The vm scientists theorized about mass-energy equivalence, quantum fluctuations, antimatter and conservative forces. Those were the expressions his father had used and had promised to explain to him when he got older. Some bulk fuel was necessary in most uses; ejected at nearly limit-speed, this fuel mass satisfied various scientific laws.

Several different applications now employed the technology. The reversing power plants that drove the larger mountaintop launch and return catapults for intercontinental and near-space travel were examples. Man's recent, although humble, venture into interstellar space was another. Vm-drive had not been practical for smaller uses. *Not safe enough*, he thought.

When he arrived back at his apartment, he inserted the disk into the home terminal. He poured a cup of coffee, sat down and listened while a female voice explained the current state of vm-drive technology. Due to various efficiency improvements, relatively small amounts of bulk fuel could provide enormous power for long periods of time. Vm-drive remained practical only for certain kinds of large applications, in airless or thin-air environments; this would not change in the foreseeable future. The much older *microfusion* engines would continue to satisfy most mobile power needs. Larger fixed-base fusion engines, supplemented by solar panels and wind generators, would remain the most efficient for geographically distributed electrical grids.

Numbers rolled down the terminal screen; a graph appeared above.

Adam frowned when the disk finished. It hadn't mentioned the new project; it was only an energy usage update. He poured the coffee back into the decanter. It was late, he told himself, and he might as well try out his new bed.

*   *   *

Adam met the other seven members of the team in the few days that followed his arrival at the administration. At eight in the morning on Friday, at the end of his first week at his new job, he attended the inaugural team meeting.

He chose an inconspicuous chair located at one side of the large elliptical conference table. He swiveled in the chair and made sure that he had a clear view of the display wall at the front of the room. While the others trickled in, he looked around. Murals and mosaics of forested hills and sunny glens graced the walls. These, he thought, showed an Earth that he had only read about or experienced via *Photronic Integrated Perception*, or *PIP*. A forest grotto on a side wall reminded him of Avery's office.

He noticed that Avery had stepped up to the podium at the front of the room and evidently was prepared to open the session. He quickly filled his coffee cup from a decanter on the table, and then swiveled his chair toward the front as Avery welcomed the seated team members.

"The government's asked me to be the official head of our group, our team," Avery continued. "To begin, I'd like to propose the acronym PANS. Let's make our unofficial name official at this first meeting." He smiled. "Any other ideas?"

Adam listened while Avery and the rest of the team debated. They quickly decided that the name would remain Population Accommodation-Next Step.

Adam took a sip of coffee while Avery took the floor again. "A little history," Avery said. "Up to the early to middle twenty-first century various factors, most notably infant mortality, disease, famine, war and pollution, limited human numbers while advancing technology allowed various rates of growth."

Adam swiveled his chair to keep his gaze on Avery. The man roamed about the room as he spoke.

"As we defeated all of these factors," Avery said, "the process, in a sense, turned around. Technology began following population growth. Our scientists, engineers and technicians provided for the needs of growing numbers—very successfully."

Adam sat straighter in his chair. "Turned around" would not be the way he would have described it, but he understood Avery's implication: Advances in technology would always solve the problems associated with human population growth. He glanced at the faces of the others around the table. Their expressions and nods told him that they agreed with Avery. Hugh Bruce looked like he agreed with Avery.

Bruce, he recalled, had confronted him at that conference a few weeks ago about the same topic. He had been embarrassed by his inability to argue the point in public.

Technology *had* been successful, he conceded to himself. He thought again about PIP as Avery mentioned that and other technological advances. The process, which Adam believed had been called "virtual reality" in its rudimentary stages a few centuries earlier, had accomplished much more than originally expected. PIP was first designed for recreation and certain kinds of training. It later helped people adapt to increasingly crowded conditions with minimal social upheaval. PIP became an outlet for aggression and satisfied a need for stimulation.

He thought about photronics. That technology had replaced the less efficient and more cumbersome electronics nearly two hundred years ago. PIP's evolution from virtual reality soon followed.

He watched Avery approach the podium, pick up a glass of water and drink deeply.

Adam glanced down at the elliptical table. This table was made of wood, so it had to be very old. It looked well maintained. His new team, he thought, held a certain high status. He looked at his coffee cup, which he had carefully placed on a square pad, picked it up and took a sip. He glanced at the paper notes in front of him. Paper, he thought, had also once been made from wood.

He swiveled his chair to face Avery, who had resumed speaking and walking. "I can't overestimate the importance," Avery said. "Many people resist imposed restrictions on procreation. It'd take a strong argument to change their minds. Many will never change."

That was evolution, Adam thought, and culture. Different cultures remained, even under earthwide government. These cultures retained very different attitudes toward birth control. Many found it easy to accept. Others would have to be forced in one way or another. He grimaced. He wanted to respect, he told himself, all the different cultures and all their different beliefs. *But something must be done.*

Earlier attempts to change basic practices, he thought, had been only minimally successful. Global equality of the sexes and reliable control of the sex of offspring had had little effect.

Voluntary methods, he told himself, held little promise with an Earth population of twenty-four billion. Effective population control now required a scientific approach and strict laws. He believed that cheap, safe and easy-to-use *sperm blocking enzyme*, or *SBE*, could provide a means that didn't force anyone to choose against basic beliefs. Someone must somehow convince enough people, enough voters, to compel the government to act. *Someone.*

Eventually human civilization must impose controls in order to preserve itself, he thought, but many individuals and groups would never think pragmatically enough to accept this. Control must be structured in a way that did not depend on any individual choice.

He looked at Avery, who stopped briefly by the podium at the front, refilled the glass with water and took it with him. "As you know, we are going to implement a new method to handle growth," Avery said. "Our elected officials have charged this team—you and I—with a great responsibility."

Adam saw that Avery had stopped pacing and fixed his gaze on him. "I'm sure Adam's presence will keep us honest," Avery said. "He wants control, not accommodation. Do you want to say something, Adam?"

"No, I guess not." Adam refilled his coffee cup from the decanter on the table and relaxed in his chair. He asked himself again if he was in the right place, in the right job.

"As we all know," Avery went on, "the last very large project in growth accommodation began over fifty years ago. I myself was a major architect of that plan."

Avery had been the *major architect*, Adam thought.

"Many of you are too young to have seen them except in old *visographs*, but long ago most of our food came from the large expanses of open land called 'farms.'" Avery brought up a visual, showing a cornfield, on the front display wall.

Adam had covered this subject thoroughly at the university, but he swiveled his chair to keep Avery in sight and listened to the man's narration. The old farms had taken up too much land area. Even with continued improvement, they had remained inefficient because they were subject to the vagaries of Earth's weather and the many insect parasites and plant diseases that could never be totally eliminated. They had also polluted the environment, particularly the worldwide fresh water supply.

In the early twenty-first century, crop genetic modification for disease and pest resistance, one of the major improvements, had finally gained acceptance by most of the world's population. This once successful process had been thwarted on the farms, eventually, by the continuing demands for increases in production.

Avery continued by describing how food was presently produced in the controlled environments of the many layered *food factories*. With nearly twenty-four hours per day of artificial sunlight, most crops grew nearly twice as fast as they had on the farms. These facilities also supplied much of the free oxygen—in the atmosphere—for breathing and other processes.

Rudimentary food factories, Adam thought, had supplemented the farm yields for decades preceding the *farm elimination plan*. Even back then the farms had been insufficient, given the population. Avery had been the first to recognize when factory technology had become reliable enough for a complete takeover. The man had written the logistical plan and coordinated the financial plan for changeover from corporate farms to corporate factories.

Adam thought about Pete MacDonald. Pete, an agricultural specialist, had been Adam's best source of information about the factories when the two were roommates at the university. Adam recalled the day, weeks ago, when he had first informed his friend that he would be working for Avery's office. He returned his attention to Avery.

"We all know the official name for our gigantic food-producing facilities," Avery continued. "Oh, boy! Many-Layered Enclosed Semi-Hydroponic Agricultural Food Production Modules? I think. But who wants to say that? And who can pronounce the acronym? They're food factories."

Avery glanced at Adam. Adam believed that Avery again invited him to comment. He shook his head.

"Let's consider one principal reason for the farm elimination plan," Avery continued. "I already mentioned it briefly. We've never been able to completely eliminate the various insect pests that plagued the open air farms."

Adam listened while Avery described how scientists in the previous century had determined that the pesticide levels needed to completely eliminate the insect pests would also poison the environment for humans. The biologists had additionally warned about unpredictable effects from the elimination of millions of species of small creatures.

Unfortunately, Adam thought, the planners had not avoided all such consequences. The elimination of the farms had had an unexpected ecological side effect. He glanced at the wall murals, and then dropped this thought in favor of another. The factories, and the associated, but much fewer in number, *meat modules*, were the key to the solution he sought. SBE could be placed in the supply of staple foods, and distributed worldwide. The centralized systems of distribution—efficient despite Louisville—provided the means to this end. The temporary antidote could be rationed globally in a numerically and ecologically sound manner.

Those who could not accept involuntary birth control would not be forced to choose between their beliefs and the law. *They would simply eat the only food that was readily available to them.* They could "protest," he thought, at the ballot box. If most others were convinced of the necessity, such protestors would remain ineffective although their consciences would be clear.

Such an involuntary procedure was certainly draconian, he told himself. He had agonized over the idea throughout his later years of study at the university, and had found no way to avoid it. Earth's huge and growing population, if unchecked, would inevitably result in a global disaster that would dwarf the localized disasters of the early twenty-first century. If generations of politicians had not sidestepped the problem, he thought, milder measures might have been sufficient.

He had had to work out a solution back at the university; he had always had little patience with those who complained about a problem but could offer no workable course of action. SBE in the food supply was the best he could offer, the most workable. The sperm blocking compounds, first formulated about one hundred and fifty years ago, worked in both the male and female body to restrict movement of live sperm. SBE in either body reliably prevented fertilization, and a century and a half of experience showed it to be without short-term or long-term ill effects.

Such a plan was straightforward enough that Adam knew that others had also thought about it; he was certain that he had not been the first. But no one, he told himself, talked of such things. Would anyone ever do anything?

His "plan," he thought again, was draconian. He wondered if just a credible threat of the government imposing such a measure would give some more voluntary method a better chance for success. Tax incentives or penalties might work under those conditions. Of course many people would then have to choose between low taxes and their beliefs. He shook his head. No solution to Earth's crushing overpopulation problem could ever be ideal.

Adam shifted his attention back to Avery. The man was bound to describe the new plan soon, he thought, and he had better listen.

"Technology tallied a great victory with the farm elimination plan." Avery said. He reached the podium again and put the now empty glass down. "I'm proud to have played a big part in it. I realize there were side effects, but it's working."

Adam glanced at the wall murals and mosaics again, and thought about the jungle in Avery's office.

"I know I'm being long-winded here," Avery said. "But I'm going over all this in such detail because I want all of you to appreciate the scope and the importance of our new project.

"The farm elimination plan changed enormously the lives of just about everyone," he said while he roamed around the room. "Of course it's a permanent change. Human numbers have now grown so large that we can never again produce adequate food in the old way. Not on Earth. Even the eventual weather control won't be sufficient anymore."

Adam took out a handkerchief and wiped his brow, although it wasn't warm in the room. *Just what are we planning to do?* He wondered if he was the only one in the room who didn't know.

"We've run out of options on Earth," Avery said.

Adam fidgeted. He took another sip of coffee.

"The PANS project will be very different from any earlier plan," Avery said. "At first it'll greatly alter the lives of only some millions of our people. But that's only the beginning. PANS will be expanded and extended indefinitely into the future. It's unlimited. We are calling it 'Next-Step' now, but in the big picture it will be the final step."

Adam saw Avery glance at him and smile. Then Avery looked at another team member and said, "Robert King will now give us the rundown on *Earth-Twin*."

Chapter 3

Earth-Twin

Avery sat down and another man got up and walked toward the front of the room. Adam shifted in his chair. He had been taken by surprise. *Maybe I shouldn't have been*, he told himself.

He had first learned about Earth-Twin from his father. That planet, a little larger than Earth, was one of several planets that orbited the star *Tau Ceti*. Tau Ceti, a relatively inconspicuous star when viewed from Earth, formed part of the constellation Cetus, the Sea Monster. It was one of only a few close single stars that were similar to the sun, and was the closest that supported a planet with advanced life.

He thought about the enormous distance to even a closer star like Tau Ceti. A group of explorers had visited Earth-Twin and returned to Earth; their odyssey had spanned just over thirty years, even though they spent only two exploring the planet. They had departed Earth eight years before his own birth.

When he was a boy, he and his father had often talked about that voyage. Together they had recorded, on a chart, the explorers' expected later progress year by year. He frowned. After the accident he had completed that chart by himself.

He recalled his father's words from long ago: "A centimeter to the Sun, eight kilometers to Tau Ceti!" *No one had talked of mass colonization then.*

Adam picked up his coffee cup and looked at Rob King, who approached the front wall where Avery's cornfield was still displayed.

He knew the engineer primarily from Avery's introduction earlier in the week, although he had briefly talked to him via voice-visual a few weeks ago as part of the job interview process.

King, he figured, was about twice his own age. He believed that King had never held that position, but the man embodied the perfect engineering professor. Tall and slim, with brown hair graying at the temples, Dr. King would have graced the classroom and laboratory and wowed the young female students.

King hit a few keys on the photronic podium and waved a hand over the control screen to queue up his own visuals, although he did not erase Avery's cornfield. "You are already familiar with most of the details," King said, "but we must look at the planet in perspective."

Adam was very familiar with the older information. An early unmanned probe had yielded atmospheric, physical and biological data. This included some inconclusive measurements on surface gravity, due to equipment malfunction. The probe, which employed space technology from a century earlier, had taken nearly fifty years to reach Earth-Twin and begin its radio transmission. It took another twelve years for the data to return to Earth.

The manned exploration mission had been commissioned soon after evaluation of that data, he thought, and had been one of the first practical uses of vm-drive. His father had helped design the exploration ship's engines.

"Space exploration," King said, "primarily by full-spectrum *interfero* telescopes, has shown that there are a number of earthlike planets in Earth's vicinity. Here I speak of Earth's vicinity as that part of our Milky Way Galaxy that scientists have so far been able to explore for the presence of life."

Adam's father had talked of Earth's vicinity. A few of the many planets in this region, including Earth-Twin, harbored life much like that on Earth. This included advanced forms, although intelligent beings had not yet been detected outside Earth's own solar system. The species *homo sapiens* remained unique, Adam thought, so far.

"The closest of the earthlike planets orbits the star Tau Ceti," King said, "at a distance of about twelve limit-years from Earth. Scientists named it Earth-Twin more than a century ago."

Adam thought of his father's explanations, and his university physics courses. A limit-year was the distance radio signals and light beams traveled in one year in the vacuum of space. Objects, and people, must move slower.

He did not have to swivel his chair to keeps his gaze on King, who remained by the podium. "Earth-Mate is the second closest," King said, "at just over twenty limit-years. Four more such planets are at distances ranging from twenty-five to fifty limit-years. Others exist farther away."

King waved a hand and replaced the cornfield on the display wall with several graphs. These showed mostly comparative distances, but a few numbers were expressed in earthbound units. The number 113,000,000,000,000 kilometers, the Earth-Twin distance, appeared most prominently. Such numbers, Adam thought, proved useful only for computerized mathematical calculations and trip estimates.

"Beyond about two hundred limit-years," King said, "present technology cannot tell us with certainty if life exists in any form. Statistics tells us that it does. Telescopes and other probes are getting better, and we will continue to expand the search area."

Adam recalled that Avery had said the new plan was unlimited. The present search area represented only a tiny fraction of the galaxy, and there were billions of other galaxies. Planets, and, to a lesser extent, large moons of large planets, were the only common classes of celestial object that could support life's genesis and evolution. They were the only places to go, he thought, but the searchers expected to find many additional earthlike planets for future colonization.

He listened while King described the conditions that classified a planet as earthlike, although this had all been common knowledge since

Earth-Twin's discovery. King briefly ran over class, age and generation of the central star, and orbit and size of the planet.

Adam sipped coffee while King talked about chemical makeup of a planet's surface and atmosphere, its rotation rate, its surface gravity and other details. He understood that the general conditions which made crowded Earth ideal existed elsewhere, but an exact match to Earth would be rare indeed. He figured that King was leading up to a discussion of the differences between Earth and Earth-Twin.

King described how the element carbon's chemistry made it the only realistic candidate for the atomic basis of life. Adam nodded when King explained that the discovery of carbon-based life on Earth-Twin, and on other planets, had simply added empirical confirmation.

He leaned back in his chair as King began to describe Earth-Twin itself. Adam knew many of the details well. Earth-Twin had a rotation period nearly the same as Earth's, so its day length was about the same. The nearly circular orbit about Tau Ceti was smaller than Earth's orbit around the sun; the Earth-Twin year was about two-thirds of an Earth year. Tau Ceti was smaller and cooler than the sun, but, since Earth-Twin remained closer, the planet had a general climate similar to Earth's.

Its atmosphere was a close match, with a slightly larger average pressure.

Earth-Twin was a little larger than Earth. A vast salty ocean covered most of the surface. Most known dry land formed one large irregularly shaped continent; its area was twenty to twenty-five percent greater than Earth's total land area.

The planet's surface gravity was about twenty-five percent stronger than Earth's.

Adam watched King bring up another visual on the display wall. King explained that this one was an actual visograph from the exploration, taken from a high Earth-Twin orbit. Adam could clearly see the great continent that straddled the globe's equator, and a small ice cap at one pole. Even white clouds were evident. He watched and listened while King briefly pointed out these features.

He glanced around the table. From their murmurs and the expressions on their faces, he wondered if some of the team members, like himself, had not seen this *viso* before. Someone whispered, "Just like Earth."

King continued his description. A large part of the land resembled the area on Earth once called the Great Plains. Mountain ranges were minimal, but a long and narrow range of tall mountains ran along the western coast.

King also mentioned some details about the life forms. Life on the planet was apparently at the evolutionary stage where that on Earth had been just before the arrival of the dinosaurs, although a few animals were similar to later arrivals on Earth. All known animals were relatively small.

King explained how the explorers were able to eat plants and animals native to the planet. Adam recalled that earlier scientists, using well-established scientific laws, had predicted this; the explorers had gambled their lives on it, although *that* risk was small when compared to other risks of their journey.

He sipped coffee while King continued. Plenty of human edible plants and animals existed on the planet, and the known predators were too small to be a threat to people. In their limited coverage of the continent, the explorers found no poisonous species.

King added, "The explorers found no native diseases that could penetrate general immunization. As most of you know, human diseases in an alien land are unlikely. Unlikely, but not impossible. The tests were necessary."

He should have seen this coming, Adam told himself again. The biologists and other scientists had belabored the human compatibility question when they reported on the exploration results. He had not even guessed that the goal was mass colonization, not at that distance. He had expected only small-scale activities, such as a research station.

Adam picked up his coffee cup; he put it down again when King asked for comments. He had been silent, and he wanted to at least say something at this time. He wondered what would be appropriate. While he hesitated, a team member, a woman a few years older than himself, asked about how the shorter year might affect the colonization. King explained that a university group had examined the problem and expected little difficulty with agriculture or with human psychology. The group had worked out a preliminary plan for food factories and field farms.

Adam still hesitated. Someone else asked about the larger gravity. King referred this question to Avery.

Avery stood up and said that he had led the group that had examined the gravity difference. He explained briefly that the explorers had adapted easily. He quickly concluded by saying that gravity would cause no problems with agriculture, and sat down.

Adam took another drink from his coffee cup, and then quickly refilled it from the decanter on the table. This was his third or fourth cup this morning. He wasn't sure which. He wondered about Avery's brief response. He would have expected his new boss to say more about a project he had led, like he had about the farm elimination plan.

He glanced at Bruce again. Bruce appeared ready to pounce on him. He could question Avery's gravity study sometime later, he told himself, since he expected that the team would address the differences in detail at later meetings. He could also talk to Avery alone.

He relaxed a little. Since others were asking questions, he figured that he was not the only one on the team who had not been familiar with the project. At least a few others, who may have known in general about the plan for mass colonization, were just now learning some of the details.

Adam decided to ask a neutral question, one to which he believed he already knew the answer and one that wouldn't be argumentative.

King's and Avery's mentions of agriculture had given him the idea. He raised his hand to get King's attention. "Tau Ceti has a more orange color than our sun," he said. "Will Earth crops grow well in that light?"

"Extensive experiments have been performed here in our own food factories," King said. "The crops tested thrived in a simulated Tau Ceti spectrum. Since food factories will also be utilized on Earth-Twin, at least in the beginning, we even have a degree of redundancy. If necessary for individual crops, internal lighting can made be similar to the sun's even while the outside light is different."

During his first talk with his new boss, Adam recalled, Avery had mentioned talking about the plan for a few years. Apparently the administration had done a lot more than just talk; many studies and experiments had been completed.

He relaxed in his chair while King brought up a visograph of Tau Ceti high in the Earth-Twin sky, taken from the planet's surface.

Adam gazed at the orange sun; he had seen actual visos only on a small computer display. *It's quite striking*, he thought. *One would need some time to get used to it.*

King displayed another visograph, with a lower orange sun. This one showed some of the landscape. Irregularly shaped but familiar objects, colored an unfamiliar green, appeared at the bottom of the display. Adam looked at the viso, and then glanced around the table. He saw team members look at the viso and then at each other. Many had certainly not seen this one before, he told himself. He looked back at the display.

The green objects, he guessed from the reports, were the large plants that the explorers had called, due to their similarity, trees. The green color looked something like olive drab, but a pea green tint made it much more pleasing to the eye. Hills colored a lighter but similar green formed the background in the lower half of the scene.

He mentally compared the visograph with the murals and the landscape mosaics on the meeting room walls, and noticed that others appeared to be doing the same. The scenes and the trees were similar, he thought, and different. The orange sun lent its own influence to other colors on Earth-Twin's surface. He looked back at King. "We will cover those and other questions in greater detail later," King said, "but we are very fortunate that the closest earthlike planet is as much like Earth as it is."

Adam recalled another fact, one that King hadn't mentioned. Earth-Twin had a moon; it was smaller than Earth's moon and its orbit was closer to the planet. This small moon had a period, from full moon to next full moon, of about 21 days. The explorers had reported that it was, when viewed from the planet's surface, about the same size in the sky as Earth's moon. They had also described a large lunar tide, with daily variations closely matching Earth's.

There are similarities and differences, Adam thought. He wondered what Pete would say about how food factories might operate on the new planet. He could contact Pete about this, so that he could be better prepared for the later discussions. He would have to make that contact only on a weekday afternoon, he thought, when Linda would most likely be busy with her applications for the medical institute.

He felt his heart beat a little faster. Her appearance on Pete's v-v could upset his careful plan to get her out of his mind. The wedding was still a few years off, but he was determined to be prepared for that.

Another question bothered him. Now that he knew something about the plan, was he going to stay with the team, with his new job? Would he have reason to question Pete about the factories?

He looked at King, who now discussed the explorer's travel experience, and took another drink of coffee. In space the exploration ship had attained a speed of ninety percent of limit. Only vm-drive, Adam thought, could impart such speed to a massive object. It had made interstellar human travel possible centuries earlier than had been generally predicted. *Many had once believed that people would never reach the stars.*

He reminded himself again that his father had helped design that ship's engines. He and his father had talked for hours on end, about vm-drive and about Earth-Twin, until the day that he had arrived home from school and found his mother alone and crying. He felt a tear in the corner of his eye. *It was ten years ago.* She had taken her only child into her arms and held him tightly for a long time before she was able to explain.

Adam briefly examined the exquisite wood grain of the tabletop, and then focused his attention back on King. King explained that the ship needed just over fourteen years to reach Earth-Twin and the same for the return trip. The explorers arrived back on Earth, seventy-five of them, three years ago. They returned younger than they would have been if they had not left Earth.

Adam understood that this was due to the well-known effects of time dilation at relative speeds near limit. As seen by people on Earth, the explorers had been away more than thirty years. They had aged only sixteen years. From the point of view of the explorers only sixteen years had passed.

King added a statistic: Two explorers had died, one on the planet and the other during the return trip. Adam nodded. Scientists had exhaustively examined the circumstances and determined these deaths to be normal for a trip of such complexity and long duration.

Adam sipped coffee while King took a quick drink of water.

"Many researchers studied that long trip," King said. "All concurred that, with a suitably sized, designed and equipped ship, it presented no real difficulties for the travelers. Of course, as we know, the trip took only about seven years in each direction, from their point of view."

King displayed a visual of the ship and Adam envisioned a bicycle wheel. His father had described it that way.

"Apparently the explorers fared well under the conditions of artificial gravity," King said.

Adam recalled, from the university, a scientific argument that gravity and acceleration, hence "real" gravity and "artificial" gravity, were essentially the same thing. He never did understand that argument, although he had remembered it well enough to answer the general relativity questions in several physics exams. He expected that King knew it well.

"We know several got married while in space," King continued. "Life was relatively normal, but they did not bear any children because of life support limitations."

Adam looked at his coffee cup. The meeting had better adjourn soon, he thought. With all that coffee, he would certainly have to use the facilities.

King asked if there were any more questions.

A team member, a woman about ten years older than Adam, asked about plant diseases. King reported that the explorers had planted some Earth crops on the surface and found no disease problems. They had planted many varieties, but nothing large scale. They brought cuttings back with them, to analyze during the return trip and on Earth.

Adam relaxed when King concluded and asked Avery if he had more to say. Avery walked up to the podium. "Thank you, Rob," he said. "I'm even more fired up now."

Adam swiveled his chair as Avery strolled around the room. "I'll add a little more to what Rob said about the explorers," Avery said. "I talked to most of them, and they couldn't say enough about the beauty of the place! It'd be difficult to repeat their descriptions, but they made frequent use of the words 'paradise' and 'heaven.' Many wanted to go back—not feasible, of course.

"A few will serve as part-time advisors on the university teams; this will be voluntary time spent away from their promised retirement and big pensions. None were asked to serve on this team."

Adam believed he understood this. Their trip hadn't been planned with colonization in mind. They had been isolated, away from Earth's quickly advancing technology and growing problems.

Avery continued. "Our elected officials are pleased with the results of the exploration. Although they don't want anything made public until we've ironed out some of the details, they've voted to make available the resources for our colonization."

They have a plan to gain the most political capital from it, Adam thought.

"A new Earth Senate committee has been formed to oversee the operation," Avery said. "But it's up to us to decide how to proceed."

Adam watched Avery walk to the podium and briefly glance at some notes. "Colonization away from the confines of the Earth's surface certainly isn't new in this last decade of the twenty-second century," Avery said. "As we all know, millions have lived well in the orbiting space stations and the colonies on the moon and Mars for well over a hundred years."

Adam also knew of the smaller groups of people who inhabited several of the moons of Jupiter and Saturn and a few asteroids, mostly for tours of a year or two. Many people on Earth weren't even aware of those activities, he thought.

All these colonies within the solar system depended on Earth for many of the necessities of life, Adam told himself. The people lived in enclosed and carefully controlled environments. There were no wide-open spaces. Human populations were severely limited.

Avery remained by the podium, and said what Adam now expected him to say. "But the PANS plan will be the first attempt to place large numbers of people in an open natural environment that need not depend on the diminishing resources of our own Earth. This is truly a first!" He smiled. "In contrast to our solar system colonies, Earth-Twin has its own suitable environment. We base the initial plan on this principle. We plan to colonize the closest known such environment outside Earth."

Adam watched as Avery brought back King's visograph of the orange sun and the alien green trees. "Earth's twin indeed!" Avery said. "A generous providence has given us another Earth!" The administrator's smile filled the room, and Adam couldn't suppress a smile himself. "Any more comments?" Avery asked. "Questions?"

Adam glanced around the room. No one responded.

"By the way," Avery added, "remember that we must continue to keep it to ourselves. Don't even tell your families. Not yet. We'll close this meeting now." He glanced at the notes on the podium again. "Relax this weekend, and think about our first major decision. We must decide how many people to send."

Adam picked up his coffee cup. It contained just enough for one last swallow.

"Senator Bitterman wants that number as soon as possible," Avery said. "He's been named head of the oversight committee."

Adam gasped. He nearly choked on the slug of coffee in his mouth.

Chapter 4

The Plan

Adam remained in his chair while the others around him gathered up their personal notes and got up. He managed to swallow the coffee that had nearly gagged him. At sixteen years of age he had debated then thirty-one-year-old Senator John Bitterman and had looked the fool in front of a worldwide audience. He had hoped he would avoid the senator for the rest of his life.

He picked up his empty coffee cup and gathered his notes. He would catch Avery, he thought, before he left the meeting room.

Before he could get up, Hugh Bruce leaned across the table toward him. "Hampton, you looked jumpy," Bruce said. "But you didn't have a lot to say. Could it be the rest of the world is finally getting through?"

Adam started to respond. "Now—"

Bruce interrupted. "You're single, like me. This evening, try The Alligator. It's by the university. Just go over to the campus and ask someone."

"Thanks," Adam said in a small voice. "I'll check it out."

He got up and joined Avery, who was near the door. "I'll walk to your office with you, Bill. I do have some comments."

"Sure." Avery smiled.

Adam followed Avery through the door. "We've never produced food fully independently except on Earth," he said, "not in large and reliable amounts."

"That's what I was explaining," Avery said. "Earth is the only place in the solar system that has the appropriate natural conditions. But that's just our solar system."

"Earth-Twin is so far away," Adam said. "How can we keep tabs?"

"It's time-tested technology," Avery replied. "Agriculture—food factories and farms—will feed them."

Other team members approached and made brief remarks to Avery as Adam walked alongside in the hallway. Adam ignored them, and tried to put his thoughts together. Non-biological sources of food had proved impractical. The manufacture of essential amino acids from basic elements had so far been a failure, he thought, at least for economical large-scale production. The same held true for other nutritional requirements.

Nature's own green plants remained the only method efficient enough to reliably feed large populations. The higher-level process of meat production was less efficient, but still much better than any artificial method.

Agriculture, utilizing the basic processes evolved over more than a billion years, simplified Earth's ancient natural food web.

Agriculture was also the only method in wide use outside Earth, Adam thought. The occupants of the orbiting stations grew limited amounts of their own food, in their own food factories, and used these crops to provide free oxygen for their artificial atmospheres. They recycled all biological waste products, but certain plant nutrients and supplementary foods were shipped to orbit from Earth.

The colonies on the moon and on Mars, he knew, also obtained some of their food from Earth. Those farther colonists produced various fruit and vegetable crops and some grains, but these were limited because of the environmental enclosures. Open farms were not practical, and the enclosures restricted the size and function of food factories. On the positive side, most crops grew very well in the low gravity conditions on both the moon and Mars, as they did in the low artificial gravity of the orbiting stations.

Adam looked at Avery when the two entered the jet lift and were finally alone. "I know it's mostly working well," Adam said, "here in our solar system."

"Mostly?" Avery hesitated, and then smiled. "Yes, I will concede that our technology's so far failed to convert Mars to an earthlike planet," he said. "But we have made some progress."

Adam recalled the old word "terraforming," and the plan to follow up on it later. The additional technology was not yet available and the proposed process, once started, would take more than a hundred years. *If it worked at all*, he thought. For now Mars colonists had to settle for the enclosures that blocked radiation and hoarded air pressure, supplemented by limited underground facilities. *This is Mars*, he thought, *the most nearly earthlike neighbor in the solar system.*

The jet lift reached the top floor, and Adam followed Avery into the hallway. Why are they planning a new and bolder venture, he wondered, when the old problems still await solution? *Terraforming? Manufactured food? Birth control?*

SBE had long been used in all the colonies outside Earth, "voluntarily" by a required contract, he thought, but on Earth only truly voluntarily. Various cultures demanded the right to reproduce at will. *But what is a "right?" Doesn't "responsibility" also fit in?* He could accept a need to replace oneself, but one or at most two children per couple would satisfy that need. *Why does anyone champion the "right" to reproduce at will on an already critically overcrowded Earth?*

He spotted the men's room as he walked with Avery down the long hall that led to the man's office. He had downed at least six cups of coffee at the meeting, he thought, and that room would come in handy in a moment.

"I'm sure you know we ran very-large-scale crop tests," Avery said. "These Mars tests proved very successful. Only minor modifications were needed. Unfortunately it was too expensive for the long term, given the present status of that planet."

"But the gravity is higher," Adam argued. "Not lower."

"We've gone over that in detail." Avery smiled. "We expect the higher gravity to be as benign as the lower gravity."

"I don't see how large-scale crop tests could've been done," Adam said. "Not in high gravity." He glanced again at the men's room door while he walked beside Avery.

"We'll cover that in later meetings," Avery said. "You'll see how the plan unfolds."

Adam nodded.

"The other needs," Avery said, "are oxygen and water. Technology solved those problems long ago, in the stations as well as Mars and the moon. Of course we need take these into account only in the space-craft."

Adam and Avery reached Avery's office. Adam glanced inside when the doors slid open, and thought he might want some live plants in his own office. *Maybe not a jungle.* He didn't need a jungle, he thought, just something green and fragrant.

He used the facilities, and then headed for his office. While he walked he thought about the economic situation. The Earth Government had given the go-ahead to start planning. This was necessary, since public financial support was required. The earlier planners had needed such support, in the beginning, for the space stations and other solar system colonies.

The free market had quickly taken over those stations and colonies, he thought, with great benefit for all involved. The costs, particularly those of catapulting people, supplies and equipment out of Earth's gravity, were easily offset by the profits gained in the various enterprises: mining, airless manufacturing, low and zero gravity manufacturing and tourism.

Could the PANS plan ever become routine enough for the free market to take over? *Could such an enterprise,* he asked himself, *ever be free of politicians like John Bitterman?*

He thought of his own economic situation while he rode the jet lift. After years of school, he needed this job even though he wouldn't be doing what he wanted to do. Avery had told him that his role was, at least in part, to exploit that skepticism, to watch for mistakes.

He exited on his office floor. He was now part of the administration, he thought while he walked, in a position where he would help make decisions. He was involved in a very important new project. He liked his new boss.

Why had Avery and the team chosen him? He had asked himself this question before. Others were more qualified, he thought, and Avery had told him that many had applied. He himself had not applied directly; the administration had picked him from a computer listing. *Devil's advocate? Dissertation topic? Were these reasons enough?* He shook his head.

His father had designed the engines for the exploration ship long ago, he thought, and would have been proud of only son Adam's participation in the follow-up. He would help make the important decisions.

He had observed the behavior of the other team members; he knew that the project needed a skeptical point of view. He made up his mind. He would not resign.

I probably won't have much contact with Bitterman, he thought. *That will be Avery's job.*

He reached his office, sat behind his desk and poured a cup of coffee. He sat still for a moment, and then decided to v-v Pete's office. He pulled the terminal close and hit a few keys. He waited, and wondered if Linda would be there. After a minute or so, he hit the keys again.

Pete's face appeared. "Sorry, old buddy. I was in the lab."

Pete was alone, and Adam relaxed. "We just had the first meeting, Pete," he said. He hesitated, and then asked, "Where's Linda?"

"She bought the initial disks," Pete said, "and she's scanning them. She just finished the applications and she's already studying."

"Remember, we found her in the disk library." Adam laughed. Linda would have no trouble gaining acceptance at the medical institute, he thought.

"Yeah," Pete said. "So what did you find out," he asked, "at the meeting?"

"I can't tell you anything yet," Adam said, "but we need to talk about the factories. I need to know more about the physical operation, and any new developments."

"So it's going to involve the factories?" Pete asked.

"I can't tell you that." Adam laughed again.

Adam and Pete briefly discussed the food factories. After the call, Adam wondered about his old friend. Pete had not shared in his laughter. He had known Pete to be hardworking and impatient, but generally lighthearted. Maybe, Adam thought, he was in the middle of a particularly difficult lab experiment.

He glanced around his office and planned where he would place a few azaleas and geraniums.

*　　　　　　　*　　　　　　　*

In the evening, Adam worried about how to dress for The Alligator. He decided not to bring his tunic; that was too professional. He chose a pair of blue jeans, since that very old style had been the newest fad just a few months ago at the main campus. In place of the tunic, he donned a lightweight shirt with many pockets; student scientists had been wearing such shirts recently.

He rode the chute to the campus, since it was away from the central government area and his apartment and too far to walk. He exited the station on the campus and asked a student for directions to The Alligator. He then walked between the academic buildings.

The structures stood rather close; only narrow walkways separated the tall buildings. The Earth City campus of Earth University appeared even more crowded than the government section of the city. The far-away main campus, he thought, at least had some green grassy areas and bicycle paths.

He heard the music from a block away, so he easily found The Alligator just outside the campus. Once inside, he struggled to adjust his eyes to the bright flashing lights. Greens, oranges, blues, yellows and reds splashed across the walls in human and animal shapes that quickly dissolved and reappeared and danced in time with the music.

Young people crammed The Alligator. Many gyrated in wild abandon on the centrally located open floor. As his vision improved, Adam noted to his relief that blue jeans were also the fad here.

He looked around.

He spotted her. He stared.

The young woman with long blond hair, on the dance floor near where Adam stood, moved in perfect time with the music. She noticed his stare, he thought when she threw him a sweet smile that challenged the light show. He felt his heart pound, and he convinced himself that her dancing partner was just a casual acquaintance. *Otherwise,* he asked himself, *why would she smile at me?*

He tried to keep her in view, but the crowd made that impossible. He soon lost her.

When the music stopped, he tried to find her. She had smiled at him, he told himself, so he had better work up the courage to talk to her. After a few minutes the music started again, and he decided that "try to talk" might be a better way to express it.

Unfortunately, Adam thought, the Friday evening confusion could make it easy to lose someone at The Alligator. *Had she left?* In the crowd, he couldn't tell. He persisted, while his heartbeat gradually fell back to normal. He absorbed the music and lights, drank a couple of beers and searched. After a few hours he accepted defeat. In the thinner crowd, he realized she was gone.

He had had her in his sight for only thirty seconds, he thought, but he remembered the details. She was neither too tall nor too short. Her long blond hair reached almost to her waist. She wore well-fitting blue jeans. She had aimed that dynamite smile directly at him. He hadn't been able to determine her eye color; he blamed that on the flashing lights.

He was past step one, the physical attraction, he told himself. He was past the necessary but probably least important step. He was ready for the next step. He was ready to meet her.

Adam asked around just before closing time, and managed to find someone who knew the young woman. He learned that nineteen-year-old Jennifer Brown, an occasional visitor at The Alligator, studied system science at the university.

System science? That smile, he thought as he sat by the bar and finished off his last beer, *didn't come from a computer.*

Jennifer, he told himself, was a pretty name, like Linda. He felt his heart rate increase again; the unaccustomed quiet of The Alligator at closing time made it more apparent. Could Jennifer Brown help him forget? Did she go by Jenny? he wondered. He stood up and got ready to leave The Alligator. He knew he would be back.

*   *   *

Adam and the team struggled with the numbers question for several weeks, and determined that the PANS project must send about two million people to Earth-Twin each year. Earth's population would still grow, but Adam observed that the rest of the team believed that advancing technology could handle the excess. He knew that the doubling per century was an average; growth had slowed in the latter part of the twenty-second and scientists expected that lower rate to continue.

He voted in favor when the team finally elected to make it exactly two million. It wasn't the way to solve Earth's problem, he told himself, but he didn't think he could change anything by starting *that* argument at this point. He could talk to Avery alone later, he thought, maybe first about the number.

He sat in his usual seat at the side of the elliptical table during a meeting break just after the vote. He sipped coffee and thought about the previous few weeks' discussions. The plan would not crowd Earth-Twin. In fifty years, that planet would have to support only a small fraction of Earth's present population.

Such colonization outside the solar system, he thought, for such large numbers, had only recently become technologically feasible; but the basics had been in place for a long time. Long experience with the space stations showed that large numbers of people could live for long periods aboard such craft. Recent developments in food factory technology and earlier work in nuclear energy conversion would make it relatively easy to feed the travelers aboard ship. The journey itself, he thought, might not be a problem.

He thought about the exploration voyage. The exploration group had relied on older technology; they departed Earth with only enough water, fuel and condensed food for the outbound trip. Eighteen of the explorers dedicated all their time and efforts, on the planet, to replenishing these supplies from native resources. A full dozen of the expedition's four dozen humanoids had assisted. The explorers, Adam thought, had relied heavily on the data sent back by the earlier unmanned probe.

After the break, King took the floor.

Adam knew that King had met regularly with a university research group that had been examining the engineering problems of interstellar ships as large as space stations. King began by stating that group's conclusion that vm-drive spacecraft, large enough to carry several million people and support them in a relatively pleasant lifestyle for the long trip, could be built as necessary.

Adam agreed when King explained that one very large ship per year would be more efficient than several smaller ones. These would achieve ninety percent of limit-speed; the large ships would cover the distance to Earth-Twin in the same time as did the much smaller exploration ship. Speedup at the beginning and slowdown at the end would provide artificial gravity for those periods. During high-speed coast in the middle portion, the wheel-shaped ships would rotate like a space station. The spacecraft would be built in and launched from Earth orbit. At Earth-Twin they would probably land on the surface, using descent rockets assisted by parachutes. Adam nodded when King remarked that the team would have to make some decisions about these arrivals.

He refilled his coffee cup. He knew that the explorers' spacecraft had not landed; shuttlecraft descended to the surface while the main ship remained in orbit to be ready for the return. *The PANS engineers are planning one-way ships*, he thought, *and the team will soon have to approve that.*

Adam sipped coffee while King sat down and Avery took the floor. "I'd like to add just a little," Avery said. "The initial ships will be built from materials mined on the moon and shipped to Earth orbit. Later we may build and launch from lunar orbit. This is one of the ways our technological advances will improve the plan.

"But some technology might not be utilized. For example, we probably won't use the cleanups that're always scampering to get out of our way. Nor other such servants. We'll have to decide these things."

Adam turned around in his chair and glanced at the previously unnoticed little silver and gray metallic being, maybe a half meter tall, that was busily picking up things from the floor. He knew it was there by its low buzzing; he hadn't noticed until reminded by Avery's mention. It moved toward him on one of its random trips. It slowed, dipped its bowl-shaped head and changed direction just before reaching his chair.

He believed he understood why such exclusions might be prudent. The colonists must not depend on something that they won't have when they spread out on the planet, and they must feel useful themselves during their long journey. The more advanced humanoids, he thought, would also be excluded in the plan for human migration.

"We're beginning a grand experiment!" Avery said. Adam turned toward him and smiled. Avery radiated enthusiasm; Adam thought of a small boy opening a birthday present. "We will show," Avery said, "that a self-sustaining human colony can be set up on a distant earthlike planet, and that such a colony can absorb human numbers quickly enough to forestall problems on Earth.

"We'll use our advancing technology for the later colonization of the more distant planets. In the far future, the colonized closer planets will be stepping-stones to the farther planets. We won't need to use Earth's and the moon's resources indefinitely."

Adam looked around and noted that most of the team members nodded in agreement. He swiveled his chair to follow Avery as the man went on. "Many years hence, science will certainly find a way to get around faster than limit. This will open the way to colonization of large parts of the entire universe. Over thousands of years, of course. But the problem will be solved forever!"

Faster than limit? Adam wondered. *That may never be possible.* Scientists and engineers had changed the designation from "the speed of light" to "limit-speed" long ago, he thought, when they first planned interstellar probes and spacecraft.

Avery concluded and dismissed the team. Before he could leave the meeting room, Adam cornered him. This might be a good time, Adam thought, to question the decision. "Bill, I think we're taking a big risk here," he said. "Can't we start smaller?"

"We have to start big," Avery said. "You participated in the discussions."

"I only agreed that it was the necessary number, based on recent growth rates," Adam argued. "Maybe we can do this for two or three years and wait to see how it works out."

"That's not politically possible." Avery put his hand on Adam's shoulder. "Adam, we can do it that way only if the government changes the laws on Earth. We both know they won't."

"But this is too risky," Adam said. The government leaders would certainly support the initial plan, he thought. They would look like they were doing something about the problem, and disregard any risk. Earth's population would still grow, but they would just point to the future expansion of the plan. The political will to impose positive control on the population now looked even more remote.

"Relax, Adam," Avery said. "We'll be using the latest and greatest. All new advances will be included. It'll work!"

"I wish I could be so optimistic." Adam walked the few steps back to his chair and picked up his coffee cup. He then looked back at Avery.

"It'll work," Avery repeated. "Just keep your eyes and ears open so that we don't make any mistakes." He picked up the few notes he had placed on the podium. "Rob tells me we'll even be able to use *hypersignal.*"

Adam departed the meeting room. In the hallway he thought about Avery's last remark. Hypersignal was new, and he knew only a little about it. While physical objects could not approach limit-speed, brief signals could exceed it. That was hypersignal, now utilized, he thought, for certain data and control communications between Earth and the more distant solar system colonies.

*   *   *

Adam and the team framed the basic features of the plan for several more weeks. The oversight committee then approved the first public announcement.

Adam sat in his office after a team meeting that finalized the agenda for the announcement, which would reach all Earth and the solar system colonies via an *earth communication,* or *earth comm.* He glanced at his terminal. He could soon, he thought, talk to Pete about the details.

He considered asking Pete to join one of the PANS research groups, since the team would need to keep up with food factory evolution. Pete was a talented researcher; he had chosen to remain on the university research staff after graduation. *That was mostly to remain near Linda,* Adam thought. Linda had been accepted for and had begun her medical studies, so Pete would not be able to relocate to Earth City right away. That would work out fine, both for the PANS plan and for Adam's plan. He decided to approach Pete just after the earth comm, which was scheduled for the next evening.

In the early evening on announcement day Adam, the rest of the PANS team and the eleven members of the senate oversight committee assembled at Communication Hall, not far from the population administration building. Adam anticipated the initial round of greetings and he wiped his palms with a handkerchief; he hadn't been face to face with Senator Bitterman in years.

He didn't approach the senator. Instead he waited until Avery introduced him. Bitterman had a firm handshake; Adam assumed "well practiced." Bitterman was cordial, but Adam knew he remembered. Bitterman was smooth, but the man appeared unable to hold eye contact.

Adam sat with the team and the committee, in a semicircle that faced both the earth comm supernet crew and equipment and a live audience of a few hundred. While he waited for the procedure to begin, he couldn't keep his mind off Bitterman. His youthful encounter with the man had also been in front of such a worldwide audience, and he had been thoroughly humiliated. The solar system colonies, he thought, had also watched and listened.

Bitterman had won that long ago debate. *Why couldn't he look me in the eye?* Adam asked himself.

The senator was, he thought, pudgy. The man had gained weight. Maybe others wouldn't notice; it may not be that apparent. He hadn't seen the senator close up for almost ten years, and he repeated the word "pudgy" in his mind when the man got up to speak. Perhaps, he thought, Bitterman used his privileged position to obtain extra food for himself. Maybe not, he chided himself. Food was not scarce on Earth. *Not now.*

Adam listened while Bitterman made a few brief remarks. Avery then explained the general plan as well as bragged about the earlier farm elimination plan, and introduced the members of the PANS team. King explained the distance to Earth-Twin and the trip time, and described the spacecraft. He showed a visual of the ship schematic, and Adam thought of a five-kilometer bicycle wheel. King continued with details about the voyage.

Adam drifted to other thoughts. His turn to speak would come up soon; he could feel it in the pit of his stomach. He took out the handkerchief and wiped his palms again, and quietly pored over his scribbled notes. He thought about coffee, but none was available at the comm. He heard King conclude his remarks. "During the coasting phase, the ship will make one complete rotation in just under one hundred seconds. This will not cause any problems such as dizziness."

After several others talked, Avery reintroduced Adam.

Adam straightened his tunic, made sure it was closed at the neck and stood up. From memory, he explained the shipboard food factories and the open-air farms. He mentioned that some of the colonists might even forage for native food in the beginning.

He concluded his intentionally short talk. "The ships will carry some stored food. Most of this will be used up by the time of arrival, with a small reserve left over. That's the nutritional plan." He looked over the live audience. "Any questions?" He hoped for none.

A number of children accompanied the adults in the audience of several hundred. A dark-haired little girl in the front row, about eight or nine years old, raised her hand. "Yes, young lady?" Adam responded.

The little girl stood up. "My name is Nola," she said. "I have a question. Since the people won't have any stores to go to, how can they buy food?"

Adam smiled. He didn't know just what she was questioning, so he rephrased some of what he had already said. He started when she responded, "But a million people! Will they have enough to eat?"

So that's what she's worried about! He hesitated, started to answer, glanced at pudgy John Bitterman and at Hugh Bruce, and then referred the question to Avery. He sat down, took out his handkerchief and wiped the fresh perspiration from his brow.

Avery got up and explained, to both the little girl and the rest of the audience, "Yes, they'll have plenty. They'll easily be able to gather wild fruits and vegetables and hunt and trap the animals, while they build their houses and start their farms. The still-operating shipboard factories will be the main food source in the beginning. They'll have plenty to eat. After a few years, the farms will be well on their way. Then people will buy food from stores."

Adam tried to relax when little Nola finally sat down. She had, he thought, just wanted some reassurance; but he couldn't forget her last question. He couldn't have answered it the way Avery had.

He calmed down while several others gave short presentations and answered more questions. After the comm concluded and the government people departed, Hugh Bruce confronted him as he stood by the door and waited for Avery. "You ducked a question, Hampton. Losing your confidence?"

Adam clenched his teeth. *I don't need this right now*, he thought. He started to answer, but Avery interrupted, "Come now, Hugh. You should be congratulating Adam for his discretion. He obviously had an answer in mind."

Bruce backed off. "Sure, Bill. You're right." He looked at Adam. "Sorry, Hampton."

"That's all right." Adam forced a smile. He added, after Bruce left the room, "Thanks, Bill. For understanding."

"That's why you're here." Avery smiled. "We need an honest skeptic."

"I'll try not to be too skeptical." Adam managed a genuine smile now. "It *is* a grand project."

"We're planning a new civilization, Adam. It's not a simple colonization like Mars and the moon."

Chapter 5

A New Civilization

Adam accompanied Avery on the brief outdoor walk back to the population administration building. The city street, in the twilight, looked less crowded than usual. Many people had gone home earlier for the comm, Adam thought, but those few on the street had not been left out. He knew most had picked it up on wrist receivers.

"The general idea was always for one-way ships," Avery said. "Everyone who goes, stays."

"I got that from the discussions," Adam said.

"We must make it an official team decision," Avery said. He hesitated, and then added, "First thing tomorrow's meeting."

Adam nodded.

"It's all about the distance," Avery said. Adam nodded again. Avery continued, "Rob educated me. We have to talk of great astronomical distances as time distances instead of space distances."

Adam glanced at Avery while he walked alongside.

"It's the shortest time," Avery said, "to transport people or send messages."

Adam now understood. He recalled that his father had talked about it long ago. Earth-Twin was more than fourteen years away from the point of view of Earth. From the travelers' point of view, seven years described the journey. Radio distance was twelve years, each way.

When they reached their destination, Adam glanced at the stone lions guarding the entrance. He followed Avery up the short stairway and entered the building. "Our human minds can't picture such space distances," Avery said. "We have nothing to compare. It's far beyond our sensory experience. We can't even visualize the distance to the sun."

"A centimeter to the sun, eight kilometers to Tau Ceti," Adam said, partly to himself. He realized he couldn't grasp the distance to the sun, other than to simply call it "one hundred and fifty million kilometers." His father's words painted a useful but not definitive picture.

"But we can visualize the time, in a sense," Avery said as the two entered the jet lift. "We adults have all lived more than twelve or fourteen years, so such time distances are part of our sensory experience."

"Eight minutes to the Sun, twelve years to Tau Ceti," Adam said. "At limit-speed. I understand."

"Rob will tell us more as we go along," Avery promised. "Of course, hypersignal changes some communication numbers." He hesitated, and then added, "We'll finalize some of this tomorrow."

"All right." Adam exited the jet lift on his office floor while Avery stayed aboard. He walked down the empty hallway, entered his office, poured a cup of coffee and sat down at his desk to think for a few minutes before going home. *New civilization?* At such a large time distance, the plan's participants can certainly be called that.

Another question stuck in his mind. *Will they have enough to eat?* It was just an innocent question, he told himself, from a child.

*   *   *

At home a little later in the evening, Adam donned his blue jeans and pocket shirt. He rode the chute to the campus and revisited The Alligator for the first time. He had meant to come back sooner, he told himself, but had been too busy.

He stood by the bar and ordered a mug of beer. The Alligator was quieter and less crowded than his first visit. He hoped that no one would recognize him from the comm. *Except her.* Would she recognize him? Would she remember that she had smiled at him? he asked himself. He looked around while he drank his beer, but in the lighter weekday crowd he saw that Jennifer Brown wasn't there. When he finished the beer, he decided he was tired from a long and hectic day. He went home.

*   *   *

At the early morning meeting, Adam listened to Avery congratulate the team for the comm and then bring up the one-way trip question. Since this had been the unofficial plan for a long time, the team quickly made it official. Adam voted in favor; he understood its practicability.

He sipped coffee while King got up to go over the technical details of a one-way voyage. The now official decision would make return trips not only unplanned, he thought, but impossible. The colonists would be unable to initiate any kind of space travel, not for many years.

He watched King bring up a visual that represented the trip with a dotted line and point out its parts. This time the incomprehensible distance numbers did not appear. He glanced down at the fine wood grain of the tabletop. He had finished his father's chart by himself. That chart, he thought, had looked much like King's visual. He picked up his cup from its square pad and sipped more coffee.

He worked with King and the rest of the team on the details. In general, the colonists would tear down parts of the ships and recycle the materials to build new facilities. Other sections would initially shelter many of them at their new home, and continue to house the food factories.

Adam refilled his coffee cup several times while he and the team worked out a transportation plan for the planet. They decided to instruct the engineers to design into the ships a number of large modular rooms and walls in a way that each could be detached and reassembled to become aircraft capable of carrying many people.

These would be human-piloted, the only choice for a primitive and uncharted planet.

A few hundred small surface vehicles, modified for the higher gravity, would go with each ship. They were primarily for convenience, for quick local hops. These "terrains," or, more affectionately, "terries," had been used on Mars and the moon for a long time.

Small and medium-sized microfusion engines powered both the terries and the aircraft. Each ship would carry enough microfusion fuel for several years of air and ground transport. Later the colonists would produce their own fuel from native resources.

Adam finished his fourth cup of coffee when Avery stood up and adjourned the meeting.

✳   ✳   ✳

Back at his office, Adam sat down and tried to relax for a few moments. His v-v interrupted. "You there yet, old buddy?"

Adam turned toward the display and hit a key. "I'm here."

"Been trying to get you all morning," Pete's face above the terminal said.

"Meeting."

"I haven't heard from you in weeks," Pete said. "I just found out yesterday what you'd gotten yourself into. Yeah, I saw it all."

"I can finally talk about it." Adam smiled.

"Sounds like Avery's really charged up." Pete returned Adam's smile.

"He is." Right now would be a good time, Adam thought, to approach his old friend about a future job with the plan. "You have to meet Bill, and I'd like you to think about something. We need a food factory expert. Maybe not right away. Let's say near future."

Pete's smile faded. "You want to hire me?"

"You wouldn't have to come to the city right away," Adam encouraged. "You can wait for Linda to finish."

"By the way, you just missed her," Pete said. "She's gone off to study. These first few months at the institute are getting to her."

Adam relaxed in his chair. He had been sitting on its edge since he had identified his caller. He picked up a touch of sarcasm in Pete's voice, at least in the last few words, but shrugged it off. "Say hello for me," he said. "And think about the job."

Adam and Pete conversed at length about food factory operation in space, until Adam noted the time and said goodbye.

*   *   *

While he walked to Communication Hall on the evening of the second public announcement, on a Friday two months after the first comm, Adam thought about some of Avery's earlier comments. Avery had emphasized that the colonists would not only become a new civilization, but would do so as soon as they departed Earth orbit.

He found it easy to think of large numbers of people while he dodged others also on foot on the crowded streets of the city. The first group of two million would use the seven-year travel time to plan the details of their initial life on Earth-Twin. They would form a government, and devise their own laws.

He pulled the high collar of his tunic tighter around his neck; a cold breeze heralded the coming winter. This reminded him, as he picked up his pace, that the team had rejected the controversial low-temperature method of suspended animation. The earlier planners, for the explorers' trip, had also done so. Such methods for space travel had not proved desirable even for the shorter trips within Earth's solar system. This imperfect technology carried a failure rate, or death rate, of more than ten percent. Instead the travelers would utilize a two-week to four-week temporary hibernation method to combat boredom and conserve food and oxygen. Hibernation lowered body temperature only a few degrees, and had worked well for the explorer group when used voluntarily throughout most of their round trip.

The colonists would be awake for a large part of their seven-year one-way trip, he thought. The PANS team would provide them with some kind of rudimentary government and ship command structure, like a medium-sized city, but after launch they would be on their own. He recalled that the team had decided to use the word "colonists" to describe those going to Earth-Twin, even though that was not an accurate description. The expressions "pioneers" and "settlers" had been discussed.

The streets emptied as he neared the government complex of buildings. Most people had gone home for the comm, he thought, so that they could see and hear it with family. Many all over Earth, he told himself, would be choosing to become Earth-Twin colonists.

*   *   *

At comm number two, Adam sat quietly in the semicircle and faced the live audience while Avery explained the details of more recent team decisions. Only unmarried volunteers in the age range of twenty-one to thirty-five years would be accepted; later in the plan the upper age limit might be increased. A million female and a million male would emigrate each year. They would be free to marry and raise families in space. All ships would carry additional food facilities and other life support for a carefully forecasted rate of population increase.

The colonists would make their own rules, Adam thought. They would recognize the limitations and at least limit those shipboard births. After all, he reassured himself, they must live with the consequences. In deep space, such consequences would be immediate and inescapable.

Avery quickly ended his talk. The man must feel restricted, Adam thought. In an earth comm, Avery couldn't move around as much as he did at PANS meetings; the comm agenda called for more structure. Presenters addressed the live audience as well as the supernet-connected humans throughout the solar system.

Adam listened while King discussed the tools and equipment the colonists would take with them from Earth. Avery had earlier informed Adam that he would be made leader of the group that would forecast development on Earth-Twin. His recent dissertation work qualified him for this job. His group would choose both the equipment and the expertise carried by each year's spacecraft. So far he and the team had decided only that each succeeding trip would carry a different mix and number of well-chosen equipment, and had made some preliminary plans for the first group. He watched King display a visual showing various tools and powered equipment, and listened to him explain each.

Adam was originally scheduled to present next, but he had asked King to fill in for him. King brought up a new visual. This one showed various tractors, harvesters, and other farm machinery that had not been used on Earth for many decades. Adam had prepared this part of the presentation, so he knew the details. He sat quietly while King talked to the world about seeds, fuels, spare parts and other supplies that the colonists would take from Earth for initial use and produce from native resources later.

He relaxed when King finished this short presentation and Avery closed the comm with, "While our political leaders fully support the plan, they're unhappy about the colonists' new independence. After all, they'll be losing two million voters every year!"

Adam glanced at Senator Bitterman, who sat halfway around the semicircle from him. He imagined a scowl on the man's pudgy face.

After the live audience and government officials departed, Avery stood in front of the still seated PANS team. Adam thought briefly about coffee, and then focused his attention on Avery.

"We must decide what to send by hypersignal," Avery said. He glanced around at the team members. "You recall that the engineers told us we'd be limited to only brief signals. Each ship will send a single short message. I have my own idea what this message must be." He smiled. "I believe you'll agree with me, but I want all of you to think about it independently. We'll compare ideas Monday."

Adam saw Avery look directly at him. "Think about it," Avery said. "We can transmit only one short message from each ship. A number or a few short words, and probably soon after it lands. What's best? What is the most vital piece of information in our grand experiment?"

*   *   *

At The Alligator later in the evening, Adam sat at the bar, nursed a beer and thought about the hypersignal during a break in the music and flashing lights. He had attended lectures at the main campus a few years back, when the early results were first publicized.

Hypersignal bent space. He knew that this explanation was just superficial; hypersignal bent space in a way that distances appeared to be much shorter. Instead of the twelve years for an ordinary radio signal, a hypersignal message would reach Earth from Earth-Twin in just under one year.

That was theory, he thought. Although they had worked out the details, the engineers had not yet tested it for that distance. They had determined only that the present state of the technology limited the plan to a very short message from each ship. Later, when the method improved, more detailed communications might be possible. *That*, he told himself, *could be a long time away*.

He glanced around. He hoped to see long blond hair, but found it difficult to focus when the flashing lights came on again. The music started and battered his ears. He looked around and squinted for a few minutes but didn't find Jennifer Brown. He could walk around later and look for her, he told himself, after he finished the beer.

He relaxed on the bar stool and tried to concentrate in the din. He asked himself what that single short message from Earth-Twin should be. He wondered what might be the most important parameter in the "grand experiment." He looked out at the crowd that had gathered on the dance floor, and he knew.

One item of information carried the message of success or failure. *The signal must be the current human population of Earth-Twin.*

Will Avery agree? Later, at closing time, Adam left The Alligator with this question in mind. He boarded the chute.

Jennifer Brown had not appeared, and on the ride home he also thought about her. Should he try to contact her at the university? Or even by computer? After all, he thought, the v-v database now made nearly fifty percent of all introductions worldwide. She was probably on line, since she was studying to be a computer specialist and would likely be inclined toward this approach. He was certainly smart enough to "engineer" a match, he told himself, even with his limited knowledge of her.

He decided against this direct approach. He told himself that she was bound to show up at The Alligator again.

*   *   *

At Monday's meeting, Adam sat in his usual seat. He watched Avery's glance go around the table, and then settle on him. "Adam, let's start with you. What should the signal be?"

Adam remained seated. "It has to be a census count of the people," he said.

He smiled when Avery agreed. He sipped coffee while a few other ideas were offered. The team discussed the subject at length and all finally agreed on the census count.

Adam helped plan the process. Each colonization spacecraft would carry a photronic *population counter* and a hypersignal generator. Each of these devices would operate only one time, at the time of ship arrival on the planet.

A population counter, he knew, received human brain waves and counted the number of separate signals. The photronics industry could easily build the counter to be sensitive enough to examine all of Earth-Twin, and do the counting, in minutes.

He understood that Earth would receive the first population count fifteen years after the first ship departed Earth orbit. After that, a census of Earth-Twin would reach Earth once each year. The first count would be the number of colonists who arrived alive on the first ship, and would give some information on the birth rate aboard that ship.

Fifteen years was a long time to wait, Adam thought, but most of that was ship travel time. He swallowed the last slug of coffee in his cup when Avery took the floor and adjourned the meeting.

*   *   *

Adam decided to have a beer or two at The Alligator in the evening. As he prepared at home, he thought about the morning's meeting. He got what he wanted for the content of the signal, but he was uneasy. The team would be able to note small trends in the birth rate or death rate, and make long-term corrections to the overall plan. That was important for routine problem solving, he thought, but it would also make it easier for the political leaders to claim that they were "minimizing risk" while "doing something" about Earth's population.

Could risk really be minimized? he asked himself. At such a time distance, could the team handle a more serious problem even if alerted? He left his apartment, entered the crowded street and headed for the chute station.

At The Alligator he sat by the bar and ordered a mug of beer. He looked around; his glance stopped at a particular table and he felt his heartbeat pick up.

Jennifer Brown sat alone. From the glasses and bottles on the table, Adam figured that she was with several others. *Her friends must be on the dance floor,* he thought.

He got up. He hesitated, and then sat on the bar stool again. He took a coin out of his pocket and placed it on the bar. *For the beer when it comes,* he told himself. He felt his pounding heart. *If the music wasn't so loud,* he thought, *everyone would hear it.*

He got up again, approached Jennifer's table, leaned over and looked at her. "Hi!" he shouted. "May I sit down?"

Jennifer looked up. Adam noted that her eyes were a brilliant green. She didn't say anything. She knew, he thought, that she had seen him before.

He smiled and shouted, "My name's Adam. I saw you sitting here all alone."

Jennifer smiled. She stood up and shouted, "Hi, Adam. I'm Jenny." She extended her hand and Adam took it in his.

Her hand felt pleasantly warm, and that smile was certainly what had kept him coming back to The Alligator. He held on to her hand. "Shall we sit?" he asked.

"It's too noisy to talk," Jenny said. "Let's dance."

Adam led her by the hand to the nearby dance floor. Her waist-length blond hair sparkled in the flashing light, and her eyes were the prettiest green eyes he had ever seen. He also liked the way she fit into her blue jeans.

On the dance floor, Adam couldn't match Jenny's gyrations and certainly not her grace. He followed the music, and, he noted, she didn't complain.

Later Adam picked up his beer from the bar and Jenny her half-full glass from her table. She introduced him to her three female companions who had returned to the table, and he then led her to a small table in a quieter part of The Alligator.

"I've seen you before, Adam," Jenny said as she sat down.

She looked at him in the same way that she had when he had first approached her ten minutes earlier, Adam thought. He sat on the opposite side of the table. He could satisfy her curiosity quickly, he told himself. "Yes," he said, "here at The Alligator a while back. You smiled at me. I couldn't forget your smile."

"No," Jenny said, "I don't remember that." She hesitated a moment, and then, "I remember! You're with the PANS group!" Her green eyes opened wide. "I saw you at the comm. The first one."

"That was I, Jenny." Adam smiled.

"You looked a little nervous," Jenny said. "Cute."

I was a little nervous, Adam thought.

"That little girl asked you some questions," Jenny added. She smiled. "I wished I could've been there. It's so exciting! And I'm actually talking to you." She laughed gently and added, "Oh, I'm just teasing. You're nice. For a famous person."

"We're just doing a job," Adam insisted.

"Yes, a most exciting job!"

"Someone told me you're studying system science," Adam said. He felt flushed and wondered if his face was red. In this quiet area away from the flashing lights, he thought, she might notice that. He took another drink of beer.

"It's system science-special applications." She traced a few letters on the tabletop with her index finger. "We just say SSSA."

Adam looked at her hand. He thought of the warmth when he had held it earlier. He shifted his gaze to her green eyes again. "Which special applications?" he asked. He told himself to talk about her interests.

Jenny reached back, lifted her long hair and released it so that it fell behind her chair back. "It's getting so long that I sometimes forget and sit on it," she said. "Which applications? Maybe PANS. I heard in a lecture that PANS would need some very special computer equipment just for the artificial gravity on the ship. An SSSA type."

Adam picked up his mug, took a quick sip and put it down. "Yes. It's more complicated now than for the explorers."

"Why is it more complicated now?" she asked.

Adam didn't want to talk about work. He could at least try to humor her, he thought. He recalled that the exploration ship just needed an artificial gravity equal to Earth's gravity, so adjustments were relatively simple. "Do you understand about the different stages of artificial gravity?" he asked.

Jenny picked up her glass, but didn't drink. "Yes, I do. We covered that in Physics. I was the best student in my class."

She sounded sincerely interested in the details. Maybe he could take advantage of that, Adam thought, and show off a little. After all, he *was* "famous."

"The difference for the colonization ships," he said, "is that we must gradually acclimate the travelers to the greater gravity."

He took a quick sip of beer and went on. "All the colonists must be physically active and productive immediately after arrival. So we will acclimate them while still en route by gradually increasing the gravity as the ship nears Earth-Twin. Even hibernation will be off limits for the last few months."

Jenny smiled, and Adam took this to mean "Go on, I'm interested."

"The computer must make the gradual change in the late term deceleration," he said, "and make corrections as the ship falls in the extended gravity of Tau Ceti and Earth-Twin."

"I'm surprised. I understood that." Jenny hesitated a moment, and then said, "I guess that might not have worked so well for those explorers, since they must have had a period of weightlessness in their shuttle ships at the end."

"Yes," Adam said quickly, "that's true." He hadn't even thought about that complication, and he wasn't sure just how it might have affected the end result, but he knew now that Jenny didn't just sound interested.

"By the way," he added, "we don't expect any big problems with human adaptation to the higher gravity. It's just that some people may be affected more than others. With such large numbers, we have to be careful. If, say, only one out of a hundred has difficulty, that's still a lot of people."

Jenny nodded. She picked up her glass again, and this time took a short drink. She then smiled and said, "Since you're so good at answering, I have another question. One of the things I always have trouble with is the aging difference for the people on the ship. I guess I understand it for the explorers. They came back younger. But for the new colonists," she asked, "how do you compare when they're so far away?"

She wanted more details about his work, Adam thought, and she asked good questions. He continued to try to show his expertise even though, on this subject, he had little. "I don't think you can compare directly," he said. "It's a problem about the concept of 'now.' It's difficult to judge the simultaneity of events, whether or not things happen at the same time. This is because of the way space and time are related instead of being separate. The difficulty comes about for very-far-away events. We just have to talk about such things as if we understood them, and plan using the proven mathematics."

Adam looked at his beer mug. It was nearly empty. He picked it up and finished it off. "We just use 'now,' 'last week,' 'next year' and other such expressions," he said, "as if things were happening right here on Earth. But we know that the meaning is obscured."

"I used to talk to my physics professor about that 'simultaneity,'" Jenny said, "when we covered relativity. It's something I never really understood."

"Rob King explained it to me. He's the senior engineer on the team. Maybe I can get him to talk to you." Adam looked at his empty mug and wondered if he should get a refill.

"Yes," Jenny said. "Please do." She hesitated, and then added, "It's nice the way we have real professors at the university—someone to talk to. In prep we just had computers. I like computers, but when I have a question, I want to ask a person." She smiled. "Like you."

"I hope my answers helped, Jenny."

"Very much." Jenny picked up her glass and took another sip.

"What are you drinking?" Adam asked.

"It's just *fizz*. I have an early class tomorrow."

Adam looked at his watch. He also had a busy schedule for the morrow. It would be best to call it an evening, he told himself, but he wanted to make certain he would see her again. He felt his heartbeat pick up. He hesitated, and then said, "Jenny, I'm sure both of us have a busy day tomorrow. Can I see you next weekend? Saturday night?"

"Saturday? Yes, I'd like that." Jenny finished off her fizz.

"Why don't we meet right here?" Adam asked. "About seven?"

"Sure." Jenny smiled.

The two talked a little longer, and then said goodbye and parted.

On the chute ride back to his apartment, Adam contemplated Jenny's smile and gave only a little thought to the big decisions he and the others would make in the next few months. The team and its subordinate groups must decide whom to send to Earth-Twin in the first ship. They must choose from the volunteer lists that were already coming in.

Chapter 6

The First Group

Adam and the others, including several newly commissioned groups guided by individual PANS team members, began to process the applications of well over a million volunteers. More came in every day. Adam sat at his desk alone in the afternoon a few days after his talk with Jenny Brown; he had just finished preparing some notes on skills selection. He filled his coffee cup, breathed in its aroma and took a deep swallow. The colonists, he thought, would certainly grow coffee on the planet.

He thought about the volunteers. Those chosen would leave crowded Earth and many of its ways forever. Families would be broken up. Young adults would abandon their parents and siblings and never see them again. They might never even communicate again. He wondered if he would lose anyone.

He thought of Pete. Maybe he could benefit from the plan by bringing his old friend to Earth City. Pete had been coy about it when approached earlier, Adam thought, but he had had some time to think it over. The research position could be arranged in a way that did not interfere with Linda's medical studies.

He took another drink of coffee, and then pulled the terminal table close. He hit the familiar keys.

Pete's face appeared almost immediately. "Adam, old buddy."

Adam hesitated a moment. He wondered if Linda might appear. He hadn't seen her in months, and he thought he might be able to handle her presence. After all, he had a date with Jenny. "Pete, I'm waiting for Linda," he said. He smiled.

"I'm alone again," Pete said.

Pete almost spit that out, Adam thought. He recalled his friend's attitude at the last v-v, but decided not to pursue it. *They've had a lovers' quarrel,* he told himself.

Adam and Pete discussed newer details about spacebound agriculture. Adam again offered Pete the research position in the city, and Pete said he would "think about it."

*   *   *

Adam and Jenny met on Saturday. After a few hours of dancing, they left the noise of The Alligator and strolled to a nearby restaurant where they could talk. Adam chose a private little booth. When they were seated, he ordered coffee.

"I have another PANS question," Jenny said after the waitress left the table.

"Sure, Jenny. It's good to talk to someone who can understand what I'm talking about."

"I like the details." Jenny smiled.

Her green eyes sparkled even in the dim light and, Adam noted, her long blond hair appeared to take on a glow. The quiet little restaurant didn't need a light show. She also smelled good.

"Your question?" Adam asked. He looked around to see if the coffee was on its way.

"What about communication?" she asked. "I know radio is restricted by limit-speed. I guess we could say they'll be out of contact with Earth."

Adam could show off again; the hypersignal plan had not yet been publicized. "We'll have radio," he said, "but it won't be like calling up Mars. We just worked out a plan to use the new hypersignal."

The waitress brought coffee. This was one of the old type restaurants, where robotic services never did take over. Adam believed they were called "quaint." The charm of the place attracted young lovers, he thought, and young hopefuls.

He watched Jenny put cream and sugar into her cup and stir. He left his coffee black and took a sip to test for temperature.

"We had some lectures on hypersignal," Jenny said. "I didn't understand it." She gestured with her hands as if she were bending something, and smiled.

Adam glanced at her small hands. He liked the tint of the red polish on her fingernails. "Very few people do," he said.

"Bend space." Jenny repeated the bending gesture. "It sounded so weird to me."

"It's going to be the only communication in the beginning," Adam said. "Radio will reach us later, of course." He explained the recent PANS decision, and then added, "Takes less than a year." He picked up his cup and took a sip.

"That's a lot faster than radio," Jenny said.

Adam put down the cup. "We still have the simultaneity problem, even with hypersignal. It just changes some of the numbers." He said this as if he almost understood it.

"That's so fascinating. Simultaneity." Jenny smiled. "I'm going to learn more about it."

Adam contemplated her smile. He changed the subject. "Jenny, I want to see you again. Often."

Jenny hesitated, and then said, "I'd like to see you, too."

Adam ignored her hesitation. *I can't stop now*, he thought. "Let's plan another night," he said. "Maybe PIP? I tried some mountain climbing last week. We could go on a hike or something. In a forest. Or that new roller coaster one. You know what a roller coaster is, don't you? Probably from Physics?"

"I'd better tell you something about me," Jenny said. She picked up her cup and took a sip of coffee.

It was her first drink, Adam thought. He didn't say anything.

"You may not want to get to know me too well," she said. She took another sip. "I've been asking all those questions for a reason. I'm going to volunteer."

"Volunteer?" Adam started to say more, and then hesitated. He picked up his cup and took a big slug of coffee, and then ordered a refill. He told himself to remain calm. The first group was scheduled to leave in about two years; he had time to do something about it.

Adam and Jenny talked for a long time that evening. The two went through many cups of coffee. Jenny drank sparingly and Adam not so sparingly.

In the following weeks, Adam and Jenny frequented The Alligator and quiet restaurants, walked in the PIP forest and even braved the PIP roller coaster.

*　　　　　*　　　　　*

Four months after the first public announcement of the plan, the PANS team held the third earth comm. While Adam sat in the semicircle, others explained the big hypersignal generators that would be built just for the plan and discussed the population counters. Adam didn't speak at this comm.

A few weeks later Assistant Professor Lynn Higami, Pete's research director at the main campus, signed on as a part-time advisor to the team. Adam hoped this arrangement would help him convince Pete to come to the city, but he knew Higami's involvement would end before the first ship departed; she had been accepted as a colonist.

Adam did not speak at the half-dozen bimonthly comms that followed the third. He managed to talk King or one of the others into including his reports with theirs, although he wondered why Avery didn't object to this.

He remained determined to bring Pete to the city. At a later voice-visual contact, while he sat at his desk with his finger in the handle of his coffee cup, he again offered Pete the research job; sixteen months had passed since he had first extended the offer. "You know we'll make a great team, Pete," he added when Pete didn't respond immediately. He picked up the cup.

"Not in Earth City, old buddy," Pete's image above the terminal said. "But I need your help. I've been going over the requirements and I may need your influence to get past the *psych profile*."

"The psych profile?" Adam put the cup back down. Fortunately it was only half full, he thought, or he might have splashed coffee on his desk. "You want to go to Earth-Twin?"

"Yeah." Pete smiled. "Can you help me?"

Adam hesitated, and then said, "I may be able to do something." Others made the many detailed evaluations and the majority of the selections, he thought, but the team members retained final authority over all choices.

"Thanks, old buddy."

"Wait a minute, Pete. I haven't agreed to anything. You know I want you here." Adam scribbled a few words on a pad. He then described, to Pete, the merits of the research job in Earth City.

After the v-v, Adam refilled his coffee cup and remained seated behind his desk. Pete, he thought, was determined. Pete had not mentioned Linda, but Adam assumed she would drop out of medical school and volunteer as a medical technician. He thought of the singleness policy; the PANS team did not exclude engaged couples, as long as both were qualified and possessed needed skills.

The groups had not yet filled all the two million slots for the first ship, and he had the power to help his friends qualify. *Or not qualify.* He could do it discreetly, either way. It was a secret system; an unsuccessful volunteer would never learn which individual or individuals rejected the application. The selection group would give only a reason, and there were many valid reasons. The team had had to make rejection easy from the very beginning, he thought, since many more volunteered than could be accepted.

He thought about Jenny, and took a drink of coffee. Her application was on hold, pending completion of university graduation requirements. He had choices to make, and time was getting short.

*   *   *

The team and the selection groups completed the list of two million plus a few thousand alternates, the first colonist group. In the afternoon, four months after Pete had asked for his help, Adam sat at his desk, went over some final notes and sipped coffee.

He looked up when Pete interrupted, this time not from the terminal. Pete didn't knock, he just walked in. "Adam, my old buddy!"

"Pete!" Adam got up.

"Yeah. It's me."

"It's been so long since I've seen you in person." Adam smiled. "But I figured you'd have to come to the city soon."

While they clasped hands, Adam chuckled and briefly broke into song. "Old MacDonald had a farm."

"Well, it looks like I'll get to see some real farms," Pete said. "Thanks to you."

"You're qualified." Adam sat back down behind his desk and motioned Pete to sit in his extra chair.

"But you had to use your influence." Pete moved the chair to the front of the desk and sat down.

"I can't tell you that. But, off the record, some people thought you might not be able to handle the long voyage. Just like you suspected. I managed to convince them about your knack for problem solving." Pete could solve PANS problems here in Earth City, Adam thought, but he said, "The farms and factories will need you."

"Yeah, I remember what you used to say. About technology holding on by a thread."

"I never could convince you." Adam smiled. "I hope things work out."

"Well, thanks again, old buddy." Pete smiled. "I'll make it."

Adam poured Pete a cup of coffee, and then refilled his own cup. "I was really surprised when you told me a few months ago," he said. "I had no idea."

"I'm excited about it." Pete picked up his cup, but didn't drink. He put it back down on the desk. "The first group."

"I feel like I'm losing a brother," Adam said.

"Yeah," Pete said. "Remember how people at the U thought we were brothers?"

"Twin brothers." Adam took a sip of coffee, and thought of the age difference. He was two years older than Pete.

"Even the dirty blond hair." Pete laughed.

"But I was always better looking." Adam chuckled. "Of course, you got the girl."

Pete didn't say anything.

"I guess Linda must be dropping out of med?" Adam asked. He had been too busy to check on Linda Donner's acceptance, and had just assumed it.

"Linda and I are," Pete said, "history." He frowned. He got up and paced Adam's office floor.

Adam stood up. "What? History?" *Had Linda even applied?* he asked himself.

"Since she started at the institute," Pete said, "she's been too busy. She doesn't have time for me anymore."

Adam recalled Pete's increasingly sarcastic attitude toward Linda and how she had not participated in the many v-v contacts. "But that's med," he said. "She'll have more time later." He momentarily ignored Pete's emigration plans and added, "Pete, you've got to be patient."

"Patience! Yeah, I know. My psych profile. It's too late now."

Adam sat down again. "But you two were so close. What did she say when you told her?"

"I didn't." Pete still paced Adam's office. "We haven't been seeing much of each other anyway."

"But she must've seen your name on the list?" Adam pointed to a disk in the disk rack on his desk.

"You know it's a long list, old buddy. Linda doesn't have time for long lists either." Pete sat down again.

"You've got to talk to her," Adam insisted.

"Maybe she likes those medical professors more than us ag specs." Pete picked up his cup, but again didn't drink. "I don't know what she's doing."

"She's working." Adam took a sip from his cup. "She's preparing for a very demanding career."

"I suppose."

"The research job in ag is still open," Adam said. "I could use your help here."

"Maybe I can help you more on the planet. I'll be your Earth-Twin connection." Pete picked up the cup again and this time took a sip.

"That's not the point," Adam said.

"I have to go now. I'd like to spend more time, but I've got a lot to do." Pete stood up. "You know prep starts tomorrow," he said, "and you guys are getting ready to pick the date."

"Yes. We've about pinned it down." Adam stood up.

"If I don't see you again, old buddy, goodbye."

Adam stepped out from behind his desk. "I guess it is goodbye. But I wish you'd at least talk to Linda about this."

"I'll think about it. Thanks again for the help."

"Keep in touch, Pete—" Adam caught his slip and chuckled.

Pete laughed. "You never know, old buddy."

"At least v-v me once in a while before you leave Earth," Adam said.

Adam and Pete engaged in a handshake that ended in a hug. After Pete left, Adam refilled his coffee cup and dumped the contents of Pete's nearly full cup into the office disposal. His old friend, he thought, had never been much of a coffee drinker.

*   *   *

The team scheduled the first departure for New Year's Day, year 2201, just over two years after the first PANS earth comm. Two months before that date, Avery announced it at the regular bimonthly comm.

After this announcement, while Adam sat in his usual seat in the semicircle and listened, Avery reminded the worldwide audience how PIP provided the only adventure available on Earth. Avery described how even life in the orbiting stations and solar system colonies had become crowded and routine.

Life is crowded and routine indeed, Adam thought. Although tourism remained popular, only large salaries and comfortable retirements attracted new solar system emigrants.

He listened only halfheartedly to Avery. As he and the others had expected, the plan to colonize a new and open planet had revived the old dream of adventure in space. Even he had had mixed-up feelings and conflicting motivations during the year just past, and had talked briefly with Avery about it.

He recalled the conversation that had taken place some months earlier, a few weeks before he had learned of Pete's decision. After a final futile attempt to talk Jenny out of her decision, he had entered Avery's office and told him that he wanted to resign from the team.

"You're serious about this?" Avery had asked.

"I'd like to volunteer for the first ship. I think I can fit into one of the odd slots. Yes, I know I'm the one who's been skeptical all along."

"Adam, please reconsider. I won't block you. But we need you here. Your dissertation work makes you unique. We chose you for the team because we need you."

"I won't argue that. But I'd still like to go."

He recalled Avery's hand on his shoulder and the man's disarming smile when he had added, "As I told you when we first met, you'll also keep the rest of us from allowing our enthusiasm to overshadow our good judgment."

He wondered if he had acquiesced too easily.

Adam continued to daydream while Avery concluded the public announcement. He heard only Avery's closing remark about "the few months remaining before the big day."

*   *   *

Adam, alone at home in the evening on New Year's Day, watched the departure at his v-v terminal. The Earth-orbiting ship slowed its rotation and started its main engines. It was bathed in full sunlight at its orbital position; he could see it clearly. He knew that walls and floors inside the ship changed places when all rotation finally stopped. The colonists, he told himself, had to be strapped in for that. Some large internal modules, like the fifteen food factory "sections," pivoted ninety degrees.

The ship gained speed in a direction parallel to the axis of its wheel shape, and he imagined a great bicycle wheel drifting off sideways. The image grew smaller as the ship moved away from its co-orbiting v-v station.

He had been invited to watch at Avery's apartment, he thought, but he had turned down that invitation. He could, alternatively, have joined several other team members at a party at one's home.

At first Adam could read the expression "PANS 1," which emblazoned the ship's panels in letters fifty meters high at several locations on the outer walls. The letters soon grew too small, and the ship shrank from his view. It entered the curved space path, a partial orbit of the sun, which allowed it to most efficiently depart the sun's gravity and the solar system itself.

Adam sat and watched, with a glass of wine in his hand, while the grand machine drifted out of v-v station range. It became a pinpoint of reflected sunlight on his display, and he soon lost it among the many stars.

He put the half empty glass down, got up and walked out onto his balcony. In the cold and quiet night he gazed at dim Tau-Ceti.

He shivered slightly. He had not felt so alone, he thought, since just after his father's death. Jenny was gone. That dynamite smile and those green eyes, that optimism, that curiosity and sense of wonder were gone forever. All would brighten another world, and never again his.

*   *   *

Adam sat in the semicircle and faced the live audience at the PANS earth comm on the day after the departure. The other comms had all been informative, he thought. This one was instead part of the celebration.

He looked at Avery, who greeted the audience and then said, "Let's talk about the people, our friends and relatives."

He saw Avery look at him and grin. "Team member Adam Hampton," Avery said, "will give you some of the details."

He hadn't expected to be called upon, but apparently, he told himself, Avery had been saving this for him. He was stuck now. He looked at Bitterman, and noted that the senator's pudgy face showed no particular emotion. He needn't say anything that would rile the man, he thought. He glanced at Bruce and detected a faint smile. He almost smiled back; he believed that, although he had disagreements with

Bruce, the man would not attack him during a comm. He expected no such consideration from Bitterman.

He straightened his tunic, got up, hesitated a moment, and then spoke up. "I'd like to first thank the many individuals who helped in the preparation. I wish I could give all the names, but I have to keep this to a reasonable time. I'll just name Assistant Professor of Agriculture Lynn Higami. She helped us with many details. Unfortunately, she won't hear this. As many of you know, Professor Higami is one of the chosen two million. Thank you, Lynn. Have a safe and happy voyage."

The applause from the live audience of several hundred gave Adam a moment to collect his thoughts. He took out a handkerchief and wiped his brow.

He mentioned the medical profession and gave a few volunteers' names. After more applause, he discussed the shipboard food factories and mentioned Pete's name. He wiped his brow again during the applause, and then talked briefly about the volunteers who had recently received old-time surface farm training. He covered several other occupations, and apologized for not being able to discuss all.

He added, "We chose a small number of computer specialists. They'll operate the shipboard computers."

He hesitated for a moment and looked toward the high ceiling of the hall. He looked back at the live audience, took a deep breath and added, "Jennifer Brown is one of those computer specialists."

He took another deep breath. "Good luck, Jenny. And happy birthday." He tried to smile. "Jenny turned twenty-one just a week before departing. She's the youngest of the two million."

The live audience again applauded.

"Administrator Avery will now say a few more words," Adam said. He sat down, wiped his brow and put away his handkerchief.

Avery stood up. "Thank you, Adam." He turned toward the live audience. "Adam's being modest," he said. "He didn't tell you how much he himself contributed. Let's give him a hand."

Again applause filled the room, and Adam hoped his embarrassment didn't show. Avery waited until the applause subsided. He then said, "Just a few more things. Then you can go to your parties. We've been especially careful with this first two million, and will be for the next several groups."

Adam recalled that the selection teams had disqualified persons with any record of criminal activity or even a tendency in the psych profile. Although crime was no longer as prevalent as it once had been, he thought, it had never been totally eliminated.

Similarly they had disqualified anyone whose profile indicated a war-like nature. Adam recalled a number of notorious names, particularly from the twentieth century, whose profiles were used to determine the parameters. He listened as Avery continued. "Later groups won't need such extensive evaluation. They'll arrive on Earth-Twin to join an established and growing civilization. We won't always need to send only our best."

Yes, Adam thought, *our best!*

"Now these first two million young people are on their way to what is certainly the greatest adventure that a large group of humans ever shared," Avery said. "There'll be no coming back to Earth and Earth's ways. I applaud their enthusiasm!"

"And their bravery," Adam whispered to himself. "Goodbye, Jenny. Goodbye, Pete." *I hope my fears are unfounded*, he thought. *But we won't know anything for a long time.*

Chapter 7

A Long Wait

Adam visited with Bill and Brenda Avery at their home, a few days after the departure. He and Avery stood and talked on the Averys' private roof patio amidst potted flowers. He could see the rooftops of nearby shorter buildings, and a taller building to the southwest blocked the sun. A retractable glass enclosure kept the cold afternoon air at bay.

Adam accepted a steaming cup of coffee from Brenda when she joined them. "She got to you, didn't she?" she asked.

"I guess so," Adam said.

"I still think about the time you brought Jenny over here to visit with us." Brenda smiled. "She's a sweetheart."

"The prettiest smile I've ever seen." Adam took a careful sip of coffee. "I tried," he said, "but I couldn't talk her out of it."

Brenda winked. "You could've disqualified her."

"But that's not Adam's way, dear," Avery said. He turned toward Adam and laughed. "The team would've backed you up. She would never have known. We want a happy Adam."

"I kind of figured that," Adam said. He took another sip of coffee.

Avery put his hand on Adam's shoulder. "Nevertheless, my boy, you did right."

Adam didn't know if his boss praised his refusal to disqualify Jenny or his decision to stay with the team and on Earth rather than follow her. *Probably both*, he thought, although he was sure that Avery knew how halfhearted had been his plan to emigrate. Both he and Avery, he told himself, have had time to think about that conversation. "Thanks, Bill," he said.

"You'll meet someone else." Brenda smiled. "You're young."

"I'm looking," Adam replied. He sipped coffee.

"And it could be someone you've already met," Brenda said. "You never know."

Adam nodded. "Jenny's mother and father were in the front row at the comm," he said. "I was going to ask them to stand up for a round of applause. But they looked so sad, I just couldn't call attention to them."

"You knew them well?" Avery asked.

"No. They didn't come to Earth City very often, since Jenny usually went up north on holidays." Adam sipped more coffee. "We did talk some about Earth-Twin last week. I'm sure it wasn't easy, but they gave their blessing. I guess they understood her reason."

Later Adam and Avery relaxed on patio chairs by a small table and watched the sun go down behind the lower buildings to the west. A bottle of creme sherry and two empty glasses sat on the table.

Adam's relaxed mood didn't last. "Can't we wait now and see how it works out?" he questioned. "Before sending more?"

"Not possible," Avery said. "You and I talked about this before."

"Send one or two more groups," Adam said, "and then wait for results."

"You know we won't even get a hypersignal for fifteen years." Avery picked up the bottle. "We have to address the problem, and we both know it won't be through population controls here on Earth."

"But it has to be," Adam said. "I want to bring this up at meetings, but I don't want another fight with Hugh Bruce."

"Don't avoid Hugh." Avery poured creme sherry into one glass. "Face up to him. If you have something specific to say, say it. Take over the meeting."

"I don't want to disrupt anything," Adam said. He watched Avery fill the second glass.

"Don't worry about that. Remember, you're the honest skeptic."
Avery picked up a full glass and handed it to Adam.

That's what I'm trying to be right now, Adam thought, but he said,
"You're right. I have to talk to the whole team." He accepted the glass
and took a sip.

"You know we'll be busy," Avery said, "even while waiting for the signals. But disrupt meetings if you must." He picked up his glass and took
a drink.

"I don't mean you shouldn't confront me in private like this," Avery
added. "If you see me doing something wrong, holler at me. About anything. Remember, I'm also the administrator."

Avery took another short drink, and put his glass down. "With the
team, it should be just PANS. But we need more than generalities. We
need to know why it won't work."

The government's "doing something" about the problem, Adam
thought, and he had no evidence to use in an argument. "Sure, Bill," he
said. "I guess I'll think about it some more."

*　　　　　*　　　　　*

On his way home from the Averys' apartment, Adam skillfully
negotiated the crowded Earth City streets. He thought about his talk
with Avery an hour earlier, and Earth-Twin's higher gravity came to
mind. More than a year ago he had briefly argued with Hugh Bruce
about just that topic. Then the team had been exploring the physical
differences between Earth and Earth-Twin at greater length than in
the earlier meetings, even as they were beginning preparations for the
first departure. He recalled how he had been unwilling, or maybe
unable, to persist in such a direct confrontation at a meeting.

Should he have confronted Avery this evening? After all, it had been
Avery's earlier responsibility; he had headed the study team. Something

about that gravity study appeared to be incomplete, Adam thought, or unexplained, but he couldn't point to anything specific.

*   *   *

At home, well after dark, Adam stood out on his small balcony and gazed toward the constellation Cetus. A cold breeze braced his face. He shivered a little and pulled his tunic tighter around his neck.

The winter night was relatively quiet. During the warmer months, he had listened to the night sounds of the city. Now it was much quieter.

In the cloudless sky, decorated by myriad stars and a thin crescent moon, Adam easily identified faint Tau Ceti. His thoughts drifted.

Jenny had listened with him, to the summer city at night. They had experienced PIP together: mountain and forest hikes, roller coasters and downhill skiing. She had been delighted when he had shown her the explorers' visos of the orange sun.

He and Jenny weren't the only pair separated by the PANS plan, he thought. *Did Pete talk to Linda? Probably not. Most certainly not, or he wouldn't have gone.*

Adam planned to call her in a day or two, and to restrict that contact to voice without visual. Linda would be studying at the faraway main campus for years, and he was busy in Earth City. Even with Pete gone, he thought, he must remain aloof.

He stood and shivered for a long time, absorbed in his thoughts.

*   *   *

The next five years passed uneventfully for Adam. He lost interest in The Alligator, and he attended official departure celebrations only as a duty. PIP and occasional private parties became his only diversions. As head of the occupation selection group, he found little spare time.

He decided to attend a private reception just after the departure of the sixth ship. He was not duty bound, but he had worked long hours for several weeks; he welcomed this diversion.

He expected only some idle chatter and a chance to make a new friend or two, but soon after he arrived at the reception hall he spotted an unexpected familiar face. Linda Donner stood near the entrance and, he thought, she searched for a familiar face herself.

She was tall, but not too tall. He recalled Pete's word from years ago: Linda was "statuesque." Her auburn hair fell to just below her shoulders. She wore a well-fitted white tunic, like his gray. His idle plan changed. *Could she be here in Earth City*, he asked himself, *permanently?*

He hesitated a moment, composed himself and approached her. "Linda!"

She turned toward him. "Oh! Adam!"

Her blue eyes reminded Adam of a summer sky. His heart rate accelerated. He told himself to calm down. "Linda, it's good to see you. It's been years."

Linda extended her hand, and Adam took it in his. "Too many years, Adam," she said. "It's so good to see you, too. You look well. Are you behaving yourself?"

"I'm behaving. I'm too busy for anything else." Adam looked into her eyes. *Sky blue*, he again thought. He let go of her hand. "You must be finished with med. What're you doing now?"

"I have an internship right here in Earth City. I guess you could say I'm busy, too."

"I haven't even talked to you since right after Pete left." Adam grimaced slightly. "I'm sorry. I shouldn't bring that up."

"It's all right." Linda hesitated, and then said, "Pete didn't even say goodbye." She bowed her head.

"I tried to get him to talk to you." Adam took both her hands in his. He felt her squeeze his hands.

"Oh, Adam! I still believe he really loved me—even after he left." She leaned closer and put her head on his shoulder.

"He's gone," Adam said. "We both know Pete's halfway to another world." He put his arms around her, and could almost hear his heart pound. He again told himself to be calm. What she needed right now, he thought, was a friend.

"It took me a while to accept that," Linda said, her head still on Adam's shoulder.

Adam looked around and wondered what the other partygoers might be thinking. The room was full of people, mostly strangers. He quickly convinced himself that they would see only two old friends who hadn't been together in a long time. "It's been so long since we've seen each other," he said. He hesitated to build up his courage, and then asked, "Why don't we plan to do something together?"

"I'd like that." Linda raised her head.

Adam released her from his arms. "Let's sit over there," he said. He pointed to a small table in a quiet corner of the large hall. He led her by the hand to the table, and held a chair for her while she sat down. "I'll get us some coffee," he said.

As he carried a tray with two cups of black coffee, a spoon, a container of cream and a package of sweetener to the table, he recalled Brenda Avery's long ago comment about someone he had already met. He sat down across from Linda. "I know we're both busy," he said, "but let's find the time to get together." He took a careful sip of hot coffee.

Linda put cream in her coffee and stirred. "What did he say?" she asked. "About me?"

"What?" Adam put his cup down on the table. "Oh, you mean Pete."

"Was he angry?" Linda asked.

"I wouldn't say angry," Adam answered. "He said that you didn't have any time for him. I tried to convince him he was overreacting." He noticed a tear sparkle in the corner of Linda's eye.

"I feel so dumb," she said.

"He *did* overreact." He reached across the small table and took her left hand in his right. "It wasn't your fault."

"What's his new home going to be like?" Linda asked. "I know he'll have a different year. But why is it shorter than ours?"

"That's an important question," Adam said. *Maybe I can help her talk it out of her system,* he thought. "It turns out that Tau Ceti is cooler than our sun. For a planet to have an earthlike climate, it must stay closer."

"That's kind of what I thought," Linda said.

"He'll get used to it quickly," Adam said. He still held her hand in his. He leaned closer over the table and looked into her blue eyes. "I've always thought you were special," he said. "I kept it to myself. But I'd like to get to know you better now."

"Will he have any trouble with the gravity?" Linda asked.

Adam let go of her hand, leaned back and took a drink of coffee. "He'll adjust easily," he said. "The exploration trip proved that. And agriculture shouldn't be a problem. I wasn't personally involved in those studies, but those who were expect no difficulties."

He stifled a frown. Winning Linda, he thought, even with Pete far away, could be a tough job.

*   *   *

Adam and Linda shared dinner at his apartment a few days later. Afterward they stepped out on the patio, and after a few minutes came back to the dinner table. Adam poured two glasses of wine. "This should warm us up," he said. "Sure is chilly tonight."

"Thanks," Linda said. "I'm still shivering."

"The winters here are milder than at the campus," Adam said. "This is just a cold night." He took a sip of wine. "Try it."

Linda took a sip from her glass. "What about Pete's weather?" she asked. "What are winter and summer like on Earth-Twin?"

He must continue to humor her, Adam thought. Eventually the wine might bring her closer to him and away from thoughts of Pete. "Better than Earth." he said. "More pleasant. The colonists will not have to face temperature extremes. There's enough rainfall in most places, but little flooding."

"Have you looked at the list of new volunteers for the next ship?" Linda asked. She took another sip of wine.

"No," Adam answered. "We just got it last week. The groups'll start in a day or two." He picked up the bottle and topped off both small glasses even though neither was empty.

"You haven't seen it, Adam?"

"I don't get to see all the names myself," Adam said. "We do have many slots left to fill. That'll keep everyone busy for a while."

Linda took a drink of wine and looked directly into Adam's eyes. Adam thought of a summer afternoon sky.

"I'm on that list," she said.

Adam's summer sky faded. He looked down at the small dinner table, at the wine glasses. They were his best glasses, he thought, and he owned only these two. His mother had given them to him when he moved into his apartment years ago. He sat in silence for a moment, and then said, "I guess I should've expected that."

"I just made up my mind a few weeks ago, but I've been thinking seriously about it for a year." Linda explained, "When he first left I tried to lose myself in my studies. I tried to forget him. But that just didn't work. I tried for years, Adam. I really tried." She added, "Oh, I hope you understand. You've been so nice to me."

Adam nodded. "I do," he said. "I understand."

Linda picked up her glass of wine, now half full, but didn't drink. "I should've caught on," she said. "I should've realized what I was doing to him."

"Don't blame yourself," Adam said. "I told you it wasn't your fault."

"Yes, it was." She took a sip of wine and put the glass down. "I blame myself. I have to find him."

"It's been a long time," Adam cautioned.

"Oh, I know it's risky. By the time I catch up, he may have found someone else. But I have to try." Linda added, "I believe you need physicians anyway."

Adam didn't respond right away. He looked down at the table.

"Adam, I didn't know at first that you—"

Adam interrupted. "It's all right. It sometimes takes me longer to catch on, too. I hope you find him." He added, "I really mean that. You and Pete are two of the best friends I've ever had."

He noticed the tears in her blue eyes. He told himself to stifle any show of his own disappointment. Linda, he thought, had struggled with her decision. He must not add his problems to hers. He picked up the bottle, topped off both glasses, and then picked up his. "A toast to a reunion in the stars," he said.

Linda picked up her glass and touched it to Adam's. "In the stars," she said. She smiled faintly.

Adam returned that smile, and both drank deeply.

Linda put down the glass and took Adam's hand in hers across the table. "You're the best friend I've ever had," she said.

"We do need more physicians," Adam said. "I'll make sure you get top priority."

"Thanks. And I hope you find someone, too." Linda leaned over and kissed Adam lightly on the cheek.

"In a few years I'll be thirty-five," Adam said. "I should think more about a companion animal. Maybe a cat." He laughed.

Linda smiled. "Not a dog?"

"I've actually thought about that. Cat or dog? I like dogs, but I guess I would've preferred the bigger dogs. Like at the zoo. My father told me my great-grandfather used to have one." Adam closed his eyes briefly.

His father had taught him many things, and told him many stories of the old days and the old ways.

"Big animals," Linda said. "I used to dream about even bigger animals. Horses. I think I would've liked horses. I read a lot about people riding them. It sounded like so much fun. I tried PIP, but it didn't measure up to what I had read about the real thing.

"I guess they don't have horses on Earth-Twin," she added. "I checked on that."

"Nothing big." Adam poured himself another glass of wine.

*   *   *

Nearly a year later, Adam watched his home v-v display while PANS 7 shrank to a pinpoint of reflected sunlight in the starry sky. Alone, he talked out loud to the display. "Goodbye, Linda. I wish you all the luck in the world. In your new world."

Maybe they'll all be all right, he thought. Perhaps the fact that he had no proof meant that he was wrong about the perils of the plan. He smiled. His good friend Pete was in for a big surprise, many years from now.

He sat for a long time and stared at his v-v screen, even after the ship had long vanished from view.

Later he drank wine and reflected. Jenny left six years earlier. Linda just departed. Both had asked him about the trip and the new world, but they had volunteered for very different reasons.

Linda had wanted reassurance, not details like Jenny. Linda, he thought, chased a past that had been taken away from her. Jenny looked for a future that wasn't available on crowded Earth.

Pete's motive? Did he regret it now? He could've stayed on Earth, Adam thought, and helped administer the PANS plan. Pete could have married Linda right here.

Millions of volunteers were now crossing the unimaginable distance to Earth-Twin. So far, Adam reflected, there were fourteen million very personal motives.

*　　　　　*　　　　　*

The busy years of the PANS plan passed sometimes slowly and sometimes relatively quickly for Adam. He noted, along with the progress of the plan, that Senior Senator John Bitterman continued to be reelected to office, and that the man remained chair of the senate PANS oversight committee.

Adam awaited the first hypersignal. He realized that it would reveal only the number who arrived alive, but it would be the first report of any kind. Later counts, one each year, would be more interesting. These would give some information on the progress of the new civilization.

Less than a year before the expected time of the first signal, Adam celebrated his forty-second birthday. When he returned home from a party thrown by the PANS team, he relaxed on his patio. The night was pleasantly cool, and he sat with his cat Moonshadow on his lap.

He stroked Moonshadow, and thought about his situation. He remained single, so he had been able to keep a companion animal. Moonshadow, a solid gray cat with a small white patch on his underside, had been with Adam since he was a kitten seven years earlier. Moonshadow now weighed fourteen pounds, but wasn't obese.

Adam recalled, with a chuckle, Bill Avery's storytelling when kitten Moonshadow had first arrived. "When I was a youngster," Avery had said, "eleven years old as I recall, I had a black cat. I asked my mother to get me a second one, so that the bad luck would cancel out. Like a double negative."

In the time of Avery's youth the laws were a little less restrictive. Back then even those under age thirty-five could keep an animal, but Adam knew that Avery's mother would have been unable to obtain the permit for a second cat. Today, Adam understood, Avery's story was an absurdity. Two cats of any color, or two small dogs, existed together only in tight security at the breeding stations.

*   *   *

As the time for the first hypersignal from Earth-Twin approached, Adam at first counted down the months. That countdown soon became weeks, days, and finally hours.

The PANS team had scheduled an earth comm to coincide with the event, and this comm began thirty minutes before the expected time of signal arrival. Adam sat in the usual semicircle and listened to Bitterman's and Avery's preliminary comments. He and the others then waited.

Soon he heard a female-sounding computer voice count off the last ten seconds. The photronic terminal, which had been set up just in front of the semicircle, beeped.

Adam listened to Avery read the number from the display. "It's as we expected!" Avery added. "Just over two million of our people arrived alive on Earth-Twin. We predicted almost exactly the number of births during the voyage. Some of you are new grandparents. And aunts and uncles."

Jenny and Pete made it, Adam thought, while Avery went on. "Of course the signal took nearly a year to reach us. It's reporting the recent past. A year ago two million of our friends and our relatives began the colonization of Earth-Twin.

"Another group of over two million will arrive there in a few weeks. We'll 'hear' from them next year."

Adam observed, mostly, the satisfied faces of the always present, at public announcements, government officials. Bitterman's face looked especially smug, he thought, and he could no longer justify the word "pudgy." The man was *fat*.

*   *   *

The second hypersignal, sixteen years after the first group of colonists departed Earth, also arrived on schedule. This count showed over four million, and Adam thought about his earlier concerns. Results looked good so far; subtracting off the number that should have arrived with the second landing revealed that births on the planet exceeded deaths by roughly the number that the research teams had calculated many years earlier.

*   *   *

The following year the third hypersignal indicated an Earth-Twin population, including new arrivals, of well over six million. Adam sat in his usual chair during a break at the team meeting on the day after receipt of this signal and sipped coffee. He thought about Jenny, and then about Pete. They had departed seventeen years ago; he tried to visualize what they might look like after so many years. The visos he kept at home were of much younger people, he thought, but they would have aged less than he had. He thought about Linda. She had departed only eleven years ago; she would not yet be on the planet.

Things still appeared to going well, he told himself. He smiled slightly, and then shrugged his shoulders. *Is it just too soon to tell?*

He was startled from his reverie when Avery, at the front of the meeting room, restarted the meeting with a personal announcement. Now one hundred and ten years old, he would retire from active work. Robert King, the next senior member of the original PANS team and its technological leader from the beginning, would take over as its head. Avery also reported that the Earth Government had chosen King to succeed him as administrator of the Earth Population Administration.

After the meeting, Adam and Avery sat on the couch in Avery's plant-filled office. "You and Brenda'll get to spend more time together now," Adam said.

"We'll keep in touch with you, and the PANS plan," Avery said. "You've all done a great job." He smiled.

Adam smiled.

"I'm pleased you stayed with the plan all these years," Avery said. "I was worried about that in the beginning. You were so restless back then."

Adam nodded. "It's been a great project," he said. He had often considered quitting, he thought, but only in the earlier years. The work had always been difficult, but never boring. Somehow it was his destiny to see it through, he told himself. He looked at Avery. "I have to admit the early results look good." He hesitated and glanced around at Avery's jungle. He added, slowly, "The very early results."

"Relax, Adam." Avery put his hand on Adam's shoulder. "Find someone and get married. You've done a fine job. And you'll continue to do so."

Adam's thoughts drifted back to Brenda Avery's comment of long ago, about "someone he had already met." *That was, maybe, seventeen years ago*, he thought. *Time has certainly eliminated that possibility.*

Avery grinned. "I may even have someone in mind for you," he said.

"Someone in mind?" Adam leaned forward on the couch. He looked at Avery.

"Maybe, my boy. But I'm just thinking out loud." Avery laughed, and then Adam watched his face take on a more serious expression. "My only regret is that Brenda and I've never had children," Avery said. "Unfortunately that couldn't be helped."

"You never said anything about that," Adam said. He hadn't known that the Averys' childlessness hadn't been by choice.

"I'm not capable. It's a medical problem, and the medical establishment with all its wonders couldn't help. They called it an 'uncorrectable genetic defect.'" Avery added, "I do wish I had great-grandchildren to see our colonization of the galaxy."

"I can understand that, Bill." Adam shifted uneasily.

"I sometimes wonder how that may have affected any of my decisions." Avery hesitated, and then added, "Knowing that I won't have any descendants to face the consequences. Could I've been careless? I hope not, Adam. I hope and pray not!"

Adam grimaced, and then hoped Avery had not noticed this. He leaned back and thought of his own forty-four years. He said, mostly to himself, "Someone to share the consequences."

Chapter 8

Nineteen Years

Two weeks after receipt of the third hypersignal, Adam entered the large government hall where Avery's retirement celebration was about to begin. He didn't get far from the entrance when Brenda Avery put her hand on his arm to get his attention.

"Good to see you this evening, Adam," she said. "I'm glad you didn't let work get in the way this time."

"Hello, Brenda." Adam smiled. "I couldn't miss this one."

"You work too hard," Brenda chided. She smiled.

"I wanted to help you plan this party," Adam said, "but I just couldn't get away. I apologize."

"Oh, hush. Just have fun."

"I expect to," Adam said, "but I don't even know who'll be here."

"Oh, there's more coming in. I'd better go greet them. Enjoy, Adam."

Adam smiled as Brenda turned away. He then looked around. Hundreds crowded the reception hall. Even though he had lived in the city for a long time, he had not visited this hall before. It was generally used for government celebrations, he thought.

He looked across the room, toward what appeared to be the head table. A hanging sign, over the table, read: BILL AVERY LEADS US TO THE STARS. He nodded.

He wandered about and greeted a few people that he knew, and then he spotted Hugh Bruce near the hall's entrance. Bruce must have just arrived, he thought. Bruce wasn't alone.

Adam stood and stared at the young woman at Bruce's side. Even in the distance, ten meters away at least, he noticed her beautiful brown eyes. Her relatively short reddish brown hair didn't quite reach her shoulders. *What is that hairstyle called?* he wondered. *Pixie?*

He watched her while she walked alongside Bruce. He watched the way she walked. He noted that she and Bruce weren't walking hand-in-hand. *I'd be holding her hand*, he thought. *I wouldn't want her to get too far away. Nice catch, Hugh.*

Adam started when he heard Avery's voice behind him. "You're staring, Adam."

He turned to face Avery. "Hello, Bill," he said. "I was just going to look for you. I like your sign."

"You remember her, don't you?" Avery asked.

"Remember her?" Adam turned to look at the woman again, but she and Bruce were lost in the crowd. He turned back toward Avery. "I don't think I've ever seen her before," he said.

Avery grinned. "You have."

Adam glanced around again. He shrugged. "I don't think so."

Avery laughed. "You look confused, my boy."

Adam smiled. "C'mon, Bill. At least give me a hint."

"You'll find out soon enough." Avery glanced at some papers in his hand.

"I hope so," Adam responded.

"Adam, I must go," Avery said. "I have to review my speech one last time."

"Sure, Bill." Adam smiled as Avery turned and walked away. He glanced again in the direction he had last seen Bruce and his companion. He spotted several other people that he wished to greet, and walked over to talk to them.

A short time later he stood alone by the punch bowl and filled his glass. He heard a soft voice behind him. "Hello, Dr. Hampton."

He turned around and looked directly into beautiful brown eyes. She was alone; Bruce was not with her now. Her voice was somehow vaguely familiar, he thought, like a voice from a long ago dream. He felt his heartbeat speed up. He stared at the young woman, and tried to think of something clever to say. Before he could speak, she smiled and said, "You look so puzzled. Why, I'll bet you don't even remember me."

"I guess you have me at a disadvantage," he said. *What a dumb thing to say!* he immediately thought.

She smiled. "I'll give you a hint," she said. "My name is Nola. It's Nola Walker, but I don't think you'd know my last name."

Adam searched his memory. *How could I forget her?* If only he had insisted that Avery tell him! He again tried to say something clever, but could only fumble. "I'm sorry."

Nola interrupted. "I'll give you another hint. When we met before, I asked you a question you couldn't answer."

Adam looked into Nola's brown eyes. Surely, he thought, he would've remembered those eyes. He shook his head. "Nola, I just don't recall."

"I'm sorry, Dr. Hampton," Nola said. "I'm teasing you." She smiled. "I think you may remember me, but I can't expect you to recognize me. When we met before I was nine years old."

Nola was an uncommon name; Adam could recall hearing it only a few times. *Or was it only once?* he asked himself. *Nine years old? That must have been about the time of, yes, that first PANS comm. About nineteen years ago?* Little Nola had asked, "Will they have enough to eat?" With the sincerity of a child, she had asked that startling question so long ago.

Adam smiled. Little Nola, whose appearance he just barely recalled, had grown up into a lovely young woman. "Yes! You were with your parents at that first comm." He added, still fumbling, "Please call me Adam." He took a drink from the nearly forgotten glass of punch in his hand, and then grimaced. "Sorry, I'm forgetting my manners," he said. "Can I pour you some punch?"

"Yes, please," Nola said.

Adam put his glass down on the table, picked up a clean glass, filled it and handed it to Nola. He picked up his glass again, raised it and said, "To earth comms."

Nola raised her glass, hooked her arm in Adam's and said, "Earth comms." Both drank, and then put their empty glasses down on the table.

"Since that comm I've been a great fan of the PANS project," Nola said. "I've just completed advanced studies at the university. I'm an extraterrestrial biologist."

"A biologist," Adam said. "You're not a little girl anymore." He hesitated, and then chuckled at himself.

Nola smiled. "Time does that."

His attraction to her, he told himself, was already more than just physical. He wondered about Bruce; she had come to the party with him. *How close are they?*

"I'll bet you haven't thought about me for all those years," Nola said. "Have you?"

She caught him off guard again, he thought. He had often recalled the encounter, but the little girl had been just another anonymous pretty face. He frowned. He certainly couldn't tell her that.

Before he could say anything, Nola smiled. "I'm just teasing you again, Adam," she said. "Don't answer my dumb question."

Adam smiled.

A faint bell sounded. Adam turned around toward the sound, but Nola spoke first. "I see that they're getting ready to seat us for dinner. Why don't we sit together?"

"Didn't you come in with Hugh Bruce?" Adam asked.

Nola smiled. "I just ran into Hugh at the door. I met him a couple of weeks ago."

"You're by yourself?"

"Yes." She added, "I'm flattered that you noticed me when I came in."

He hadn't meant to confide that. *No harm done,* he thought when she smiled again.

"Oh! Maybe I'd better ask," she said. "Are you with someone?"

Adam grinned. "I'm also alone," he said, "and it'll be a pleasure to sit and talk with you at dinner."

They strolled side-by-side to the tables, and Adam thought of taking her by the hand. He didn't follow up on this thought, although her manner assured him that she wouldn't object if he had.

No longer distracted by her brown eyes, he concentrated on other things. She was about average height for an adult woman. She did not wear the usual tunic worn by all the men and half the women in the room. Instead she wore a one-piece colored frock, similar to Brenda Avery's, that was designed to be feminine yet not advertise body shape. Adam noted that it failed in the latter, and smiled.

Idle chatter filled the time between bites at dinner. Nola talked a lot more than Adam, but it was mostly with him and only a little with the other guests who sat nearby.

After dinner and Avery's speech, Adam and Nola danced. While standing on the dance floor after a waltz, Adam briefly thought about the age difference. He looked into Nola's brown eyes, and convinced himself that she didn't care about age differences. *Sixteen years isn't that much,* he told himself.

Nola interrupted his thoughts. "It looks like the band's getting ready to take a break. Let's sit down. I'd like to talk to you about something anyway."

"Sounds good to me." Adam took her by the hand and led her to a table in a quieter part of the hall. At the table he said, "I'll get us some coffee."

"I don't drink coffee," Nola said. "Ice water will be fine for me. I don't think you'll find herb tea here." She sat down while Adam held her chair.

Adam grinned. "All right," he said. He left the table, and soon returned with a cup of black coffee and a cup of tea." He put the tea in front of Nola, smiled and said, "Elderberry. Brenda Avery drinks it, and she planned this party." He sat next to her.

"Why, you're resourceful, too," Nola said. "Thank you, Adam."

"My pleasure."

Nola picked up her cup and took a sip. "Could I pick your mind for a while?" she asked. "I have some questions about Earth-Twin."

"Uh, Oh." Adam's smile faded. Old memories stirred.

"The crops, the initial crops, are ordinary Earth crops, aren't they?" Nola asked. "We've gone over some of this. They said something about native plants. But I get the impression that they won't be used as crops."

Adam stifled a frown. "You're right. Native plants won't work for extensive farming. They can't give the necessary yields."

He couldn't talk Jenny out of it. Linda had been an entirely different problem. Could he change Nola's mind? She hadn't even mentioned the plan at dinner, he thought. Right now he could only try to humor her. They had just met as adults, and he didn't want to offend her. She was a biologist, and she was asking a biological question. He took a sip of coffee and added, "And native plants won't have much of a chance in the factories. Not until they've been modified."

"What about the native animals?" Nola asked. "I recall that some people will hunt. But will they try domestication?"

Something was different. She asked good questions, but, to Adam, it appeared that she was more interested in him. *Wishful thinking?* he asked himself. *Mental fatigue catching up?*

"We don't expect that to work either," he said. "Domestic animals on Earth, like food crops, were bred over many years for fast growth and fast reproduction." He took another sip of coffee. "Again, the colonists will work it out in time. But at first those who want meat will obtain it only by hunting. We couldn't send animals with the ships."

"Why not?" Nola asked. "I suppose the life support systems would be kind of overworked?"

"Yes, that's true," Adam said, "and the facilities take up too much space, although we could use limited suspended animation. But we also don't want to chance upsetting the natural life systems on Earth-Twin any more than necessary. If Earth animals escaped, they might cause big problems. We can control the humans, so to speak."

These were interesting problems, Adam thought. The team and its subordinate groups had struggled with them, but he wondered where she was going with the conversation.

Nola smiled. "Why, I'm the biologist," she said. "I should have thought of that. I'm still kind of new to extraterrestrial. And I'm trying to learn something about agriculture and its problems." She picked up her cup and sipped elderberry tea, and then turned the conversation over to other topics.

As they prepared to part later that evening, Adam said, "I hope I answered your questions. Earlier, that is." He had better clear this up now, he thought while he helped Nola with her coat.

"Yes," Nola said. "Thanks for the answers. Hugh and the others went over a lot, but some of it wasn't clear when I thought about it later."

"Hugh?" Neither Hugh Bruce, Adam thought, nor any of the other PANS team members briefed new volunteers. Another group had been commissioned long ago for just that purpose.

"He gave my group a talk on the basics," Nola said.

Adam looked questioningly at her.

"Why, I'll be working on these things. Remember, I'm joining a new biological group at the university." She hesitated, and then added, "Oh, maybe I forgot to tell you."

Adam sighed. "I don't remember. I guess you've had me quite distracted." "Enchanted," he thought, was a better word. "Which group is it?"

"We're going to study the plant life, and then the animals later," Nola said. "We want to make up an initial classification scheme, matched as much as possible to Earth's. We're going to start with the stuff those old explorers brought back, and then work from their reports."

"Whew!" Adam relaxed. He had been so busy with his own direct responsibilities that he hadn't been able to keep up with the details of the rest of the program. *Nor with new researchers*, he thought.

"That's how I know Hugh," Nola said, "and I interviewed with him and Dr. Avery a couple of weeks ago."

Adam thought of Avery's earlier evasiveness, and the man's sly grin. He nodded. "Nola, welcome to PANS," he said.

"I'm really happy to be with the program. I've wanted it for so long." Nola smiled.

"I guess we'll see a lot of each other," Adam said while he walked Nola to the door.

"I hope that it won't be all work, Adam."

"Not if I can help it." Adam grinned. "Let's have dinner tomorrow."

At home later that evening, Adam sat on his couch and nursed a small glass of wine. It had been quite an evening, he thought, and it might be a while before he could even try to sleep. He couldn't get Nola's brown eyes out of his mind.

He thought again of Bill Avery's sly grin, and recalled his talk with Avery a few weeks earlier. Avery had said he had "someone in mind."

Avery had become, he thought, almost a substitute for his father. The team and the administration would miss his leadership, but the personal relationship would continue. Even at a hundred and ten years of age, Adam told himself, Avery appeared vigorous and would certainly live and thrive for many more years.

His thoughts quickly returned to Nola's eyes. He refilled his wine glass.

*   *   *

Adam's optimism about Avery proved wrong just nine months later. Bill Avery died after a short illness.

Adam and Nola rode bicycles in a local park, on a sunny day a few weeks after Avery's funeral. The two had taken time away from their busy PANS schedules to don sport shorts and pocket shirts and ride their two-wheelers.

The bicycle path weaved among dense stands of shrubbery and small grassy clearings. The park was one of very few places in the city with outdoor greenery, Adam thought, and one of the few places where people could go outdoors and enjoy the company of friends and family.

While he rode beside Nola, he noticed a young man who appeared to be teaching a small boy to ride a two-wheeler. *Father and son*, he thought, and recalled a long ago but similar scene with his own father. "Let's stop for a moment," he said. "This reminds me of something." He hesitated, and then added, "Of one of the many reasons I was so attached to Bill."

Adam and Nola braked to a stop, remained atop their bicycles and watched the simple drama in the park path. The father walked alongside and held the bicycle lightly while the boy tried to balance. A few moments later, the boy finally rode unassisted. Adam looked at the father's face. The man smiled broadly. Adam thought again of his own father.

"Tell me," Nola said. "Reminds you of Bill?"

Adam hesitated. Nola would certainly be a good listener, he thought, but he said, "It's nothing. Some other time."

Nola put her hand on Adam's arm. "But you sounded like you wanted to say something."

"It's just that Bill was almost like a substitute father to me, and now this reminds me—" Adam didn't finish.

"Adam, do you want to talk about him? We've never talked about your father."

"I guess not. No. Let's just continue riding." The two started pedaling again, and Adam changed the subject. "Oh, we can have dinner with my mother and Brenda this evening if you want." The two older women had hit it off when he had introduced them, he thought, just after his mother moved to the city a year ago. She had been a big help to Brenda in the past few weeks.

"They make a great pair," Nola said. "Those shopping trips?"

"We won't talk about their shopping trips." Adam managed to laugh.

"You worked with Bill for a long time," Nola said.

"Yes, he was one of the first to propose the plan," Adam said while he pedaled. "He was so proud of it. I'm happy that he got to see the early results."

"Brenda seems all right. It looks to me like she's taking it very well." Nola continued, "Oh, about dinner. Yes, let's visit with them." She smiled.

Adam smiled back, and the two continued pedaling. Another couple of loops around the park, he thought, and then he would have dinner with three beautiful women.

*　　　　　*　　　　　*

Two months later Earth received the fourth hypersignal. It indicated a population of over eight million, but Adam noted a small discrepancy in the number. According to the earlier calculations, he thought, the exact count should've been a few thousand larger. He and the team discussed the possible problem at length on the same day that they received the signal, and reported it to the senate oversight committee.

The next morning Adam sat at his desk in his office. He sipped coffee and considered the number. Either the birth rate on Earth-Twin had decreased, he thought, or the death rate had increased. Or both. Or things had happened differently, not according to prediction, on the fourth ship.

The others did not believe that the signal was cause for alarm, he told himself. The team had, so far, simply recorded it for comparison with future numbers. Adam tried to relax. He realized that the calculated birth and death rates, statistical predictions, need not be matched exactly. He sipped more coffee.

Bitterman's oversight committee also hadn't reacted. "Not a problem," the chairman had announced. *That doesn't encourage me*, Adam thought.

He thought of the brevity of the signal, keyed his terminal and reread engineers' reports that he and the team had considered years earlier. He then summarized them in his mind. Hypersignal required tremendous energy to create a gravitational aura that could bridge the Earth-Twin distance. The concentrated energy would destroy the internal workings of the transmitter. The distance demanded very large and heavy equipment. The result: Each ship would send only one short signal. At present, he thought, the single number disclosed all that Earth could know about the progress of the colonists on Earth-Twin.

He looked toward his window briefly, and then glanced at some charts on his wall. He hit a few more keys on his terminal, and then looked closely at the colored charts and tables that appeared in the space just above the screen. He frowned. *Of course nothing has changed since yesterday*, he thought. Count number four was indeed several thousand less than predicted.

What will the next signal show, a year from now? It will be a long year, Adam told himself.

Chapter 9

Questions

A few days after Earth received the fourth signal, Adam stood beside Nola on his balcony and gazed at the southern night sky. He noticed that she shivered slightly even though she wore a light pullover. He put his arm around her.

"It's so quiet," she said. She leaned against him.

"Not a breeze. Not even the usual city noises." Adam raised his hand and pointed to a group of stars just above the horizon. "I wonder how many times I've looked at it."

"I'm having trouble finding Tau Ceti tonight," Nola said.

"The bright moon washes it out some." Adam glanced up at the quarter moon.

"I guess our sun must be difficult to see from Earth-Twin, too." Nola said.

"Yes. But the sun may be a little more prominent. It's bigger and brighter." He turned toward Tau Ceti and squinted. "What's happening there?" he wondered out loud. "I wish we had more information."

"Don't be such a worrier," Nola said. "Most people don't think anything's amiss."

"We have to wait so long for another signal," Adam said.

He removed his arm from Nola's shoulders and took her hand in his. She turned toward him and smiled. "You may be worried over nothing," she said.

"I know," Adam said. "Maybe I've been expecting trouble for so long I can't see it any other way."

"You could be right," Nola said. "But what if you're wrong? You must think about how that could affect your career."

Adam squeezed Nola's hand. "I'm sorry. I'm spoiling the mood."

"You're not spoiling anything." She kissed him on the cheek.

Adam looked into Nola's brown eyes. He looked at her reddish brown hair, at her shoulders covered by the pullover, at her slightly turned-up nose. He regarded himself. He was forty-five years old. He had noticed wrinkles forming around his eyes. Not a lot, he thought, but enough for him to take stock. Nola didn't notice, or at least she didn't let on that she did. That was another thing he loved about her, another reason he should ask her. He made up his mind.

"Nola, will you marry me?"

She looked surprised.

"I love you," Adam said. "I want you to marry me. You don't have to answer right now if you don't want to."

Nola smiled. "I'm sorry. You startled me. We were talking about something else. I love you, too. Why, yes, yes. I will marry you."

Adam grinned. "I hate to sound corny, but you just made me the happiest man in the world."

"That's my intention," Nola said.

Adam and Nola held each other for a moment, and then agreed to talk about most of the details later. Adam had not yet consulted the genetic database; he and Nola would have to do so before making further marriage plans. The two did decide to put off having children for at least the first few years; they would make a final decision on that later.

*   *   *

A few weeks later Adam, with Nola, prepared dinner in his eat-in kitchen. He stirred a pot of soy chili, and then held the spoon up to his nose. *That smells good!* He liked to cook, and was happy that this was one of the many likes he and Nola shared. Most people just used the *autoprep* with packaged meals, he thought, but he did only when pressed for time.

He looked at Nola and smiled. Tonight it was simply chili, but even chili, by candlelight, could be romantic. "What'd your group do today?" he asked.

"We went over the rest of the calculations." Nola opened a cabinet and took out two candles. She smiled. "I've been waiting for you to ask about it."

"Must be about the signal," Adam said. He knew that King had asked Nola's group to take some time away from their main project to do some statistical calculations. He stirred the chili, and then looked at Nola again.

"Yes. We finalized it today." Nola explained, "We believe that the latest population number shows just a coincidental change in the birth or death rate on Earth-Twin. It's a statistical anomaly, a perturbation." She placed the candles into silver holders on Adam's small dining table.

"I'm trying to convince myself." Adam knew that Nola would perform an accurate and meaningful calculation. He stirred the chili again, and then picked up a little in the spoon, blew on it and took a sip. He added a pinch of pepper to the pot.

"After all, we see only a relatively small difference from a number we can't predict exactly anyway," Nola said.

"I'll try to look at it that way," Adam replied. "But let's drop that for now. We have more pleasant things to talk about." He stirred the chili one last time, took the pot off the heatpad and carried it to the table. "Sure does smell good," he said.

"Mmm." Nola put two bowls on the table next to the pot.

"Since the machine's accepted our genetics, let's set a date," Adam said. "Maybe early next year, say two months after the next signal. What do you think?"

"Sounds good to me," Nola said. "That'll give us plenty of time to prepare."

"Let's light the candles and eat. Then have some wine to celebrate." Adam smiled. "I'm famished."

*   *   *

The rest of the PANS team, Adam observed, accepted Nola's group's explanation. They remained convinced that the hypersignal did not warn of a problem on Earth-Twin.

Adam and Hugh Bruce lingered after a meeting, several months after receipt of the fourth signal. They sat by the elliptical table and drank coffee.

"Take it easy, Adam," Bruce said. "Nothing's wrong."

"I wish I could believe that." Adam took a sip of coffee. "I suppose the next signal could show I'm uneasy about nothing."

"Sure." Bruce drank the last few drops in his cup. He gathered the few paper notes in front of him on the table.

"But I keep getting this feeling that we missed something." Adam drank deeply, emptied his cup and reached for the decanter. He poured a half-cup.

"I don't know," Bruce said. "We were careful, but I suppose we can never be absolutely sure. I understand a lot more now about the complexity of our plan, about your anxiety even back in the early days." Adam looked at him, and he went on, "I hope I'm getting wiser as I get older." He twisted one end of his moustache, which was still dark and not yet graying even though his hair at the temples did show some gray streaks. "I regret giving you such a hard time back then."

"That's in the past, Hugh." Adam smiled. "Could be we kept each other in line."

"Or the opposite," Bruce said.

Adam straightened in his chair. "The opposite?"

"A distraction. And something slipped by. Adam, I'm going to think about that number again. Let's talk more often." Bruce picked up his papers and stood up.

"Sure, Hugh. I need someone who'll listen to me." Adam finished off the coffee left in his cup and stood up. "Nola listens, but I can't convince her."

"I'm not convinced either, not yet," Bruce corrected. "But, maybe?"

*   *   *

Adam lay in bed wide-awake the night after talking to Bruce. He thought about a particular meeting early in the PANS planning.

The team had been discussing Earth and Earth-Twin differences, and Bill Avery had added some details. Adam started to comment. He barely got the words out when Bruce countered with a remark that Adam believed was more personal than substantive. An argument ensued, and he had disengaged himself from it by, as he now put into words in his mind, "clamming up."

What was that issue? What had Avery been explaining? Adam remembered the incident, but couldn't recall the details. *Of course,* he told himself, *that was long ago. Was it important?*

He fell sleep while still trying to resolve that question. The next morning, when he awoke, he thought about it again. He failed again to answer it, decided it hadn't been important and went on to other things.

*   *   *

The months passed slowly for Adam, even though his PANS duties and marriage preparation kept him busy. Finally he sat with the team around the elliptical table on hypersignal morning and waited for King to bring in the number. For the previous three counts, the second, third and fourth, the head of the PANS team had received the signal in his own office and announced the number to the team at a meeting that commenced immediately afterward. The fifth was planned to be the same.

Adam recalled that an earth comm and worldwide countdown had accompanied only the first hypersignal, four years earlier. For the succeeding counts, the team scheduled a public announcement later in the day.

He glanced at the clock on the back wall. King was late. The team waited.

"That's not like Rob at all," Adam finally said. "I'd sooner expect the sun to come up late." He traced his index finger along one of the wood grains in the tabletop.

"Nearly twenty minutes now," Bruce, who sat next to Adam, said.

"I know he's in the building." Adam started to get up from his chair. "Maybe I'd better look for him."

"There he is now," Bruce announced. "He looks a little shaky."

King entered and approached the front of the meeting room. The team members fell silent. Adam looked at King and sat down. King took a drink of water, and then broke the silence. "We may have a serious problem," he said. "The number is again just over eight million, not much more than the last count."

"What the hell?" someone whispered. Adam glanced around the table. Other team members looked at each other and murmured. Adam returned his attention to King.

"According to the signal," King said, "the increase is just over ninety thousand, much less than the expected two million plus."

Adam felt a chill. He shook his head. He then looked at King and asked, in a small voice, "Rob, the signal? Could it be wrong?"

"No, I do not think so," King answered. "The hypersignal is such that if we receive a readable signal, it is the one sent."

Adam unconsciously picked up his coffee cup, and then put it down without drinking. He didn't trust his stomach right now. He looked around the table and saw some very pale faces.

"But what about the population counter?" Bruce asked. "Could that have malfunctioned? To count such a low number?"

"We will have to go over that," King said. "I have been considering the possibility."

Adam looked around the table again and saw that most of the team members had relaxed in their chairs. A few faces were still pale, but he could imagine the sighs of relief. He grimaced. *Are we going to call this instrument error?* he asked himself.

"I believe we must postpone the scheduled communication," King said. "Let us reschedule for tomorrow. We have to decide what to tell the people."

Adam tried to relax, while the routine meeting became an emergency session. The team was at full strength, since a replacement had filled King's previous position. Two others on the original team had recently retired. They had also been replaced, but all seventeen currently on the team, Adam knew, were seasoned veterans of some part of the PANS project.

He hoped that his teammates would look beyond the possibility of equipment malfunction, but, during the emergency session, most agreed that this was the most likely explanation. They decided to reveal both the number and this conclusion at the earth comm. Although Adam argued against it, the team voted in favor of keeping the next ship on schedule. He cast the only dissenting vote. Bruce abstained.

Bruce grabbed Adam right after the emergency session, as both got up from their chairs. "Adam, I'm really thinking your way now. I was the one who suggested counting failure a couple of hours ago, but only because I didn't think Rob answered all of your question."

"It can't be that simple, Hugh." Adam picked up his cup from the table.

"I don't think Rob believes it either," Bruce said.

Adam accompanied Bruce out of the meeting room. In the hallway he said, "We have two consecutive anomalous signals. I realize that everyone—almost everyone—thinks they're unrelated."

"Like I said before, Adam," Bruce said, "let's talk more often."

"Sure, Hugh. We will. But right now I'd better v-v Nola." Adam and Bruce turned and departed in opposite directions.

*   *   *

On his way home in the crowded city street later that day, Adam thought about population counters. Such devices had long been used to take an Earth census.

He recalled that some of his friends at the university had likened the counter to an extrasensory perception mechanism that somehow entered a continuum of human consciousness. Others had talked of mind control. His scientific inquiries had debunked such fears. The counter could not read or change anyone's thoughts. It simply detected many brains' electrical activity at a superficial level, and did so very well.

The technology is mature and reliable, he told himself.

*   *   *

At the rescheduled earth comm, Adam sat in the semicircle while King announced, "Yesterday's hypersignal shows just over eight million people, even though we expected more than ten million. We have examined this, and we believe it is only a malfunction of the counting equipment."

Adam knew that King had asked the comm crew to keep his face in the shadows for this announcement. Even the live audience, he thought, couldn't see King clearly.

"I know you will be concerned about your relatives and friends," King said, "but we do not yet know if anything is amiss on Earth-Twin.

Until we have more information, the PANS plan will continue. I hope this will reassure you."

After a short and uneventful question and answer exchange with the live audience, King terminated the communication. During the entire session, Adam recalled as he left the hall, he had not been able to read any reaction from Senator Bitterman's face. He shrugged. *Why would the man react? No plans had changed.*

*   *   *

Two weeks after receipt of the fifth hypersignal, Adam sat at his desk in the morning and sipped coffee. He thought about the next ship; it was due to be launched from Earth orbit in two weeks, on the usual New Year's Day.

All chosen volunteers and alternates for PANS 20, he recalled, had viewed a recording of the PANS team's emergency session. The new colonists had been given much more information than had the general public. He had hoped that his arguments at the session would cause a stir among the volunteers, and at least delay the departure. *No such luck,* he now thought. Only a few hundred of the two million had chosen to remain on crowded Earth. Alternates had quickly replaced them and now hurriedly prepared for the journey.

He mulled over the official handling of the situation during the past two weeks. Most in the Earth Government, as on the PANS team, believed that the population counter had malfunctioned. "Reduced sensitivity" remained the major argument, since this would mean a short count where some of the people farthest from the landing site were not counted. The PANS team had recommended that an engineering group be commissioned to perform an extensive evaluation of the older model population counters, and the oversight committee had approved.

To add some confusion, early in the debates Senator Bitterman had suggested that the colonists themselves, for selfish motives, might have modified the signal in order to force the PANS team to limit their population. The team had rejected this. The signal, Adam recalled from the discussions, would not arrive on time if the colonists had tampered with the equipment; the team would have noticed even a short delay. Another discussion had concluded that the colonists would have no practical way to shield part of their population from the counter. Bitterman, he thought, had not known enough about the technology to challenge these arguments.

He looked around, first at potted geraniums and azaleas on the front corners of his desk, and then out the window. *The population counters are very reliable*, he told himself again. He shook his head, and then took another sip of coffee.

*   *   *

On departure day Adam and Hugh Bruce sat in front of Bruce's home v-v display and watched PANS 20 fade into the starry sky. "I don't think the engineering group'll come up with anything," Adam said.

"Who knows?" Bruce shrugged. He poured two glasses of wine. "This is not for celebration. It's to calm our nerves."

Adam accepted one glass and took a drink. "I hate to keep belaboring this," he said. "I just have to talk about it. The two problems occurring in sequence can't be just a coincidence. About two thousand are missing from the fourth count, almost two million from the fifth. Is there a connection?"

"I don't know," Bruce said. "I can't come up with any explanation."

Adam took another drink. He didn't feel calmed, he thought. "No one else agrees with me—us—on this," he said. "Maybe Rob, but he isn't saying anything."

"Adam, if something went wrong, it must be on Earth-Twin itself or on the ships near the planet. Or we'd have received radio."

Adam nodded.

Bruce took a big drink of wine, and then refilled his glass.

∗   ∗   ∗

Later that evening Adam and Nola discussed the situation at Adam's apartment, over a light meal of sandwiches.

"I think we should wait," Adam said. He had been too busy for the past month, he thought, but he had better do something about the wedding date now.

"Wait?" Nola asked.

"Postpone our wedding," Adam said. He looked at her. "It's not what I want. But I'm too mixed up to go through with it now. Let's plan to get married right after the next count, no matter what it may be." He could hope for a normal census, he thought, and, given some time, prepare himself for more bad news from Earth-Twin.

Nola closed her brown eyes and did not speak.

Adam reached across the small table and took Nola's right hand in both his hands. *Did I offend her?* he asked himself. *That's the last thing I want.* He tried to think of something more to say.

Nola opened her eyes and looked at him. "I love you," she said. "I'll wait. Let's not talk about it anymore."

Adam forced a smile. He had been sure she would understand, but he also knew that he had upset her. He saw her look directly into his eyes, and he felt like she could read his thoughts.

"How can I not wait? I've loved you from that very first day," she said, "when I was nine. You were so different from everyone else at that comm, the other team members and the senators. You were like a little lost boy."

Adam grimaced, and then smiled. He had often felt like a "little lost boy," and he certainly had at the first PANS comm. He squeezed her hand gently, and felt her squeeze back.

"I don't yet know what to think about the latest problem," Nola said. "I'm not so sure now as I was about the fourth count."

"Hugh and I've discussed it," Adam said. "We can't come up with anything. We could use the help of the full team, but no one else seems to recognize the problem. Maybe Rob King, but he's not talking about it." He released Nola's hand, and then picked up his autoprep-produced sandwich and took a small bite.

"But he's administrator," Nola said. "He has to go more with the consensus."

"Maybe." Adam put the sandwich back down on his plate.

"I remember Rob at dinner last week," Nola said. "He *is* worried. Very."

"I guess we can only wait and see," Adam said.

Chapter 10

Crisis

The sixth hypersignal arrived on schedule. Adam sat with the team around the elliptical table while King announced a census that was again much lower than expected: nearly fifty thousand fewer than the fifth count. The number had actually decreased, Adam thought, when more than two million should have arrived. He grimaced, and then shook his head. He knew that the engineers had determined that equipment failure in this manner was unlikely. The team and the government, he told himself, must now accept the evidence. More than four million colonists had died.

He looked around the room. Bruce's, he thought, was the only face that did not register surprise. Or fear. He listened while King again postponed the public announcement and turned the scheduled meeting into an emergency session. This time all agreed that the next colonization ship must be held back.

"So we agree," King concluded. "Let us decide now what we will tell the public. Then we can use the rest of the meeting to plan our next steps. I will talk to the oversight committee this afternoon. I am sure I can convince them."

Adam sipped some coffee. He then put his cup down and asked, "Convince them, Rob?" King, he told himself, could handle Bitterman more effectively than he could.

"That we must suspend the plan for the near future," King said. "I do not think any of us doubt we will get approval, but I must go through the channels."

Adam shifted in his chair. "I was hoping it was something more than that."

"Do you want to come with me?" King asked. "You are certainly welcome."

Adam hesitated, and then said, "No, I can't talk to politicians." He picked up his cup again and took another sip of coffee. Suspension was all he could realistically expect at this time, he told himself. They wouldn't let go altogether, not the officials who were "doing something" about Earth's problem. It was a plan for the future.

"For the public announcement," King said to the team, "I believe we must simply tell the truth. We must preserve the credibility of the PANS team and the administration."

The team discussed the topic; all agreed.

"I will prepare the public statement later," King said. "Let us now decide how we will handle this situation. So far we have only the hypersignals, six of them. The last two—or possibly three—indicate a problem. That is it. We will not receive radio for at least seven years—from the planet itself."

"We don't know when the difficulties may have started," a team member said. "Did they encounter the problem, whatever it may be, right away? Was it a gradual deterioration? Or did something happen suddenly, later?"

Adam nodded.

"We will have later hypersignal counts to help us, of course," King said. "I will organize a group to talk to the explorers, and another to look at the full database. Perhaps we can gain some insight."

Adam shook his head. He had already talked to a few of the old explorers, and had gained no insight.

The team's next decision was unanimous. A small ship, with a small crew and a well chosen mix of specialists—ninety people total—would be sent in place of the twenty-first colonization ship. This "rescue" ship would carry a new communications technology called programmable hypersignal. Adam knew only that *P-hyper* was much more capable than the earlier equipment.

The team concluded the emergency session by working out a timetable for further discussions.

*   *   *

The next morning Adam sat in the semicircle at the earth comm and listened to King tell the public about the signal and the team's decisions, including the rescue craft.

"Of course," King added, "suspension does not mean that no more colonists will arrive on the planet. The fourteen ships now in transit cannot be called back. One of those will arrive in just a few weeks.

Adam knew that the time necessary for radio signals to catch a fast-moving and distant ship must be determined by a complicated calculation. Most could not be reached before they landed.

Communication with the one-way ships could not help the situation, he thought. The travelers would not be able to return to Earth even if they became aware of the crisis. They carried only enough nuclear fuel and other life support supplies for the one-way trip. The more recent departures were not yet past the point-of-no-return determined by such supplies, but none of the ships carried the extra vm-drive fuel needed for a turnaround.

Adam wished for a drink of coffee. He glanced around the semicircle at several faces. Most showed dismay. Bitterman just looked puzzled, he thought, or maybe he just measured that fat face on a different scale.

"We will send a radio message to Earth-Twin," King said, "to inform them about the suspension, and will send more later when we know more about the situation. Of course, radio will take twelve years. The colonists have no hyper receivers, and will not have any until the rescue ship arrives there."

The rescue ship would set up a communication link that was much faster than radio, Adam told himself. *Fourteen years from now.*

"I apologize for my bluntness." King said. "We on the PANS team, and the Earth Government, want to be perfectly candid.

"Questions?"

Someone in the live audience asked, "When will we know more?"

"Fourteen more population counts will return to Earth, one each year," King said. "These signals will be the only information from the planet until we start receiving radio seven years from now."

Adam thought again about coffee, and listened.

"The rescue mission will be ready to leave in about two months, since we will use an exploration-type ship that is already in inventory," King said, "in orbit. So we will receive P-hyper in about fifteen years. Of course we will announce publicly anything we may be able to figure out here on Earth."

Another in the live audience asked, "When will colonization be resumed? When will more people go to Earth-Twin or another planet?"

Adam grimaced.

"We have no definite plans yet," King said, "but we will send no more people anywhere until we solve the problem."

*   *   *

In the evening Adam and Nola discussed the new development. They sat at the small table in Adam's eat-in kitchen. Adam sipped coffee and Nola herb tea.

"Your call yesterday really shocked me," Nola said. "Why, you were right all along."

"Thanks for sticking by me." Adam took her hand in his.

"Oh, it's not your being correct that shocked me." Nola smiled.

Adam chuckled. "I know," he said. He relaxed. "We have no idea what the problem might be, but at least people are working on it now."

"Adam?"

Adam knew her question. "Let's do it as planned," he said. He looked into her brown eyes. "We've already made the arrangements. We don't have much time now, but this crisis means we might have even less time later."

*   *   *

Adam and Nola got married a month after Earth received the sixth count. Brenda Avery, with the help of her now best friend Anna Hampton, planned and hosted the reception that followed the marriage ceremony.

Adam and Nola talked to Brenda at that reception. "You miss him, don't you?" Adam said.

"Bill loved these celebrations so much," Brenda said. "And he loved you, Adam. Like the son we never could have."

"I miss him, too," Adam said. "Perhaps he's looking in on us right now, from up above." He glanced toward the ceiling of the party room.

"I know he looks after me." Brenda smiled.

Adam said to Nola, after Brenda left them to attend to her host duties, "I hope Bill's not looking in on the PANS plan."

Nola nodded. She then reminded him that he had an obligation. "Adam, remember? We must find Moonshadow a new home."

"Let's look for Hugh," Adam said. "I think he's the right one. I've already hinted about it to him."

"Why, yes." Nola smiled. "Hugh'd be perfect."

They found Bruce near the punch bowl.

"Thought we'd find you here, Hugh." Adam picked up two glasses. "We'll join you."

"The happy couple! Congratulations, you guys." Bruce smiled.

"Why, thank you, Hugh," Nola said. "Where's Carla?"

Adam finished filling one glass, and then looked at Bruce.

Bruce glanced around. "She's around somewhere," he said. "Probably looking for you two."

Adam filled the second glass, and then looked at Bruce again. "We've talked about cats, Hugh."

Bruce nodded.

"I know you don't have a companion animal anymore," Adam said, "not since your Calico died. Have you thought some more about Moonshadow?"

Bruce wrinkled his brow.

Adam handed Nola one glass of punch, and took a drink from the other. "He's a good kitty," he said to Bruce. He smiled.

"I believe I'll take you up on that," Bruce said. "Carla and I've been seeing each other a lot, but we have no plans for marriage in the near future."

"Thanks, Hugh. Of course I'm quite attached to the little guy." Adam put his free arm around Nola. "Nola and I would like to visit you and Moonshadow once in a while—in his elder years," he said. "He's eleven."

"That's fine with me," Bruce said. "I'll welcome the company." He glanced around again. "I'd better find Carla," he said, "and tell her the news."

*   *   *

After the reception, Adam and Nola took a short honeymoon trip to a PIP resort just outside Earth City. They walked among dense stands of shrubbery, under an early afternoon sun.

Adam noted that the shrubs were planted in a terraced, or step, arrangement. The background, the farther greenery, loomed taller than that closer to the walkways. In some places the terraced shrubs grew above even the five-meter-high brick and composite PIP enclosures.

"It's pretty here," Nola said. "There's more green than in the parks. But it's so crowded."

Adam looked around. "Everywhere's crowded," he said. "Everywhere on Earth. And it's going to get worse. The plan was at least holding it back a little. But now?" Adam hesitated, and then said, "I'd better stop being so negative. Maybe something can be done about it now."

He put his arm around her, and the two continued down the path.

*   *   *

Adam and Nola returned to Earth City a few days later. Adam visited King's office in the morning of his first day back at work.

"Coffee, Adam?" King got up from behind his desk.

"Sure. Thanks." Adam poured his own. "Rob," he said, "we have to do something right now, other than figure out the Earth-Twin problem. We're right back where we started over twenty years ago."

Both stood next to King's desk, Adam with the cup of coffee in his hand. "What do you suggest?" King asked.

"We need to look for ways to solve our problems right here on Earth," Adam said. "PANS isn't going to bail us out." He took a drink of coffee.

"We cannot be sure of that," King replied, "and our job here is just PANS." He smiled. "But you are welcome to join me the next time I speak to the senate committee. Or we can set that up anytime you desire."

Adam took a big gulp of coffee. He wasn't ready for that, he thought. "Maybe later, Rob," he said.

King poured himself a glass of water from the pitcher on his desk. "Just let me know when," he said.

"I'd like to get the support of the team, at least on the future of the plan," Adam said. "That'd be a beginning. I don't think I can convince the government by myself." He thought of Bitterman's fat face.

"Like I said, Adam, anything other than PANS is not the team's job. But as administrator it is in my area of concern," King said. He took a drink of water. "I will go to the government with you whenever you desire. Just get your arguments together."

Adam nodded.

"But we can see what support you have on the team," King said. "Maybe that can help. Let us discuss that, then, before we get back to problem solving."

"At this afternoon's meeting, Rob?" Adam asked.

*   *   *

At home hours later, Adam stood outside in the cool and cloudless night. He gazed in the direction of Cetus and quietly questioned. *Jenny? Pete? Linda? They left here so long ago. What's become of them?*

He wondered if Pete was using his problem-solving skills. Pete could have been useful on Earth, he thought, but maybe he was more useful on Earth-Twin. *That depends on the nature of the problem,* Adam told himself.

"Oh, there you are." Nola stepped out onto the balcony, stood next to Adam and turned toward Cetus. "I should've expected to find you out here thinking."

"So far away, Nola darling." He put his arm around her.

"I hope that we can solve the PANS problem soon, dear," Nola said. "I'm really beginning to understand about the coming crisis on Earth."

"I don't think we can solve it." Adam looked at faint Tau Ceti, and tried to explain his comment. "I believe we'll have to somehow work around it." He looked at Nola. "We'll just have to make our future plans with Earth-Twin as a guide. An object lesson."

Nola looked at him.

"I'm thinking out loud," Adam said. "I guess I don't really know what to think. Just that we can't solve our problems by exporting them, I guess."

Adam felt Nola take his hand in hers and squeeze it gently. "I know you want to stop the colonization entirely," she said. "Maybe it'll come to that."

"I don't have a lot of support from the team. We talked about that this afternoon." Adam added, "Rob said he'd set up a government meeting for me, but I don't think I can accomplish anything now. We have to find out what happened."

*   *   *

The PANS team, with the approval of the oversight committee, organized a number of study groups in the few months following the sixth signal. Individual members of the team chaired many of these groups, and each was charged with investigating a possible cause for the colonists' population losses. Adam took charge of the "food supply failure" group. He suggested that Nola's research group form a "disease" group at the university, where it could readily consult with appropriate departments.

Other groups, Adam noted as he organized his group, would consider predators, failures of mechanical equipment, shipboard failures of life support systems and various other deep space hazards, unexpected radiation sources from Earth-Twin's sun or from the planet itself, and inadequate protection, from cosmic and other radiation, by the planet's atmosphere. Also included were attack by alien intelligent beings, criminal activity and war among the colonists themselves. All of these had been examined, in one way or another, early in the PANS planning; now they would be examined with the specific population losses in mind. A general group was formed to look for other possibilities.

*   *   *

The groups worked for the better part of a year; at the end of that time Earth received the next population count. Something about that latest number caught Adam's interest.

The seventh hypersignal indicated an Earth-Twin population of roughly thirty-five thousand less than the sixth. He sat in his office just after the team meeting where King had announced the count. *Do the numbers follow some kind of pattern?* he asked himself. It was almost as if the later ships didn't arrive, he thought, but the on-time signals meant that all had arrived intact. He wondered if those ships could have landed with most colonists dead.

He shook his head, and thought about shipboard life support systems failure or unknown space radiation for the fifth, sixth and seventh ships. These were not new theories, he told himself, just some of the possibilities the team already considered. Only a few living people were needed to operate the ships during the arrival stage.

He grimaced. *The seventh is Linda's ship.*

He took a sip of coffee. The "dead-on-arrival" theory had a flaw, he thought. The expected birth rate for those already on the planet should still have increased the total population. Instead Earth observed a decrease, at least for the last two counts. He wondered if the pattern of *about* two million missing colonists each year implied something else about the arriving ships.

*   *   *

Adam and Nola lingered at the table after dinner at home. After discussing the morning's seventh census, Adam thought of Avery. "Bill liked this," he said. He took a drink of creme sherry.

"Like you do, dear." Nola smiled.

Adam shook his head. "Long ago Bill convinced the others on the original team to accept me as a new member," he said. "He believed that my distrust of such a plan would keep the team from making mistakes.

He told me that. Called it a 'healthy skepticism.' But it appears that I didn't help."

"You can't blame yourself. You tried. I know you did your best." Nola got up, sat on Adam's lap and put her arms around his neck. "I know that you, my Adam, will figure out what's happening. Long before we get anything by radio."

Adam smiled, held Nola close and said, in his noblest voice, "With you by my side, I can accomplish anything. Even this impossible thing. Nola darling, you'll be the one who'll lead me to the answer."

She smiled. "How will I do that?"

Chapter 11

The Numbers

Adam lay in bed at midnight, wide-awake, the night after receipt of the seventh count. He shook his head. He eased out of bed so he wouldn't disturb Nola, and donned his robe and slippers. He glanced at her in the semi-darkness and smiled. *Sound asleep,* he thought. He left the bedroom and walked out onto the balcony.

He stood still. He felt a cold breeze on his face, and detected the faint chemical smell of Earth City's scrubbed air. He looked at the sky.

In the moonless night, the countless stars resembled diamonds scattered on a bowl-shaped sky. Over the millennia, he thought, human observers had mentally arranged many of those stars into patterns. He gazed at the particular arrangement of stars called Cetus. This arrangement was peculiar to an Earth view of these stars. From elsewhere, he told himself, far from Earth's solar system, they would not trace out the shape of a sea monster.

He saw the constellation clearly, halfway up in the southern sky. Viewed from Earth-Twin, he thought, those stars would be randomly scattered, with Tau Ceti missing.

He knew that he saw some of the stars, those much farther than Tau Ceti, because of the light energy that left those stars hundreds of years ago. Tau Ceti's light had departed that star some twelve years ago. Even the most advanced telescopes could examine only the history of Tau Ceti and Earth-Twin. Hypersignal remained the sole source of more recent information.

The answer had to be in those numbers, he thought. *What are the numbers saying?*

All of a sudden he understood what had kept him awake. That afternoon he had followed a false lead when he had concentrated on the arriving ships. Instead the signals told him something about the colonists already on the planet. The latest three counts were all nearly the same. *No. Four counts.* The small discrepancy in signal four might also fit the pattern. The numbers were not exactly the same, but they indicated that not many more than eight million people remained alive on Earth-Twin, even though over two million arrived each year.

He had recognized that number pattern earlier, but until the seventh count had confirmed it he had not thought it significant. Earlier, he told himself, others had believed it showed only equipment failure.

Adam started when he heard Nola's voice behind him. "You're thinking again," she said. "Will it help if I hold your hand?"

Adam turned and took Nola's hand in his. "How long've you been standing there?" he asked. "I didn't mean to ignore you." She looked very pretty in her new purple robe, he thought. Her brown eyes looked half asleep.

"I have this habit, dear," she said. "I sneak up on you when you're looking at the stars."

"Did I wake you when I got up?" he asked.

"Yes, kind of." Nola smiled.

"Sorry about that," Adam said. "I had to come out here to think about it."

"Any new ideas?" Nola asked.

"Let's talk about numbers," Adam said. He looked toward Tau Ceti, although he kept hold of Nola's hand. "Why does it remain at about eight million? No. Six million." He looked at her and exclaimed, "It's six million!"

"Six million?"

"If one can assume that each ship arrived intact with its more than two million living people," Adam explained, "the critical number is really about six million or so." He hesitated, and then added, "It's the number alive on the planet when each ship lands."

"Yes, of course," Nola said.

"What's magic about six million?" Adam asked. He let go of Nola's hand and turned toward Tau Ceti again. "Of course it's changing by a few tens of thousands, but it still looks like a pattern."

"A strange pattern but, yes, it could be a clue," Nola said. She stood beside him, her shoulder against his arm.

"The answer has to be there," he said. "Counter error's been ruled unlikely. And then the seventh ship had the new design." The morning's hypersignal had definitely ruled out equipment malfunction, he thought. The seventh ship carried a newer model counter and signal equipment than the earlier ships, built with a newer technology. If the counting equipment malfunctioned, one couldn't expect the same error.

Adam went on. "The equipment can't be the problem. The counts must be accurate." He shrugged. "The numbers have the answer." He tapped his fingers on the side of his head. "It's in here somewhere, darling."

"You may be right," Nola said. She looked at him. "I'll make sure that my group considers those numbers some more, too."

Adam noticed that she shivered a little. "Let's go back inside," he said. "It's cold out here."

        *   *   *

Adam sat by the desk in his study, two weeks after he and Nola had first talked about the number "six million." He prepared, in the evening, for the PANS meeting to be held the next morning. He picked up his cup and took a sip of coffee, and then perused some handwritten notes. He looked up when Nola came into the study and sat down next to him.

"So you'll be the rep," he said. She had told him earlier that she would give a talk and answer questions on behalf of her group.

"They drafted me this morning," Nola said. She inserted a small disk into the terminal on the desk and looked at tables and graphs in the space above.

"They could've chosen anyone," Adam said. He smiled. "But they chose you, my Nola, to be PANS spokesperson. Now I'll be seeing you at most of the important meetings." Adam winked. "The little girl from the front row."

Nola smiled. "I'm glad you'll be there."

"You don't need my help," Adam said. She was the intellectual equal of any member of the team, he told himself.

"But I've been kind of isolated from most of the PANS work," Nola said, "and you know everything that's going on."

"Except how to solve the problem, darling. We have studies, research, discussions, everything. But no real answers." Adam removed Nola's disk from the terminal, inserted his own and glanced at his graphs.

At tomorrow's meeting, he thought, the team would evaluate all of the possible explanations for the crisis. They would hear reports from all the individual study groups. "I'm anxious to hear more about your group's conclusions," he said.

"I'm a little scared," Nola confessed. "Not about our ideas. I understand them. I'm just not used to presenting to a top-level group."

"You'll be fine." Adam took another sip of coffee. "You know everybody."

"Why, yes." Nola smiled. "Everybody's nice."

Adam removed his disk. "I'd like to convince the team," he said, "to make some kind of decision over the next few weeks. Earth's overcrowding problem is just getting worse. With the plan on hold, nothing's being done.

I'd like them to ask the government to abandon the PANS plan and look for other solutions."

"But you still don't have any proof that technology can't keep up," Nola suggested, gently.

"Maybe when we know exactly what's gone wrong," Adam said. "But I'm convinced it can never work." He picked up his coffee decanter, intending to refill his cup. The decanter was empty. He put it back down on the desk. "I'm sure the answer lies in the number—the six million."

"You know we've looked at some disease explanations involving numbers," Nola said.

"Why don't you tell me more about that, and then we can let it all go until tomorrow." Adam stood up and picked up the decanter again. "I'll refill this first."

*   *   *

Adam sat with the PANS team and the group representatives by the now rather crowded elliptical table. Nola occupied the seat just to his right. He drank coffee. It tasted good, he thought, after a sleepless night; he hadn't been able to let the problem go. He listened while King opened the meeting, introduced the reps, described the agenda and told Nola that she was first.

Adam smiled when she got up and walked to the front of the room. She looked very professional in her blue tunic, he thought, and beautiful at the same time.

He listened while she described the consequences of an alien disease that may have penetrated the general immunization that all humans on Earth received just after birth. She explained how a long latency disease and the particular timing of arrivals might account for the number pattern. He frowned slightly. He had talked to her about that explanation the previous evening, but he had later rejected it.

He sipped coffee while she continued. "The exploration team," Nola said, "stayed on the planet for two Earth years and found no killer diseases. But a new disease, as I already said, may require more than two years of constant contact in order to infect humans.

"It could be," she added, "that the disease organism also required large numbers of hosts to become effective and deadly. If it had to mutate before it could affect humans, it may have needed many infected people. The relatively small number of explorers would have remained immune."

Adam frowned again. Disease, he thought, could not give a simple explanation of the numbers.

Adam put his cup down on the table. He knew that Nola was about to finish. "We looked at one more possibility," she said. "The explorers could not have covered all of the surface area of that large continent. Perhaps the colonists, as their population increased, entered an isolated area and encountered the deadly disease organisms." She hesitated, and then asked, "Any comments?"

Adam stood up. He remained by his chair. "Nola, I don't think disease is the problem," he said. He then addressed the whole team. "This disease theory can't explain the number pattern, the apparent stabilization of the Earth-Twin population at just about six million."

If a disease was killing the colonists, he thought, the population could not be expected to remain at a particular number. Either the colonists' technology would overcome the disease and the count would increase again, or the disease would conquer the colonists and the count would decrease.

He went on. "Nola and I did discuss her group's explanation of the numbers last evening, but later last night I thought about that some more. It's possible that a long latency disease may kill people only after they've been on the planet for several years, and this could be responsible for the number pattern. That could happen.

"But I'm not convinced that it did, since there should still be some small total increase due to the birth rate on the long journey and on the planet."

He concluded, "Maybe death by disease could give that particular number pattern by some coincidental series of events—somehow involving things like long latency and the particular number and timing of new arrivals and births. But this gets too complicated. Nola's group may turn out to be correct, but right now I believe that the answer will be simpler than this." He sat down.

He winked at Nola when she returned to her seat. She winked back and he smiled. He had rejected her explanation, but he knew that she was not convinced that disease was the problem on Earth-Twin. She and her group, he thought, had simply performed the study assigned to them. They had attempted to fit the observations to a disease theory and, in his opinion, had done a fine job.

Adam, the team and the reps examined other possibilities. A rep talked about a predatory animal, larger and more dangerous than those the explorers found. The team concluded that the highly educated and skilled colonists would have found a way to control such a predator; it would certainly have to be a very primitive animal. Adam also argued that the number pattern didn't fit a predator scenario.

A team member, head of the subgroup that examined the possibility of lethal radiation, reported. Adam listened while the man described how both the explorers' lack of problems and the hypersignal numbers could be explained by radiation that could effect humans only after five of six years of exposure.

Adam smiled when Nola stood up and disagreed. She explained that such radiation would also affect the native animals. The animals on the planet are chemically much like Earth animals, she argued, and evolution could not create stable species in an environment of killing radiation.

She was very insightful, Adam thought. He smiled at her when she sat down, and she smiled back. He stood up.

Adam presented the same argument against radiation that he did against disease. The number pattern could be adequately explained only by a complicated series of coincidences.

He listened while others discussed attack by intelligent aliens. No intelligent alien life had ever been detected, even with the most advanced sensing technology, but he knew that all reasonable explanations must be examined.

One team member suggested that aliens might be able to mask their radio and other signals, or used a very different form of communication. Another argued that the population counters may have detected alien intelligences, and that many more colonists had died since the alien count was filling in. That would be possible, Adam thought, only if their brain waves were much like that of humans, an unlikely possibility.

Adam got up and countered that aliens couldn't explain the number pattern, at least not in simple terms. He used the same argument to dismiss two other possibilities: war among the colonists themselves and massive criminal activity.

Earth had eliminated war long ago by various measures, Adam thought, including PIP. He listened while Rob King got up and added to the discussion of war. "The colonists have not had much time to organize into large opposing groups, and they took only a relatively few weapons with them. But those on different ships may have set up different sets of laws, and groups could have gone to war over those differences.

"We must admit that, from earliest recorded history to the early twenty-first century, various human groups had been almost constantly at war in one place or another on Earth. But I must accept Adam's argument. War, and similarly crime, cannot explain why the population remains at six million. These would kill too erratically, too indiscriminately, to result in any pattern."

Adam saw King look at him. "Adam," King said, "let us have your presentation now."

Adam got up, walked to the front and stood by the podium. He did not bring his coffee cup with him. "Let's consider a food supply problem," he said. "Could the colonists be starving?" He hesitated a moment, and then went on. "Several of us examined this possibility, but I must admit we haven't yet found a way that food shortage could account for the pattern in the signals.

"We looked at outdoor farming failure and food factory failure. But if one failed, they'd have the other. Both failing, food factories and farms, gets us back to the multiple coincidences problem."

He looked at his coffee cup on the table far from the podium, and then ignored it. "I think it'll be simpler than that," he said. "One problem that the colonists haven't yet been able to solve.

"I'm biased toward an explanation that involves a shortage of resources," he confessed. Food, he thought, was humanity's most basic need. Air and water, while also basic, were available in abundance as long as they weren't polluted, or a planet wouldn't be called earthlike and wouldn't be colonized. Heat energy, a mild climate, was also there for the taking on Earth-Twin.

He glanced at the faces around the elliptical table. All looked like they ate regularly, he thought, but people have always had to work to obtain food. This meant society collectively, not necessarily each individual. Some would always be the supporters and others the supported. The supporters would always have to work in one way or another to obtain or produce food. For that reason, food would remain the most important commodity. *Always*, Adam said to himself, *for any size population.*

He noticed that the well-fed faces around the table waited for him to continue. "As I said, the food shortage theory suffers from the same deficiency as the other theories," he said. "We can't explain the pattern, at least not in simple terms." He winked at Nola. She winked back and he knew that she understood. He had rejected his own presentation, at least for the time being, for the same reason he had rejected hers. "I'm still working on this," he concluded. He returned to his seat.

He listened and sipped coffee while the group considered other scenarios. These included, along with other possibilities, various kinds of natural disaster on the planet, planetary or spacecraft encounters with space debris, and other space hazards. None proved very compelling. None could provide a simple explanation for the pattern in the signals.

Adam was not surprised when the team did not reach a conclusion; most members agreed only that they would require more population counts to confirm the number pattern. Adam believed that such a pattern was already established, but he knew this thinking was not unanimous.

*   *   *

Adam headed for his office alone after the morning meeting, since Nola had gone off to report to her group. He made a mental note to congratulate her later, perhaps with a special dinner.

He thought she had handled herself well in her first high-level meeting. She had been apprehensive the night before, but that hadn't shown in her performance today. Even though young and inexperienced, Nola had acted very professional in a setting unfamiliar to her.

She had given an excellent presentation. She had handled herself much better than he ever had, especially in the early days. Today even he had been much more talkative than he had ever been, he thought, probably spurred on by Nola's demonstration of confidence.

He recalled the time when he had first seen her. Then just a bright-eyed nine-year-old, she had asked, so long ago and so sincerely, "Will they have enough to eat?"

Adam entered his office and stood by his desk. Little Nola's question stuck in his mind. *Will they have enough to eat?* She had asked that question in a particular context, he thought. She had been concerned that the Earth-Twin colonists would have no stores at which to buy food.

He sat down and filled his coffee cup from the decanter on his desk. He mulled over the question again. *Will they have enough to eat? No stores at which to buy food? Is* this *the key?*

The first few shiploads of people, he thought, would initially obtain a very small portion of their food from the natural bounty of the planet—by hunting and gathering; that is, a very few would live, at least partially, off the land.

For most colonists, the still-operating shipboard food factories would be the main source of food in the beginning. Open-air farms would soon follow. These farms were scheduled to be in place and operational by the time the first several ships had arrived. Within a few years, the colonists would establish a free market with individual or corporate farm ownership. *Then* stores would sell food.

Such was the plan, he thought.

He leaned forward in his chair, with his elbows on his knees. He held the full cup of coffee lightly between his hands.

What if some single but persistent problem caused both the farms *and* the food factories to fail? he asked himself. He had rejected that possibility earlier, he thought, or at least had not considered it likely. *But what if? What would happen then?*

What must *happen then?*

Will they have enough to eat?

Adam's cup of coffee slipped from his hands. Coffee and cup fragments scattered all over his office when the cup hit the hard tile floor. He glanced at the mess, and then ignored it.

The numbers had revealed their secret. The pattern could be explained. Circumstances, he thought, had somehow forced the colonists to live *totally* off the land.

He wondered when they discovered that they had a problem. It could have been a number of years ago. It could have been when the first ship,

Pete's, arrived on the planet. Pete had his work cut out for him, Adam thought. For the first time since his old friend had departed Earth, Adam knew that Pete was where he was needed most.

Chapter 12

Pete

Pete MacDonald sat in the warm control room with the factory journal in his hands and glanced around at computer terminals, gauges and chart covered walls. He sighed, and closed his eyes. His local region of space, he thought, lay a vast distance from Earth. What would the ship, that oasis of comfort for himself and more than two million others, look like from the cold blackness of space outside?

Certainly it moved at great speed. However, all motion was relative. Did it move, he asked himself, when existed no nearby objects that could attest to this movement? Earlier, and for a number of years, it had rotated. Now the great silver wheel no longer performed that noticeable motion, although he knew its instruments measured a slowing down, a deceleration.

Other than the slowing down, it must now appear to just float in the blackness. It was, he thought, too far from any lighted star for a visual observer to detect any relative motion. Even the closest star, the ship's destination, was still too far away. That star remained only a bright speck in the blackness, although the talk in the ship's halls insisted that it was getting brighter.

The sun was only a speck of light in the opposite direction, nearly seven years away. To Pete, it might as well be a million.

He opened his eyes, and then looked down at the journal, at the numbers he had, a few minutes earlier, transferred from the computer.

Daydreaming won't change the facts, he told himself. He scrutinized the data.

He had been correct. The minor production problem he had first noticed a week earlier was getting worse.

He looked up when his assistant entered the control room. "Something isn't right here, Andy," he said.

"Oh, put that journal down, Pete," Andy Landis said.

"I don't know," Pete said. "We may have a problem."

"It's almost time for the evening crew to take over," Andy said. "Most of our people have already left. Relax. You fret about the smallest things in the section."

Pete stood up with the journal in his hand. "This is different," he insisted. "Why don't you check the parameters? I may have missed something."

He watched Andy glance at the large humidity and pressure gauges on the wall next to the control terminal, and check those readings against the computer's numbers and graphs. He noticed Andy and himself reflected in the gauges. Andy, he knew, was a few centimeters shorter than his own 186-centimeter height, but Andy's mass of curly brown hair made him look almost as tall.

"Physical parameters are normal," Andy said, "and I just tested nutrient and microbe concentrations."

Pete placed the production journal on the terminal table. "Maybe you're right," he said. He picked up his jacket from the back of the chair he had just vacated, and slung it over his shoulder. It was relatively warm in the factory, even in the dehumidified control room, but he knew it would be cooler outside in the hallways. He leaned over and shut off the computer terminal where he had checked the recent production figures, and then looked at Andy.

Andy shrugged. He hit a few keys on the control keyboard. Graphs, suspended in space above the control terminal, faded away.

Pete didn't let it go. "But production of fruits and vegetables has been stable for nearly seven years. Why is it dropping now? Grains too. I'll have to talk to the other managers and see if they've noticed anything."

"I haven't heard anything," Andy said. "You might just be having some end-of-journey jitters. You know how the excitement's building up all over the place." He smiled. "Only six more weeks."

"At long last," Pete said.

"We'll be the first people to actually live there, Pete. Aren't you getting excited too?"

Pete frowned. "I suppose so."

"I'm even having trouble sleeping now." Andy picked up his jacket from a hook in a corner of the control room. "I can't stop thinking about it."

"I'm not jumping up and down like you," Pete said, "but I guess I'm looking forward to the bright open sky."

"I liked the ship at first, but it's been so long," Andy said.

"Yeah." Pete sat down, his jacket still slung over his shoulder, and made some entries into the main section computer. He then turned off the big terminal. Numbers and letters floating in space above that terminal slowly faded away. Now all terminals were off, he told himself, to conserve ship's energy. This completed his usual preparation for shift changeover.

He got up and donned his jacket. "I guess we're secured," he said. "They should be here in a minute."

"An Earth minute?" Andy laughed. "I guess the minute will be the same, but we'll have to change our counting of weeks, months and years soon." He hesitated, and then added, "Of course we won't have to change the day from the ship day."

"Yeah," Pete grunted.

"Having our artificial day and night here on the ship always seemed so ludicrous to me." Andy shrugged. "Like we're fooling ourselves."

"Yeah." Pete looked at Andy. "I guess it keeps things normal."

"Outside the ship it's always the same, the permanent night of deep space," Andy said. "In here normal." He glanced at the hallway door.

Pete turned around toward the door. A man and a woman entered the control room. Pete greeted the newcomers, his "night" assistant managers, and gave them some instructions. Then he and Andy departed shipboard food factory section three and entered the dimly lit hallway.

"See you later, Pete." Andy turned right.

Pete turned left. "Yeah, Andy," he said. "Have a good 'evening.'"

Pete walked down the narrow hallway. He soon reached one of his favorite places in the giant ship. He stopped and stood in front of a large viewing port, and the star-filled permanent night of deep space loomed before him. This port, about a meter wide and just over two high, fitted into a curved section of the spacecraft hull; although the thick transparent shielding panel was flat, the upper end was closer to his head than was the lower end to his feet. It slanted toward him. He could look up in the present artificial gravity, in the general direction of the sun and Earth.

He heard a familiar female voice a few steps behind him. "You're here again, Pete. I can always find you here."

He turned around.

The young woman's long blond hair reached to her waist and bounced as she approached. She smiled.

"Hello, Jenny," Pete said. "I'm on my way from work."

"I know," Jenny said. "You always take this same route past this same port."

"You planned to intercept me?" Pete smiled.

"Maybe."

Pete turned back toward the port. "It's a fascinating view," he said.

Jenny stepped up alongside him.

"Look at it," Pete said. "The star patterns have hardly changed since we left Earth. Even though we've traveled a tremendous distance, the galaxy is so vast that I can't notice any change in most of the star positions."

"Oh, yes," Jenny said, "fascinating."

"Except for Cetus, of course, since we've been moving in that direction," Pete said. "Of course we can't see it from this port."

"Sure, Pete."

"You can see three constellations right now," Pete said. "They look just like they looked from Earth."

Jenny turned toward Pete. "I know what you see," she said. "It's not constellations."

Pete continued his star discourse. "The patterns are easier to make out now that we've slowed down a lot—that relativistic effect."

"I know all about the constellations, Pete," Jenny said. "I also know what pattern you see in the stars. You see a face. You see the same face all the time."

Pete turned toward her. She looked almost as pretty when she pouted as when she smiled, he thought.

"And you don't look at constellations," she said. "You always look back toward Earth. At our old sun."

Pete sighed. "I guess I do sometimes," he said.

"Remember when we met, Pete?" Jenny smiled. "It's hard to believe it was only a few months ago."

"I remember," Pete said. It had been during one of his rare visits to The New Alligator, he thought, and a crowd had played a matching game. He had reluctantly agreed to participate.

"Out of a hundred people," she said, "we got matched because we have a mutual friend back on Earth. Someone we both care about a lot."

"Good old Adam," Pete said. He hesitated, and then asked, "Do you miss Earth?"

"Can you picture a hundred trillion kilometers?" Jenny asked. "You can't even see Earth. But I'm here. And you're here." She looked directly into his eyes.

Her eyes were a pretty green, Pete thought. That was one of the first things he had noticed about her months ago. "Yeah, Jennifer Susan," he said, "we're right here."

"You never did tell me your middle name, Peter A. MacDonald," Jenny said. "Just what does 'A' stand for?"

"It's a funny name." Pete grimaced. "Most people don't think it's funny. But I do."

Pete felt Jenny take his hands in hers. "Oh, c'mon," she said. "I promise I won't laugh."

"Maybe when we know each other better, Jennifer Susan."

"I hope that's soon," she said.

Jenny's hands felt warm in Pete's. He tried to ignore that, and her pretty green eyes as well. He liked her, he told himself, but to show affection would be unfair to her. She was correct about his seeing another's face in the stars.

"Will you be at the rec center later?" she asked. "Maybe we can play some racquetball. We haven't played for a couple of weeks. I'll bet I can beat you this time." She let Pete's hands go, but still faced him.

"You never win," he said. "You can dance better than me, but I'm better at racquetball."

"I think I know something you don't know." She smiled. "I'll beat you this time."

"No way," Pete said. He laughed. "Some games are close, but I always win."

"Not this time." Jenny turned to leave.

"All right," Pete said. "I'll be there."

"See you then, Pete."

He watched her walk away. She turned once and waved, and then continued down the hallway.

He turned back toward the viewing port, looked up and stood quietly for a moment. *Of course I can't see Earth,* he told himself. Even the sun was difficult to pick out. Just a pinpoint of bright light, it looked like any other of the countless stars.

So long ago! he thought. He had walked out on Linda without saying goodbye. He told her that he was going to Earth City for a few months, to help Lynn Higami. Then, after a talk with Adam, he halfheartedly planned to v-v her. He put that off until the last day, and then "chickened out" entirely. He boarded the shuttle catapult like a robot. He had entered Earth orbit fighting to keep the tears from his eyes.

Sometimes it really seemed like seven years ago. Sometimes a million years. Other times only yesterday. After the ship had departed from Earth orbit and its motion had stabilized, he had stood and watched through one of the viewing ports as the great blue orb that had been his home for his then twenty-five years slowly shrank into the distance. Many others had also watched through that port, but he hadn't joined in their conversations. He hadn't even eavesdropped.

How many times had he relived that departure? Even his occasional four-week hibernation periods had not helped, he told himself. He awoke to the same thoughts he had when he entered the hiber. Now he did not even have hiber; no one could hibernate during the last six months of the voyage. He remembered from the briefing back on Earth that this involved physical activity in the months just before arrival. There was more to it, he thought, but he couldn't recall the details.

No matter. He had responsibilities now. As a senior agricultural specialist, presently manager of shipboard food factory section three, he was soon to take part in the greatest agricultural experiment ever.

The greatest agricultural experiment ever? He wondered how that might play out, and what his contribution might be. He sighed. Had he been sensible, he would be on Earth, married to Linda and helping Adam administer the plan. He shook his head.

He thought of his more immediate responsibility. He turned away from the viewing port and walked to the nearby main food factory office complex. He found the managers of several of the sections seated at a small conference table, drinking coffee. Pete liked the smell of coffee, although he drank it only occasionally.

He sat down with them. After a round of greetings, he said, "I may have a problem. Have you noticed any change in your production recently?" Before anyone could answer, he added, "Three's producing smaller fruit and vegetables."

"I haven't noticed any difference," the manager of section one, sitting next to Pete, said. "I'll check again."

Pete looked around at the others.

The managers of sections four and seven also hadn't noticed anything, but the manager of section nine had. "Nine's fruit is smaller," she said. "Not everything, but a lot of undersized fruit for about the last week or so. I haven't checked the vegetables or grains. Willie's been handling those. I'll talk to him." She looked at Pete. "I'm glad you brought this up, Pete. I've been a little puzzled about it." She took a sip of coffee.

The managers of sections ten and fourteen reported undersized fruit and vegetables. Fifteen, exclusively grains, reported a small decrease in total production.

Pete tapped his fingers on the table. "Let's have a meeting of all the managers," he said. "Maybe in a few days? Let's all record our production and compare with the past. We can match notes when we get together."

The other managers agreed, and would pass the word to the section managers not present. Pete got up to leave, and said he would talk to Lynn.

He hurried to food factory director Lynn Higami's nearby office and told her of the problem. "So that's the situation, Lynn. I talked to the managers of some of the other sections and some of them've seen it, too."

"Hmmm. Yes." Pete's former professor and present boss got up from her chair and stepped over to a chart on her wall.

He watched as she eyed the chart briefly. Her shoulder length brown hair, clean good looks and average height belied her professionalism, he thought. Although she was seven years his senior, he had always considered his boss to be one of the prettier women in his life. "We're going to get together later and compare notes again," he said.

"It looks like you're going at this correctly, Pete," Higami said. "We should look into it. Even if only to see if there really is a problem. Keep me informed."

Pete nodded, and then said goodbye and left.

*   *   *

Later, on the racquetball court, the questions still crowded Pete's mind. *What's gone wrong,* he asked himself, *in the factories?* He raised his right arm and tensed his whole body. His left arm and empty left hand moved outward for balance, and he shifted his weight.

Why, after so long with no problems, is food production falling off? It couldn't be just his imagination, he thought, since others had also noticed it.

The ball flashed by and Pete swung at it too late. He missed.

"Your mind's not on the game," Jenny said.

"Sorry, Jenny."

"I won our first game, and this looks like it'll be number two. C'mon, try harder." She smiled. "I'll win anyway."

Pete noted how pretty Jenny looked in her racquetball outfit, as he had when he had joined her on the court fifteen minutes earlier. He started to say something about that, but said, instead, "I'll try. I can't let you keep winning."

Pete lost anyway. He couldn't follow the ball. It didn't seem to bounce, or fall, correctly. "Looks like I'm mister clumsy today," he said.

"I told you I know something you don't know," Jenny said. She smiled. "I know because I helped check out the main ship computer and the, oh, some peripheral computers a few weeks ago so we could start the automatic sequence. Let's play another game. See if you can figure it out." She served the ball. It bounced off the front wall and then again off the floor.

Pete got ready to hit the ball, and then stopped abruptly. It flashed past and hit the back wall. He dropped his racquet arm to his side and watched Jenny retrieve the ball. *What is she talking about?*

"It's been so long since we were all briefed on this," she said. "You probably forgot."

Pete's eyes opened wide. "Forgot what?"

"It's so subtle. You and I won't notice it. None of the people will notice it." She hesitated, and then added, "The change is so gradual that we won't notice anything. We adjust. But the ball can't adjust."

Pete looked at her. "But, what?"

"I've been practicing, so I can follow the ball now and you can't," Jenny teased. She held on to the ball, and smiled.

"You mean there's a change in the whole ship? What is it, Jenny?" Pete shouted. "What's different?" He gestured with his arms, and dropped his racquet. It made a loud bang when it hit the floor.

Too loud, he thought. *Too loud!*

Jenny's smile faded into a puzzled look. "It's just the gravity," she said. "The artificial gravity is increasing so that our bodies will be accustomed to it when we arrive."

Pete stood with his mouth open.

"You must remember from our briefings on Earth," Jenny said.

Pete now recalled that he had seen a small "reminder" in the "Ship's News" a few months earlier. He had not been particularly interested then, and it had, apparently, slipped from his mind. "Yeah, I remember now," he said. "The gravity has to get stronger. Could that be doing it?"

"Doing what?" Jenny asked. "What're you so excited about?"

Pete picked up his racquet. "Jenny, you said that the change started a few weeks ago," he said. "How much greater than Earth gravity would it be by now?"

"It was four weeks," she answered. She hesitated, and then added, "It should be about ten percent greater than Earth average."

"Ten percent?" Pete asked. "Could that do it? Most crops've grown well in weaker gravity. But stronger gravity?"

Jenny stared at him.

"I guess they assumed the larger gravity wouldn't be a problem for Earth crops," he said. "They must've checked it." He noticed Jenny's puzzled expression, and realized he hadn't told her of the problem. "Some of the fruits and vegetables are growing slower. In my section and a few others. This just started about a week ago."

Jenny grimaced. "I didn't know there was a problem, Pete," she said. "I would've told you." She hesitated, and then said, "I'm sorry. I should-n't have played silly games with you."

"It's all right, Jenny. We don't yet know what's happening."

"Could that be a problem for us?" Jenny asked.

Pete retrieved his racquet cover from the corner of the court. "I don't know," he said. "If it doesn't get any worse, we won't have a problem." He was talking and thinking. "We do have some stored food left, and we'll be on the planet in only six weeks." He added, "I'm going to try to find Lynn right away."

"Won't it wait until tomorrow?" Jenny asked. "It's late. Dr. Higami is probably at home."

Pete fumbled with his racquet, and started to put on the cover.

"The gravity change is gradual, so there can't be any big failure in the factories overnight," Jenny said. "You don't really know it's the gravity, anyway. Like you said, Earth must've checked it. They wouldn't have sent us without making sure."

In her expression Pete read "Would they?" He asked himself the same question, and then said, "No, it can't wait." He zipped up his racquet cover. "I have to talk to Lynn now."

"But you said it wouldn't be a serious problem." Jenny picked up her own racquet cover."

"Sorry, Jenny." Pete turned toward the small door in the back of the court.

Chapter 13

Failure

On his way to Higami's office, Pete considered the situation. A ship-board food production shortfall might be only the beginning. If gravity was indeed causing the problem, agriculture on the planet could be in jeopardy. Plans would have to change, he thought, for both the factories and the open-air farms.

The gravity increased a little every day. He thought of the hibers; gravity was the detail he could not recall earlier. Hibernation at this late stage in the journey would defeat the purpose of the gradual change in artificial gravity. Earth's scientists had planned carefully for that. *Had they for the crops?*

Maybe this is premature, he thought. *Maybe it isn't the gravity.* He realized that the situation wasn't critical, and might not get worse. *Earth must have checked it.*

Earth! It made him think of Linda.

He had first met her at that Spring Dance. She had brown hair and blue eyes, and was somewhat tall. He had called her "statuesque," and she had laughed.

Linda had been Adam's date, but she and Pete had hit it off from the beginning. Adam had been gracious about that, Pete thought, and had given in easily. Adam had never been very assertive; Pete knew he had taken advantage.

He wondered what Adam was doing now. Adam had been troubled about the colonization plan. Had he checked the gravity? Had he been too busy with other things? Perhaps gravity had been someone else's job.

Adam had even asked him to join in the PANS research, Pete thought. *On Earth.* Why hadn't he accepted the offer? He knew why. *Stupidity.*

Pete reached the food factory office complex, focused his mind on the problem at hand and knocked on Higami's door.

"Yes?"

"It's Pete again, Lynn."

"Come in, Pete."

Pete quickly entered the small office. "I didn't know if you'd still be here. Am I interrupting anything?"

"No. I was hoping I'd see you again this evening." Lynn remained seated behind her desk. "We need to talk, and now would be just fine."

Pete sat down in front of the desk. "I have an idea what may be causing the problems with production."

"Good. After our earlier talk, I took a more careful look at the past few weeks' figures." Lynn pointed to some charts on the wall. "Production is down a little in nine of the fifteen sections. Just enough to be significant."

"I expect we'll have problems in all sections, Lynn."

"The drop is so small that I didn't notice it before," Lynn said. "For once your impatience may be a help rather than a hindrance." She smiled.

Pete laughed. "Yeah, maybe I did something right." He didn't pause to take a breath. "Anyway, I was playing racquetball with a friend just a few minutes ago. I couldn't follow the ball! At first I thought I was just getting clumsy, but she reminded me that our artificial gravity is increasing."

Lynn looked at him. She nodded, and then said, "Yes, I suppose it is—for several weeks now."

"Could that be causing the problems in the sections?" he asked. "If so, we can expect it to get worse."

"When I worked with the PANS people," Lynn said, "we talked mostly about conservation of resources in the factories, and irrigation and fertilization on the field farms." She hesitated, and then added, "Apparently they had already hashed out the details of the gravity difference. They said Earth-Twin's higher gravity would be no problem for agriculture."

"Who did the experiments?" Pete asked. "What did they do?"

"They didn't say much about the experiments," Lynn answered. "I recall that I thought *that* was a little curious. But we were so involved with the other issues." She nodded. "We'll have to keep careful watch on everything. If gravity turns out to be the cause, there's nothing we can do to change the situation. On the ship."

Pete believed he understood. The artificial gravity, determined by the ship's deceleration, must be continually increased for the remainder of the journey. The dynamics of the entire trip had been carefully planned, he recalled, and a change at this time could mean that the ship would reach the new star system at too great a speed. They would risk being unable to slow down and land before using up all life-support nuclear energy reserves. In a classic "lost in space" scenario, their dead ship would become a small new planet in orbit around Tau Ceti.

The ship was not designed to operate in space on just "solar." Massive photovoltaic arrays would be deployed inside the ship circle for full operation of the food factories and other necessities when on the ground. The ship must land as planned, he told himself, on time.

"I hope we can do something about this, whatever the cause," Lynn said. "So far we've managed to produce enough food for everyone, including all the new babies."

More than ten thousand over the past few years, Pete thought.

Lynn scribbled a few notes. "Let's set up a meeting of all section managers for tomorrow morning," she said. "I'll get some of the engineers, too. We can look at any other changes in the ship's environment, and then decide what to do next."

Pete stood up. "Yeah. And I'll start thinking about what the problems might be once we reach our destination and are stuck with the planet's gravity." He left the office.

*   *   *

The next morning Pete, Lynn, the other food factory managers and several of the ship's engineers debated the problem. They found no other significant recent changes in the ship's environment, and accepted the increasing artificial gravity as the most probable cause for the decrease in food factory production. "Watch and wait" was the decision, and do what they could to keep up production.

*   *   *

A week later Pete entered Lynn's office. She was seated at her desk, entering data at her terminal.

He said, nearly out of breath, "Lynn, I just checked the latest figures. All fifteen sections are showing production shortfalls."

"Yes, Pete, I've been on top of that all week," Lynn said. She picked up the cup of coffee on her desk and took a sip. "I had to ask the Council for authorization to start using the remaining stored food, or we would-n't have been able to meet the demand over the past few days."

"I have a proposal," Pete said. He paced the office floor. "I'd like to take section three off production and use it for experimentation. Try some different crops. Maybe some varieties won't be affected. We need to know what to plant on Earth-Twin." He hesitated, and then added, "I know this could make us run out of stored food."

"I hear you," Lynn said. "You're the best qualified to do such experiments in the short time that we have. But I don't know if I can get approval. We aren't certain that the gravity is causing our problems."

· 157 ·

"We have to do something," Pete insisted, "now." He still paced the floor.

Lynn stood up. "We're going to need all the production we can get," she said. "Can you do this with only a small part of the section?"

"I've thought about that," Pete answered, "but it may be inconclusive. We have to try every crop that's not presently being grown. I'll need the whole section." He turned toward the door.

"I'll bring that up with the Council," Lynn said. "I'm meeting with them in an hour to discuss our situation."

As he left the office, Pete said, "Thanks, Lynn, but I'm going to start preparing right away. We have only five weeks."

"I'll come over to three as soon as I have something definite to tell you," Lynn said. "Don't terminate your routine production just yet."

*   *   *

Pete found his assistant deep in the bright and fragrant interior of section three. Andy emerged from the greenery with a few plant stems in his hands.

"Well, it's about time you got to work, boss." Andy laughed.

Pete laughed halfheartedly. He hesitated, and then said, "Let's take the section off production. From now on we'll be experimenting."

"Is it all right to do that? Does Lynn know? Does she approve?" Andy put the plants down on a nearby table.

"I told her," Pete said. "She wants to consult the Council first. I'm sure they'll approve."

"Maybe we'd better wait." Andy wiped his hands with a towel.

"I'll take responsibility," Pete said. He turned and headed back to the control room.

"Relax, Pete," Andy said. He followed Pete. "There's a Council meeting that should be starting just about now. Let's wait a few hours."

"Yeah," Pete said. "Lynn told me about that meeting. But we can't wait. I'll have to take the chance that we'll get approval." He glanced back at Andy.

Andy shrugged. "You're the boss. I'm only assistant manager."

In the control room Pete gave his initial instructions. "Let's get out seeds and cuttings for everything we have that's not currently being grown in one of the sections. Something may grow all right."

"We'll need more help, Boss," Andy said.

"I'll get it," Pete said. "I'm sure Lynn will give us more people. Now let's start the harvesters to clear out the current crop."

An hour later the Council approved his plan.

*　　　　　*　　　　　*

Over the following weeks Pete watched food production plummet in all sections. Two weeks before the scheduled landing, fruit and vegetable harvests dropped to less than twenty percent of normal and grains to twenty-five percent. A week later, production was down to five percent for all, and even the edible leaves were in short supply.

He considered the good news and the bad news.

Oxygen supply wasn't affected as much as human-edible production. The ship's atmospheric oxygen remained adequate for breathing, but the factories produced mostly inedible leaves and stems. It was as if all the genetic selection and modification of thousands of years on Earth, and especially the intense modification of the past few hundred years, had been wiped out. *The shipboard food factories*, Pete told himself, *now cultivated weeds.*

Such thoughts filled Pete's head as he watched all of his experiments in section three fail.

The stored food lasted until three days before arrival.

*　　　　　*　　　　　*

The great spaceship PANS 1 swept around a partial orbit of Tau Ceti, and then entered a wide Earth-Twin orbit. Pete monitored these early maneuvers on his control room computer while he prepared section three for arrival. The space path became parabolic, and then elliptical. The craft slowed and aligned on the path that would lead to atmospheric entry and parachute-assisted rocket descent.

A few hours before landing, Pete completed his section preparations and then met with Lynn in her office for the last time in space. He had no trouble standing next to her wall charts while he discussed the situation with her. He knew that he would experience no noticeable changes as the trip computer continually adjusted the ship's deceleration, hence its artificial gravity, to include the gravitational influences of Tau Ceti and now Earth-Twin. He thought a lot about gravity now, he told himself.

"I guess we'll have to believe that it's the gravity," he said. "What else could it be?"

He and Lynn, Pete thought now as his stomach growled at him, had agreed earlier not to talk about their hunger and how long that condition might last.

"We have a big job ahead of us." Lynn said, "At yesterday's Council meeting we talked about radio to Earth. Some wanted to tell them that we have a problem, but they were voted down."

"Why voted down?" Pete asked.

"It's because we don't know for sure what the problem is," Lynn said. "Radio takes twelve years to reach Earth anyway."

"But we have to let them know." Pete frowned.

"The Council doesn't want to panic the people on the ships following us," Lynn explained, "prematurely. They're certainly listening on the frequencies. They'd have to be curious."

"I'd be listening," Pete said.

"The Council decided that the risk wasn't worth the possible benefit," Lynn concluded. "By the way," she said, "what do you think of our new home? From the viewing ports?" She smiled.

"I haven't looked." Pete shrugged.

"Oh, it's *beautiful*, Pete! It's just like Earth. And so big now that I felt like I could almost touch it through the port."

"I'll look when I get a chance," Pete said. He looked at Lynn's wall clock. "I'd better get back to three now." He turned toward the office door.

"I have a few things to clean up, too," Lynn said.

Pete entered the hallway. "See you later, Lynn."

"Yes, Pete. On the ground!"

Pete rushed past his favorite viewing port. Just then Jenny approached from the opposite direction, grabbed his arm and steered him back to the port. "Look with me for a minute, Pete," she said. "This port is in a good position right now. We can see the star and the planet."

Pete complied. "Yeah, Jenny. But just for a minute."

"Our new sun looks a little orange," Jenny said, "even from here in space. Just like they said." She smiled.

Pete noted that her face looked orange from the sunlight. He turned toward the port. He had not, he told himself, looked outside for three or four days. "Yeah. I can see the orange." He understood that the orange color would be even more noticeable from the planet's surface, due to atmospheric effects.

Pete stepped closer to the port and the planet loomed up to the right. He turned toward it. It was so close now that it filled nearly half of his field of view.

"Look at our new home," Jenny said. "Isn't it pretty? It's just like Earth."

Pete felt Jenny take his hand in hers. "It's so bright out there now," he said.

"It's our bright future." Jenny squeezed Pete's hand.

It's not just like Earth, Pete thought. "I guess that's our continent," he said, "with the funny greenish color where there are no clouds." The planet appeared to rotate slowly, and he understood that this was due to the ship's motion.

"The pretty greenish color," Jenny said. "It looks like a giant Australia."

"So big it wraps around into the dark night side," Pete said.

"I'll bet you never noticed that my eyes are green like the continent." Jenny looked at him and smiled.

Pete looked into her eyes. "Your eyes are a prettier green."

Jenny turned her smile into a pout. "But you didn't even know I had green eyes until I told you just now."

"Yes I did," Pete insisted.

"But you never said so."

He might as well play her friendly little game, Pete told himself. "I just figured you already knew you had green eyes." He chuckled.

"All right. I'll accept your explanation." Jenny smiled again. "I'm going to like it here. I do already."

"I guess our minute's up," Pete said. "I have to go and monitor three for the rest of the arrival."

"I have to go, too," Jenny said. "We have to secure the computer center before we get belted in."

*　　　　*　　　　*

Pete, seated in the section three control room alone, checked his leg, lap and shoulder belts for security. He didn't expect to be tossed around, but he understood that atmospheric entry had some uncertainties. He knew that everyone else was also belted in, even the monitor pilots.

The ship entered the thin outer limits of the planet's atmosphere. It fired its descent engines, slowed and deployed its parachutes. Pete felt the brief deceleration from the engines, and a few bumps when the parachutes opened.

He listened to the public address speaker. The deep voice of Alan Thackaray, president of the Council, narrated the arrival. "The parachutes are fully opened. Artificial gravity is no longer a factor. Your weight is the real thing now."

Pete tried to picture the five-kilometer silver wheel slowly descending through the thickening air. After a few minutes he heard Thackaray count down the last few seconds. Then he felt a light jar. "On the ground," Thackaray said. "Welcome, fellow space travelers, to a new world. Our new home."

*   *   *

It took Pete nearly an hour to get off the ship, since more than two million had to evacuate over only fifty exit ramps spaced around the five-kilometer circle. He finally stood on solid ground and looked around at the openness. The orange sun beamed in the late morning sky. He had, he thought, grown used to metallic and composite floors, confining walls and artificial lights.

He stood in a milling crowd of thousands and heard someone with a loudspeaker apparently trying to organize the chaos. All two million adults aboard, he thought, had had the same goal: Don't be the last to set foot on Earth-Twin. Now he saw that they shook hands, congratulated each other and ignored the speaker.

He too ignored the loudspeaker instructions. He had arranged to meet with Lynn in an hour, and later with Jenny. He glanced around, away from the looming ship. The landing area lay in relatively flat terrain with low rolling hills to the west. He recalled some of Thackaray's earlier narration on the way down. The first fifty of the five-kilometer wheels would fit into the generally flat area to the east of the present landing site, a roughly circular region of over two thousand square kilometers. This region had been chosen for its flatness and for its location near the geographical center of the large continent.

PANS 1 now lay at the western edge of the circle. Pete could see only one curved edge of the ship from where he stood, but he knew that it looked like a wheel on its side. It would lie flat on the terrain, with automatic supporting legs to make up for small elevation differences. He turned to the west, away from the ship and from the sun. The growing hills in that direction, he thought, made that area unsuitable for landing the giant ships.

He noticed a group of people, several hundred meters away, gathered around a large green plant that loomed well above their heads. *It must be what the explorers had designated a tree*, he thought. He walked over, worked his way through the small crowd and stood close to the tree. He estimated that it was about five or six times his own height. He recalled Adam's description of the color of the leaves: olive drab with a pea green mix.

The explorers had reported that the leaves were not edible, he recalled, at least not by humans, and he could see that this tree did not bear any fruit. He felt hungry. Very hungry. He looked around at the others gathered around the tree. He knew that they were hungry, too. Only the very young children had eaten in the past three days.

He thought about the thunder that had echoed through the ship soon after touchdown. The hypersignal generator had sent its signal to Earth. *That signal*, he told himself, *will deliver only a head count.*

Chapter 14

At First

Eight weeks after the arrival, Pete stood with Jenny at the top of a hill. Small purple flowers decorated the grassy growth underfoot, and a few scattered trees stood nearby. He looked to the west. The height gave him a commanding view of the surrounding plains and low rolling hills. Meandering streams sparkled in the early afternoon yellow-orange sunshine. In the distance denser stands of trees bordered the stream banks.

He turned around. The great silver ship blocked his view to the east. Its closest edge lay about a quarter kilometer from the base of the hill. Its three hundred meter height rose just above his hilltop elevation.

That once-crowded ship was now nearly empty, Pete thought. Over a period of several weeks its complement of twelve aircraft had transported people to widespread locations all over the continent. A few thousand people, mostly those with agricultural expertise, had migrated on foot so as to be close and readily available.

Most of the two million were now dispersed in small groups of a hundred or two each. They would feed themselves by hunting the animals and gathering the edible plants. This was the new plan, he told himself, until someone found a solution to the crop problem.

He looked around, and thought about the vastness of the continent. The Council had, for its initial administration, divided it into four regions called "quadrants."

"I'd like to stay here," Jenny said, "by the ship."

Pete looked at her. "I don't yet know how everything will be set up here," he said. The population of the landing area, he thought, was limited to the small number that the food factories could now feed. "Maybe they'll need a computer specialist."

Jenny smiled.

Other people resided at recently named Landing-One, Pete thought, in addition to food factory operators. This included the Council and other government workers, a small medical group and aircraft crews and support personnel. "Since I know Lynn well, I'll talk to her," he said. "She may be able to help. Or the aircraft people may need some computer work for maintenance scheduling. They have some catching up to do."

"Thanks, Pete," Jenny said. She looked to the west, and then turned toward him again. "Isn't it pretty here? So many real trees. Everything's so green. It's a different green, but there's so much of it. And everything smells good. It's like putting my nose up to a flower."

"Yeah. " He recalled Earth's "scrubbed" air, and the faint but always changing chemical smells.

"I'm glad you finally agreed to come up this hill with me," Jenny said.
"Yeah."

"I really like it here." Jenny turned away from Pete and spread her arms as if to embrace all the open land to the west.

"Jenny, something's different about you," Pete said. "I can't put my finger on it."

"That's the clue." She turned and faced him again.

"The clue?" Pete asked.

Jenny put her hands behind her back. "Fingers," she said.

"Fingers?" Pete shrugged. "I give up."

"At least you noticed something," Jenny said. "It's my fingers—no more red polish on my nails." She held up her small hands for inspection.

"Why not?" Pete asked. He glanced at her fingernails. "It was a nice red."

"I ran out," Jenny said. "We just don't have any more."

"I guess we've run out of a lot of things." Pete shrugged. "No one's producing anything," he said, "but absolute necessities."

"I can do without," Jenny said. She smiled. "I guess I just finally have to give up some of my girlish habits."

"Yeah." Pete nodded. "At least everybody's *eating* now."

"Those first few weeks—I was always so hungry," Jenny said. "I'm glad that's over." She turned and looked again to the west, away from the looming ship. "Isn't this a great view? I think we're on the tallest spot in this nearby area. All the other hills look small and flat."

"We are kind of high up," Pete said.

"And listen to the birds." Jenny cupped her hand to her ear.

Several small feathered creatures perched in the closest tree. One sported bright red and blue feathers. The others, Pete could see three, were black and gray. "Yeah," he said. "A lot of them on this hill."

"I guess it's all right to call them birds," Jenny said. "They look a lot like birds. And they *do* fly."

"I've seen only small ones," Pete said. He glanced around, and then looked at Jenny. "No big ones like crows."

"Small ones have a more musical tone," she said. She looked upward and closed her eyes. "Isn't that a nice breeze? It feels so good on my face." Her long hair stirred lightly, although it was held somewhat by the wide-brimmed hat that hung loosely across her back.

"Yeah." Pete hesitated, and then said, "I'm going to talk to Lynn tomorrow, about what she and the Council are doing about the field farm plans. I'll ask her about a job for you then."

Jenny smiled.

Pete knew that he would stay with the ship to tend section three. It would be good to keep Jenny's pretty smile around, too. He thought of telling her that, and then he thought of Linda.

"You probably have a few more weeks, anyway," he said. "For the trip data."

Jenny sighed. "The Council gave us only a short time to finish evaluating."

"Yeah," Pete said, "I think more will have to join the hunters soon." He looked at Jenny and smiled. "I'll try to keep you here. But the hunters are eating better than we are." People who never ate meat before, he thought, were enjoying it.

"They like it out on the plains," Jenny said. "We don't get many messages, but the few on the comm-computer are so ecstatic."

The two million on the plains shared only a small number of short-range wrist comms, Pete thought. These were not very useful in the vast land, and power supplies were limited. Communication with those far from the landing site had quickly become a problem. "I'm surprised you get any at all," he said.

"The messages tell what I've already been thinking," Jenny said. "About what Earth must've been like a long time ago. They said, their words, 'but without the large predatory animals and bad weather problems.'" She smiled.

"Sounds like you found what you came here for," Pete said.

"Well, not yet. Not everything. I'm working on that." Jenny hesitated, and then asked, "What do you think of the new name for our continent? I like it."

"I guess I understand the reasons for choosing *Pangaea*," he said. The Council had finally decided on the name just the previous day; it had been considering several alternatives. He turned toward the path the two had used to gain the hilltop. "Jenny, duty calls. I'd better get down off this hill and back to work. I don't have Andy to help manage three anymore."

"Me too," Jenny said. She turned to follow Pete. "I hate to leave this place, but we have a lot more to do today."

"We'll be back, I guess," Pete said. He felt Jenny take his hand in hers as she walked alongside him down the hill.

*   *   *

Late the next morning Pete dropped in at Lynn Higami's shipboard quarters. He stood with her in her small work room. "So you're going to direct all the open air farming projects, Lynn? And right away?"

Lynn nodded. "I'll be based in the East Quadrant," she said.

"I was at your office," Pete said. "Looked abandoned. And it looks like you're getting ready to go here." He pointed to a trunk on the floor. "Can I help you pack?"

"I'm done," Lynn said. "I'm not taking much. It'll be primitive in the beginning."

"I guess you'll be glad to leave this section," Pete said. "I think you're the only one left here." His living quarters were in another area, near several of the food factory sections and near a few other remaining residents.

"Have a seat, Pete. We need to talk." Lynn pointed to a trunk, and then sat on another trunk herself. "This is quite important."

Pete turned the trunk so that he could face Lynn, and sat down.

"The Council and I would like you to take over all fifteen factory sections here," Lynn said. "Call it 'general manager.'"

"General manager? Me?"

"You're the best qualified to manage the tests on Pangaean plants." Lynn smiled. "I know you can do the job."

She has already assimilated the new name, Pete thought, but she had worked with the Council on the choice. "Lynn, I don't think I can manage the whole thing," he said. He stood up.

"Pete, you must. We have to get agriculture started."

"I don't know." Pete paced the small room. Such a managerial role, he thought, would be a long-term commitment to Earth-Twin, to Pangaea.

"We need your talent," Lynn said. "We all know another group of two million will arrive in not much more than a year. And that's only the beginning."

That was Earth-Twin year, Pete thought.

He realized he had to give Lynn an answer. He could work out his own problems, his thoughts of Earth, later. He sat down again. "Yeah, Lynn. I'll accept the job."

"Thanks, Pete." Lynn smiled. "I know we can all count on you."

Pete nodded.

Lynn hesitated, and then said, "My plans? In the fields we'll try to cultivate both Earth crops and native plants. I've worked out some short-year adaptations for the north and south.

"Here in the factories," she added, "your experiments should be only on the native Pangaean plants. We have to know which of the edible varieties are adaptable to mass production. And you'll have to feed everyone here with your experimental production."

"Yeah. But those we're trying to grow now produce much less than Earth crops did—as we expected." Pete hesitated, and then added, "Earth crops in Earth gravity."

"We both know that's because people have cultivated Earth crops for a long time," Lynn said, "and have bred them for the desirable characteristics. We want you to look at how it all started."

Pete nodded. He watched her get up and step over to a group of diagrams on the work room wall. She pointed to a graph that showed estimated gross agricultural production on Earth, going back to agriculture's beginning. She indicated the left end, where the curve first started to rise.

"Most scientists believe that agriculture got off to a good start when people found wild strains of wheat that were amenable to their early attempts at cultivation," she said, "and primitive modification. In other places on Earth it was corn or rice. And others. I'm sure you remember this from your courses at the university. We hope you can do something like it here."

Pete got up for a closer look at the graph. "Yeah," he said. "I remember." Apparently she did not want him to attempt genetic modification, his specialty, at least not at present.

Although Lynn had mentioned only the seeding crops, he understood that she also expected him to consider those native plants that may be best propagated with cuttings or tubers. He would also seek new methods that may be extant in this world although unknown on Earth.

Lynn stepped away from the wall. "That's why you must concentrate only on native plants," she said. "I suspect Earth crops will need many years of genetic manipulation to overcome the problem—gravity or whatever. We can't wait that long." She hesitated, and then added, "And we can't feed the researchers."

"I guess I can try." Pete nodded.

Lynn sat down again. "You're the one who can do it," she said.

Pete looked back at the graph. The time scale at the beginning, where agricultural production first appeared above zero, read "minus ten thousand years" followed by an asterisk. He saw that someone had scribbled in "Earth" above the word "years."

He understood the asterisk. It meant "best scientific estimate." The number could be off by up to a few thousand years.

"Pete, we have many thousands of edible plant varieties here, probably millions," Lynn said, "that we know nothing about. If you just keep trying to cultivate random varieties, the search could take decades. You'll have to narrow it down somehow."

The explorers, Pete thought, had cataloged only a few thousand. He sat down on the trunk again. "That's a big order," he said. "I haven't done any statistics or prediction since we left the U. And that was on genetics."

"I remember your work." Lynn smiled. "That's why I know you can figure it out," she said. "And you have the ship's computing facilities, mostly to yourself. Learn as much as you can. We'll use your results—as you get them—on the farms."

"How much emphasis on Earth crops in the fields?" Pete asked.

"It'll be a minor effort," Lynn answered. "I don't expect good results, but we'll try everything. We must solve this problem."

"We have time," Pete said. "There's plenty of food here."

"For now," Lynn said.

"You seem to be in a hurry, Lynn."

Lynn pointed toward the graph on the wall. "We need agriculture to feed a large population," she said. "You know very large numbers can't continue to live off nature's bounty."

Pete looked at the graph. "How much time do you think we have?"

"A number of years, I guess." Lynn hesitated, and then added, "We have to keep in mind that our population will increase by more than two million each Earth year."

Pete got up and took another close look at the graph, but didn't expect it to help him. He shrugged. "I'm sure we'll have fifteen or twenty years anyway."

"I believe we must plan for less," Lynn said. "But you'll have to do your experiments with only a few workers. We'll also be using small crews in the fields. Only what we can feed."

"Yeah." Pete had learned just this morning that the Council, with Lynn's help, had recently called some people back in from the nearby plains and sent them to all four quadrants to get ready to start the farms. His former assistant manager, Andy Landis, had gone to the East Quadrant.

He thought of another question he had wanted to ask Lynn. "Lynn, what's come of the radio messages to Earth?"

"Nothing so far. The Council's undecided." She explained, "Since everyone's eating, they don't want to risk it. President Thackaray is adamant about not taking a chance on panic aboard inbound ships. He did appoint a small committee to try to work something out."

Pete sat down on the trunk again. "Earth should be told something," he said.

"The president said 'we cannot forget Louisville,'" Lynn said, "but he had to explain that to the rest of the Council."

Louisville? Pete vaguely recalled something about that Earth city. It was back when he and Adam were still roommates. The citizens had somehow believed that they weren't going to get their food, and the resulting riots had caused many deaths. Adam had talked about the incident, long after it was no longer newsworthy.

Lynn stood up. "I'd better get going," she said.

Pete got up. "I'll help you carry this stuff out," He said. He grabbed the handle on one end of the largest trunk.

Lynn took hold of the other handle. "None of it's heavy," she said. "Just papers and manuals. Some clothing. My decanter."

As he helped Lynn carry the trunk down the ship's hallway, Pete wondered about the Council's role now that it was "settled" in the new world. Its job was difficult to pin down in a world where the people were spread out in small self-sufficient groups. Lynn met with the Council regularly, he thought. "The government people—what are they going to do while you run the farms?" he asked. "Other than argue about messages to Earth?"

"They have to plan for the future. It won't always be like this." Lynn hesitated, and then added, "We do have a planned economy here at Landing-One and will have for the first farms."

"Yeah." That was part of the plan from the beginning, Pete now recalled as he and Lynn stepped outside the ship and under the orange sun. They would change to a free market system only later when the farms were well on their way. That would give the Council another job: establish a new monetary system. He and Lynn carried the trunk down the exit ramp to her parked terrie.

"I'm not sure when that'll change," Lynn said, "in this situation. We don't want a planned economy any longer than necessary. We hope we'll be able to set up some kind of private ownership on the farms within a few years."

"I agree," Pete said. He recalled what he had once read about Earth's economic failures in the late twentieth century. Many so-called *socialist* economies had failed catastrophically; they had recovered, albeit slowly, only by adapting to the free market.

"I don't know what we can call it on the plains right now," Lynn said. "Cooperative?"

Pete helped Lynn work the trunk into the back of the vehicle. He let go of his end and rubbed his hands together. Then the two headed back up the exit ramp.

A few minutes later they entered Lynn's residence and picked up another trunk. The humanoids that the explorers had utilized, Pete thought, would have been useful here. He helped Lynn carry and load this and the two remaining trunks.

After he helped fit the last trunk into the terrie, he said, "Well, I guess I should get going, too. I'll have to meet with the people in all fifteen sections—the few that are left—and get things organized here."

"Will you need my help to get started?" Lynn asked.

"No, I don't think so. You have your hands full already."

"We'll talk again soon, Pete. Thanks for the help with my stuff." Lynn got into the terrie, engaged the microfusion engine and turned toward the nearby aircraft staging area.

"So long, Lynn," Pete said as she pulled away.

She waved to him.

He watched the terrie until it disappeared behind a mound, too small to be called a hill, a few hundred meters from the curved side of the great ship.

He turned toward the exit ramp and looked at the opening to the ship. He was now, he thought, manager of all fifteen food factory sections in that ship. Was he, he asked himself, up to that challenge? He hadn't really wanted the job, but he had accepted it. That was his situation for now.

Pete stood for a moment, and then climbed the ramp, entered the ship and walked down a deserted hallway. He had considered asking

Lynn about a local job for Jenny, he thought, but such authority was his now—as were other authorities and responsibilities.

The edible native plants weren't responding well, so far, to cultivation. Should he test many different varieties, in some as yet unknown ordering scheme, as Lynn suggested? Or should he try to modify the more promising plants? The growing tests would take time, but genetic modification in this situation, although more interesting, would require more time and many more workers.

He had used, back at the university, many of the common genetic procedures; he had been the one and only genetics specialist in Lynn's group. A few of the procedures had been used for centuries. Others were more recent developments. Many could be used in combination. All were labor intensive. He would first have to learn more about the local genetics, which would itself be quite a task even though the basic genetic code was the same as on Earth.

Genetic modification had been the original long-term plan for the native plants. His assignment, when he was first accepted as a colonist, had been to help implement it. That had been Earth's plan for him: operate section three for Earth crop production in the early years on Earth-Twin and use the section to experiment on native-plant genetics later.

Lynn's "new" plan made sense, Pete thought. Machines did most of the work in the factories. Only small crews were needed, full-time, for basic operation. Time and resources demanded that he seek those "wild strains of wheat," like Earth long ago.

Earth. So far away. What is Linda doing now? She would be a practicing physician, he thought, and very good at it. She was always dedicated, and he had misinterpreted that. *Stupidly.* Did she ever think about him?

Pete told himself to get back to the problem at hand. It was time for him to try to be dedicated. He turned a corner and headed down the hallway that led to section three.

Progress would be slow, he thought, and each result would certainly take months. The hunters on the plains saw results every day, as did those gathering and eating native fruits. The hunters, to conserve their limited modern ammunition, were building primitive traps and weapons from native resources. The few hunters he had talked to had mentioned such things.

He reached his old office, the section three control room. He could move some of his belongings to Lynn's office, he thought, or he could work from section three. He could decide that later.

He stood just inside the door and thought again about the hunters. He wondered if any hunted in snow. The colonists' clothing protected them in the colder weather areas, although extremes were not expected. He looked at his "uniform." The machine-produced garment was made of a light but strong and well-insulating material; it was just a little heavier than what everyone had worn during the space journey. It had a pleasant semi-gloss appearance, but it was all white. Only different colored trim and pockets, he thought, allowed for some individuality. Lynn usually wore red trim. Jenny preferred yellow. He himself wore green.

These low-maintenance uniforms that everyone wore, he thought, were designed for protection in the initial period, the few years needed to start building a civilization. Now, he realized, they might be used for a long time.

The footwear? He remembered, from the briefings, that they used to be called mountain hiking boots long ago when people on Earth did such things. His wide-brim hat was called "western" or "outback." All in all, he thought, he liked the colonists' low-maintenance clothing.

He sat down by the control room terminal table and hit a few keys. He needed a list of those factory specialists from the other sections who remained at the landing site.

The hunters, he thought while he waited for the list, led a pretty good life on Pangaea. They roamed a wide-open world. They ate meat, without paying Earth's *meat tax*.

Adam had once explained that it wasn't really a "tax." It was the cost of producing meat.

Pete's own studies had covered primarily the food factories, and hadn't included the meat producing facilities. He recalled, from Adam's explanation, that the meat modules were sufficiently large and equipped, thus expensive, to afford the "condemned" animals a pleasant and comfortable life while they awaited their humane slaughter. Years ago society, in its collective guilt over the loss of all Earth's wild animals larger than a rat or a crow, and of all range-roaming domestic animals, had demanded humane treatment. The inefficiency in using the already human-edible grains as animal feed compounded the issue. Those few on Earth who chose to eat meat, he thought, had to cover all these costs.

The list came up on his display. He proceeded to fashion a manpower schedule for all factory sections, his new "laboratory."

He would have to be careful when setting up future schedules, he thought; he wasn't quite used to the change from the Earth calendar. Ignoring the 21-day "lunar" period, the Council had artificially divided the Earth-Twin year into nine equal months of twenty-eight days each, and subdivided each month into four seven-day weeks. He decided he would ask Jenny to fix his computer programs to take care of it automatically.

He thought of that lunar period. He was pleased that the local moon looked so much like Earth's moon. He and Linda used to look at Earth's moon. Except for the odd pinkish color, he could imagine he was viewing the same moon; it showed the same phases, although they changed more rapidly.

*   *   *

A few weeks after Pete took over as general manager of the food factory experimental facilities, he played racquetball with Jenny.

"You keep winning, now that I don't have my secret," Jenny said. "Although this game is close."

"Yeah." He had practiced alone just enough, Pete thought, to handle the gravity.

Jenny smiled. "By the way, thanks again for getting me the work. I'll make sure that your experiments are all properly recorded and evaluated on the computer."

"I know you will." Pete smiled. "Yours is one of the very few jobs we were able to establish here. But it's essential. I chose you not only because I like you, but also because you're the best computer person around."

"I like you, too, Pete!"

"There are also very few of you around," Pete said. He laughed.

"So we're in great demand." Jenny turned away from Pete and served the ball. She faced him again and smiled.

Such a pretty smile, Pete thought, and those green eyes—the ball! He swung and missed.

"You missed again!" Jenny said. "I win! I got your mind off the game for only a moment, but it worked. I finally won a game."

Pete raised his a racquet in a mock display of anger. "Jennifer Susan!"

"Admit it, Petey. You like me a lot."

Pete hesitated. "I guess so," he said. He closed his eyes and dropped his racquet arm to his side.

"You can't go back," Jenny whispered.

Pete felt her take his free hand in hers.

"You know you can't," she added.

He opened his eyes and looked at her. "I need a little more time," he said. "Sorry, Jenny."

Jenny smiled. "Peter A, you're not ready to tell me what the 'A' stands for, are you?" She put her head on his shoulder.

*　　　　*　　　　*

A few weeks before the expected arrival time of the second ship, Pete welcomed Andy Landis at the food factory experimental facilities. The two met in the section three control room.

"You've changed a few things," Andy said.

"I've been using this as my main office," Pete said. "If you've completed those errands for Lynn, why don't I show you what we're doing here."

"I'm finished," Andy said.

"Come on. Let's look at some of my experimental crops." Pete motioned Andy to follow, exited the control room and entered the green and humid interior of section three.

Andy followed. "More than two million new people are going to arrive in a few weeks," he said, "and we still haven't made any progress in the fields."

"I hear you, Andy." Pete pointed to a particular section of dense greenery. "We call this crop wheat. It doesn't grow like wheat. Just looks a little like it."

The wheat grew in four layers, each with its own nutrient barrier. The plants in the topmost layer nearly reached the five-meter-high ceiling. In the narrow spaces between plant tops and nutrient barrier bases, the greenery spread as far as Pete could see in the intense orange light. Only a little grain, a few seeds, topped the longer stems.

Andy shrugged. "Like the fields."

"Yeah. We can't plant them close enough together to increase yields." He and his small crew, Pete thought, had tried over a hundred different varieties of native crops so far, and the results had been the same. A particular volume of space produced the same small amount of food no matter how much they tried to plant in that volume. "Can't call this agriculture," he said. "What about Earth crops in the fields?"

"Total failure," Andy said. "Lynn told us not to waste the time and energy any more."

Pete nodded.

"She said the other quadrants aren't doing any better than we are in the east," Andy said, "on the native crops."

Let's go over to four," Pete said. He led Andy through the control room and down the hallway. After a few hundred meters he opened another door. The two passed through a control room and into section four crop space. "What do you think we call this stuff?" Pete pointed to the crop; the three layers accommodated taller plants than in section three. He looked at Andy.

Andy looked over the greenery. "Looks like cornstalks," he said.

"Yeah. We call it corn," Pete said, "but of course it won't produce like corn." Corn was one of the most highly modified crops on Earth, he thought, and the most improved from natural. "Jenny does the naming. I'll show you her soybeans in a moment. That's in five. And carrots and beets in two."

"We haven't been naming in the fields," Andy said. "Not yet."

"It's Jenny's idea here," Pete said. "She insists on names for her computer records, and uses names of Earth crops which they sometimes resemble a little. She says that may help us later." He shook his head. "I don't know how, since it's all being rejected."

"I don't know Jenny very well," Andy said, "but she seems to be smart. Trust her."

"We're using compound names," Pete said. "We would've run out of singles. This is rainbow corn. As you noticed, the leaves look like those of corn. I don't know where she got 'rainbow.' She even started putting up signs."

He pointed to a small white rectangle, of a kind of plastic material, attached at a corner of the lowest nutrient barrier wall. It read, in maroon colored removable letters: CORN, RAINBOW. Although all the factory managers had used them regularly in space, Pete thought, he hadn't been concerned with these signs for the experimental crops.

Andy shrugged. "I guess names are a good idea. Even if the stuff doesn't produce."

"At least no one's going hungry," Pete said. "I sometimes wonder if we're the only ones worrying about this. The hunters are having a good time." Pete turned toward the door to four's control room. "Let's go over to five."

"I don't think they're having that good a time," Andy said. "You know I hunted for a few weeks when we first got here. And we had to hunt some in EQ, before the farms got going."

Pete led Andy through the control room.

"It was hunt all day," Andy said. "Prepare the fields all night. Get little sleep. A hectic and exhausting life. I don't think we could've kept it up more than a few months."

Pete entered the hallway and turned left toward section five. "I guess they are all kind of busy," he said. He realized, from his conversations with a few hunters, that hunting on the planet was a full-time job. It wasn't just the hunting, he thought, but also the vastness of the land. The hunters, and the gatherers, were almost constantly on the move.

"But I understand your comment," Andy said as he followed Pete. "Lynn's worried, too—thinks that people are getting complacent."

Compared to his job in the factories, Pete continued to believe that the hunters lived a better life. The new world appeared to be bountiful. "I don't know if I can muster up the patience to keep on trying different varieties," he said. "Progress is so slow."

Andy shrugged. "What choice do we have?"

"Genetics would be a lot more interesting and exciting," Pete said. "I know more about that. But genetics requires people." The search for the proper native plants was, as he had expected, not labor intensive. He spent a lot of time waiting and monitoring, he thought, but didn't have the resources to start anything else. "I guess you have the same situation in the fields," he said. "Your manpower is restricted to the number you can feed with your meager production." He opened the door to the section five control room.

"Kind of a bootstrap process," Andy said.

"Yeah." Pete led Andy through the control room and into the growing area. "These are triangle soybeans," he said when they reached the crops. He pointed to the lowest of six layers. "Look at the shape of the leaves. But there aren't many beans, and the few we can see are small."

"I see Jenny's sign," Andy said.

Pete nodded.

"Pete, you should come to the East Quadrant for a short visit. To get away. You sound bored."

"Yeah, bored," Pete said. "I haven't been out to the quadrants at all."

"We have larger creeks and rivers in EQ." Andy smiled. "Bigger than the little streams you have here. And valleys. Bigger trees, too. It all reminds me of my old visographs. I think these were called photographs. Remember those of Earth a couple of hundred years ago? The ones my dad gave me when I was a kid?"

"I think so." Pete pointed toward the door. "Let's go to two."

"I showed you them when we first started working together in three," Andy said. "The ones for which I could never find the right PIP."

Pete led Andy through the control room and into the hallway. "Yeah," he said, "I remember." They climbed a metal staircase to the next higher level and headed down a long hallway toward section two.

"I used to read a lot about the days when they were settling the western part of the North American continent," Andy said. "Most of my visos were from those days. Not actual, but the same places—shot a hundred years later for those old 'movies.' I think that's what they called them."

"Yeah." Pete led Andy around a corner into another hallway.

"A year ago we drove our terries over some large areas in EQ, looking for the best places to start the farms," Andy said. "We looked for the naturally irrigated areas, but those with fewer trees. You know how people still don't like to cut them down."

Pete understood that the farmers were restricted at present to only the most favorable areas, since they didn't have time to construct irrigation systems. He nodded.

"A lot of it's like those 'vast vistas of the old west,'" Andy said. "I used to find it hard to believe that Earth was once like that. But I believe it now, Pete. I believe it now."

Pete glanced back at Andy. Andy was smiling.

"My favorite story was about the Lewis and Clark expedition," Andy said. "Lately I've been thinking about that. Like the explorer group that first came to this land."

"Lewis and Clark?" Pete led Andy around another turn.

"I'm sure you studied that in school," Andy said. "The early nineteenth century? Lewis and Clark were gone for a couple of years without communications with the 'home base.' Like our group was gone for thirty years without communications."

"Yeah, I suppose," Pete said. Andy was getting carried away, he thought.

"Of course, Lewis and Clark explored the land with help of people already inhabiting the place," Andy said. "But I like to think of us as the pioneers that followed—the Oregon Trail of deep space."

Pete grimaced. "Oregon Trail of deep space? Lewis and Clark? Andy, you're a romantic." He shook his head. "The way you're carrying on, I think you like it here."

"You know, I'm very busy," Andy said. "The work is hard and frustrating. I complain a lot about our lack of progress. But I'm happy."

Pete stopped by the door to section two. He looked at Andy.

Andy grinned. "I told you earlier that Cindy and I are getting married," he said. "Like I said a moment ago, come out to the quadrant. I want you to meet her."

"Yeah, I'd like to," Pete said. "And I'd like to see the quadrant. We've been here for over a year and I haven't wandered more than a few kilometers." He opened the metal door. "I've done some hunting, but only nearby, and I've gone out to choose native plants and gather seeds. But the other guys do most of that, the more distant forays."

Pete led Andy through the section two control room. He greeted one of his crew, a man seated by the main section terminal, as he passed.

Once inside the brightly lit growing area of two, Andy said, "So it's set, Pete. How about right after the ship arrives? Come out after you and Lynn talk to the leadership of the new arrivals."

Pete thought briefly about those planned meetings. "Maybe they can tell us something," he said. "Maybe Earth thought about it some more after we left." He pointed to the right. "These are crimson beets," he said. "Over on the other side we have golden carrots." Both the beets and the carrots grew in six layers, like the soybeans. Pete looked at Andy. "I can understand those names," he said.

Andy nodded.

"Let's head over to one, to see the rice," Pete said. "It's rancho rice." He shook his head. "Don't ask." He added, "Later we can take a shuttle over to six to see the mushrooms. You remember how they had a part set up for fungi."

*　　　　　*　　　　　*

After Andy left, Pete looked for Jenny. When he didn't find her at the computer center, he climbed the big hill just west of the ship; he knew that she often spent a few spare moments there. He found her at the grassy summit, facing the southern sky. She turned toward him when he approached, and the two exchanged greetings.

"I just talked to Andy," Pete said. "They're getting married, Andy and Cindy."

"Married? I didn't know Andy—Oh, I guess you did mention that he met someone a few months ago." Jenny smiled. "That's wonderful."

"Yeah, he's really happy," Pete said. "What're you looking at? Off into space?"

"Stay here with me awhile," Jenny said. She turned to face south again. "This is such a beautiful place."

Pete stood next to her and felt her take his hand in hers. *Such a warm hand*, he thought. A freshening breeze caressed his face. "I guess so," he said.

"You've got to start looking around you," Jenny said. "Listen to the birds. Smell the flowers."

"I've looked at the trees," Pete said. He glanced at a nearby tree, partway down the southern face of the hill. *The source of the birdsong*, he thought.

"Of course you have, and they're pretty trees," Jenny responded. "But that's not really looking. You've got to experience the rest of it."

"I'll try," he said. He meant that, he told himself.

Jenny turned toward him. "Have you met Cindy?" she asked.

"No," Pete said. "Andy said she's a surface agriculture specialist like he is. They met for the first time right out in the fields."

"We'll have to go out there to meet her," Jenny suggested.

"At least they'll be easy to find," Pete said, "because they're at the farms."

"Yes." Jenny turned away from Pete and faced south again, although she held on to his hand. "We don't know where most people are."

"Small groups spread all over," Pete said. "It's a big place."

"Like tribes," Jenny said. She continued to gaze at the sky, in the direction of Tau Ceti shining brightly high over the southern hills.

Pete saw her glance up toward the new sun under the brim of her "western," and felt the warmth of her hand in his. Her long hair moved with the breeze and scattered the sunlight. A few strands of shiny blond hair wafted in front of her eyes.

He watched her brush away the blowing hair.

"The tribes," she whispered, "of the orange sun."

Chapter 15

Other Plans

As he climbed the ramp at one of the many entrances to Landing-One, Pete glanced around the great curve to his left toward Landing-Two. One's curved side and the clear morning air created an illusion that Two was close, but he had covered the distance many times in the five weeks since that ship had arrived. The visible segment of Two was six kilometers away.

He entered One, and then walked down a curved hallway to the main food factory office complex where he was scheduled to meet with Lynn Higami. She had flown in from the East Quadrant for a series of meetings with the Council and to talk with him. He found her sitting at the conference table; a few papers and a half-filled cup of coffee lay on the table in front of her. The two exchanged greetings, and he sat down beside her.

They traded progress reports. Lynn then took a sip of coffee and asked, "You also wanted to talk about a manpower problem, Pete?"

Pete nodded.

"I'm sorry," Lynn said. "I know you're short-handed."

"I have the people I need to keep both the One and Two factories going," Pete said, "but I may have to do some genetics. I'm just not finding anything that works." He shook his head. "I don't know what I'm asking for."

"I'm still short-handed in the quadrants, too," Lynn said. "I know it's frustrating, but you must keep trying new varieties. I believe that's the only way right now."

"I guess I already knew that." Pete shifted in his chair.

"We'll have to do the best we can," Lynn said, "with the resources we have."

"Yeah." He could have been back on Earth, he thought, doing less frustrating work for the PANS plan in Earth City.

"You'll have to narrow down your search." Lynn smiled. "I know you can do it. Just think about your work back at the lab."

"I'm trying," Pete said. He thought about the lab at Earth University, he told himself, all the time. He frowned, and then asked, "Are you going to try any more Earth crops in the fields?"

"No. I'm convinced that's not the way to go at this time."

"Yeah," Pete mumbled. He could have been checking out that gravity problem, he thought, back on Earth. He got up and paced the floor.

"Your work here is the most crucial." Lynn pointed to the door that led toward several nearby factory sections.

Pete nodded, and then asked, "What did you talk to the Council about yesterday afternoon?"

"Mostly about complacency," Lynn answered. "I'm trying to convince them that we're facing a big problem."

"People are still complacent?" Pete asked.

"Many are," Lynn said. "Everyone's eating adequately in one way or another."

"So far so good. For the hunters." Pete sat down next to Lynn again.

Lynn nodded. "At least the nomadic lifestyle's kept the birth rate down on the plains," she said.

The births were down, but the number of hunters had doubled, Pete thought, due to the recent arrivals. He recalled the debriefing. "The second ship," he said. "You know we didn't learn anything from them that could help. We have only our ideas." The second group had arrived in about the same hungry condition as his first group had, he thought. The newer colonists had not suspected the gravity, nor could they offer any other suggestions. Except for the few he was able to keep with the Landing-Two factories and the four small groups sent to the quadrant farms, the newcomers had quickly dispersed onto the vast plains to form new nomadic groups. Jenny, he recalled, had called them "tribes."

"We can't be absolutely sure it's the gravity." Lynn hesitated, and then added, "But no one's come up with anything else. Not yet."

No one has had the time or resources to look into it, Pete thought. "That hypersignal must've read well over four million people," he said. "I don't think there's any way Earth can know we have a problem." He turned his palms up in a gesture of resignation. "Like you said, even most of the people here are acting as if we're all right."

"We must recognize," Lynn said, "that it doesn't look like a crisis to them."

The hunters ate well, Pete thought, and, while busy, generally lived well. They roamed a wide-open and unspoiled world, a novelty for modern earthlings. They ate where they found the plentiful food; they cooked it over an open fire. They slept under the stars, and required little protection from the benign weather and no protection from predatory animals. They had established some small camps, but nothing permanent. The few he had talked to had enthusiastically described such things.

Lynn continued. "People call Pangaea a beautiful place. I agree with them. You've seen the red sunsets."

"I guess I haven't paid much attention," Pete said. He had thought often about being out on the plains, he told himself, but not about the esthetics.

Lynn shrugged. "I suppose even some of the councilmembers are getting complacent."

"Yeah," Pete said, "I've seen Thackaray's watered-down progress reports. Earth'll have to read between the lines to find out what's happening here. Twelve years from now, anyway."

"But we know why he's doing that," Lynn said.

"Lynn," Pete said, "something else. I'm curious about living on the farms. Two months ago Andy just described things as 'primitive.'"

"We still haven't had the time or the manpower to complete any permanent shelters," Lynn said. "So far our small makeshift buildings have been adequate." She didn't mention furniture, but Pete understood that the basics had been supplied for the farms: chairs, tables, beds, desks and other simple items, all made of a tough but light composite material and easily carried in the aircraft.

"I guess we're fortunate here," Pete said. "We don't have to build anything."

"We're getting along," Lynn said. "Not ideal, but livable." She stood up. "I have to meet with the Council one more time before going back to the quadrant, so I'll have to leave you now. But remember that you can always call on me if you need help."

"Yeah." Pete stood up.

"By the way," Lynn added, "Andy's getting married next week. He asked me to make sure you come to the wedding."

"Yeah, I promised him I'd visit."

"So long, Pete." Lynn turned toward the metallic door.

"So long, Lynn. Tell Andy I'll be there."

*　　　　*　　　　*

A week later Pete and Jenny disembarked from the aircraft that had carried them to the East Quadrant. Red-orange Tau Ceti, about to set, hovered just above the western horizon. A few dark clouds gathered overhead.

"Cindy and Andy. That almost rhymes," Jenny said. "Thanks for bringing me with you."

"Wouldn't be the same without you." Pete put on his western, and noticed that Jenny just left hers loosely draped across her back.

Pete and Jenny were the only passengers to disembark, although about a dozen boarded. The two stood at the edge of the landing area, a flat clearing maybe a quarter kilometer square, and watched the aircraft depart. When it was out of sight, they turned and followed a path into the surrounding trees and shrubbery.

A large sign on a post near the edge of the clearing read: EAST QUADRANT COASTAL AIRPORT, ESTABLISHED IN THE YEAR 1.

Jenny commented, as they passed, "I like their sign."

"Yeah, clever," Pete said. "But 'coastal'? Andy told me the ocean is over forty kilometers from here." He glanced to the east, away from the low orange sun. A full pink moon floated just above the horizon.

"Forty kilometers isn't far," Jenny said. "Not in this big place. It's close enough to be 'coastal.'"

"I guess." Pete led Jenny down the path; he followed verbal directions Lynn had given him a week earlier.

"It's so pretty here," Jenny said. "Look at all the big trees. They're different than where we live. And the moon looks so big."

"Yeah."

Jenny stopped abruptly, put a finger to her lips and whispered, "Listen."

"What? That insect sound?" Pete stopped alongside his companion. Creatures similar to Earth's insects were plentiful in Pangaea, and people had called them just "insects." There were yet no individual names for the many varieties. Very few, he thought, have been bothersome to humans.

"It's a chirping sound," Jenny whispered. "Crickets." She crept toward a particular clump of bushes, with one hand cupped to her ear.

"It's not how I remember Earth crickets," Pete whispered. He followed.

"I hereby officially name them 'crickets,'" Jenny whispered. "They sound the same at the Landings, and I've seen them. They're black and look a lot like Earth crickets. But smaller." She stopped by the bushes, but didn't disturb them. The chirping had stopped.

"Why the interest in these bugs?" Pete asked. "I never paid any attention. They're not an agricultural problem."

"Crickets sang outside my window at home when I was growing up." Jenny smiled. "They used to serenade me to sleep."

"I think they'd keep me awake," Pete said.

"I like their chirping," Jenny said. "Adam and I talked about what night sounds I might hear when I got here. We talked a lot about things like that." She hesitated, and then said, "He tried to talk me out of coming here."

Pete looked at her.

"He tried," Jenny said. "But he, I guess, didn't follow through. I liked Adam. I thought about him a lot while we were on the ship. I believe that if he had tried harder, I would've stayed on Earth."

"Jenny, Adam's a great guy. And it sounds like you got to know him."

Jenny smiled. "He was responsible for us meeting. Remember?"

"Yeah."

"I'm sure that people who know both of you," Jenny said, "have told you that you and Adam look a little bit alike."

"Yeah, at the university." Pete looked up at the clouds. "It's starting to rain. We'd better get going."

"All right. It feels like a nice warm rain. But, yes, let's go meet Cindy." Jenny put her western on her head.

✳　　　　　✳　　　　　✳

The wedding ceremony was arranged to take place in a small clearing near the wooded main shelter area and away from the more open farm fields. After greeting some of the people he knew, Pete stood with Jenny and waited for Andy and Cindy to appear. Others stood and talked nearby, or sat on chairs taken from the shelters. The orange sun beamed brightly in the late-morning sky.

Pete noted that he was surrounded by more greenery than he had seen anywhere near the Landings. The strange green color of the trees and shrubs combined with the bright yellow-orange light of the sun to create a scene that he could describe only as "unearthly." The flowers also displayed unearthly tints in the foreign sunlight, and the "bees" that accompanied the flowers sported unearthly colors. Others often talked of the beauty of these colors, Pete thought, but to him they were just "different from Earth." *Will I ever get used to this planet?*

Jenny took Pete's hand in hers and held it tightly. "Isn't this precious? Out here in this beautiful spot?"

"It's nice," Pete said. "I like the breeze."

"The only thing that's missing is the music," Jenny said. "We need something when they come out."

"Yeah. Another thing we've had to do without." Pete pointed to a pair of unused chairs. "Let's sit."

The two sat down.

"I'm glad Cindy found the time to make herself a white veil," Jenny said.

"Yeah." Pete smiled. "I'm sure she'll look great in it. Andy's really a lucky guy."

"Cindy's cute," Jenny said. "I like her red hair. Only I would grow it a little longer. I like her, Pete. I'm happy for Andy." She took Pete's hand in hers again. "It's hard to believe they've known each other for less than a year. They were on our ship together for so long and never met. But here in this beautiful place they found each other."

"Yeah. They look like they belong together." Pete felt Jenny gently squeeze his hand.

"Just like you and I," she said. "Remember? We didn't even know each other for almost the whole trip."

"Yeah."

"I rarely saw you at The New Alligator," Jenny said. "Only that time when we played the game, and those few times I got you to dance with me afterward."

"I guess not," Pete said. "I almost never got around to it. But you had Phil to dance with. He struck me as a nice guy."

"Yes, he is." Jenny smiled. "But you know I'd rather be with you."

Pete held Jenny's hand, but his thoughts drifted elsewhere. What would his wedding, with Linda, have been like? *Probably not out in the open like this*, he thought.

She had not really ignored him. Linda had just been busy, he thought, dedicated to her studies. The long trip had given him a lot of time to think about his folly.

"Oh, Pete," Jenny said. "You're thinking about *her* again."

Jenny's small hand felt warm in Pete's. He replied, "Jenny, I promise. I'll think about you from now on."

"I could make you happy. Don't you like me?" She smiled. "At least a little bit?"

"I like you a lot," Pete responded. "I just have to sort things out in my head. I know I've been sorting it out for a long time. You've been a big help."

Jenny leaned over and kissed Pete lightly on the cheek.

He smiled. Then he heard someone in the crowd say, "Here they come." He and Jenny stood up, as did others nearby.

"We don't have any music for Andy and Cindy," Jenny said, "except for a few birds. But maybe we can get people to sing. I have a good voice. I'll start." She raised her voice and made a brief announcement, and then started to sing a wedding song. Pete and the others joined in.

✳   ✳   ✳

During the return flight to the Landings a few days later, Pete and Jenny sat close together in the nearly empty aircraft. "I like the East Quadrant," Pete said. "I didn't tell you before, but I want to get away from the factories permanently."

Jenny looked at him. "Get away from the factories?"

"I think I'd like the hunting life," Pete said. He glanced out the window, at the forests far below. "It'd give me a sense of accomplishment. I need closure."

"But you're needed." She took his arm in both her hands. "You have to stay and get the crop-growing problems solved."

"I've tried," he said. "But it's not working." He raised both hands in a gesture of futility.

"At least you're finding out what doesn't grow," Jenny said. "That's a kind of progress."

"If I can remember it all," Pete complained. "A lot of details."

"You don't have to," Jenny encouraged. "I'm recording every little detail. They may be important someday."

Pete looked at her. "Even with the worst failures?"

"I like to think of those as 'negative successes.'" Jenny laughed. "It'll work." She shook Pete's arm lightly. "I know it will."

Pete looked into her green eyes. "Why don't you come with me, Jenny?"

"Pete?"

"We could stay near Andy and Cindy in the East Quadrant," Pete said. "They'll farm and we'll hunt. The hunting's supposed to be good."

"Pete, I'd go anywhere with you," Jenny said. "I'd go to the ends of Pangaea with you. But you would worry about the factories. You know you're needed."

Pete noted that Jenny had a pleading expression on her face. *Such a pretty face*, he thought. He agreed to stay on the job, at least until the next ship arrival; he could talk her into going with him later.

*   *   *

The third group of colonists arrived on schedule. The three ship-cities formed a triangle of a number of kilometers on a side. Pete picked up additional sections for his food factory laboratory and a few more workers.

Six weeks after the arrival, he visited Lynn at the farms. After greeting, the two sat down in the small makeshift shelter that Lynn called the East Quadrant farm headquarters. The mid-morning yellow-orange sunshine beamed through a small window and lighted the room as they exchanged brief progress reports. Pete called them "lack of progress" reports.

Afterward, Lynn poured herself a cup of coffee and offered Pete a cup. He thanked her and declined.

Lynn took a sip of coffee, and then put the cup down on her desk. "Andy said you talked to him about relocating here permanently," she said. "I'm glad you haven't done that."

"I meant to tell you," Pete said. "I'm not trying to keep it secret."

Lynn nodded. "I hope you'll remain with the factories."

"It's a bigger job now that we have the three," Pete said. "I spend a lot of time just commuting between them. I haven't had a chance to think much about leaving."

"Good. We need you right there." Lynn added, "And something else. You know the Council's trying to decide about sending an explicit distress signal to Earth, to at least let them know about our problem. A few more are in favor now."

Pete sat a little straighter. He knew that she hadn't been to the Landings recently, but the East Quadrant had a rudimentary communication link with the government. "What'd they say?"

"We know radio takes too long and could be intercepted by incoming ships," Lynn said. "It's hypersignal now."

"Hypersignal?" Pete stood up. "Can we change it?"

"I don't know," Lynn said. "An engineer is checking on that."

"That'll get their attention." Pete paced the dirt floor of the small shelter.

"They know they'd have to interrupt the scheduled signal," Lynn said. "Most think it's more important to send the count that Earth expects, at least for the next ship or two, and then modify a later signal when we know more about our situation."

Pete's thoughts drifted. Adam and the PANS group would receive and evaluate each signal. Adam had always worried about food and other supply difficulties, back at the university and about hypothetical problems. Then it had been about Earth.

He and Adam had even talked about it while preparing for that Spring Dance. The subject had quickly changed, since Adam had been anxious to talk about his date. Both Pete and Adam had spotted Linda earlier in the disk library. Adam had then been the first of the two to meet her, in a fortuitous encounter at the library. Adam's advantage hadn't lasted long. Pete had taken over soon after he and Linda had shared a few slow dances.

Pete returned to the present. "Our situation," he said. He shook his head. "Thing's just aren't working. I've tried over five hundred different varieties."

"You'll have to keep at it," Lynn said.

"I know we have many thousands more to try." Pete sat down again. "How long will it take?"

"I don't know," Lynn said. "We haven't done any better here in the fields. We can only hope that the natural bounty remains bountiful." Lynn hesitated a moment, and then asked, "Pete, have you been able to narrow down your search? Are you heading in any particular direction?"

"Not really," Pete answered. "I just haven't come up with any kind of plan."

"What about the techniques you developed at the university?" Lynn asked.

"I don't know, Lynn. I'm not progressing at all."

Lynn smiled. "If you need help, just call on me."

"Yeah." He knew that she was willing to help, even though she was very busy. *But what can she do?* he asked himself. *What can I do?*

*   *   *

Pete returned to the Landings in the late afternoon, after a short visit with Andy and Cindy. Jenny met him at the aircraft staging area. "Thanks for meeting me, Jenny." He donned his western.

"Happy you're back, Pete." She smiled.

Pete announced, while they walked away from the aircraft, "Cindy's expecting."

"Oh! That's wonderful!"

"Yeah," Pete said. "I'm happy for them. They're really excited."

"Is it a boy or a girl?" Jenny asked. "Do they know?"

"A boy. But they said they'd keep him anyway." Pete chuckled. He looked at his companion.

"A boy!" Jenny glanced at Pete. "It's nice to hear you laugh." Her western swung loosely across her back while she walked.

"I don't get a lot of good news," Pete said. "How can you be so cheerful all the time?" That cheerfulness always showed in her pretty smile, he thought.

"Look around you, Pete." Jenny gestured with her hand to point out the hills to the west. "Pangaea is so beautiful. Look at the hills. The trees—so many real trees. The grass. Everything's so colorful. And so clean. It smells so flowery. And wide open spaces." She hesitated, and then added, "Yes, I know I'm always saying those things."

The two reached the closest entrance to Landing-One and Pete glanced around. Out to the west, away from the ship, the rolling land and growing hills appeared to go on forever. *It's not like Earth,* he thought.

They climbed the ramp and entered the giant structure.

"I have to get back to the computer center now," Jenny said, "for another hour or two. Are we going to do something together this evening?"

"Yeah. You think of something. I'll come get you later."

"See you then, Pete." Jenny waved. She then turned and walked away down the ship's narrow hallway.

*   *   *

The fourth ship arrived, and the hypersignal generator sent the census off to Earth. Two weeks later, while Pete sat at his desk and worked on his manpower updates, he thought about that signal. He could not know the number, just as he had had no practical way to determine the second or the third census count. For various reasons the equipment had not been designed with a local readout. He understood all too well one of those reasons: The PANS planners had expected the colonists to be more centrally located at first, where they could readily count themselves.

Many of the more than two million newcomers had already spread out over the continent of Pangaea. While Pete made plans to include the additional factory sections in his laboratory, he thought of those dispersing colonists and what they might encounter on the plains. Lynn had been concerned about how long the land would remain bountiful, and communication remained poor since newcomers had continued to spread across the vast landscape much faster than originally planned.

He realized that he could only guess how the hunters and gatherers might be faring in the more remote regions of the quadrants. He told himself they were doing well.

Chapter 16

Body Count

Seven weeks after the fourth ship's arrival, Pete was checking the progress of maturing crops deep in Landing-One factory section five when Lynn came in and greeted him.

"Hello, Lynn." He smiled. "I'll be with you in a second." He wiped his hands with a rag. "I didn't expect to see you until next week."

Lynn returned his smile, but to him it appeared forced. *It's hectic on the farms*, he thought.

"Charlie told me where I could find you." Lynn said. "I have something to tell you."

"If I knew you were coming, I would've been waiting in my office," Pete said. He hesitated, and then said, "Lynn, you look tired. Why don't we go to the control room so you can sit down?" He added, "By the way, this is the twenty-ninth different crop that we called wheat." He pointed to the plastic sign, which read: WHEAT, GREAT PLAINS. "It's not producing any better than the first twenty-eight."

"I think we both better sit," Lynn said. Pete followed her into the less humid control room. He saw that her hand shook when she put some papers on the terminal table.

"Can I get you come coffee, Lynn? You look like you need it." Pete looked toward the metallic door leading to the hallway. "Charlie always has some brewing."

"No, but thanks." Lynn glanced at her watch. "I can't stay long."

"What's wrong?" Pete asked.

"My news is not good. Please sit down."

"All right. I'll sit." When Lynn was troubled, Pete thought, she had good reason. He sat down in front of the main terminal and swiveled the chair so that he faced her.

Lynn sat in a chair by the terminal table, near several gauges and wall graphs. "Some of the newcomers moving into the South Quadrant made a grisly discovery," she said.

Pete came to full alert.

Lynn hesitated, and then said, "They found hundreds of shallow graves, and a number of bodies that the people must not have had time to bury."

Pete shifted in his chair. He opened his mouth, but didn't speak.

"Later they did find some survivors," Lynn said, "who were near death themselves. They told of not being able to find food."

"What was," Pete asked, "the area like?" He told himself to try to stay calm. "What kind of vegetation was growing there?"

"I don't think the location's the point," Lynn said. "I'd better continue. It turns out that this isn't an isolated incident. Soon after I found out about it, other newcomers made similar discoveries in two areas of the West Quadrant." She hesitated, and then said, "To be blunt, the body count is one thousand two hundred and sixty seven."

"That many?" Pete stood up. "And some not even buried?"

"There could be more," Lynn said, "in other places."

"Damn! We've heard nothing here."

"The Council's trying to keep it quiet," Lynn said. "But I got their approval to tell you, and you can inform your crew. The Council understands that it can't be kept secret for long."

"But you're sure it wasn't disease?" Pete paced the control room. "I thought we had a lot more time. Are we already outgrowing the natural food supply?"

"Most of the bodies were emaciated, the fresher ones where one could tell. They found no obvious sign of disease."

"Yeah."

"I suppose there may have been some disease brought on by diminished immunity." Lynn sighed. "And you know the medical people haven't been able to immunize all newborns in the more remote areas." She hesitated, and then added, "There were some children and infants among the dead, but not a disproportionate number."

"So it's not disease?" He could try to convince himself otherwise, Pete thought, but he had to accept the evidence. He sat down.

"They reported more men than women or children among the dead," Lynn said. "I don't know if that means anything."

Pete frowned. "But this can only get worse—with the new two million."

Lynn shook her head. "I'm sure it's already worse than we can know."

"Earth," Pete said. "Lynn, Earth will know."

She looked at him.

"The signal," he said. "It'll have to show the decrease. Or the lower increase."

"But will they notice a difference?" Lynn questioned. "It'll be lower by only some thousands. They're expecting over eight million."

"Adam will notice," Pete said. He got up and paced again.

Adam would be looking for just such a discrepancy, Pete thought, so he could not fail to notice. Would he be able to convince anyone else? Lynn was correct. The number was not statistically significant. Adam would be warned of Pangaea's dilemma, but might be unable to do anything about it.

"Pete, our work just took a critical turn."

"I have more facilities for experimentation now, with the addition of Four." Pete continued to pace. "Of course we still have the staffing problem." He stopped and looked at Lynn. "By the way, how's the Council responding? What're they doing other than keeping secrets?"

"They've been trying to decide on growth control measures," Lynn answered, "but most councilmembers aren't yet convinced that we have too many people—that the planet can't feed them."

Pete shook his head. "What're they doing about the hypersignal?" he asked. Adam could use some more definitive information, he thought. "Did they decide?" He sat down.

"That's still under discussion," Lynn answered.

"Earth should be told about this situation," Pete said. "More than just the census."

"Most want to wait," Lynn said.

"Wait?" Pete stood up again. "They can't still be complacent. You just told me people are starving to death."

"Not everyone thinks we've reached the crisis point," Lynn said. "Many, including President Thackaray, believe that the reported deaths resulted from attempts to populate unsuitable areas."

"Thackaray needs a reality check," Pete said.

"He's doing his best, Pete. His problems are different than ours." Lynn went on, "But what can the Council do, other than inform Earth? It's up to us to produce the food."

"What else do we have going for us?" Pete paced the floor. "You said a few months ago that some people in the quadrants were trying to domesticate native animals." He believed he knew what she would say.

"They failed," Lynn said. "The animals here are too primitive."

The situation was similar, Pete thought, to that with the plants: no history of domestication. Domestic animals, to feed large numbers of people, must grow faster and reproduce faster than wild species. They must be adapted to this, and their human "keepers" must learn the "secrets" of caring for each species. That could take much longer than the present plan with the crops.

"I believe the native plants are the key to our survival, especially for the next ten or twenty years," Lynn said. "We're still failing in the fields, but we must keep trying."

"And in the factories." Pete grimaced. "I'm more discouraged than ever." He stopped pacing and reoccupied the swivel chair by the main terminal.

"You must keep experimenting," Lynn insisted. "Look at the bright side. Our machines are working well."

Farm breakdowns had been minimal, Pete thought, and the factory machinery performed flawlessly. He expressed it in his own terms. "Yeah. We have all the best technology. And the people are starving."

Lynn took a deep breath, put her hand on the terminal table and stood up. "I have to get back to the quadrant," she said. "I'm sorry about the bad news, but I thought you'd better know."

"All right, Lynn. Thanks for filling me in. I'll do my best here." Pete got up and walked with Lynn the short distance to the door.

"We'll get together again soon, Pete." Lynn left section five.

Pete sat down again, and for a while just stared at the chart-covered walls of the control room.

He was going to quit the food factories and go to the East Quadrant, but the situation just changed. *A lot.* Maybe he'd better wait, he thought, until the next ship arrived.

He must tell Jenny about the "body count," he told himself. He completed his interrupted progress check by logging the results. He then got up and left the control room.

He found her at work in Landing-One's computer center.

She looked up from her terminal as he approached. "Pete! You hardly ever visit me here." She smiled.

"Jenny, I have to tell you something."

"You sound strange," she said. "Pull up a chair."

The terminal beeped when Jenny gave the hand signal that terminated her work session. The display went dim, although its numbers and letters remained visible. *Ghostly looking*, Pete thought. *Dim numbers suspended in space.*

He sat next to her and took her hands in his. "It's started." He forced the words out quickly. "People are starving to death. Over a thousand counted."

Jenny's smile faded.

"It's really happening," Pete said. "I just got the news from Lynn." He recounted everything, as Lynn had described it to him.

Jenny sat quietly for a moment. Then she couldn't stop talking. "Those poor people! Could it be anyone we know? Can we do anything to help? I know we're trying to find a way to grow enough food. That's our job here. But maybe we can share our food. Oh, now I feel like I've been eating too much."

"It may come to that," Pete said, "real soon. But we won't be able to feed very many. If Lynn's right, thousands could die in the next few months." He let go of her hands.

"We've got to do something," she said.

"Right now we can only wait and see," Pete said, "and help when and if we can."

"I guess you're right." Jenny looked at Pete. "At least we won't be going to the East Quadrant. You'll certainly stay with the factories now."

"I've been thinking more about that," Pete said. "I may stay here for a while. But maybe we can do more good if we go to the quadrant and help the hunters." To get away from the ships would be his only chance to get away from his memories of Earth, he thought. He stood up and paced the main computer room floor.

"Pete, please try," Jenny pleaded. "It's got to be more important now. We've got to think about the future. You said yourself that you've only tried to grow a small fraction of the native plants."

"Of course you're right," Pete said. He could talk her into going with him later, he thought.

"I'll help you," Jenny said. "We've got to work together." She smiled. "Together we can win this."

"Jenny, you're an optimist to the end. The end? Poor choice of words. Or is it?" Pete shrugged.

"Pete, did I ever tell you why I came here?"

He sat down and looked at her. "You didn't."

Jenny smiled again. "I wanted to do something big," she said. "I never did anything big. My sister Alicia won first prize in the All-Earth literature contest. She's younger than me. But what did I do? My biggest accomplishment was third prize in the Podunk City Schools Junior Science Fair."

She hesitated, and then added, "I still believe we're doing something big here. I don't think I'll ever have a city named after me, but this colonization is big and important."

"You had a better reason than I had," Pete said. He smiled. "Maybe you'll get that city."

"But you're doing something big," Jenny said. "You have the most important job in all Pangaea. You know you do."

I have the most important job in the wrong place, Pete thought.

*   *   *

The weeks passed, and Pete's life at the Landings didn't change much except for the new food-sharing program. Although it was difficult to get full agreement, the residents agreed to eat somewhat less and share any leftover factory production with the people on the nearby plains whenever they couldn't find enough native food. Pete knew that the meager factory output, his experimental crops, could help only a few.

Little news came in from the field farm projects, and he wondered how they were handling the situation. He thought about this while he and Jenny finished a round of racquetball.

"You're getting better at this, Jenny. I'm bushed." Pete put his racquet down on the court floor, sat against the wall and motioned her to join him.

"So am I." She smiled and sat next to him. She kept her racquet in her hand. "But it sometimes feels good to be eating less. I think it's both physical and psychological."

"As long as we have enough," Pete said. "We've been able to share some food here. But out in the quadrants?"

"I'm worried about the quadrants, too," Jenny said. "I do get really hungry at night sometimes, but I always know that I will get to eat at least something the next day. The people out on the plains don't have any kind of assurance."

"I get hungry at night, too," Pete said. "I know what you're talking about." The hunters could be having a rougher time, he thought, but he still envied them.

"Drinking water sometimes helps," Jenny said.

"I'll try that," Pete said. He picked up his racquet cover and reached for his racquet. He started to put the cover on. "I wonder how they're doing at the farms," he said. "I haven't heard from Lynn in a while. Over three weeks. Why don't we go the East Quadrant for a few days?"

"Sounds good." Jenny leaned over and retrieved her racquet cover. "I want to see Andy and Cindy's little boy anyway."

"Yeah, me too," Pete said. "Andrew Junior. A lot of babies have been born here, but not to any of my close friends."

Jenny leaned against Pete, and put her head on his shoulder.

Taking her to the quadrant again, he thought, could make it easier to talk her into going there permanently later. He could then get Linda out of his mind. He could concentrate on Jenny. He still felt that any real show of affection would be unfair to her, but out with the hunters it could be a very different situation.

Sometimes, he told himself, he didn't know what he wanted.

He had to do something soon, he thought. Jenny appeared to be willing to stick with him, but he couldn't expect her to wait too long. She had waited so long already. Her body felt warm against his. She cared for him, he knew, but she was a young and healthy woman and other men were around. She used to dance with Phil Bassett, who worked with her on the main computer during the voyage. Pete believed that Phil had gone to the North Quadrant as a hunter years ago, but he could come back. There were others, too.

He had to do something before it was too late, he thought. There was a way: He would find someone else to run the experimental facilities. Then Jenny would be happy to leave with him.

*   *   *

Pete and Jenny boarded an aircraft and departed for the East Quadrant. Taking a large aircraft with only two passengers presented no problem. Pete knew that there was no shortage of microfusion fuel, and his job gave him a certain authority.

When they were settled in cruising flight, Pete tried to relax. He watched Jenny turn and look out the aircraft window. "Look how the sun shines off the wing," she said.

Pete glanced past her, out the same window. *Another reminder of the old days*, he thought. The aircraft basic design was the same as had been used on Earth for hundreds of years. He had built and flown models when he was a child, and he remembered it well. Although the power sources and the techniques of transition from rest to flight and from flight to rest had improved a lot, basic aerodynamics dictated that the primary shape change little. These were true aerodynamic craft, not the ballistic hybrid vehicles long used on Earth for distances longer than a few thousand kilometers.

The low early morning sun reflecting off the wing cascaded yellow-orange light through the window. Jenny turned and faced Pete. "You have an orange face," she said. She smiled.

He chuckled.

"What kind of animals do they hunt in the quadrants, Pete?" she asked. "You've been talking to hunters."

"I believe it's mostly turkeys, chickens and rabbits," Pete said. "Some snakes and lizards. That's what they call them. And I've been told that some areas have bigger animals that look like small deer." He wondered if she was interested, or merely curious.

"I like the way the hunters name the animals," she said, "for the ones they resemble on Earth."

"Like you with the factory crops," Pete said. "But I question the resemblance. The turkeys are just the bigger animals with feathers and two legs. Chickens are the smaller ones."

"I've seen rabbits," Jenny said, "at the Landings."

"I guess animal evolution does follow some particular paths," Pete said. "It depends on the environment."

"Like only the littlest birds really fly?" Jenny asked. "Because of the gravity?"

"Yeah," Pete said, "and that may be why there aren't any really large animals. At least on the land." He might be able to get her to come with him, he thought. First, he told himself, he must find his replacement.

∗   ∗   ∗

When Pete and Jenny arrived at the East Quadrant and stepped off the aircraft, the cleared docking area was deserted. All was quiet, except for a light wind that rustled the leaves in the surrounding trees and shrubs. Pete heard some far off birdsong, but the birds appeared to be fewer in number than heard during previous visits to the quadrant. "It's strange no one's here," he commented.

"Yes," Jenny said. "The last time we came in here, the place was at least a little busy."

"A few people," Pete said. "There was some travel—between quadrants." He put down the small piece of luggage he carried and looked around.

The pilot stepped out of the aircraft and joined Pete and Jenny. "Quiet, isn't it? It was the same here the day before yesterday," he said. "I came in to take some people to the West Quadrant—three of 'em. They didn't want to talk to me at all except to ask me to take 'em to WQ."

"What'd they talk about, Steve," Pete asked, "among themselves? Did you overhear anything?"

"No," Steve said. "They spoke only in whispers."

"Was there anything else odd about them?" Pete asked. He squinted in the early-afternoon sunshine, and put on his western.

"They kept looking around," Steve said, "just like you're doing now. They were in a hurry, not acting friendly at all. You two're much better passengers."

"What about the West Quadrant?" Pete questioned. "When you landed there?"

"Deserted just like here," Steve said. "Looks like something strange is going on. I haven't been doing a lot of flying in the quadrants in the last few weeks. But something strange."

"Yeah." Pete looked at Jenny.

She picked up her small bag. "We'd better go find Dr. Higami right away, Pete. I'm getting scared."

"I hear you, Jenny." Pete turned to the pilot. "Thanks, Steve. For the ride. And for the info." He picked up his bag.

"The warning," Jenny whispered. "'Bye, Steve."

"Be back for you day after tomorrow," Steve promised. "Or maybe I should wait?"

"No," Pete said. "We'll be all right. See you in two days."

"S'long." Steve gave a quick salute and boarded the aircraft.

Pete and Jenny headed out of the clearing and onto the path through the shrubbery.

"The sign's still there," Jenny said. "That's a good sign." She hesitated a moment, and then added, "Ooo! That's kind of a pun, isn't it?" She tried to laugh.

The two walked the half-kilometer to the small group of makeshift shelters where Lynn usually stayed and performed her farm management tasks. Here the low shrubbery gave way to larger bushes and the trees were more numerous than near the "airport."

"It's deserted here, too," Jenny said. "What's going on?"

"At least we haven't found any bodies," Pete replied. "That's a good sign, too."

Jenny nodded.

"We can walk to the main crop area in about twenty minutes," Pete said. "Lynn's probably there."

"I guess we'd better," Jenny said. She donned her western; it had been draped loosely across her back. "We certainly aren't learning anything here."

The two followed a narrow path through the shrubbery and trees. Occasionally the path widened into a clearing. From such clearings Pete saw plowed fields in the distance wherever the low hills gave way to widespread flat areas. Flowers bordered the path and clearings and flowery smells permeated the air. Only the rustling of leaves and the scattered singing of birds broke the silence.

The shadows were short, since the orange sun hovered just past its zenith. It was about an hour past local noon, Pete thought as he and Jenny walked down a narrow section of the path and rounded a corner.

A loud shriek blasted from the nearby shrubbery.

"What was that?" Jenny exclaimed.

A half dozen two-legged animals, each about a half-meter tall, scampered across a wide spot ahead in the path. They shrieked as they ran, and left a few gray and white feathers in their wake. They disappeared into the brush, and Pete said, "Those're turkeys. I guess we scared them."

"*They* scared *me*," Jenny confessed.

"A few that escaped the hunters," Pete said.

"They're weird-looking," Jenny said. "Short necks. I haven't seen anything like that at the Landings.

"They sound more like loud chickens," she added.

✳   ✳   ✳

Pete and Jenny completed the trek of nearly two kilometers. As they approached their destination, two armed men stepped out of a narrow wooded area that separated two farm fields. One man held a photronic multipurpose weapon, a "zapper," that could stop or kill. The other held a much older device, a rifle. Pete quickly observed that their mannerisms appeared more defensive than aggressive. They had not pointed their weapons at him.

The man with the rifle asked, "Who are you and what's your business here?"

"I'm Pete MacDonald. From the Landings. Where's Lynn Higami?"

"MacDonald?" the man asked. "You manage the experimental facilities, don't you?"

To Pete the man appeared uncomfortable in his apparent role as a guard. *A farmer recently drafted for a new duty*, he thought. "Yeah," he said, "and this is Jenny Brown. What's going on? Is Lynn all right?"

"She's all right," the man said. "I apologize for the armed reception. We've had some problems."

"What problems?" Pete asked.

"Dr. Higami is over there." The man pointed to a rough shelter a few hundred meters away, nestled in a small grove of trees and adjacent to a farm field. Pete turned in that direction.

"What happened to the crops over there?" Jenny asked. "It looks like they were trampled or something."

Pete looked at her, and then at the man with the rifle. "What's going on?" he asked.

"I think you'd better ask Dr. Higami."

Chapter 17

Capitulation

Pete and Jenny left the guards and walked the short distance to the small farm shelter-office that serviced the main East Quadrant fields. They found Lynn seated at a desk, writing what looked to Pete to be a government report; he had prepared many of them in the past few years. She stood up and greeted her visitors.

Lynn's white outfit looked like it hadn't been cleaned in weeks. That was unlike her, Pete thought. She was usually impeccably attired, even under these primitive conditions.

"Lynn, I'm happy to see you're all right," he said. He looked at Jenny. She looked at him and smiled.

Pete turned back to Lynn. "What's going on? You have armed guards out there."

"It's been hectic," she said, "but at least there've been no attacks on people. Not here, anyway."

"Attacks?" Pete asked.

Lynn pointed to two chairs. "You two must've walked a long way."

Pete, Jenny and Lynn sat by the desk.

"They've been coming in from the hills and plains and raiding the crops," Lynn said.

"So discipline is breaking down?" Pete grimaced.

"I hate to stop them," Lynn said. "They're just hungry."

"Yeah, I suppose," Pete said. She was more generous than he could be in her place, he thought.

"They come in mostly at night," Lynn said. "We don't have enough people to guard the whole place. The other areas have the same problem." She hesitated, and then added, "It's worst in the West Quadrant. The guards there were attacked with weapons."

"I believe it," Pete said. "The guards here looked like they were afraid of us."

"They've had a lot of violence in the West Quadrant," Lynn said. "Both raiders and guards have been killed. It's still going on, so I can't give any numbers. A group came here a few days ago to talk to me about it."

"We haven't had any trouble at the Landings." Pete put his hand on Jenny's shoulder.

"I just reread the South Quadrant's latest report," Lynn said. She picked up a sheet of paper from the table. "Raids like here, some violence. But less than West. North's been quiet so far, except for some crop damage. I'm expecting their latest report this afternoon." She looked at Pete. "The Council may abandon the field farm projects. President Thackaray wants my opinion."

Pete reflected for a moment. The farms lacked the manpower to effectively guard against raiding, and they weren't accomplishing much anyway, not now. He wasn't pleased about abandoning them, but it looked inevitable. He might as well, he told himself, use the situation for his own advantage. Lynn was the best person in Pangaea to take over his job. His personal plan was complete.

"Lynn, we've got to have an overall plan, a new plan," he said. "Why don't you come back to the Landings with us. We can meet with the Council right away."

"That might be the best next step," Lynn agreed.

"You can help me with the factories," Pete said. "You know so much more than I do." He didn't expect to fool Lynn for long. He could, he thought, just get her to relocate back to the Landings and have her where he needed her.

"Yes," Lynn said, "but you have a special talent."

"The two of you together should make an unbeatable team," Jenny said, "if you don't waste too much time complimenting each other."

She smiled. "Dr. Higami, you can stay in my quarters," she said. "I have lots of extra space. Eight of us lived there when we were in space." She hesitated, and then added, "The rest of the ship is kind of empty and lonely."

"Thanks, Jennifer. Jenny." Lynn smiled. "Please call me Lynn. After all, we might be roommates."

Jenny looked at Pete. "Pete, you're too late now. I've invited you a hundred times, but you just keep thinking about Earth."

"I'm forgetting. I know I'll never—" Pete turned toward Lynn. "Excuse us, Lynn. Private problems. But you'll come back with us?"

Lynn looked at Pete. "Yes, for now. I'll have to talk with the Council before I make any permanent plans." She hesitated, and then said, "Your factories are our most important project, since everything grows so much faster."

She went on, while Pete nodded in agreement. "And, if it becomes necessary, they can be guarded with fewer people. Once we make some progress, we can take the results back to the fields."

"We'd better go as soon as possible," Pete said. "Lynn, why don't you get ready while Jenny and I visit Andy and Cindy?"

"Sure," Lynn said. "It shouldn't take me more than a few hours to tie things up here."

Jenny looked at Pete. "Steve won't be back with the plane until day after tomorrow," she said.

"Yeah," Pete said. He looked at Lynn.

"You two go ahead," she said. She smiled. "You've got to see little Andrew. I'll arrange for another aircraft to take us. There's one due from North in a few hours—a small delegation with that written report."

★　　　　　★　　　　　★

Pete and Jenny quickly reached the cropland nearest the shelter-office. "Looks like we can cut across here to Andy's place," Pete said. The sparse crops, broken and fallen, presented no obstacle.

It was quiet. The recent unusual human activity, he thought, had scared away the songbirds.

The two entered the cultivated section, and detoured around piles of broken stalks. The farm workers, Pete thought, hadn't had time to complete their cleanup. The scent reminded him of fresh hay in the bulk ag lab at Earth University.

He led Jenny around a large pile, and a group of a dozen or so large birdlike animals started and scampered away. The black and white mottled creatures cackled as they ran, and flapped small and evidently flightless wings.

"Chickens," Pete said. The animals were smaller than the "turkeys" they had flushed earlier, but had somewhat longer necks.

"They look almost like real chickens," Jenny said. She smiled. "I can guess what they taste like."

"Yeah. Those leftovers will probably be caught and eaten soon." He led her into another field where a few patches of a crop still stood among the broken stalks. He stopped to survey the damage.

"Last time we were here," Jenny said, "the stuff in here was taller than I am. Before it got trampled. We would've had to go around the long way."

"Yeah," Pete agreed. "Tall but with little fruit, or whatever they called that crop. This one doesn't look familiar, what's left of it."

"Short with no fruit." Jenny bent down to get a closer look.

Pete looked down at the plowed rows. "A lot of exposed soil now." He watched Jenny pick up a handful of soil.

"This soil looks so much different than on Earth," she said. "Kind of sandy, with black speckles. Only a little dust." She held it up to her nose. "It smells organic. I think that's the right word."

"That's mostly nutrients—the speckles," Pete said. "This is good soil, Jenny, better than anywhere on Earth. Earth's is all worn out." The nutrients in this soil were somewhat more complete than at the Landings, he thought, but even the "plains" soil back at the landing site was a great improvement over Earth's.

Earth!

Jenny looked at him. "You mean we should be able to grow good crops here?" She smiled.

"Yeah," Pete said, his beginning daydream of Earth cut short. He hesitated, and then said, "We'd better get going."

∗   ∗   ∗

Pete and Jenny arrived at Andy's small wooden shelter a few minutes later. Cindy greeted them at the door.

"I hope you can stay awhile," she said. "Andy's doing some guard work. He'll be home in a few hours."

"We'd like to," Pete said, "but we can't." He watched Cindy brush back her red hair. Small puffs of dust caught the sunlight near where her fingers touched her hair.

Cindy invited her guests inside the one-room shelter.

"It's so sad that it's come to this," she said. She closed the door behind them, and the room darkened considerably.

"At least you have Andrew," Jenny said. "Can I hold him?" She smiled.

Pete watched her step over to the crib in one corner of the small dark room. Those at the quadrant farms, he thought, did not have photronic lights or any other such conveniences. Most of their small self-contained chemlights, brought from Earth, had long ago lived out their twelve-month lives and had not been replenished. Only a narrow shaft of early-afternoon sunlight came in through the one tiny window high on the west wall.

"He sure is a quiet little guy," Jenny said.

"That's because we're all awake," Cindy said. "You should be here in the middle of the night." She picked up the boy, wrapped a light blanket around him and handed him to Jenny. "I packed him all morning while I drove the tractor, so he's tired now."

Jenny accepted the baby, and held him close.

Pete thought of the dust in Cindy's hair. Life on the farm was so busy, he told himself, that she hadn't had time to clean up after her morning's work. He noticed a backpack, modified for carrying an infant, draped over a corner of the crib.

He stood close to Jenny and inspected Andrew. "Jenny, you look like a natural." He looked at Cindy. "Andrew looks well fed."

"Yes," Cindy said, "so far he's been eating regularly. But I've lost some weight. Andy's lost only a little more, but those poor people far from the farms are having a really bad time."

Jenny handed Andrew back to Cindy. "We'll make it, Cindy," she said. "I know we will. Andrew will grow up big and strong."

Cindy stepped into the shaft of sunlight, and Pete noticed that she had a tear in the corner of her eye.

"I came here to Earth-Twin," she said, "so that I could have a good clean wide-open home for my children. I didn't want them to live on crowded Earth. Pangaea is so beautiful. I want Andrew to grow up here. We could all be so happy. But now I don't know what will happen."

"He will," Jenny promised. "We'll be happy and proud. And I think Pangaea is beautiful, too." She turned to Pete and said, softly, "But you've never been able to see that."

"It's been good to visit with you, Cindy," Pete said, "and to meet Andrew. We'd better go now. Lynn's flying back to the Landings with us." He hesitated, and then said, "She needs to talk to the Council."

Cindy and Andy might have to join the hunters, he thought, if the farms were abandoned. The Landings would be able to handle only a small fraction of the farm people, and many had small children. The Council had devised a lottery system for the Landings, which they used primarily for new arrivals from Earth. Lynn would probably have to use it now.

He could keep track of Andy's family's whereabouts, if they "lost" in the lottery. He and Jenny could join them on the plains later, when he talked her into going with him. They could help find food, and this would help to feed Andrew. It was one more argument, he thought, he could use to convince Jenny.

He watched Cindy put Andrew back in the crib.

"I'm glad you came." Cindy looked at Pete, and then at Jenny. "I'll tell Andy you said hello."

"'Bye, Cindy," Jenny said. She looked at Andrew in his crib. "'Bye, Precious." She turned to Pete. "See! He smiled at me."

*   *   *

On the way back to the Landings, Pete sat between Jenny and Lynn in the nearly empty aircraft.

Jenny, who occupied the window seat, leaned across Pete and looked at Lynn. "I'm happy you're coming with us, Lynn," she said. "I hope you stay."

"Thanks, Jenny," Lynn said. "I probably will."

"Yeah," Pete said, "I'm sure the Council will abandon the farms." He looked at Lynn.

Lynn touched her fingertips together in front of her. "It all hinges on my recommendation, and I'm going to recommend that we do it," she said. "I'll reassign some people to help guard the factories. I'm afraid the rest will have to join the millions."

"Yeah, I guess we'll have to stretch the factory production a little more." The limited food-sharing with the people on the plains, Pete thought, would probably have to be suspended. It was getting difficult to keep it going, anyway. Hunger and the survival instinct, he told himself, had an edge over altruism.

"We'll have to go back to the farms eventually," Lynn said. "Who knows how many are starving to death."

Pete grimaced. "I'd hate to see the latest body count," he said. "I agree that we'll need to get back to the farms." Only the farms could offer the needed mass production, he thought, at least for the foreseeable future with unmodified native plants. "If we can at least find something that grows better than what I've tried so far," he said. He looked at Lynn. "As soon as we get back to the Landings, I want to show you exactly what I've been doing. Let me tell you about the recent stuff."

Lynn interrupted. "Relax, Pete. We'll talk about the details later."

"Sure," Pete said, "and once we have a solution, we'll have to find a way to keep raiders off the farms."

"I hope it won't come to any more deadly force," Lynn said, "like in the West Quadrant."

"I don't know if we'll have a choice," Pete said. "We'll have to stop the thieving—"

Jenny cut in. "Body counts! Deadly force! I don't like those expressions." She hesitated, and then said, "Isn't the Council considering some kind of birth control? I'm kind of glad that Andy and Cindy were able to give birth to Andrew, but things are getting really bad."

Pete looked at Jenny, and then back at Lynn. "Birth control?" he asked. "How can the Council enforce any such rules? The people are so spread out over this land."

"I believe it will be a voluntary restriction on births," Lynn said, "and the Council will try to get the word out to as many as possible. They'll recommend just enough to minimize problems later on, and hope that people will obey." She hesitated, and then added, "We already know that the lifestyle on the plains has its own effect. The scarcity of food will have a greater impact." She shrugged. "Enforcement, if these persuasions aren't enough, will come later when we're better organized.

"That reminds me," Lynn said. "The Council talked about being more explicit in the radio messages to Earth—hoping now to limit shipboard births while keeping the other problems in mind. But they voted it down again."

"Again?" Pete raised his arms in a gesture of resignation. "What's Thackaray thinking about? And the rest of them?"

"They decided it wasn't worth the possible panic." Lynn sighed, and then added, "Earth itself will learn something from the next hypersignal."

"Yeah, they'll certainly know we're in some kind of trouble," Pete said. "It'll be minus a big body count this time."

Pete saw Jenny glance at him, but she didn't say anything. "Sorry, Jenny," he said.

"The plan right now is to try to alter the following signal," Lynn said.

That would be the sixth, Pete thought. He knew that Adam would be alerted by the next signal, the fifth. He wondered how others on Earth would respond. People had been so enthusiastic about the plan. Would they just find some excuse to continue? Or could they have already done some rethinking about the whole plan?

The count carried so little information. Earth would know only that people were dying. Earth couldn't help anyway, he told himself, at least not with the immediate problems. *Earth, and Linda, are so far away.*

He had to get away from it all. Jenny might go to the quadrant with him. Although the situation there was bad, he thought, anything would be better than his hopeless quest for the proper native crops. Lynn had often tried to encourage him. She had insisted that his failure so far was not unexpected, that the search might take many more months or even years. He could accept this no longer. He could never, he thought, match Lynn's patience.

He looked at Jenny, and her face broke into that sweet smile that so affected him. They could make it on the plains together, he thought. Lynn was going to help in the factories, and she could handle his job better than he had handled it.

Lynn interrupted Pete's daydream. "Right now our greatest concern is growth due to the new arrivals of adults from Earth."

"Looks like I need to cheer you guys up," Jenny said. She looked out the window. "Look at the sunset. It looks more red than orange. There are red streaks through all the clouds. It never got so red on Earth. Pete, look at it!"

"You want me to say it's pretty, Jenny." Pete looked past her and out the aircraft window, "Yeah. Beautiful."

"Oh, Petey. You noticed."

*   *   *

Two days later Pete attended his first Council meeting. He listened while Lynn recommended that the farm projects be abandoned for the near future. He smiled when the Council approved. Later he and Lynn worked out a plan that divided the food factory duties, although, at Lynn's request, he remained head of the research effort. He told himself to accept this for the time being. She was in the factories; he could abandon the job any time, he thought, with a clear conscience.

*   *   *

Two months after Lynn relocated to the Landings, Pete and Jenny planned a rare spare moment together. The two met at their favorite Landing-One racquetball court.

Pete stared at Jenny when she first arrived. *She's so thin!* "Are you eating regularly?" he asked. "I didn't notice how skinny you are until now—in your racquetball outfit."

"I'm all right," she said. "I don't want to eat too much. This way there's more food left for other people."

"Damn it, we're all doing that," Pete said. He forced himself to lower his voice. "But you're sacrificing more than anyone."

He watched her thin hands remove the cover from her racquet.

He realized that everyone at the Landings, now that the sparse factory production must feed more people and in spite of the cancellation of the sharing program, had lost considerable weight. He had seen it in his own face in the mirror, in the hollows around his eyes and the prominence of his cheekbones. He saw it in the thinness of his once muscular arms. He felt it deep in his gut.

In his nightly dreams, he thought, he often sat down to a full meal and turned down second or third helpings. These "full meal" dreams sometimes included his parents and brother and sister at the table; he had forced himself not to think of them after he left Earth, but the memories lingered awhile after those dreams. In other dreams he sat down alone before an empty plate.

His duties, and authority, in the factories had given him opportunities to take a little extra food before general distribution. So far he had not succumbed to such temptation; he had to set the example, he told himself, for his small crew. *And what if Jenny found out? Or Lynn?*

"I want you to eat more," he said.

"It's good to know you care about me," Jenny said. She smiled.

"Of course I do," Pete said. She hadn't, he told himself, taken offense at his outburst. He smiled. He was so close, he thought, to taking her away with him. "How are you and Lynn getting along?" he asked.

"We've become the best of friends." Jenny hesitated, and then said, "Lynn has a lot of confidence in you. So do I.

"I'm glad she's here permanently now," she added. "It hardly seems like a couple of months already."

"Yeah." Pete removed his own racquet cover. "The Council did the right thing in abandoning the farms."

"Let's stop jabbering and play some racquetball," Jenny said.

*   *   *

Spacecraft five arrived on schedule with its more than two million hungry people. A few weeks later Pete attended another Council meeting at Landing-One. He sat with Lynn and the twenty-seven councilmembers around a rectangular table. After a round of discussions and reports, and several votes, President Thackaray stood at the podium at the front of the room. "Earth will certainly learn something from the latest census," he said.

Adam would, Pete thought.

Thackaray continued. "As we've been discussing this afternoon, our population has to be much lower than ten million. We may never know that number. But we're in agreement that we'll stop the next signal and alter it to let Earth know why people are dying here. Of course we may expect new arrivals for many years to come."

He looked at Lynn and added, "We will not resume open air farming until there's some real progress in the experimental facilities." He looked at Pete. "Mr. MacDonald, your report?"

Pete stood up by his chair and gave a short report on the progress, or, as he described it, the lack of progress, in the food factories. He concluded, "Since we don't have enough people, especially for guarding the facilities, we won't use Landing-Five's factories for experimentation. We'll plant what we can to feed the additional people here, and maybe a few stragglers from the plains." He sat down.

He took a drink of water, and daydreamed while several councilmembers gave additional reports on unrelated subjects. He and Lynn had agreed that she would manage Five and attempt to maximize production with any edible native crop that would grow. This way they would be able to feed a few more people and relax the guard on facilities that would not require careful monitoring.

He had asked her to be co-manager of the experiments, but she had continued to insist that he manage by himself. He didn't accept her argument, he told himself, that he was the only one who could do the job. She had argued that others, including herself, might solve the problem in a decade or two, while he could do it in only a few years. He could save millions from starvation, she had maintained, and she could only act as his advisor.

Lynn had always expected much more from him than he could deliver, he thought, but this time he had gone along with her. The two had worked out a plan that maximized both experimentation and production, and minimized guarding while taking into account the increased distances between the ship entrances as the later five-kilometer ships arrived. Since they had worked it out together, he told himself, she could take over his end at any time.

After the reports Thackaray adjourned the meeting.

*   *   *

Later that day Pete met with Jenny at the racquetball court.

"I'm a little tired," Jenny said. "Let's just sit and talk for a while."

"All right," Pete said. "I need to talk to you about something anyway."

The two sat down on the floor in the rear of the court, and did not uncover their racquets.

She's getting even thinner, Pete thought. He had been angry about this a few months earlier. If he could get her out on the plains with the hunters, with Andy and Cindy, maybe he could get her to eat more. After the vigorous exercise on the plains, she would be hungrier. They would find the places where food was still available. *After all*, he told himself, *it* is *a big continent.*

"Are you eating like I keep telling you?" he asked. "Maybe that's why you're tired."

"I'm all right," Jenny said. "I'm eating enough."

Now was the time, Pete thought. He glanced around, even though they were alone on the court. He then looked at Jenny. "Let's keep this between us for now," he said. "You remember when I asked Lynn to come here? I had a reason, other than just needing her help."

Jenny's green eyes opened wide. "What do you mean? Why the secrecy?" She hesitated a moment. She stood up. "Oh, *no*, Pete!"

"I made my decision." Pete stood up and faced her. "I'm going to join Andy and Cindy's hunting group in the East Quadrant. Tomorrow."

Jenny looked into his eyes. "But—"

Pete interrupted. "I have to get away."

"But you know you're needed here," Jenny said. "We talked about this so many times."

"Lynn can handle it all," Pete insisted. He had considered that many times, he thought, and he knew she could. He was not essential to the project.

"We both know she can't," Jenny said.

Pete had planned for some argument. "She'll do better than I have," he said. "I've made no progress at all. I want you to come with me, Jenny."

"I know I said I'd go anywhere with you," Jenny said. "But this is wrong. Can't I talk you out of it?"

"Not this time," Pete said.

"You'll regret it later. *Please*, Pete!"

"My mind's made up," he said. "I don't want you to just come with me. Jenny, I want you to be my wife."

She didn't respond right away, so Pete continued. "We can get married in the quadrant." He hesitated, and then added, "I know life will be rough. But we'll be together."

"Oh, Pete, you're making this so difficult for me."

"It's not difficult. It's easy. Just say 'yes.'" He took both of her hands in his. "Jenny, marry me." He noticed a tear in the corner of her eye. "You're crying?"

"No! I'm not! I never cry." She looked directly into his eyes. "I *refuse*," she said. "I can't let you do this."

"We can help Andy and Cindy find food and feed Andrew."

"You can help Andrew by staying in the factories."

Pete let go of her hands. "I'm going, Jenny. Tomorrow. Even if you don't go with me." He turned away. He hadn't intended to threaten her like that, he thought, although he had decided that he would leave even if he had to go alone.

He turned toward her again. She lowered her eyes.

I'm sorry. I didn't mean to threaten you, he thought. "I *can't* do this work anymore," he said. "All our results are failures. And it takes so long just to fail again."

Jenny wiped a tear from the corner of her eye with her hand. "Do you remember Phil," she asked, "who worked with me on the ship's computer?"

"Phil—who you used to dance with?" Pete said. "Yeah, I remember. He's a nice guy."

Jenny looked up at him. "He's a *dead* guy," she said. "I found out a few months ago that he starved somewhere in the North Quadrant."

Pete grimaced. "Oh, no—"

Before Pete could say more, Jenny added, "And Steve, our pilot friend. He's dead, too."

"Steve, too?"

"He got caught in the middle of a raid," Jenny said, "while they were harvesting the last few fields near the West Quadrant airport."

"Damn." Pete shook his head. Jenny knew much more than he did about these things, he thought. Scattered obituary data existed on the main computer, and she had full access.

"Pete, only *you* can stop this," she said.

"I can't stop anything."

"It'll work soon," Jenny insisted. "I know it will."

"I know what I have to do," Pete said. "Come with me. Please!"

"And I know what I have to do," Jenny whispered. A tear rolled down her cheek. She quickly wiped it away with her hand. "Stay here with me," she said. "In Pangaea. You can't go back to Earth. And you can't change things by abandoning everything."

"At least think it over until tomorrow," Pete pleaded.

"Can't I talk you out of this, Pete?"

"Not anymore." He bent over to pick up his racquet. "I'll come by your place to get you in the early morning."

"Pete, I—Oh, nothing." Jenny picked up her racquet.

The two departed the court and entered the hallway outside the rec center. "Goodnight, Jenny," Pete said. "First thing in the morning. Please decide to come with me." He kissed her on the cheek. He then proceeded in one direction and she in another.

He did not sleep well that night.

Chapter 18

Jenny

In the morning Pete walked to Jenny and Lynn's residence, about a quarter-kilometer from his own. The two lived in one of the larger of the nearly empty complexes, near One's main computer center. He knocked on the metallic door.

Lynn opened the door. "Good morning, Pete."

"Hello, Lynn. I need to see Jenny." Pete entered, and stood just inside the doorway. "I have to talk to you, too."

"Coffee?" Lynn asked.

I could probably use some coffee right now, Pete told himself. He hesitated, and then said, "Later. I need to see Jenny first." He looked at Lynn. "What's the matter? You look like you've been up all night." He knew he looked no better.

"Just tired." Lynn stepped over to the table in the middle of the room and poured herself a cup of coffee. She put the decanter back on the table, picked up her cup and took a sip.

Coffee, Pete thought, was one of the very few items that remained from the five ships' stored food. Few users resided at the Landings, and the vacuum packing kept it fresh. The old wake-up beverage was always available, for those who liked it black.

When Lynn put her cup down, he asked, "Where's Jenny?"

"Jenny's gone."

"Gone?" Pete asked. "What do you mean?"

"She left."

Pete wasn't sure if he understood what Lynn was trying to tell him. "Where did she go? Do you know when she'll be back?" he asked. "We were supposed to get together this morning."

"I don't know where she went," Lynn said. She picked up her cup again. "She acted strange last evening."

"Strange? How?"

"I tried to get her to talk," Lynn answered, "but she was preoccupied. Later, when I went to bed, I said 'goodnight.' She answered 'goodbye.'"

"Goodbye?" Pete stepped away from the door and up to the table where Lynn stood.

Lynn took a sip of coffee. "I asked her about it," she said. "She just said that I was one of her 'best friends ever.' She wouldn't say anything else."

"Lynn?" Pete now understood. Jenny had not just run an errand or gone to the computer center.

"When I got up this morning," Lynn said, "she was gone. I guess she took a small bag with some of her belongings."

"You don't have any idea?" Pete asked. Jenny had been angry with him, he told himself, but not *that* angry.

Lynn picked up a folded piece of paper from the table. "She left this for you."

Pete took the note from Lynn. He unfolded it and read silently at first. He could almost hear Jenny's voice.

Pete,

I'm going away for a while. I'm afraid that if I
stay I'll give in. I almost did yesterday.
I don't want us to do something we'll both regret
for the rest of our lives.
Please stay at the Landings. If you need help on
the computer, get George from the Council.

Don't try to find me. I'll get a message to you.
I'm sorry I was so abrupt with you yesterday.
I love you, Pete. I'll always love you.

Jenny

"Going away? Where?" Pete asked.

Lynn didn't respond. She hadn't read the note, Pete thought, since it had been addressed only to him.

He read the short message aloud. Then, "We were supposed to get together." The Landings was a big place, he thought. She could be anywhere in any of the five giant ships.

Lynn sat down next to the table.

"I guess I'll have that coffee now." Pete picked up a cup from a small rack on the table and filled it from the decanter.

His thoughts raced. What did he really know about Jenny? She was always playful and cheerful. She made a big project out of small activities where he wouldn't bother, like carefully naming all the experimental crops. He would have just numbered them in sequence. She sincerely enjoyed doing those things.

What else did he know? She was never careless, he told himself, and never thoughtless. *What happened?*

He would still talk her into going to the East Quadrant with him, and she would marry him. They would live as hunters in the wooded hills and plains of the quadrant, under the orange sun and away from the reminders of Earth. He would get away from thoughts of the Spring Dance; he would get out where he wouldn't have time to think so much.

At night they would sleep the deep sleep of the physically exhausted. *No more sleepless nights.* It would certainly be a rough life at first, he thought, but together he and Jenny could make it. "I'm going to look for her," he said. He put the cup down on the table. It was still full.

Lynn nodded.

"I'll get back to you as soon as I can," Pete said. He turned toward the door.

"You said you also needed to talk to me?" Lynn asked.

"Later."

✶   ✶   ✶

Pete was exhausted when he returned to Jenny and Lynn's residence, in the afternoon, two days later. "Lynn, I've looked everywhere. Asked everyone. No one saw her. I even questioned all the available pilots."

"I've been checking, too," Lynn said. "*Nothing.*" She shook her head. "I'm really worried." She sat down by the table.

Lynn would be very thorough, Pete thought, and neither she nor he had learned anything. He wondered if Jenny had gone out on the plains alone, afoot. He felt a chill. She was already very thin, he told himself. *Did she take any food with her? How much? There isn't much available.* He shook his head, and paced the floor.

The five giant ships were mostly empty, he thought. Jenny was probably in one of them and not alone on the plains. She would be able to get her usual ration. *Yes, that's it.* He, and Lynn, just hadn't been able to look everywhere, ask everyone. He glanced around the room and spotted two white uniforms with yellow trim hanging on a coat tree. She hadn't taken everything; she was close by, he thought. *She's safe.*

He sat down next to Lynn. "Jenny's been around so long that I guess I took her for granted. Now every place I go is just full of her absence. I was just at the computer center here at One." He hesitated, and then said, "I'd better tell you what she and I talked about the evening before she disappeared." He told Lynn the full story.

"I suspected that was why you were so enthusiastic about my coming back here," Lynn said.

"I apologize, Lynn. I owe you something better than that."

"It's all right," Lynn said. "I understand. We've all been under a great strain."

Lynn smiled, but to Pete that smile appeared a little forced.

"Yeah," he mumbled. He got up.

Ten minutes later, as he walked down the ship's hallway, he wondered if Lynn knew more than she had told him. He shrugged. Lynn and Jenny slept in separate rooms; Jenny could easily leave without waking Lynn.

*   *   *

Several months passed, and Pete found no trace of Jenny. He talked to more people, but no one had seen her. He remained at the Landings; the central location gave him a better chance, he believed, to find her. He would be around to receive her promised message. He would be around to welcome her back.

He continued his work in the factories. It was something to do while waiting and worrying, he told himself. He performed the computer evaluation and documentation himself, although he knew he could match neither Jenny's skill with that photronic machine nor her love for detail. He did contact George at the Council, but only to ask if he had any knowledge of Jenny's whereabouts.

Earlier Pete organized several forays out onto the plains, but he soon gave that up. The vastness made such a search pure folly, and the personnel and other resources were limited.

He worked, waited and slept little.

*   *   *

Four months after Jenny's disappearance, in the late afternoon, Pete was at work deep in the interior of section four at Landing-One when Lynn rushed up to him. "Pete! I have news about Jenny!"

He stood up, his measuring tools in his hands, and looked at her.

"I just talked to some people who were trying to get food from Five," she said. "They came from a small valley at the edge of the South Quadrant, just over a hundred kilometers from here. They said that a woman from the Landings came to their valley about four months ago. They described Jenny."

"Lynn, we found her!" Pete smiled. "What'd they say?" He put the measuring tools down on a nearby table.

"They didn't say much—just very long blond hair and Jenny's height," Lynn said. "None had talked to her. They left the valley a few days later to look for food. They wandered, and eventually turned up at Five." She sighed. "All weak from malnutrition."

"They were in bad shape?" Pete asked. They were wandering around, he told himself, and that's why they were in bad shape. Jenny would be smart enough to stay near the valley.

Lynn shook her head. "They buried half their small group."

"I need to talk to them," Pete said.

"They went back out on the plains after we fed them," Lynn said. "You know the rules."

Pete nodded. "But you did get the valley's location?"

"Yes, Pete. I do have some sketchy directions."

"I'll go in the morning," Pete said. "As early as I can."

*　　　　*　　　　*

The valley lay in a rugged region; a large aircraft couldn't fly all the way. After a short flight to the closest suitable clear landing area, Pete asked the pilot to return for him, and another passenger, in two days. He watched the craft depart, and then put his pack on his back and began to hike the last ten or so kilometers over rough and rocky hills. It looked like a good place for hunting, he thought, although he didn't see any "game."

He wondered if Jenny could have walked the full hundred kilometers. *That would take days,* he told himself, but he knew she hadn't boarded an aircraft, and no terrie was missing. *How did she find the valley? Did she know where it was, from messages on the computer? Or did she just stumble onto it?*

A few small birds sang. They sounded different, he thought, from those at the Landings and the East Quadrant. Jenny, he told himself, would like the musical quality of these birds.

They would soon be hunting together in the East Quadrant. *Or here? Maybe the valley?* He was almost there.

While he walked he glanced around and vowed that he would appreciate the beauty of his new home. He and Jenny would appreciate it together. He would forget about Earth. They would hunt all day and fall asleep exhausted every night.

Lynn could take care of the experiments at the Landings.

He pulled his western down so that the brim shaded his eyes. The early morning orange sun *was* bright. Jenny usually kept her western hanging loosely across her back, he thought. She looked pretty that way.

Pete walked for about two hours.

He saw larger hills ahead of him; Lynn's directions told him he was nearing his destination.

He noted a particular form of plant growth on a rocky hillside. Some bean-like vines grew among the rocks. They appeared to barely cling to life, and they held a few of what looked like Earth's lima bean pods.

He climbed a short way and picked a pod. He then stripped it and ate the beans raw. *Not bad.* He would have to stretch the little food he brought with him to last several days, so he picked and ate the few remaining beans. He spotted more growth higher in the rocks, and planned to gather those beans on the way back. There could be enough, he thought, for a light meal for two people. He turned and continued on his way.

As Pete approached the valley, he picked up his pace. He tried to ignore the fatigue brought on by his incomplete diet.

He entered the valley. Tree-covered hills, bigger hills than even in the East Quadrant, now surrounded him. Some of the trees resembled Earth's evergreens, he thought, but they were not as tall as those "pines" in Earth's old coniferous forests. He had read about them long ago. He thought of Andy's "photographs."

A potpourri of wild flowers grew in scattered patches at the bases of the hills. Their reds, oranges, yellows, blues and purples complemented the green hills. Jenny would like those flowers and their fragrance, he thought. She always liked the flowery smells. She and he could live here. He didn't have to go back to the Landings, or to the East Quadrant.

Since the valley appeared to have more shade than sun, he removed his western and allowed it to hang across his back. It bounced as he walked.

He reached the edge of a sunny clearing. He halted. The clearing was full of dirt mounds. *Graves! So many graves!* He looked around. Some were marked, but most were not. Some looked fresher than others. Hundreds of the small mounds sprouted amid the flowers.

He proceeded again, and skirted around the clearing. He had better plan on the East Quadrant after all, he told himself.

All was strangely quiet, he thought. No birds sang in the valley.

He entered what was apparently a living area, and encountered a small group of people who appeared to be looking for something in a grassy clearing. All were emaciated. *No one is that thin,* he thought, *at the Landings.*

Pete approached one man, who greeted him, "Welcome to Hope Valley, stranger." He explained, "The name tells you about all that's left here. Somebody named the place a few months ago."

The man's hair appeared to be falling out in random patches. Pete had noticed that he was losing a little hair from his own head, but he hadn't connected that to malnutrition.

The man wore ragged clothing. Pete's uniform was worn, but he could access the manufacturing facilities at the Landings and had replaced his garments several times since arriving on the planet. Those away from the central area must make do with what they wore on arrival, he thought, for years if they survived that long.

Pete inquired about Jenny, but the man knew nothing.

"They come 'n go," he said. "Not much here."

While he and Pete talked, the man continued to search the tall grass and nearby shrubs. Pete followed, and started when his companion bent over and grabbed something from the grass, popped it into his mouth, chewed briefly and swallowed.

"That's four today," the man said.

Pete started to ask, "What—"

"Grasshopper. A few this time o' day."

"Is this all you have here?" Pete asked. "Just grasshoppers?"

"Where're you from?" the man asked.

"The Landings," Pete said. He followed while the man again searched the bushes. "We haven't been eating bugs."

"We've other insects, too. We started on 'em after we ate all the birds. It's survival. Oh, a few berries 'n things." The man turned, bent over, and grabbed another grasshopper. "A good day today. But a funny thing for a trained open-air farmer—being grateful for insects. This one's for my wife."

"You're a farmer? Has anyone tried farming here?" Pete asked.

"No equipment. No time. Too tired." He put the grasshopper into a small pouch on his belt. "The few of us who stay here spend all our time 'n energy just scrounging around for enough to stay alive."

Pete asked again. "You haven't tried anything?"

"A time back," the man said, "a few of us worked with the berries. Farther down the valley. We planted cuttings 'n tried to get the bushes to propagate. Didn't work."

"Sounds like the quadrant farms," Pete said.

"Gotta get this 'hopper to my wife. Maybe see you around." The man pointed a skinny finger. "Some of the people over there've been in this part of the valley longer," he said.

Pete turned and looked. He spotted a small group of rough shelters near a grove of evergreens, a few hundred meters from where he stood. Several people looked like they were searching a nearby bushy area. He turned back to the man. "Thanks," he said. "I hope you find more grasshoppers."

"Try 'em." The man smiled. "By the way, I'm Rip."

"Pete here. Thanks again, Rip."

The two shook hands. Rip then raised his hand in a wave that resembled a salute. Pete returned it and turned away.

He headed toward the bushes to query the other people, and passed more graves. The late-morning sunshine fell on his face and neck, but it didn't warm him. He felt a chill.

He hadn't before been, he thought, in any such isolated area of Pangaea. He hadn't seen such deprivation, although he knew life had to be that way on much of the vast continent. He hadn't seen graves numbered in the hundreds.

He reached the bushes; they held a number of what appeared to be unripe berries. He picked a berry, popped it into his mouth and started to chew. He spat. *Bitter!* Probably just needs a few days to ripen, he thought, but certainly inedible now.

Pete questioned several people and finally found someone who knew Jenny. The woman busily searched the bushes, but she stopped when Pete introduced himself and mentioned Jenny's name. The others had not interrupted their searches.

"A few ripen each day," she said. "Some of us come here every morning. We go to other areas in the afternoon—a lot of walking. You see us all here together. We've agreed not to search alone."

From her tone, Pete understood that this was so that no one would take advantage of an early start. "But you know Jenny?" he asked.

"Yes."

Pete felt his heartbeat speed up. "Where is she?" he asked.

"Mr. MacDonald, I—" The woman hesitated, and then said, "Can I call you Pete? I feel like I already know you. I'm Sylvia."

Know him already? Yes, he *had* found Jenny, Pete told himself. He looked at Sylvia. Like Rip, she was losing hair in clumps. From what was left, he guessed that she must have had long black hair at one time.

Her uniform was not quite as ragged as Rip's, although still in rough shape. Pete surmised that she would have come with a later group from Earth. "Pete's fine, Sylvia," he said. "I've got to see Jenny right away."

"Jenny arrived a while ago," Sylvia said. "Three months? Four? There was still some frost in the mornings then."

"But where is she?" Pete asked.

Sylvia sighed. "The poor little dear. When Jenny came here, she was so weak. She could hardly speak."

"But—she *is* all right now?" Pete's heart beat even faster. He felt a knot form in his stomach.

"I remember that little smile," Sylvia said. "As tired and weak as Jenny was, she could still smile. She smiled a lot while she was here. And her long hair. So beautiful. My hair used to be long."

Pete interrupted. "*While* she was here? But—*where* is she now?"

"How long was she here? I don't know. A few weeks. Just long enough to get to know her. She had a certain power. Jenny gave us hope." Sylvia hesitated, and then added, "She talked a lot about you, Pete. You're special."

"But—" Pete's hands started to shake.

"Jenny said you'd solve our problems," Sylvia said.

"But—"

"I know I'm evading your questions, Pete. I'm talking a lot and not answering you. I just can't find the right words."

Pete fell silent.

"Why don't you come over here with me." Sylvia took him by the hand.

He followed her out of the bushes and into a wooded area. He could see a small clearing ahead. It wasn't far. It was a sunny spot in the middle of a lot of shade.

He tried to speak, but the words didn't come out. His breath came in short gasps. He stumbled as he walked, as if he didn't want to go where she led him, but he didn't resist her pull on his hand. He stumbled, and followed.

"Pete, I just can't say it," Sylvia said. "I have to show you."

They reached the clearing, and Tau Ceti's yellow-orange light again fell on Pete's face. Again he didn't feel its warmth. Tears flooded his eyes. He tried again to speak, but could manage only a stutter. "This—this is a—graveyard."

Sylvia stopped by a mound of Pangaea's rich soil. Pete saw, as if through a haze, that it was partially grown over with red, yellow and orange wildflowers with the cheerful look of Earth's marigolds. He felt Sylvia's hand still holding his, but she did not speak.

He tried to focus. A short inscription, laboriously chipped and scratched on a flat rock, adorned the mound. It was one of the very few graves that were marked at all. He read: JENNIFER BROWN, AGE 32 EARTH.

Pete pulled his hand from Sylvia's, fell to his knees and buried his face in his hands.

✳   ✳   ✳

Pete gazed out the aircraft window on his way back to the Landings. The vast land spread out before him. He viewed green hills and flat plains, woods and meadows, and sparkling streams and lakes that reflected the orange sun. No cultural features such as roads and cities marred *this* land; it was nothing like Earth's paved-over landscape. He saw nothing like Earth's solar energy collection fields and windmill forests. Energy extraction plants did not clutter the lakes. The streams and rivers were not dammed; no lakes were "man-made."

He had seen Earth from the air. He had flown often between his parents' home and the distant main campus. He had often looked out the window at Earth. Now he viewed a new world.

It was a short flight, and he had been away for just over two days. Back at the Landings, he departed the aircraft, donned his western, walked a short distance and climbed to the grassy clearing on the big hill near One. From the summit he viewed parts of all five giant spacecraft. They were arranged in a vee shape, and One was at the vertex of the vee; he could see only bits of the others. He turned toward orange Tau Ceti, which shone brightly high over the southwestern hills.

Jenny had liked this view, he thought, from this hill.

A year earlier she had erected a metal sundial in the middle of the clearing. She had cleverly fit together pieces of spare equipment into a workable and attractive device. Pete gazed at the sundial for a moment; it was mid-afternoon. He felt a hot tear escape from his eye and run down his cheek. Another soon followed.

He looked around. The yellow-orange light from the sun painted the surrounding trees and hills with varied colors, mostly oranges and strange greens. In a freshening breeze, shadows of scattered clouds dusted the hills to the west. A rainbow graced the darker northeastern sky.

It must be raining up that way, he thought. The rainbow looked different from those he remembered on Earth: more intensity in the red band and less in the violet at the other edge. Why hadn't he observed that before? Why hadn't he seen rainbows in Pangaea? There had been plenty of rain.

He removed his western, and held it in his hand.

He felt the breeze caress his face. The smell of flowers invaded his nose, and the birds sang their cheerful songs. None of these could dry his tears.

Pete MacDonald, no longer able to keep his thoughts inside, faced the northeastern rainbow and whispered plaintively. She had asked him, many times, but he had never given her the answer. "It's Albert. Jennifer Susan, it's just—Albert."

Chapter 19

A Goal

Pete descended the hill, entered One, checked the notices on his computer for Lynn's whereabouts and walked to the living quarters that she now occupied alone. He stood in the main room just inside the entrance and shared his news from the valley with her.

"Now she's gone, and it's my fault," he added.

Lynn was silent. She hadn't said anything, Pete thought, since she had greeted him a few minutes earlier.

He looked around the room. Many of Jenny's belongings remained. He noted a number of small animal figurines and two computer disks on a wall shelf, and the two clean but worn white uniforms with yellow pockets and trim still hanging on the coat tree.

He stepped over to the shelf, picked up a black Earth rabbit made of glass and looked at it for a moment. "I'm going to keep this," he said, "and get the rest of them later." He turned and looked at Lynn. "I should've understood. I tried to force her to make a decision she couldn't make."

Lynn put her hand on Pete's shoulder. "Jenny wouldn't want you to carry on like that."

She did not look him in the eye. He wondered about that, and then shrugged it off. "I didn't even listen to what she was telling me," he said. He shook his head. He had never listened to anyone, he told himself.

"It's nobody's fault, Pete."

"She died three months ago," Pete said. "I didn't even know."

"Let's have a small get-together," Lynn said. "Jenny had many friends here."

Pete noticed that she still kept her face turned away from him. He ignored that. He simply welcomed her suggestion. "All right. I'll talk to everyone." He turned to leave.

Lynn stopped him. "Pete, I have to ask you something. I know this is a bad time."

He turned toward her again. "Yeah, Lynn?"

"What are you going to do now, with the factories?" she asked. "You said you'd leave after you found Jenny."

"I—" Pete hesitated, and then said, "I'll stay and continue the work here."

"Thanks, Pete."

"Lynn, she made a promise," Pete said. "She told the people in the valley—" He didn't finish. He turned and walked out the door.

As he walked down the narrow hallway, he wondered if that was the message mentioned in Jenny's note: She made a promise and expected him to keep it. He had read that note many times in the past four months. She had not written that she would "send" a message; she had used different words.

Certainly she had understood just how slim were her chances for survival. Had she "hedged" in her note? Then, later, when she was unable to send a message, had she "planted" the promise?

But how, Pete questioned, could she know he would receive it?

He grimaced. Jenny had run away, and then died, because he had been so clumsy in trying to talk her into going to the plains with him. *I must keep her promise, not question how I found out about it.*

*　　　　　　*　　　　　　*

Pete was glad that Lynn helped him arrange Jenny's ceremony. She also invited one person whom he didn't know but had seen around the

Landings recently. Just before the get-together, held the morning after his return, she introduced him to Harry.

The three stood near where friends were gathering in the mid-morning sunshine on the big hill near One. "Pete MacDonald, this is Harry Sigcrist," Lynn said. "You two will want to talk later."

"Hello, Harry," Pete said. "I'm happy to finally meet you."

"It's good to meet you, Pete. We've seen each other and said hello, but we've always been rushing in opposite directions." Harry smiled and extended his big, although thin, hand.

Pete had to look up. Harry stood five centimeters taller.

While Pete and Harry shook hands, Lynn said, "Harry's an engineer. He's going to try to modify the census signal from the next ship when it arrives."

"Yeah, Harry," Pete said. "We'll have to talk about it. You must've taken over from the earlier guy."

"The earlier guy didn't make it," Harry said. "I was told he was trying to set up better long-range communications in the quadrants when he succumbed. I have that job now, too."

"I didn't know John very well," Pete said. "It was like you and I, just saying hello." He shook his head. "I didn't know he died."

"Just another victim of starvation," Harry said. "I'm not sure just how it happened, but apparently he wasn't able to take enough food with him." He hesitated, and then added, "I wanted this work, Pete. But, like I told Lynn, I don't like how I got it."

Lynn nodded.

Pete looked around. "About two dozen," he said. "I think everyone's here. I'm going to gather everybody and say a few words. We'll talk later—about the hypersignal, Harry."

*   *   *

Pete gave a short eulogy. Others said a few words. Later, after most had gone on their way, Pete stood on the hilltop and gazed at the western hills. He heard Lynn's voice behind him.

"You're a lonely figure there, Pete."

He turned and looked at her. She was alone. "This is a nice place, Lynn," he said. "Look around. At how the sun's shadows carve up the smaller hills. At the shiny edges on the clouds."

"It *is* a beautiful view." Lynn stood next to him.

He turned to the west. "There used to be more birds here," he said, "but there are still a lot. Listen to their music." He glanced up at the clouds and took a deep breath. "I can smell the rain coming. I think it'll be here soon." He turned toward Lynn again. "By the way, what's going on between you and Harry?"

Lynn looked at him. "It's that obvious?"

"Yeah," Pete said. "I like him. I'm happy for you."

"Thanks, Pete. I met him just after you left for the valley. I was at the old Landing-One central rec area sitting over a cup of coffee. I guess I looked like I needed someone to talk to."

"They call it Hope Valley," Pete said. "A strange place, but beautiful."

*   *   *

The next morning Pete stood with Harry in his photronics shop at Landing-Five. "I've been looking over this equipment that I got from John's shop," Harry said. "Look." He leaned over a partially dismantled population counter on his worktable and pointed. "There's a small triggering mechanism on the counter. It triggers a relay that sends the count to the signal generator, and this activates the hyper generator. If I can interrupt the relay, I can stop the signal. Then modify it for our own purposes, to submit to the generator later. And I can decode the original count."

"I'm not sure I'd like to see the count." Pete frowned.

"Yeah, but it'll be useful information for the Council," Harry said. "Lynn told me that you're particularly interested in the signals sent to Earth."

"Adam Hampton, my best friend from the university, is on the PANS team," Pete said. "He'll help evaluate those signals."

He watched Harry pick up a screwdriver and start to remove the triggering mechanism. "Adam always talked about things like this," he said. "About failures of technology, where people were deprived of basic needs. I used to think he was a little far-fetched on that subject." He looked up at the shop ceiling. "Now here we are stuck in the middle of his theory." He nodded. "Adam, old buddy, you really nailed it!" He looked at Harry again.

Harry put a few screws on the table and proceeded to remove more. "Yeah," he said, "I suppose we can consider this to be technology failure. We have all the best that Earth could give us, but you're looking for a new beginning."

"It's back to square one," Pete said. "Like Earth ten thousand years ago. But tell me more about the signal. The latest technology."

"We can modify it," Harry explained, "but we're limited to twelve characters at most. We're going to send just the word 'starvation.' How's that sound to you?" He put a few more screws on the table and jiggled the mechanism to loosen it.

"That'll give Earth the message," Pete said.

"We plan to send 'high gravity' with a later signal," Harry said. "I know we have to wait a long time, but this does give them the opportunity to piece it together." He lifted the now detached triggering mechanism and held it in his hands. "This is about five kilos, so it doesn't weigh much even here."

Pete looked at the mechanism. "Of course we still don't have any proof that high gravity is the cause of our problems. Somebody talked about a kind of penetrating radiation from Tau Ceti—so that our crops would start absorbing it as we got closer in space. Of course it would have to be something that isn't blocked by the ship's shielding, and no one knows what that might be."

"Yeah, it's got to be something that's different in this environment," Harry said. "I guess it could be that way on any new planet." He put the mechanism down on the table. "I'll check this over later."

"I talked to Lynn about that radiation possibility," Pete said. "She said that it might be a kind of radiation that selectively wipes out the most recent genetic modifications. Something about 'incomplete attempts to improve on nature.'"

"She hasn't said much to me about it," Harry said, "but she sounds a little frustrated about the 'cause.'"

"She's still questioning, and I guess will be for a long time," Pete said. "Since radiation is random, how does it affect all Earth crops so quickly? And why doesn't it affect us? If indeed it doesn't." Pete picked up the triggering mechanism. It was about the size of a flowerpot, he thought, and light for its size. He looked at Harry.

"I haven't heard of any abnormal births," Harry said, "or abnormal growth in children." He picked up his screwdriver and a few other tools and placed them in the tool rack on the table.

"I suppose it could be limited to only plants," Pete said. "There are a few other theories, but gravity and radiation are numbers one and two." He turned the mechanism in his hands and looked it over. It had several small access doors attached by screws.

"The Council's accepted gravity as the specific cause," Harry said. "It's the 'official' explanation, and they've instructed me to send that to Earth." He looked at Pete. "Lynn told me you came up with it first."

"I had help from a friend," Pete said. He put the triggering mechanism down on the table.

"You sound like you're not so sure now," Harry said.

"It could be the gravity," Pete said. "But it isn't directly affecting my work, so I haven't had to think about it much." He shook his head. "We abandoned Earth crops long ago."

"I see," Harry said.

"Our present problem is finding the correct native crops, and we'll do that," Pete said. "I guess the gravity does affect us in other ways. If we were eating regularly, we might feel heavier."

Coordination, he thought, could also be affected by the higher than "normal" gravity. Weight increased while inertia remained the same as on Earth or anywhere else in space. Nerves and muscles required some time to adjust to this anomaly, but did so very well during the later stages of ship deceleration when the artificial gravity was slowly increased. He recalled that he had not noticed any effect on everyday activity, although his unused racquetball skills had deteriorated; the ball hadn't adjusted. He felt a tear enter the corner of his eye.

He went on. "You weren't here when we were eating regularly. I did feel heavier sometimes, but it was no problem. You may have felt it when you first arrived, before the weight loss."

"I didn't notice," Harry said. "I just thought about food."

Pete figured he now weighed only about eighty percent of what he had on Earth, even in the Earth-Twin gravity. Harry, and everyone else at the Landings, he thought, fared no better.

"Lynn said that life was good here in the beginning for most people," Harry added. "But I've been trying to do some hunting nearby. I never even see any game. And those months I spent on the plains?" He grimaced. "I feel so lucky to be sharing in the factory food now. I'm always hungry, but not like out there."

Pete looked at Harry. The man's tanned face betokened an outdoor existence even though, Pete thought, Harry had to be spending much of his time in the shop at present. "It'll be good again, Harry," he said. "And someday I'll do the experiments on Earth crops. Someday I'll know about the gravity."

*   *   *

A few hours after talking to Harry, Pete sat down by the main terminal in his "office" to review some of his notes from the university. He
loaded and perused a particular disk, one of many he had packed long
ago but hadn't looked at since he left Earth.

This disk described his statistical system for predicting the results of
genetics experiments. The method examined results from all earlier
related experiments; the computer program could utilize the data from
several hundred years' work. He determined to adapt that program to
his present very different search, and base it on only a few years of
unsuccessful experiments.

Statistics is statistics, he thought. The underlying strategy was the
same for many dissimilar problems; only the tactics need be different.

He decided to use One's main computer. This was a truly formidable
machine, he thought. It was "overkill" for his new purpose, as it had
been for Jenny's, and now his, record-keeping. With its generous com-
putational capacity, he would not have to restrict his method in any
way. He downloaded the old program, leaned back, propped his feet up
on the table and got started.

In the following months, while he prepared the modified program,
Pete and his small crew continued the crop experiments. He performed
all the record-keeping himself, as he had just after Jenny's disappearance. The Council offered to support another computer specialist, but
he refused to concede that she could be "replaced." The long hours
deprived him of some sleep, but he slept more soundly during the few
hours he managed to catch.

∗   ∗   ∗

Six months after Lynn introduced him to Harry, Pete attended their
wedding. Only the timing surprised him.

A week after the wedding, in the early afternoon, he met with Lynn
for their regular discussion of the progress in the factories. Afterward

she accompanied him to Harry's photronics shop, and then left to attend to other tasks.

Pete and Harry stood by the worktable.

"I need someone to help me with that sixth signal," Harry said. "Lynn and I thought you'd like to do it."

"Yeah." Pete smiled. "It'll be a pleasure."

Harry grinned. "We can plan for it now. We have a few weeks."

"The sixth," Pete said. He shrugged. "That number doesn't mean a lot to me anymore. How long will they keep coming?"

"At the time I left Earth, enthusiasm was high," Harry said. "I'd say the project was getting even more popular."

Pete recalled that Harry had explained in a previous conversation that he had had to wait in line for his assignment. He was an alternate for the fourth ship, and considered himself lucky, at the time, to get on the fifth. At thirty-five, he had just slipped by on the age limit. "Yeah," Pete said. "I guess we'll just have to plan for a lot more people."

Harry leaned over his worktable. "I've gone over this some more," he said. He picked up the triggering mechanism that he had removed months earlier, held it in one hand and pointed to an opening. "Look here. All we have to do is open the access panel and cut these two fibers."

Pete looked at the mechanism.

"We can do it while it's still connected," Harry said. "That'll stop the automatic sequence. I'll teach you more about this over the few weeks."

"Yeah." Pete took the mechanism from Harry and looked into the panel opening.

"Our real problem is getting to the equipment and into the mechanism quickly enough," Harry said. "Once the ship touches down, a timing device turns on the counter. It takes a few minutes to count, and then it triggers the relay."

"Can't we radio the incoming ship?" Pete asked. He put the mechanism back on the table. "Have them disconnect it for us? I'm sure we can find a frequency."

"I suggested that," Harry answered, "but Thackaray didn't think we could do it without causing panic aboard any ship that might receive the message. We may have to include a lot of explanation before they'll agree to disconnect."

Pete understood. The message would have to explicitly describe the planet's plight, and this information could also reach the following ships. "What can I do to help?" he asked.

"At the time we do it," Harry said, "I'll need you to hand me the right tool at the right time." He pointed to a small tool bag on the workbench. "You're the tool man. It's not a glamorous job, but it's critical because of the timing."

"I don't need glamour." Pete picked up the tool bag and dumped its contents onto the workbench.

"We'll have to practice," Harry added.

"I'm busy at the factories," Pete said, "but I'll find the time to get this perfect."

Harry grinned. "Great, Pete."

Pete looked over several screwdrivers, pliers and combination wrenches. "Old designs," he said, "but still useful."

"I've already consulted the charts and calculated just where the ship's entrance will be after landing—the one nearest the counter," Harry said. "I marked it with a flag. We'll stand behind a small mound nearby and watch the arrival. Then we'll do a three-hundred-meter dash. We'll start far enough away to be safe from the rocket blast and ground debris, but we *will* get showered with leftovers while we run."

*　　　　　　　*　　　　　　　*

In the evening Pete stood on the big hill. The orange sun had just passed below the horizon and darkness now crept over the low hills to the west. Stars began to decorate a cloudless Pangaean sky, and a quarter moon glowed pink overhead.

He knew well Earth's sun's location in the star patterns; he had stood and gazed at it for hours many times in past years. This time he gave it only a cursory glance.

Just this afternoon, he thought, Harry had invited him to help alter the hypersignal and send a message to Earth. Long ago Adam had asked him for help on Earth. *Maybe this message?*

He had his own goal, he thought, regardless of how Earth reacted. He was going to find those "strains of wheat." He stood still and listened to the darkening land all around him while a cooling breeze caressed his face.

A cricket or some other insect chirped somewhere in nearby low brush. He decided that it had to be a cricket; Jenny had given it an "official" name.

The cricket chirped. Leaves rustled in the breeze. Pete stood on the hill and listened.

Chapter 20

Beans

Pete and Harry stood behind the chosen mound, with the mid-morning orange sun at their backs. They watched the ship descend.

As soon as it touched down and settled, Pete forced his malnourished body to sprint behind Harry. The two passed through three hundred meters of falling dust and debris, and then ran under the edge of the circular hull and up the ramp that had lowered into position during touchdown. They rushed through the large door at the top just as it started to open.

Once aboard the two slowed down as they pushed their way through the crowd of newcomers who now rushed in the opposite direction. Pete brushed debris from his clothing and followed Harry through the ship's hallways.

"They're in a hurry," Pete said between breaths, "like us."

"They have no idea," Harry said, "what they're in for." He stopped at a T-intersection. "This way!" He headed right.

Pete caught his breath and followed.

"They look," Harry said, "so well-fed."

"Fat faces." Pete dodged newcomers and kept just behind Harry.

"They're hungry," Harry said. "But they don't look like us."

"Not like us," Pete mumbled. Even in the rush, he pictured how thin Jenny's face had been that last evening on the racquetball court, and how she must have looked on that later day when starvation took her away from him. He thought of the others in Hope Valley, of Sylvia and of Rip. The newcomers, he told himself, had better get used to what he and Harry must look like to them.

"It's in here." Harry stopped by a metal door.

Harry opened the door, and Pete followed him into a large well-lighted room. A few gauges and terminals lined the side walls, and bulky cylindrical shapes covered much of the back wall away from the door. A small cluster of silver and gray cabinets stood in the center of the room.

Harry pointed to the cabinets. "There it is!"

Pete pulled a screwdriver from the tool bag on his belt and handed it over. He watched Harry deftly remove a small panel from the attached triggering mechanism. He took back the screwdriver with one hand and started to hand over cutting pliers with the other when he heard a low rumble. It sounded like distant thunder. Then close, a roar! He felt a minor quake pass beneath his feet. Then, suddenly, all was quiet. Wisps of smoke appeared around some of the larger equipment at the back wall.

"Damn!" Pete clenched his fists and felt the tools still in his hands. He smelled burning fiber and metal.

"The sound of space when it bends." Harry sighed.

"We were so close." Pete took a deep breath, and then relaxed.

"We failed," Harry said. "Now we have to wait more than a year."

"Be patient," Pete said. "We'll just try again next time." He shrugged. His initial anger at failure had disappeared as quickly as it had come. He put the tools back into the bag and unhooked the bag from his belt. "At least Earth will be sure we're in trouble," he said, "even though they won't know the details."

"Yeah," Harry said, "I guess I'm relieved that I don't have to see that count." He took the tool bag from Pete and hooked it to his own belt.

"Me too." Pete looked at the counter and relay.

Harry sat down on the floor and leaned against the counter. "I sure need some rest," he said.

"I have an idea," Pete said. He pointed. "Look. There's an optical cable connecting the mechanism to the relay. The next time we try, maybe we can cut the cable first. Would that work?"

Harry turned and looked at the equipment. "Might work," he said. "With an axe, we could sever it in a few seconds and block the signal. Then repair it later."

"Yeah, a few seconds," Pete said. "We could make that."

"I'll look the whole thing over later," Harry said. "I'll make sure that we'll still be able to reconstruct the signal."

Pete sat on the floor next to Harry. He looked through the open door into the ship's hallway. Hungry newcomers still crowded the way back to the exit. He had no desire to tangle with that crowd again. "They keep looking in at us as they pass by," he said.

"I hope we're not scaring them too much," Harry said. "Skin and bones? Hair falling out? And I didn't have much to begin with."

"Yeah." Pete grimaced. "The expressions on some of those fat faces when they first see us." He realized also that his clothes were still covered with ground debris kicked up by the ship's descent rockets. He hadn't been able to brush it all off.

"Puzzled looks," Harry said. "Scared looks."

"The sad part is that most of them won't live another year," Pete said. He sighed. He knew that he could do nothing to help, at least nothing timely. "We're going to solve this problem," he said, "but it won't be soon."

Harry nodded.

"These new arrivals do have a small advantage," Pete said, "with the Earth seeds. The Council did the right thing."

"Lynn mentioned something about that," Harry said.

The Council, Pete thought, had recently decreed that newcomers could eat most of the seeds they brought with them. Only a certain amount from each ship would be saved for later research and modification. Most were very nourishing and rather easy to carry in small bags.

"The way I understand it," he said, "they can just carry their seeds with them when they fly to their new areas. Each person gets enough food for a week or so."

"I guess beans are the best," Harry said. "Big edible seeds—cooked or even raw."

Harry's remark reminded Pete of the native beans he had eaten near Hope Valley. His thoughts drifted, and then raced. He had planned to gather more on the way back from the valley, but had forgotten to do that. Nature had conditioned those beans, he thought, for a very peculiar existence in the rocky hills. Might he be able to make use of nature's work? How would the beans respond to a steady supply of water and nutrients? He suddenly sat up straight and looked at Harry. "Beans! Harry! The beans!"

Harry gave him a puzzled glance.

*   *   *

More than an hour later, after the crowd had cleared, Pete and Harry got up and left the ship. Outside the two had to maneuver around a crowd again; the new arrivals hadn't gone far. A member of the Council used a loudspeaker, just outside the exit, to address the gathering.

Thousands, Pete noted, stood and listened under their new orange sun. He hadn't seen the councilmember when he had rushed the ship; the man must have waited behind another mound.

The earlier looks of apprehension, in the sea of fat faces, had changed to despair and even terror as the crowd assimilated the skinny councilmember's grim words. Some hundreds had gathered around a few nearby trees; these newcomers had initially been curious, Pete thought, but they now regarded the speaker and evidently ignored the trees.

A similar drama, Pete told himself, was being played out at each of the many other exits.

He didn't linger. Harry left him to get more tools to remove the now inoperable counting equipment for further study, and he rushed over to Landing-One to get ready for his new tests.

*   *   *

Just over eight months after the arrival of the sixth ship, Pete got into a terrie at Landing-One in the late afternoon and drove to Harry and Lynn's new home at Landing-Six.

The couple had relocated to Six so that Harry could be near a larger photronics shop. Pete knew that Harry needed more space for his work on a global communications system, and that Harry had available all the equipment and resources that came with all six ships. He and Harry had also talked about manpower; Harry could have used help in the project, but the people he needed couldn't be fed. Harry, Pete thought, was on his own.

Pete was anxious to see the new shop and new residence, but he thought instead of his own news while he parked the terrie.

He carried a small package, and he smiled as he entered the spacecraft. Once inside, he looked at his handwritten directions, searched a maze of hallways and soon reached his destination. He knocked and Harry came to the door. The two greeted each other, and Lynn soon joined them.

Pete noticed that she looked tired. He figured that she had spent the day trying to distribute the small production from the factories at Five and Six. "Been rough?" he asked.

"I can give only so little to each," Lynn said.

Harry looked at Pete. "We haven't seen much of you lately."

"Yes, Pete," Lynn said. "It looks like you brought something for us." She added, "You look unusually chipper."

"I've been busy too," Pete said. He smiled and started to open his package. "Let's sit down. You've got to taste this. You'll find out why I'm chipper."

Pete, Lynn and Harry sat down by a table near the door, and Pete placed the open package on the table. "Just dig in," he said, "with your fingers."

"That looks like the seeds you showed me a few months ago," Lynn said. "Like small lima beans." She ate a few of the cooked but now cool beans. "Mmm! Hey, that's good."

"Smells good, too." Harry tried some beans. "I wish you could've brought more. This is great."

"It's our first success story!" Pete exclaimed. "I'm now using all fifteen sections at One to grow just these beans. You've got to come and see it."

"These are the beans from the valley?" Lynn asked.

"Yeah." She had been too busy with Five and Six, Pete thought, to keep up with the details of his work. He had mentioned the beans in his reports, but only in a general way.

"And they respond well to cultivation?" Lynn asked.

"They sure do," Pete said. "One is full of beans. I'm going to start handing some out to the people soon. We've had to keep it quiet and well-guarded until now."

Lynn smiled. "This is just what I needed to perk me up." She looked at Harry. "You won't have to live with a grouch anymore."

Harry smiled.

"It took several plantings before we were able to grow a large crop," Pete said. He recalled how few seeds he had been able to gather from the sparse growth near the valley. "That's why it took so long. Once we got them on a steady nutrient supply, they really took off." He stood up. "Let's go have a look."

He smiled when Lynn and Harry stood up.

"I can't wait," Lynn said.

"Of course they don't grow as well in the factories as Earth crops once did," Pete said as he led the way out the door. He had never expected that they would, he thought. He knew he would have to adapt the beans to the factory conditions, and that could take a long time. "But they should do fine in the fields right away. I've worked out some general rules that should help."

*　　　　*　　　　*

After he showed them the bean crop at One, Pete invited Lynn and Harry to his residence. He quickly brewed some coffee, and then brought out his decanter and three cups. He sat down with his guests by his dining table. He poured full cups for Lynn and Harry, and a half cup for himself.

Lynn took a sip of coffee. "We'll get your beans out to the fields right away," she said. "I'll talk to the Council as soon as I can get them together." She took a notepad from her pocket and scratched out a few notes.

"Good," Pete said. "It won't be easy. We know you'll have to guard everything. But it's a start."

"Yeah, a good start," Harry said. He grinned. "Can we eat some more valley lima beans now?"

"How'd you know?" Pete asked. "I guess you just put two and two together."

"And I read your signs," Harry said, "in each of the four sections we visited. Beans, valley lima."

"Oh. Yeah." Pete smiled. "I do have some left over from analysis," he said. He got up and left the small room. He soon returned with a crock half full of cooked beans, still in their pods. He put the crock on the table, brought out three plates and sets of utensils, sat down and dished out three generous portions.

Harry took a few bites. "The pods are chewy." He looked at Pete and smiled. "I'm not complaining."

"They're very nourishing," Pete explained. "Almost as good as the beans themselves. We've done only limited analysis so far, but the results look good. For obvious reasons, I guess people will eat pod and all now. Maybe later we can process the pods in some way." He looked at Lynn.

"Yes, possibly animal feed when we start domesticating," she said. "We'll use everything." She hesitated, and then asked, "I'll get the beans to the fields, but you'll continue your search?"

"Yeah," Pete said, "we both know we can't rely for long on a single crop." He dished out more beans to Harry's plate.

"Good." Lynn scratched out a few more notes. "We'll have to terminate food sharing for a few months. The small production from Five and Six must feed the farm crews in the beginning. We'll fly it to the quadrants."

Pete understood. The farm workers would not be able to feed themselves by hunting like they had before. "I guess I'll be taking over from you there," he said. "I'll convert to the beans in Five and Six, section by section, and keep One in beans for a while. I'll continue to experiment in Two, Three and Four."

"Sounds like you have it all planned out." Lynn smiled.

"There's more," Pete said. "I didn't tell you about my new idea." He smiled.

"Can we do that later, Pete? I—" Lynn hesitated and looked at him. "Tell me about it," she said.

"I think I can speed it up," Pete said. "I can do in a day or so what's been taking months—the initial test of each new variety."

He took a quick breath. "Here's my idea," he continued. "I can check the characteristics of the plants I've tried. We have all kinds of data. Plant heights, leaf counts, and leaf shapes and sizes. Shapes, sizes and colors of blossoms and fruits. Roots. Vines. Seeds." He took another quick breath, and then added, "Jenny cataloged everything, all the smallest details, and her naming makes it easy to track things by relating to similar varieties of Earth crops." After Jenny's death he had followed through with the newer tests. *Not as skillfully as she*, he thought.

"We have measurements and observations throughout the life cycle," he said. "Seedlings, growing plants, mature and producing plants, plants gone to seed." Any of these multiple pieces of information, he thought, could be important in any particular case. "It's all there," he said, "and I'm going to use all of it."

"Use all the tests you've made so far?" Lynn asked.

"I know they're all failures," Pete said, "except for the beans. But there are degrees of failure." Jenny, and he, had also cataloged in detail how well each variety performed. "I'll try to find the common characteristics of the better ones." With several thousand varieties tested so far, he knew had a big enough sample.

"You'll be using all the results of the past years then?" Lynn asked again.

"Yeah," Pete said. "Without that I'd have nothing."

Lynn smiled. Pete noticed that she also had a tear in her eye.

"I haven't yet put any actual runs together, but a while back I converted some of my old programs," he said. "I've been busy with the beans." He hesitated, and then added, "If it works, I'll be using a modern computer to help solve our ancient problem."

Harry grunted and Pete looked at him.

Harry continued to munch on the valley lima beans. Between bites he said, "Only the computer is modern, Pete. The basic way of thinking is ancient."

"Yeah, I see what you mean," Pete said. The computer just made it more efficient, he thought, and made it possible to handle the more complicated problems. "More beans?"

"No, but thanks." Harry said. "This is the most I've eaten in one sitting since I got to this planet." He hesitated, and then said, "By the way, we have to start getting ready for the seventh ship." He finished the last of the beans on his plate.

"We need to learn how to quickly and accurately swing an axe," Pete said, "and I don't mean that as a joke."

"It'll work," Harry said. "I've examined the mechanisms."

"Yeah, Harry," Pete said. He smiled. "You and I make a great team. How can we lose?"

"Yeah." Harry smiled. He looked at Lynn. "Maybe we should get back to Six."

"Yes. I'll have to put together a Council presentation for restarting some of the farms," Lynn said. "I'm tired, but I have plenty of coffee."

Harry looked at Pete. "I guess we'll show you around our new home some other time," he said. "And my bigger shop."

"Our new home at the Landings," Lynn said, "and you saw only one room. But it looks like I'm going to spend time in the quadrants again."

When his guests had gone, Pete left his quarters and the ship. He climbed to the top of the big hill, and then stood quietly under a cloudy evening sky. He looked first at Jenny's sundial, and then up at the sky. He felt a tear in the corner of his eye. "I'll keep the promise you made," he whispered. "I will."

*   *   *

Spacecraft number seven arrived on schedule. Pete and Harry ran their three-hundred-meter dash and rushed aboard. As before they worked their way quickly, decorated with blast debris, through a sea of anonymous puzzled faces. Pete carried the axe in his hand, but he tried to keep it hidden from the newcomers.

He bumped into a newcomer, a woman, but he didn't stop to excuse himself. He didn't even look at her.

He rushed behind Harry and said, mostly to himself, "All those fat faces. They don't look like us." He mumbled, between breaths, "I hope I didn't scare her."

He felt compelled to look back. He took a quick glance, but the woman was lost in the streaming crowd. He shrugged off the strange feeling.

He and Harry quickly reached the location of the equipment, but didn't find what they had expected. All was different. Pete stood with the axe in his hand; he didn't know what to do with it.

He heard the rumble, and then the thunder. The minor quake passed across the spacecraft floor. Acrid smells filled the air. Smoke appeared by the cylindrical shapes at the back wall.

"You might as well put the axe down." Harry took a deep breath.

Pete looked up toward the ship compartment's ceiling. "There's another count for you, Adam, old buddy." He sat down on the floor to rest and catch his breath.

He watched while Harry, taking deep breaths, looked over the new equipment. Harry soon explained that the single silver and gray box in the center of the room housed both a population counter and a signal generator. The triggering mechanism was internal; there was no connecting cable to cut.

After a short rest, Pete helped Harry disconnect the device from the much larger hyper generator whose accessible parts covered most of the back wall. This time they had carried the few additional tools in tool belts. They also removed the leads from the counter's widespread outside and inside antenna systems.

Later, after the crowd had cleared, they, with the help of two others from Pete's crew, loaded the device into a terrie and took it to Harry's shop.

*   *   *

A few days after the arrival of ship number seven, Pete took some time away from his factory duties, in the afternoon, to visit Harry in his shop. He was curious about the new equipment, and he knew Harry would leave the Landings in a day or two to spend some time with Lynn in the East Quadrant. She was at the Landings for a series of Council meetings, but she was due back at the farms.

Pete stood and looked at the device lying on the shop floor.

"It's a totally new design," Harry said. "I'll figure it out and we'll know what to do with the next one." He looked at Pete. "This new counter is faster, so we'll also have to be."

Pete smiled. "We'll make it." He looked over the device, which was about two meters long, a meter high and half a meter wide. He thought of a silver and gray filing cabinet or disk locker, now lying on its side, with part of a middle drawer missing.

Harry stepped over to one end of the device. "Let's put it on the worktable," he said. "I think the two of us can lift it." He bent over and grabbed the end.

Pete grabbed the opposite end, and the two lifted the device from the floor. "The darn thing's heavy," Pete said when they had raised it about a quarter meter. "Wait!" He hadn't taken a good hold. His end slipped and fell on his right foot. "Damn!"

Harry lowered his end and helped Pete lift the other end from his foot. Pete mumbled a few well-chosen words.

"We'd better take a look at that foot," Harry said.

"It hurts like hell," Pete said. He limped, with Harry's help, to a chair, sat down and removed his boot and sock.

Harry took a quick look. "I can't tell if anything's broken," he said. "Let's get you to med."

"Yeah, to med," Pete mumbled.

"I'll get some people from—I guess it's Seven now," Harry said. "They just moved the medical people over there."

"It's at Seven now?" Pete grimaced. "I'd better sit still."

"They were getting crowded at Six," Harry said. "One of the new ship's dispensaries had more space."

*   *   *   *

Pete got into a terrie with the help of two men from the medical facility, and the trio departed for Landing-Seven. Pete grimaced every time the terrie went over a bump in the primitive new road, better described as a fresh set of tire tracks, from Six toward the appropriate entrance to Seven.

When they approached their destination the driver said, "You might be lucky, Mr. MacDonald. You might get the new doctor."

The other man smiled. "I'd like to break a finger," he said, "just to get the new doc to hold my hand."

Pete tried to smile, but his foot hurt too much.

"I hope you do get treated by the new doctor," the driver said. "You're a hero to all of us."

"Yeah," the other man said, "because of you we might get some meat on our bones again."

Pete watched the man curl skinny fingers around a skinny forearm.

He grimaced when the terrie hit another bump. He didn't care who treated his foot, just as long as it was done soon.

The driver brought the terrie to a halt. "Then we'll get back to being full-time medical technicians instead of armed guards for the factories."

"We haven't had to shoot anyone yet," the other man added, "but I've been seeing that in my dreams." He helped Pete get out of the terrie.

Pete tried to take a step without help. "Damn!" His foot had stiffened while he rode.

The two men helped him up the ramp and into the ship, and he sat down on a bench just inside the entrance.

"Good luck, Mr. MacDonald," the driver said. "We have to get back to guard duty. Be back later to return you to One."

"Thanks," Pete replied. "And drop the 'mister.' I'm just Pete."

Chapter 21

New Doc

Pete waited in the empty hallway near the entrance. His foot throbbed, but he felt a little better when he sat still.

A med tech named Sally, whom he knew casually, soon greeted him. He leaned on her and limped the short distance to the medical facility, and then sat down on a couch in the cramped waiting room.

"I believe the doctor is available now," Sally said. "I'll get your information later. Be right back."

Pete watched her disappear through a doorway on the opposite side of the room. He tried briefly to find a comfortable position for his foot, and then looked up when she returned. He started to stand up.

"I'll help you, Pete. Dr. Donner can see you right away."

Pete froze.

"She's new," Sally said. "Just came on the ship. This one."

Pete remained speechless, and in a half crouch supported by one hand on the couch. His foot hurt, he thought, but was it enough to cause delirium?

"Put your arm on my shoulder," Sally said. "Let's get your weight off that foot."

Pete complied. He limped, with Sally's help, into the examining room. He could've moved a little faster, but he dragged along and tried to compose himself.

When he entered, he looked at the new doc from across the room.

She looked at him. "Good morning, Sir. I'm Dr. Donner." Then, to Sally, "Why don't you help him into *that* chair, Sally." She pointed to one of several chairs, and then turned back to Pete.

Pete glanced around quickly to get his bearings. He saw chairs and a desk, an examining table, several photronic diagnostic machines, a small but busy disk rack next to a computer terminal, and a few shelves filled with medicine containers and various small instruments. He then studied the doctor.

The new doc was tall, with brown hair. *Or is it statuesque, with auburn hair?*

Pete maneuvered with Sally's help into the chosen chair. He kept his gaze on the new doc and sat down.

Dr. Donner glanced at Pete's foot, still from a distance. "That's good," she said. "You took your boot off already. Before the swelling. That'll help. I'll give you something for the pain, and then take a look at it." She picked up a photronic thermometer from a shelf. "I'll need your temperature first."

When the new doc came closer, Pete looked into her eyes. "Blue," he said. "Like I remembered. Deep blue."

"That's the bruise, Sir. It'll—" She dropped the thermometer. It broke into pieces when it hit the floor. "Oh! Oh, Pete!"

"Hello, Linda."

Linda Donner looked down at the shattered thermometer, and then ignored it. "It's you, Pete! I didn't even recognize you."

"It's me." Pete thought of his skinny and weathered face, and broke into a wide grin. "I've lost some weight. I'd like to get off this diet. It's killing me."

"Dr. Donner, you know Pete?" Sally asked. "I would've told you it was him."

Pete glanced at Sally. He then stared at Linda's well-fed face, which contrasted sharply with Sally's; Sally had been on the Pangaean diet for a long time. He felt his heartbeat pick up. Linda was just like he remembered. Old feelings stirred.

"You look so—" Linda hesitated, and then said, "I'm sorry. I'm still trying to assimilate what's happened here."

"That's all right," Pete said. He looked into her eyes again. "I can't believe this. I never expected to see you again."

"I'll leave you two alone," Sally said. "Be in the waiting room if you need me."

Pete tried to relax and engage in small talk while Linda picked up another thermometer and took his temperature. He took the oral painkiller she offered and sat still while she examined his foot.

"It's only a small fracture," Linda said. "The bruise is the worst part of it." She then bound foot and ankle with a simple flexible bandage.

"You'll have to keep your weight off that foot for three or four weeks at least," she said when she finished. "We'll get you a pair of crutches. That'll work better than a brace for now."

"Yeah, I'll manage," Pete said. "That's not as long as I expected."

"You've changed, Pete," Linda said. She pulled a chair close to Pete's and sat down. "Oh, not about the weight loss."

"I understand," Pete said. "And you haven't changed." She hadn't changed at all, he thought briefly. She was still the young university student who had been so excited about the medical institute. He smiled. Of course she had aged, he chided himself; his imagination was playing tricks on him.

"I haven't seen you in over thirteen years," Linda said. "Oh, it's so good to see you. I didn't know if I'd find you." She hesitated a moment, and then said, "You'll have to tell me about everything that's happened. The briefings didn't say much."

Pete noticed her well-fed face turn a little red. "Here we'd call it twenty years," he said. Linda, he thought, had not shown any interest in PANS when the plan was first announced. *Could it be that she came here just to be with me?*

"Pete, are you—"

He thought he knew what she was trying to ask. "I'm not married," he said. "Are you?" He believed he knew the answer; she wore no ring.

"No," she said. "I—"

Sally came back. "Excuse me, Dr. Donner. I hate to break up this reunion, but you have another patient."

"We'll talk later," Pete said. "I have a lot to tell you. I'm happy to see you, but I wish you hadn't come here. Don't take that wrong."

"Oh, it's all right, Pete. I understand. I'll find you as soon as I can get away." Linda stood up, and helped him get up.

Pete's heartbeat, which had almost returned to normal, picked up again when he felt her touch. "I'll be at One," he said. "Sally can tell you how to get a terrie and locate me. I have a meeting in a few hours, but we'll have some time to talk."

Linda gave Sally brief instructions about Pete's crutches.

Pete then leaned on Sally and limped to the outer room. She took some information from him while he sat, and then brought out a pair of crutches and showed him how to use them. She then accompanied him to the entrance where the other medical technicians had left him an hour earlier.

He sat alone and waited for their return. His foot felt better; the painkiller worked well.

He hadn't thought much about Linda for a long time now, he told himself, even though he had dreamed about little else during the voyage and his first few years in Pangaea. *What is* she *thinking?* She looked happy to see him. During their short talk she had seemed to be ignoring the grim reality of her new home.

That won't last, he thought. He had seen her next patient. While fitting and adjusting the crutches, Sally had explained that the man had fallen out of a tree while trying to reach some small pieces of fruit. The new doc would not need her scanner to locate the fracture in his bony arm.

Pete managed a smile. He was on his way toward changing all that. His broken foot would slow him down only a little.

*   *   *

Two hours later Pete sat by the main computer terminal in his office, the section three control room at One, and examined the results for some new native plants. He looked up and smiled when Linda arrived. He greeted her, used his new crutches to ease himself up from the chair and asked her to sit in a chair next to his desk. He then hobbled around behind the desk, sat down and laid the crutches across his knees.

"I stopped by some trees on the way over here," Linda said. "Oh, what a sight! Even in this situation." She smiled.

"I'll show you around the facilities sometime," Pete said, "and the surrounding area." He pointed to the crutches. "When I get used to these things." He half-smiled and added, "I'd ask you about Earth, but you've been long gone, too."

"A hundred trillion kilometers," Linda said. "I talked to Adam about that before I left. It was so incomprehensible, but now I'm here on Earth-Twin." She corrected herself. "I guess it's Pangaea now."

"Linda, welcome to Pangaea." Pete smiled. "That's our continent. The planet is still Earth-Twin." He hesitated, and then said, "About my departure from Earth. I apologize."

Linda interrupted. "Let's not dwell on that. It was my fault, too."

She was too generous, Pete thought. It was his entire fault, from the beginning. "I regretted it," he said.

Linda interrupted again. "Sally said you're a hero."

"Yeah, I've been getting that treatment," Pete said. He shook his head. "It doesn't really belong to me. We have a lot to talk about."

He explained some of the situation, and added much to the scant information Linda had obtained during her few days in Pangaea. All newcomers received a series of briefings, but their numbers were great and their immediate needs were pressing. Only minimal information could be given. Sally and other medical people may have filled in some of the details, he thought, but he wanted her to hear it from his perspective.

"So that's how it is," he concluded. "Now you can see why I'm not as happy as I could be to see you. You'd be better off on crowded Earth." A few years ago, he thought, he could not have *imagined* saying something like that to Linda. Now he wasn't sure what he imagined, but those blue eyes still intrigued him just like they had so long ago at that Spring Dance.

"Oh, Pete, I'm right where I belong." Linda wiped a tear from her well-fed cheek. "I didn't know what to expect when our food factories broke down a few weeks ago. I didn't anticipate anything like this." She hesitated, and then said, "I only started to understand when those two ragged men rushed aboard just after we landed. One of them bumped into me and just kept going."

Pete now recalled that collision, and that strange feeling of recognition even though he hadn't even looked at her. He had ignored it then. He had been in a hurry. Out of two million rushing people, he thought, he had bumped into Linda.

He could explain that later, he told himself, when he had more time. "We do need more medical help here," he said. "I'm sure you already know that. But let me tell you what we're doing about it. We've started to make real progress."

"You've really—" Linda hesitated. "Oh, never mind my babbling. Tell me."

"It took a long time," Pete said. He smiled. "But I found these native beans."

"Beans?"

"They look like the lima beans we used to grow on Earth," Pete said. "I've been able to grow them in the ships' factories, and we've started growing them on the field farms." He hesitated, and then added, "It's difficult to keep other people from picking them before they're fully mature, so our initial yields have been small. We use only small fields so we can guard them."

"You mean they steal the beans?" Linda asked.

"Well, yeah," Pete said, "but they're not thieves. They're just hungry."

Linda shifted in her chair. "I'm sorry, Pete," she said. "I guess I still need some adjustment."

Pete propped up his crutches so that he could use them to help him get up from his chair. "It *is* good to see you, Linda, but I have to meet with Lynn now. You probably have work to do, too."

"I have time to talk a little longer," Linda said.

"You remember Lynn Higami, my agriculture professor? Lynn's in charge of all the farms. She's here now to discuss some policy decisions with the Council. She keeps me up-to-date." Pete eased himself up.

"What policy decisions?"

"They're kind of complicated," Pete said. "We can talk about it when we have more time."

Linda got up from her chair. "All right, Pete. It's so great to talk to you. Just to be close to you again. We'll talk again soon." She glanced at his bandaged foot. "And I'll look after your foot." She looked at him.

"Yeah." Pete hesitated, and then said, "I just can't believe you're here. I mean, I'm astonished!" He balanced on his crutches as Linda made ready to leave. He thought about taking her into his arms and holding her close, but he made no move toward her. It wasn't the crutches, he told himself, since that wouldn't have stopped him. Her look invited him, but he couldn't follow through.

*   *   *

Pete met with Lynn in his office soon after Linda left. The two sat by his desk.

He explained his injury and Linda's arrival, and got to the subject of the meeting. "Tell me about the new policy on raiding."

"The Council has given their official approval for deadly force," Lynn said, "in cases other than straight self-defense."

"Yeah, the edict." Pete grimaced. The unofficial "suggestion" had now become law. "We've had rumors here."

"Pete, I'm in a quandary. I don't want to order the killing of hungry people."

Pete nodded.

"I did manage to keep the final authority," Lynn said. "For now." She shook her head. "But if I can't control it, the Council may take it out of my hands."

Pete understood the situation. While they delayed, people starved. They might have to kill now to allow greater numbers to survive later. "What can we *do*?"

"There just has to be some other way," Lynn said. "But I gave the managers of the quadrants the authority to do what they must."

"We'll have to hang in there," Pete said.

"West is the worst now," Lynn said, "like before."

"Yeah," Pete said, "and we know it's going to be rougher everywhere for the next few months with the new arrivals."

He thought of Hope Valley and the people who struggled just to live another day. *Is Sylvia still alive? Rip? His wife? Have the grasshoppers and the ripening berries run out like had the birds?*

"The Council directed the air crews to fly most newcomers to locations far from the farms to try to minimize raiding," Lynn said. "I guess we'll all just do what we have to do."

Pete grimaced. *What we have to do?* He had heard rumors about cannibalism in some of the more remote regions of all four quadrants, but so far none had been substantiated. He decided not to bring this up with Lynn. "By the way, how're you doing with the beans?" he asked.

"We've had to adapt some new methods," Lynn said. She nodded. "But they're growing just fine."

"New methods?" Pete asked.

"In a way it's easier." She explained, "Wild strains almost grow themselves. They don't need as much care. The major problem is that they try to propagate themselves. Natural reproduction. We have to make sure they don't do this in the wrong place at the wrong time."

"Like growing weeds," Pete said.

Lynn nodded.

"But this time we have the correct weeds." Pete smiled.

He was silent for a moment. Then, "Lynn, my matching system! I finished it and did a test. I scored a direct hit."

"Direct hit?" Lynn asked.

Pete's system, which he recalled he had partially explained to Lynn back when he was still working out his procedure, examined all the crop data and sorted the common characteristics of the "better" of the many crop tests. It then perused all the data that he had been able to gather for a subject new sample, compared with the sorted data and gave a probability of success based on the old tests.

"I chose twenty of the old tests—our failures—at random," he said. "I removed their data from the database, one set at a time, and entered that data as a 'new' crop. Each came up with a probability of less than ten percent, as I expected. Then I tested the beans. Direct hit! Eighty-six percent probability!"

"Pete, what can I say?" Lynn smiled.

Pete wasn't finished. "I can screen new plants in not much more than the time it takes to measure them and enter the data." He could now, he thought, perform the one-month to three-month planting experiments only for those with a good score. He told himself that it would work, although he understood the peril of working with statistics rather than with fundamental principles. He expressed this simply: "There'll be false alarms, but I know it will speed things up a lot in the long run."

He noticed that Lynn had a tear in the corner of her eye. He had seen that before when he first told her of his progress: a smile and a tear. He shrugged it off. She was just happy about it, he thought.

"I have to go now—back to the quadrant," Lynn said. "I was going to wait a day for Harry to come back with me, but he's going to be delayed for a while." She stood up.

"Yeah, I guess he needs more time on the new equipment." Pete stood up and balanced on his crutches.

"I'll have to talk to Linda sometime," Lynn said. "I wonder if she'll remember me."

"She does," Pete said.

*   *   *

When the initial shock of Linda's arrival subsided, Pete was still unable to renew their old relationship. He got together with her and talked over old times at the university, but something always held him back. When he no longer needed his crutches and medical attention, he saw her only occasionally.

A few months after her arrival, he dropped in at the medical facility at Landing-Seven in the early evening. He found her alone. "Linda, do you have time to talk?"

"I'll make time for you, Pete." She smiled and pointed to a chair in the waiting room. She sat on another.

Pete sat down. "I need some help from the medical group," he said.

Linda's smile faded away. Pete noted how much thinner her face had become.

She nodded.

"You already know about the beans," he said. "I'm trying to look now at some rice-like plants. When I find the right ones, could you get some people to do some analysis?" He tried to avoid looking into her blue eyes, but was unsuccessful.

"Yes, I'll be glad to help," Linda answered.

"I've been narrowing down my search," Pete said. "If I can concentrate now on the rice-like plants, I have a better chance to find something in less time. At least to keep people alive until I can find other things later."

"That sounds workable." Linda smiled again.

"Good," Pete said. "This gives me a focus." He had to avoid her eyes, he thought again. "Thanks. I'll see you later." He stood up.

"Can't we visit a little longer, Pete?" Linda rose from her chair. "I don't expect any patients this evening."

"Maybe later," he said. He turned toward the door. "I have to get back to work."

*   *   *

Pete arrived back at Landing-One. He parked his terrie and walked to the big hill. He climbed to the summit and stood in the clearing near Jenny's sundial. He looked west, toward setting Tau Ceti. Half the red-orange globe was visible. A bright red color tinted the scattered clouds, and the hills slowly faded from light green to dark green, toward black.

He gazed at the setting "sun" and the array of colors displayed for his eyes alone. He imagined that Jenny was out there somewhere. *She turned on this display for me. She always tried to get me to look at the colors.*

He was making progress now, he told himself. Her "tribes of the orange sun" would become a great civilization in a beautiful new land, just like Earth had planned so long ago.

He thought about Linda, and he now knew why he could not get close to her. He had asked Jenny to marry him, and he had been sincere about it—although clumsy. He had wanted her with him on the plains, and she had died because he had not communicated with her. He fancied that he could communicate with her now, on some psychological plane; he could somehow overcome the great gulf that separated the living from the dead. He would lose that attachment, he thought, if he renewed his old relationship with Linda.

He stood quietly for a moment and listened to the evening sounds, but he found no solution to his problem. When he tried to think of Linda and Jenny at the same time, reason failed him.

He looked at the sundial in the semi-darkness, and a strange thought came to mind. Jenny's small metal sundial was trying to tell him something. Or Jenny was, via the sundial. *Why did she erect it? What message did she leave for me?* He gazed at the sundial for a few moments, but gained no insight. He turned and headed back down the hill toward another late night in his "laboratory."

As he walked he thought of Jenny's note of long ago. Could she have "planted" her message to him a year before she wrote the note? Back when she had erected the sundial? Maybe his earlier—and very questionable—interpretation had been wrong. He shook his head. *Do any of these thoughts make sense?* It was all so cryptic, but Jenny had always been careful with details. Everything in that note, he told himself, meant something.

*   *   *

A few months later Pete was well on his way in his rice search when Harry Sigcrist came over from the East Quadrant. There, Pete knew, Harry had worked on the communication link between the East Quadrant and the other areas as well as helped Lynn.

Pete met Harry in the photronics shop at Six, in the late morning, and they stood by the worktable.

"It's good to be back at the Landings again," Harry said, "but I'll miss Lynn. I hated to leave her at this time, but we have to get ready for number eight."

"Yeah, I heard she had to order the killing of some people a few weeks ago." Pete didn't know the details.

Harry added these. "Seventeen were killed, all raiders. Others were wounded, including guards. We tried to avoid killing, and we didn't want to use the rifles. But *they* had some weapons—and used them. Everything was so chaotic."

Pete grimaced.

"More of the wounded died later," Harry said, "because of their poor condition. We couldn't save them. Lynn was devastated. She couldn't sleep for days afterward."

"Yeah." She had tried so hard to avoid killing, Pete thought, but she had to act.

"I was one of the shooters," Harry said. He hesitated, and then added, "I was the 'captain.'"

Pete looked at him. "You, Harry?"

"I took the job because Lynn found it so difficult to assign it to anyone," Harry said. "I couldn't let her do it herself, and there wasn't any time to work something out."

"I suspected it would come to that in the East," Pete said. "Like the other quadrants." He raised his hands in a gesture of futility.

"After the shooting, they got the fields planted again," Harry said. "They're growing well now, but when the new people arrive?" He looked at Pete. "Lynn needs to expand the fields, so the guards will be spread more thinly when we'll need them the most."

"Yeah." With his new rice she might have to expand even more than she expected, Pete thought.

"We weren't expecting *that* raid," Harry said. "We thought we'd be at peace for a time since it'd been a while since the last arrival. But a group of more than a hundred just came in out of the hills. We had to shoot because they were destroying a large part of several fields. They were eating everything in sight and wouldn't stop. They fired at us when we ordered them to stop." He grimaced, and then added, "Pete, I keep finding myself making excuses."

Harry, Pete thought, also did only what he had to do. He changed the subject. "Harry, we need to talk about the ship."

"Yeah," Harry asked, "are you still interested?" He picked up an axe and cutting pliers from the worktable. "I know you're busy."

"I'll help," Pete said. He smiled. "We're on a new track now, and I *am* busy. But we've narrowed it down to two rice varieties." He took the tools from Harry.

"Rice now?" Harry asked.

"Yeah, rice," Pete said. "They're a lot like what used to be called 'upland' rice on Earth. I believe they'll do well on the farms. I think I mentioned it before, at least to Lynn. I'll have to talk to her, so we can get it to the fields." He looked at the axe and cutting pliers in his hands. "Yeah, I'll help you with the signal."

"Great!" Harry pointed to the tools. "We'll both carry these. We'll have to run as hard as we can, and start a little closer than before. Maybe two hundred meters. We'll have to shield ourselves under tarps during the touchdown.

"Whoever gets to the equipment first," he added, "has to take off a small panel with the axe and then cut one fiber. We'll have to practice."

Pete nodded. He may be the one to get there first, he thought. He was sure that he had been eating a little better than Harry recently, since Harry had been in the quadrant. Pete already felt stronger than he had in several years.

"I'm still interested in the signals, Harry," he said. "I believe there's a lot more to our struggle than just our survival here. We have to get the information back to Adam. He'll need all the help he can get."

"You and Adam must've been great friends." Harry smiled.

"Yeah," Pete said. "It's curious. In our last face-to-face talk before I left Earth, Adam had a slip of the tongue. He started to say 'keep in touch.' I joked about it. I guess I said 'you never know,' or something like that." He shrugged.

*   *   *

When the ship touched down, Pete, in the coolness of early morning, threw off his tarp and raced Harry to the entrance. He ignored the dust and other blast debris. He quickly took the lead and rushed aboard the ship. He pushed past well-fed faces, lost track of Harry and reached the device. He located the panel and swung the axe. He reached inside and cut the fiber, and then fell to his knees. He was exhausted.

Harry arrived.

"Think I," Pete asked between breaths, "made it?"

Harry chuckled. "No rumble," he said. He took a breath. "No quake."

Pete, still on his knees, looked toward the ceiling. "Adam, old buddy," he said, "this one will be a little late."

Harry sat down on the floor, next to the silent equipment. "You sure showed me up," he said. "This race was no contest."

"Yeah." He owed that to the Landings' now slightly more adequate diet of beans and rice, Pete thought.

He rose to his feet and looked up at the ceiling again. In his mind he associated Earth with the local "up" direction, a psychological direction of interstellar space. Harry would send the 'starvation' message in a few days; Earth would get that message an Earth year from now. Until then Earth would have to go by only the census numbers. Was there anything in the later numbers, he asked himself, other than just their being much lower than expected? Could anyone make any sense of it?

If anyone can, he thought, *Adam can. Adam had expected something like this.*

Pete sat down on the floor and leaned against the wall of the equipment room. He glanced at the rushing crowd outside the door. "Looks like it'll be a while," he said. He leaned back and closed his eyes.

Chapter 22

A Perfect Experiment

Adam skipped his usual lunch at the office and left early. He believed he could show that starvation was killing the colonists, more than a hundred trillion kilometers away, by the millions. He must, he told himself, work out the details before he presented his idea to the others. He planned to consult some very old disks in his home library. Once he obtained the data, he thought as he exited the building, the calculations would be simple.

He negotiated the city street, and ignored the noon crowds. Counts four through seven had all come in at just over eight million, he thought, so the colonist population was apparently stabilizing at around six million. He had tossed that around in his mind at least a hundred times in the past few weeks. Now, would his calculation give that number? Something close? All depended on this; it was all Earth knew about the situation on Earth-Twin. The team had not reached a conclusion at the morning's meeting, he told himself, simply because no one could give a satisfactory explanation for the number pattern.

At home he sought, found and dusted off several disks. He perused them at the computer terminal in his study. He gathered his data and performed the few simple, but necessary, calculations.

Later in the afternoon he was still in the study when he heard Nola arrive. He stood up, stretched and rubbed his neck. He walked into the living room and looked at her. "Nola, the colonists *are* starving to death," he said. "I'm sure of it now."

She looked at him.

"I did some calculations this afternoon," he said. "Let me explain it to you. I want to see if you agree."

Nola nodded.

Adam stepped up close and kissed her. He then turned his head toward the study. "Let's go in there," he said.

As he led her into the study he heard her say, "I was in your office just before coming home. Coffee all over the place."

"A little accident," he said, "when I had my revelation."

The two sat by the desk, where a number of papers were spread out. A small stack of disks lay near the edge of the desk closest to the terminal. He picked up a paper, glanced at it, and then put it down again.

"If you recall," he said, "the exploration team reported that a large part of Earth-Twin's land looks very much like the area once called the Great Plains right here on our continent."

"I remember," Nola said.

Adam pointed to the stack of disks. "I looked at a few of my old disks. One especially."

He picked up a disk from the stack. "I scanned the chapters describing the middle and later parts of the nineteenth century, the time of the great migration westward.

"The text is a treatise on how the newcomers made much of the land productive. The earlier inhabitants, before the migration, had required considerably more Great Plains land to support each human individual, since many of those earlier groups lived off that land without agriculture. I needed estimates of that." He put the disk back on the stack.

Adam's disk had given a series of numbers for the acreage per person, which was reckoned home range area divided by population. The varying amounts of tree and brush cover, water availability, details of climate and other local differences meant that no single number could be characteristic of the entire Great Plains region. Even the series of numbers was uncertain, he thought, since in those days any census would have been, at best, just a close guess or an anecdote from tribal "memory."

He assumed that availability of food, rather than disease, war or predation, had been the primary factor limiting the populations that didn't farm. He wanted to get to his conclusion, so he didn't voice the details. Nola never needed excessive explanation anyway, he told himself.

He continued. "Earth-Twin has an estimated land area in the range of one hundred and seventy-eight to one hundred and eighty-six million square kilometers."

Nola nodded.

"By analogy with Earth's Great Plains, let's assume that it takes about thirty square kilometers to support each colonist in a hunter/gatherer lifestyle on Earth-Twin." This number was near the upper limit from the disk, he thought. He had, in the afternoon, converted from acre measure.

He picked up the paper that he had glanced at earlier. "We can then calculate how many people the planet can support without agriculture," he said. "I'm assuming that all of the great continent on Earth-Twin is usable for hunting and gathering. We can expect that the colonists can spread quickly over the entire continent and take advantage of all available natural food. They have the aircraft. They have that technology."

He also assumed that his chosen divisor, thirty square kilometers, characterized the Great Plains people who didn't use horses. The Earth-Twin colonists were, once distributed over the continent, afoot. The engineers had designed Earth-Twin's aircraft only for mass transport; the craft could not help in hunting and gathering. The all-terrain land vehicles, the "terries," were few in number and limited in capability.

He held up the sheet of paper and showed the scribbled notes to Nola. "Look at these results," he said. "Using my assumptions, Earth-Twin's natural resources can support a human population in the range 5,900,000 to 6,200,000. In rounded numbers."

He realized that his result was open to serious questions. He didn't know the character of the entire Earth-Twin continent; it wasn't all like the Great Plains. The time scale was distorted; such a limit might be valid only over much longer time periods. His calculation was not fully objective; he had picked the number from the disk that gave the result he needed. He summarized these concerns simply: "It's all a guess. I hope an educated guess. I just wanted to see if I could get close."

Nola nodded. "Earth-Twin's not exactly like Earth," she said. "Different animals and plants. But this is intriguing." She hesitated a moment, and then looked at Adam. "Why, it's incredible!"

"This match is too compelling," he said. "I have to believe that the human population on Earth-Twin is stabilizing at a hunter/gatherer limit—a fundamental limit imposed by nature."

A fundamental limit? Yes. He grimaced. Theory or history might suggest a number, he thought, but the only way to be sure would be to do the experiment. He hadn't thought of it that way.

The PANS team had inadvertently set up a perfect experiment. The experimenters controlled how people and supplies could get on, or off, the planet. Except for a relatively small number of births, the experimenters increased the population at a known and fixed rate. They measured exact results.

Adam picked up his coffee cup from a corner of the desk. It was empty. He picked up his decanter. It also was empty.

The experimenters had their results, he thought. Earth-Twin's great continent could support six million people, more or less, as hunters and gatherers.

The PANS experiment was also a test of human ingenuity. The subjects, he told himself, must find a way to adapt. How many more lives would be lost before they accomplished that? Would they continue in this way until all ships arrived? This experiment could end with just six million left out of the forty million sent. *Thirty-four million could die. Or more, counting shipboard births and births on the planet.*

Bill Avery had called the whole thing an experiment.

Nola's voice brought Adam back to their conversation. "What could've happened to the farms and factories?" she asked.

"I haven't pinned that down," he said, "but I carried my number research another step. I looked up the estimated population for early Earth, before crop growing and animal domestication. For a long time—up until about ten thousand years ago—the population remained very near ten million. Or less. A very rough estimate, of course." He pointed to his scribbled numbers again. "Given the differences, even this close a match is amazing."

"The PANS groups made those plans so carefully," Nola said. She shook her head.

"I don't know yet what went wrong," Adam said, "but I'm working on a couple of possibilities. You can help me sort them out."

He smiled. "By the way, darling, you're the one who gave me the answer. Just as I once predicted you would."

Nola sat a little straighter. "I did? How'd I manage that?"

"Your question from that first earth comm," Adam said, "overcame my mental block. That's when I dropped my coffee in my office."

"I was serious when I asked that question," Nola said. "When I was little, I didn't understand about the food factories or the old farms. Food just came from stores. And photronic storage bins." She got up, and picked up the coffee decanter. "I'm going to refill this," she said. "You look like you need it."

Adam smiled when she returned from the autoprep with the full decanter a few minutes later and sat down again. "Thanks, darling. I sure do need it." He filled his cup and took a deep swallow.

"What went wrong?" he thought out loud. "A mistake in planning? Maybe. Or in motivation." He shook his head. "There's a flaw in our great plan," he said, "and now the colonists must be living from day to day. Like wild animals." *Those wild animals are armed with a few modern weapons*, he thought, *but they are still wild animals.*

He picked up the paper again and looked at it. "I guess they could go on like this and slowly increase their numbers while they put the pieces together, so to speak," he said. "They're all well trained and highly motivated." He shook his head again. "But the plan is dumping more than two million hungry people into their midst each year."

He looked at Nola. "What does a biologist think about all this? You know more about such things than I do."

"If you're right," Nola answered, "they could be living like wild animals. A hunting and gathering human population would certainly be limited by its natural resources. It's called the 'carrying capacity of the natural environment.'" She hesitated, and then added, "As far as I know, no such natural population-limiting processes such as starvation have been observed on Earth in my lifetime." She looked at Adam. "Or even in my biology professors' lifetimes. At least not for large animals."

"Yes," Adam said, "I guess we lost much more than we realized when the large wild animals disappeared from Earth."

"Very few people appreciate that anymore," Nola commented. "My professors did mention something, but they talked only about insect populations."

"We may be learning that old lesson all over again," Adam said. He nodded. Earth was still home to the small wild animals, including insects, he thought, but it wasn't intuitive to relate their populations to that of people even though they obeyed the same natural laws.

"Adam, I just had a terrible thought," Nola said. "Just what we need right now."

He looked at her.

"Humans are not natural to the Earth-Twin ecosystem," she said. "If they're living like wild animals, they could unbalance that natural world. Remember what you said about not taking domestic animals? We don't know how delicate the balance may be. If they destroy the ecosystem, things could get a lot worse."

"I see your point," Adam said. He grimaced. "The next few signals could be very enlightening."

Nola nodded.

Adam picked up his cup and took a sip of coffee.

✻   ✻   ✻

After a light evening meal, Adam contacted Rob King via voice-visual and set up an emergency team meeting for the next morning. He prepared a few visuals for the meeting, and then sat is his study and waited for Nola, who was attending to other duties.

He thought of Pete; he wanted to ask him what could go wrong with the factories. If Pete was still alive, Adam told himself, he was right in the middle of the problem. Pete was where he could do the most good, Adam concluded, as he had earlier in the day.

Nola soon joined him. The two stayed awake half the night and discussed possible reasons for the failure.

One possible cause was most compelling; the planet's high gravity had bothered Adam in the past. He wondered if it could have slowed progress just enough to make the "careful" plan go awry. Both the farms and the food factories would be affected. There would be no escape.

Adam tried to catch a few hours of sleep in the very early morning, but the question would not go away. He recalled that the team had discussed the gravity difference several times long ago, and that even he had glossed over it when he had talked to others outside the team. How could the team, and he, have missed something that should have been so evident?

Chapter 23

Expedience

Adam watched Administrator King walk up to the front of the meeting room, and then looked at his cup. He would need his coffee, he thought, after a nearly sleepless night. He picked up the full cup and glanced at Nola, who sat next to him. She smiled. He put the cup down and looked back at King.

"I appreciate all of you showing up at this early hour," King said to the team and the reps. He looked at Adam. "Adam says he can explain the numbers. So we will get right to it. Adam?" King sat down at the head of the elliptical table.

Adam picked up his cup and walked to the front. He took a quick sip and placed the cup on the podium.

He pushed the podium buttons that operated the front display wall, and then waved his hand to bring up the calculation he had explained to Nola the day before. He looked at his hastily prepared visual of the arithmetic and recalled how, twenty-three years earlier, he had first seen full-scale visuals of the orange sun on the same wall.

He described his calculation, and then waved his hand again. One of the old orange sun visuals appeared on the lower half of the wall, below his arithmetic. This one showed the low orange sun over rolling hills and scattered trees.

He pointed to the arithmetic. "So that's what I put together after our meeting yesterday," he said. "The calculation is simple and inexact, but I believe it's adequate when we consider the limited information we have. I know this isn't proof, but the close match has to make it worth pursuing."

He mentioned the early human population on Earth. "We've had a similar situation here. For a long time, Earth's human numbers remained stabilized at about ten million. This number increased only after our ancestors started growing crops and domesticating animals."

Adam waved his hand again, and the number 10,000,000 appeared next to the Earth-Twin numbers. He picked up his cup and stepped back, to give his audience a moment to question all he had displayed.

He knew that the numerical Earth comparison was questionable, but he felt comfortable with it. He and Nola had discussed many of the details the previous evening. Earth's land area was somewhat smaller than Earth-Twin's, but it had apparently supported a larger non-technical human population. Large rain forests and other kinds of dense forests had covered much of early Earth. Such forests changed the situation, but he wasn't sure which way. They were sparse on Earth-Twin.

Stage of evolution might also play a part. Even for early people, he thought, Earth was at least a hundred million years farther "advanced" in biological evolution than present-day Earth-Twin.

Nola had given him more reason for early Earth's larger number. Humans evolved on Earth, and thus were able to fit in. They had time to learn the local tricks of survival, as they slowly spread over the Earth.

Another complication remained. On both early Earth and present-day Earth-Twin, some land was not livable, not suitable for hunting and gathering. Simple comparison of total land areas was certainly inadequate.

No one raised an immediate question, so Adam stepped back to the podium and said, "Six million observed on Earth-Twin? Ten million estimated for early Earth? For our purposes, they're the same."

He took a quick drink of coffee, and then put the cup on the podium. "Despite all our careful planning," he said, "I now have to believe that our colonists on Earth-Twin are starving to death."

Adam watched the team members and reps glance at each other, and then look back at him. Even Nola grimaced.

He went on. "I believe that the early attempts at agriculture, both farms and factories, were unsuccessful. In a moment I will explain what I think may have caused this failure." He glanced over the whole audience and added, "Please speak up if I say anything you don't believe. I realize this is speculation."

He paused for a few seconds, and then went on. "So let's assume the colonists are forced to live off the land. After they reached the apparent limit of around six million, the arrival of more than two million new people each year must've caused massive starvation until the population again stabilized near the limit." He looked at King, who had raised his hand. "Rob?"

"They do have technology other than agricultural facilities and equipment," King said. "They are not fully dependent on nature."

"I suppose they're able to use most of the equipment we sent with them," Adam agreed. "The aircraft must be performing as we planned, since otherwise they'd be on foot. The few terries wouldn't be sufficient.

"Afoot, the new arrivals couldn't spread out and take advantage of the vast continent quickly enough to avoid even greater starvation. The time scale demands modern transportation simply to take advantage of what nature has to offer.

"They do have a few weapons for hunting," he added, "but even the most sophisticated weapons aren't much good when they run out of things to hunt. I don't expect much help from fishing. We haven't yet included that part of our technology." Adam's group had chosen no one with boatbuilding expertise for the first twenty colonization ships.

"The situation is similar for other exploitations of the waters," Adam said. PANS did not include Earth algae and seaweeds and their facilities in the shipboard food factories, he thought, because that technology had not been ready for space use. Sea farming equipment and personnel had also not been included, although that was in the plan for later ships.

No one appeared to have another immediate comment, so Adam continued his earlier argument. "A technological civilization on an earthlike planet can support many more than six million people. Consider the twenty-five billion now on Earth." He recalled that he had referred to Earth's situation as "holding on by a thread," when he had first talked to Bill Avery more than two decades earlier.

"It takes time and effort to put it all together," he said. "Enough people have to have enough free time, even while they solve the initial problems. But hunting and gathering on primitive Earth-Twin, for such large numbers, must impose an *enormous* opportunity cost."

Earth's population had advanced from small hunter/gatherer groups to a much larger technological society over thousands of years, he thought. The attempt to populate Earth-Twin had been in progress only a few years. The team had planned for the shipboard factories and the early farms to feed the people. That would have freed up the labor and talents of many, who could call on knowledge and technology that early humans on Earth had not yet possessed. Instead, he told himself, most, if not all, of the colonists must now wander the land in a desperate search for food.

Adam looked at his audience. Several people were writing notes. He took another sip of coffee.

"I suspect that," he said, "after the fourth and each of the later ships landed and unloaded its passengers, massive starvation cut the numbers until the total population reached at or just below the six million, and then stabilized somewhat until the next shipload."

He glanced at Nola. "I say just below because the hungry humans might have depleted the natural food supply by overhunting and over-gathering. But this may be just a temporary setback." Earth-Twin was a pristine planet, he thought, and the continent was very large. The relatively small number of humans could not hunt and gather everywhere at the same time. Areas deserted because food became scarce would have time to recover. The plants could quickly grow back, and the mostly small animals could quickly rebuild their populations to near original.

He glanced at Nola again. "That is, if the new human predators didn't upset the natural balance too much. But the great size of the continent may mitigate such damage."

Adam picked up his coffee cup but didn't drink. Not all this was new to him. He had considered a starvation scenario a long time ago, as an academic exercise at the university. That study had been about Earth, about what could happen after a massive technological failure. He had considered a number of causes, primarily global natural disasters, and a number of failures that could result in widespread and persistent shortages of food. A number pattern in the results, when dealing with a very large technology-dependent population like Earth's, had intrigued and worried him back then: The larger the initial population, the smaller the final number of survivors. *Very hungry survivors.*

Only yesterday, he thought, was he able to tie that old exercise to the present Earth-Twin crisis. It wasn't easy to make the connection. On overcrowded and wilderness-barren Earth, the situation was not so clean cut and the calculation not so straightforward. The few million people left alive, he told himself, would have to "hunt" rats, crows and cockroaches. *And each other.*

He took a sip of coffee, and then looked at Nola and winked. The insight had come from a little girl's innocent question. She winked back, and he wondered if she knew what he was thinking about.

Adam looked over the team. "I'll finish this up," he said. He mentioned birth rate on the ships and on the planet, possible birth control and an assumed nomadic lifestyle. He concluded, "Our observed number of just over eight million can be expected."

A team member commented, "People aren't going to starve willingly. Things could get pretty rough, in addition to hunger."

Adam thought of Louisville. That had been only a threat of hunger, many years ago.

"But please continue, Adam," the man said. "You said that you have an idea about why agriculture may have failed."

Adam stood next to the orange sun visual on the lower half of the front display wall. He looked at it briefly, and then back at the team and the reps. "Yes, I do." He told himself that he must use "the cause" to prove that the PANS plan could never be a way to handle excess human population. He must show that the plan had been doomed to failure from the beginning.

He took a deep breath, and glanced again at the orange sun visual. "We must examine the major differences between Earth and Earth-Twin. I think the best possibility is the larger gravity. Ordinary crops thrived in the lower gravity of Mars and the moon. And the orbiting stations. But we may've been misled by those easy successes." Adam looked at Hugh Bruce, who had raised his hand.

"Didn't the explorers try some growing experiments?" Bruce asked. "I remember we did talk about the high gravity."

"I plan to look over some of the early records right after this meeting," Adam answered. "We must've assumed it wouldn't be a problem." He knew that a group, led by King, had perused the full PANS database a year or so earlier. That group had also questioned some of the explorers, as had he. Back then the focus had not been on anything specific.

"We must consider, while we try to figure this out, a simple fact," Adam said. "Before PANS, we hadn't tried to colonize any planet or satellite, natural or artificial, with gravity stronger than Earth's." He looked at King. "Any ideas, Rob?"

"A number of researchers performed small-scale high-gravity experiments in the breweries long ago," King said. "They reported satisfactory results." He went on, "Before you joined the team, Adam, we did discuss large-scale experiments in the orbiting space stations. We had to reject that plan because we would have had to build one or more additional stations just for that purpose."

Such stations, Adam thought, required much stronger basic structures; it would have been an expensive engineering project. The stations already in orbit had been built for an artificial gravity of less than half Earth's.

"We needed our resources kept in reserve," King added, "for the PANS spacecraft construction."

Adam recalled that the PANS ships were built to handle the higher gravity only in the slowdown phase. They could not be used to test crops at Earth-Twin gravity levels while rotating in Earth orbit. "Did anyone try to get funding for experiments?" he asked.

"Yes. The committee, the senate technology committee, refused," King answered. "Several times. I do not recall just where it went from there. We did have some follow-up."

Adam leaned on the podium. He searched his memory, but it had been a long time. He recalled only that Bill Avery had led a gravity study group. He picked up his cup and drank the few remaining drops of coffee.

King stood by his chair at the head of the elliptical table. "I should mention another possibility, something else we talked about years ago," he said. He pointed to the display wall. "We know Tau Ceti's light is different from the sun's, best seen in it's yellow-orange color as compared to the sun's whitish yellow." He hesitated, and then added, "But we did those experiments, and they showed that many Earth crops grew well in light like Tau Ceti's. We even set up large-scale tests in our food factories."

Adam had already rejected that possibility for another reason. The food factories taken to Earth-Twin could provide inside light identical to that from the sun or, as an option, identical to that from Tau Ceti. The colonists, at least for the shipboard factories, need not rely on a particular spectrum.

"For this and other reasons," King concluded, "at this time I would favor your gravity explanation." He sat down.

"I think I see where this is leading," Bruce said. "Whichever the cause, gravity, spectrum, maybe year length or something else, Earth crops may have failed. The native plants would then be the alternative, but we know that's not a quick solution since there's no history of cultivation."

"Yes, that's the idea," Adam said, "especially in the crowded factories. We expect the colonists to overcome such difficulties over time, but the short time available to them just wasn't enough." He hesitated, and then added, "I have several reasons for favoring the high-gravity cause over the others. Any others."

Although he wasn't sure why, he felt that he must pinpoint the exact cause. It was, he told himself, something more than just proving that PANS was not the solution to Earth's population problem.

What about other possibilities? Insect pests or plant diseases, he thought, not discovered by the explorer group, could have crippled the new open-air farms. Here again the shipboard food factories, as with the star spectrum, should have kept operating.

"The food factories are well protected," he said, "but gravity is pervasive. We have no way to keep it out. We can eliminate light, sound, electric fields, magnetic fields, various other radiations and even biological agents. But we've never been able to block gravity."

He understood that even orbiting non-rotating spacecraft, with their apparent weightlessness, participated in a form of free fall that merely masked gravity. It was still there. Gravity affected the orbiting craft and all its contents in the same way; all free fell at the same rate.

"This is why I favor gravity," Adam said. "It's a single straightforward explanation, and one that can affect both the factories and the farms." He concluded, "That's all I have to say, until I can look at the old records." He picked up his empty cup and stepped away from the podium.

"Thank you, Adam," King said. He stood up and said to the team and the reps, "Unless you have more comments or questions, let us adjourn until tomorrow morning." He hesitated, and then added, "Let us make that a team-only meeting."

Adam nodded. Standing by his chair, he said, "I guess I'd like to make just one more comment. I believe this is telling us that the PANS plan is doomed to failure." He had wanted to say that all morning.

Bruce looked at Adam. "I wouldn't go that far," he cautioned. He stood up and picked up his notes from the table.

"We can talk about that some more later, Hugh," Adam said, "after I've had time to go over the records."

*   *   *

In the early afternoon Adam began his search of the PANS records. He smiled when he thought of his second day of confident discourse, but his elation didn't last. He realized that today's and yesterday's meetings had been with mostly close associates, and, in the records, he found the information he sought.

At home in the evening he sat with Nola in the study to discuss his findings while the autoprep prepared dinner. "I was supposed to keep this kind of thing from happening," he said as he poured a cup of coffee.

Nola looked at him.

Bill Avery had always been so confident, Adam thought, and so competent. How could he have made such an error? *How could I?* "He once told me it was my job to make sure no one allowed their enthusiasm to overcome their good judgment," he said. He shook his head. "He even told me to watch *him*."

"You mean Bill Avery?" Nola asked. "Bill did the gravity follow-up?"

"I'm afraid so," Adam said. "At least he chaired the group, but I already knew *that*. I recall now that we did discuss it in the earlier planning. Hugh and I got into some arguments." *I should have pursued it back then*, he thought. "I guess I just shut it out."

Nola looked at him. "You can't blame yourself."

"I don't know who's to blame," Adam said. "I hate to bring this up with the team. Bill meant so much to me. But I don't have a choice."

"What did Bill do?" Nola asked.

"He, his group, made two wrong assumptions," Adam said. "They assumed that the successes in low gravity meant that high gravity would cause no problems." He grimaced. "They also assumed that satisfactory small-scale tests in high gravity predicted large-scale success." What had they meant by "satisfactory"? he asked himself.

"And they were wrong?"

"It's hogwash, Nola," Adam replied. "What was I thinking back then?" He still wondered how Avery's group could have been so careless, and planned to look into more records in the early morning before the meeting. "By the way," he said, "you're invited to tomorrow's meeting even though it's just for the team."

Nola smiled.

*   *   *

Adam rushed into the morning meeting a few minutes late. "Sorry," he said. "Been on the computer." He touched Nola's shoulder when he passed her. She smiled.

He sat next to her in his usual chair while King stepped up to the podium. "First, does anyone have anything about Adam's starvation theory?" King asked. "Can we agree that this is the only good explanation so far, and go on from there?"

Everyone on the team agreed to pursue the starvation scenario.

"Gravity appears to be the most probable cause," King said. "Does anyone have anything else?"

"I thought some yesterday about mechanical failure," a team member said. "But both, the factories and the farms, would have to experience such failures. I concluded that gravity is more likely—a single and more fundamental cause."

"Anyone else?" King asked. Then, after no one responded, he looked at Adam. "Adam, the floor is yours." He sat down.

Adam stood up. "I checked the old records, and I did find out how it could've happened."

He picked up his coffee cup and walked to the front of the room. "I hate to bring this up," he said. "Bill Avery was the most dedicated person I've ever known."

He expected that everyone on the team, even those who had joined it later, would know that Avery had headed the gravity study group. That group had completed the project about six months before he himself had joined the PANS team. "As far as I could determine, Bill's group made a wrong assumption," he said. *It's really just one assumption*, he thought, *not two.*

"This was after they realized that large-scale tests would not be funded.

"We know that the explorers performed some small-scale experiments on the planet—very small. They planted a few Earth crops, on a couple hundred square meters of land, and reported the results as satisfactory.

"Bill's group also looked at the *satisfactory* results of the old brewery experiments that Rob mentioned yesterday. They apparently then assumed that large-scale crops, such as in food factories and on farms, would also be successful." His examination of the records, Adam thought, indicated that no one in the group of nine had dissented. The younger and fresher people and the older and more experienced people had all concurred.

Adam took a quick sip of coffee. "But small-scale success rarely guarantees large-scale success, in almost any endeavor. A satisfactory result in small scale does not—in general—mean the same as one in large scale." He shook his head and added, "They apparently looked at how small-scale experiments did *predict* a favorable large-scale outcome in low-gravity farming. I believe that case was just fortuitous." He took another sip of coffee.

The records had also indicated that the group had performed an extensive literature search and consulted many experts, but, like Adam remembered King to have said the previous day, expense, time and political pressures had, from the beginning, ruled out the definitive large-scale experiments. Later the group did commission a few new small-scale tests, similar to the old brewery experiments but of a more quantitative nature; those results were then extrapolated to large-scale. Adam mentioned all this to the team, but didn't elaborate. The government officials had found a way to "do something" about the population problem, he thought, and wouldn't have let caution change their plans or their timetable.

He had discovered, just this morning, that ambitious young Senator John Bitterman had headed the technology committee that had refused to fund the large-scale experiments. Bitterman and his committee had, early in the study, rejected three separate requests for funding.

The information he had obtained this morning was somehow incomplete, Adam thought. The older records had mentioned an "earlier setback," but he found no details. He told himself that he would have to go over them again.

He took another sip of coffee, and then stepped away from the podium. "I guess that's all I have right now," he said. He returned to his seat.

King stood up. "I will talk to the committee about those large-scale gravity experiments," he said. "Perhaps we can get funding now. I will also look into commissioning a genetic study of the preserved Earth plants that the explorers brought back, although that could take a long time and might not yield any useful information."

King cautioned the team members to keep Adam's findings to themselves pending further investigation, and asked for comments.

Hugh Bruce stood up and looked at Adam. "Adam, you said yesterday that this gravity-caused failure must doom the entire PANS plan. Why? If gravity's indeed the cause, isn't this just an Earth-Twin problem?"

"I don't mean to put you off, Hugh," Adam answered, "but I have to think about the overall implications some more, and do some more research." He again thought briefly about the mention, in the records, of an earlier setback; he wondered if that could affect his arguments. "It's too important, and I can't present a half-baked idea." He glanced around the room at all the team members. "But it does doom the PANS plan."

"All right," Bruce said. "But I'm curious."

Adam looked at Bruce. "Give me a week or two to go through the records in more detail and do some more thinking, Hugh. We can talk about it then."

Bruce agreed.

*   *   *

Alone in his office just after the meeting, Adam sat down at his desk. His thoughts drifted a hundred and thirteen trillion kilometers away.

The colonists must deal with their situation, even while Earth debated the future of the PANS plan. The problems could be multiple. Survival itself was basic. Individuals would try to survive the present, even when that was detrimental to the future of the group. "People aren't going to starve willingly" was the way someone had expressed it at yesterday's meeting.

He thought of his friends, friends he hadn't seen for many years. *Jenny. Pete and Linda. What's happening to them?*

He leaned back in his chair and closed his eyes. He was so tired. So very tired. He dozed off.

Chapter 24

Gone Fishing

Pete prepared to fly to the East Quadrant with Harry. While waiting the week or so that Harry needed to modify the signal and the equipment for the "starvation" message to Earth, he finished the documentation for his two rice crops. He then arranged for his small staff to prepare a few tons of seeds for the fields. A week after the eighth ship's arrival, he was sitting at his desk in the section three control room in the late morning and finalizing some notes for Lynn when Harry dropped in. He noticed that Harry looked troubled and asked about it.

"I decoded the population number last night," Harry said. He put a sheet of paper on Pete's desk.

"It's that bad?" Pete asked. He squinted at the paper, and pointed to a chair in front of his desk.

Harry sat down. "That's what I came here to tell you. I matched the new count with the arrival tallies for all eight, and used the Council's estimate for Pangaean births." He pointed to the paper, shook his head and said, "Pete, we lost nearly *eight million.*"

Pete opened his mouth, but didn't speak. *Eight million is about half of total arrivals!* He grimaced. Half of all the colonists who had, to date, set foot on Pangaean soil had starved to death. Deaths from other causes such as farm-raid violence, he thought, accounted for only a very small fraction of the total.

"I reported that to the Council this morning," Harry said.

"Eight million," Pete said. He thought of the hundreds of graves he had seen in tiny Hope Valley. "I guess," he added, slowly, "we should've expected that."

"I'm going to stay here another week," Harry said. "The Council wants to talk to me some more, and I need to do a little more work on the long-distance comm link. I think I can finish the Landings station." He hesitated, and then added, "Why don't you come to Eight with me when I send our message to Earth tomorrow? I don't need help, but I'd like the company."

*   *   *

The next morning Pete threw Harry's makeshift switch that blasted the "starvation" message to Earth. He insisted that it was addressed to Adam Hampton.

Later that day, while sitting alone at his desk, he thought about the next signal. He recalled that Thackaray and the Council had directed Harry to alter it to send the words "high gravity."

Politicians needed an explanation, he thought, any explanation. Science and technology must find *the* explanation, and someday he would do that. The Council might have to change that directive about the next signal. "Causeunknown" or "crop failure" would be more honest than "high gravity." They could always send Earth the details later, he told himself, when they knew more about it. That could be many years from now.

Later in the week he helped Harry, from the shop at Six, turn on the communications link at the Landings. This completed the initial phase of the long-range system. All farm communities came on line. Most of the people remained on the plains far from the farms, Pete thought as he drove his terrie back to One, but now word from the Landings or any quadrant farm could reach a large fraction of the population. Wrist comms, those with still functioning power packs, would receive the new strong signals even though they could not answer back long distance.

Harry had told him that the Council had decided that the first world-wide broadcast would be a "no nonsense" reminder of the farm-raid deadly force directive. How unfortunate it was, he thought, that the first message on Harry's new system would be such a negative one. He knew Harry would have to send it soon, after a few more tests.

*   *   *

Pete and Harry boarded one of the later aircraft that took newcomers to the East Quadrant. Soon after arrival, in the late morning, Pete visited with Lynn at her farm office shelter. Harry, after greeting Lynn, had gone off to test the quadrant's comm station.

Pete put a package on Lynn's desk and opened it. He pulled out three one-liter cans of vacuum-packed coffee and several decanter fuel capsules and put them on the desk.

"Thanks," Lynn said. "It helps when I put in long hours."

"I know you like it," Pete said. "We got some from the eighth ship's storage." She looked even thinner than she had been, he thought. He knew that he didn't look much better, even though he had been feeling stronger. Even with his successes at the factories, a long time would pass before anyone regained original body weight. Full relief could come only from increased farm production. Lynn was under a lot of stress, he told himself, trying to accomplish just that.

Lynn sat behind the desk. "I'm sorry I couldn't talk to you about it before, Pete. About the shootings."

Although another chair was available, Pete didn't sit. "It's all right, Lynn. I understand. What's the situation now?"

"It's been quiet," Lynn answered. "The beans are growing well." She shook her head and added, "But the new people are on the plains now."

"Yeah."

Lynn shook her head. "I'm afraid—"

Pete interrupted. "You don't have to say it. We expected this and, yeah, may have to do it again." He moved the other chair next to the desk and sat down. "Let's talk about rice."

"Yes," Lynn said, "you told me you have two varieties. I know that's why you came here. But let me tell you about something else first."

"All right." Pete leaned back in his chair. "We can get to the seeds later."

"I talked to Andy Landis a few days ago," Lynn said.

"Andy?" Pete sat up straight. He hadn't seen or heard from Andy in years.

"They're not hunting anymore," Lynn said. "They're fishing now. By the ocean shore."

"Fishing?" Pete asked. "You mean like Earth fish?"

"A little," Lynn said. She scribbled a picture of a fat fish on a piece of paper and handed it to Pete. "Andy drew it just like this."

Pete took the paper and looked at it. "They're surviving on these fish?"

"I believe it's more than just surviving," Lynn said. She smiled. "Andy was quite optimistic."

Pete got up and paced the small room. He recalled that Lynn couldn't find Andy and Cindy when she restarted the farms more than a year ago. *Cindy? Little Andrew?* Lynn just said Andy was "optimistic," he told himself, but he hesitated to ask about Andy's family.

"Apparently a few small groups are doing all right," Lynn said. "Andy just recently found out I was here, that we were farming again."

"Yeah, I guess most people are still incommunicado," Pete remarked, "but Harry said that's changing." He thought about the planned first broadcast. *The fish? Is there something positive here?*

"He came right over and told me about the fish," Lynn said. "They're not too far away. He said they found a few places along the shoreline where these fish are relatively abundant."

"People have tried the oceans already," Pete said, "and the rivers. They never found much food. What's different *now?*" He still paced the floor.

"Apparently these types of fish are attracted to certain rock formations at the shoreline," Lynn answered. "Andy said they're easy to catch, now that they know just where to look." She shrugged. "Of course we don't know how long they'll last."

Pete was silent for a moment. Then he stopped his pacing and exclaimed, "A new food source! Maybe this is better news than we might think." He had better ask, he thought, for the other news. He looked at Lynn. "What did he say about Cindy and Andrew?"

"They're both still with us." Lynn smiled.

"Yeah." Pete relaxed. He hesitated, and then said, "I'm going out to see them. I've been away from my friends too long."

Pete drew a small map from directions that Andy had given to Lynn. He then gave her the details about his two rice varieties, handed her his written comments and helped her arrange to get the seeds to all the quadrant farms.

"By the way," Lynn said as Pete prepared to leave, "you've said nothing about Linda."

"Linda's all right," Pete said. "I guess she's busy, too. I'll be on my way. Be back in a few days, Lynn."

*　　　*　　　*

Pete drove a terrie and followed his map. He expected that the trip of more than forty kilometers, mostly over rough terrain, would take three or four hours. He encountered no roads, or even paths, once he had driven a few kilometers away from the farm shelter area.

Lynn had told him that Andy had walked the entire distance to her shelter. A farm worker had driven him back, so Pete utilized the occasional fresh terrie track to check his navigation. Those fish must have given Andy the energy to walk, Pete thought as he drove, and the fishing group must be doing very well if Andy was able to leave his family for the time necessary to visit the farm.

After nearly two hours of driving, Pete stopped and got out of the terrie at what he figured was the halfway point. He relaxed, contemplated the changed scenery and listened to the birds. He was anxious to talk to Andy, but he wasn't rushed. He could think more clearly when he was not negotiating the terrie around rocks, trees, shrubs and weeds.

He pulled the brim of his western down to shade his eyes and leaned against the terrie.

The greatest agricultural experiment ever? He had thought about that expression years ago. Now he cultivated native beans and native rice in an alien land, in an exotic environment; he had restarted Earth's ten-thousand-year grand experiment. This would soon be done on a worldwide scale if the farms could control the raiding. Surely there was a way to do it without killing the raiders, he thought. *The "greatest agricultural experiment ever" must not be marred by terrible expedience.*

He wondered about the fragmented reports of cannibalism from the remote regions. They had not yet been substantiated.

The solution to these problems could be at the shore, he thought. He got back into the terrie, engaged the engine and drove on.

✶   ✶   ✶

Pete arrived in the early evening. He parked the terrie at the base of the hill, nestled among other hills, that his map claimed was his destination. He exited the vehicle, glanced at the orange sun low in the western sky, and then looked around. He quickly sighted the small building at what he figured was the location marked with an "X" on the map.

The makeshift shelter, from a distance of a few hundred meters, appeared barely large enough to house one person. It stood about halfway up the hill in an acre of trees. Pete glanced around and spotted a few similar shelters on another hill.

While he secured the terrie, he glanced at the leaves on a couple of nearby trees. He had memorized leaf shapes from computer displays when he had studied, at the university, the dwarf fruit and nut trees developed in the early food factories. Those dwarf trees had become so highly adapted to the factories, he thought, that even in the early days they could grow nowhere else. The term "apple shrubs" came to mind. None of the dwarf trees had been included in the shipboard factories, since they were not expected to grow on the open-air farms. He shrugged. *How little Earth had known!*

He had also learned other leaf shapes. He classified the local trees as a close match to oaks and maples in Pangaean green. They were dispersed in small "forests" over all but the very top of the hill and the relatively clear area where he had parked the terrie. A few leaves were beginning to turn red, orange and gold, showing signs of the coming cooler season.

The shortest route to Andy's shelter was not over the top of the hill, but Pete decided to climb the peak anyway. While he ascended, he noted that such climbing was getting easier. He thought of his race with Harry a few weeks earlier.

When he reached the nearly treeless summit, the ocean appeared in the distance. He stopped for a moment and glanced around. The green hills to the north and south were splashed with patches of red, orange and gold. A thin white beach separated those hills from the blue ocean. He detected a faint salt smell in the breeze that blew in from the water.

Except for the space view upon arrival many years earlier, he had not seen an Earth-Twin ocean. He had not come this way on his other visits to the quadrant. In the fading evening light the dark blue ocean looked much like, except for the absence of shoreline energy-extraction facilities, Earth's oceans.

He felt the diminishing ocean breeze on his face and neck while he gazed at the scene before him. The ocean and its white beach stretched from northern horizon to southern horizon in his view. It was enormous, he thought, bigger than all Earth's oceans combined.

He reminded himself that the continent of Pangaea, Jenny's "giant Australia," had a huge shoreline. He now viewed only a tiny part of it. He lingered awhile and listened to the breeze rustle the leaves of the oaks and maples. He savored its cool caress.

*   *   *

Pete approached the small shelter. He knocked on a board next to the rough door, and Andy answered almost immediately.

Pete spoke first. "Andy, old buddy!"

"Omigosh! Pete!"

Pete and Andy started to shake bony hands, but this greeting quickly evolved into a hug.

Andy then grabbed Pete's arm with both hands and almost dragged him into the room. "Come on in," he said. "Cindy, it's Pete!"

Pete hardly recognized Cindy.

"Pete! Oh, please forgive my skinny look," she said.

Pete smiled, and tried to stifle his expression of surprise. Cindy's red hair was shorter in some places than in others, he noted, like much had fallen out and now attempted to grow back. The room was light enough for him to see clearly, since the evening daylight came through the still open door and one small window. The low sun formed an image of the off-square window on a side wall just above the dirt floor.

"You're beautiful, Cindy." Pete hugged her.

A small boy ran up to Pete. "Hi, daddy 'n mommy's friend! I'm Andrew." Andrew's hair was red like his mother's, and curly like his father's.

Pete picked Andrew up, held him briefly, and then put him down again. Even though the boy was the correct height for his age, he didn't weigh much. "My name's Pete. You met me a long time ago, when you were little."

"We're having a small birthday party for Andrew," Cindy said.

"I'm six!" Andrew exclaimed.

That's Pangaean years, Pete thought.

"We just cooked a couple of fish." Andy pointed through the still open door to the remains of a fire. "You're just in time to finish off the party."

"I've been looking forward to that," Pete said. He wondered if Andy and his family had enough for themselves. Could they afford to share with him? Then he recalled Lynn's comments about Andy's optimism. He could help catch more fish the next day, he told himself.

All sat down to eat, in rough chairs around a rough table. The table was made of flat rough-cut boards nailed on top of a tree stump. Andy, Pete thought, had cut a dead tree at the proper height and then built the shelter around the stump table.

"Try it." Cindy passed a piece of fish, skewered on a stick, to Pete.

Pete took his first bite, chewed, and swallowed. "It's great," he said between bites.

"I wish we had more to give you." Andy shrugged.

Pete smiled, "I hope you'll show me how to catch more tomorrow," he said.

"I'll help! I'll help!" Andrew waved his thin arms.

After they finished the fish, Pete helped clean up. Then all sat again around the table. Pete told about his successes in the factories and learned about the challenges of hunting and gathering. He soon noticed that Andrew was having difficulty keeping his eyes open, and saw that Cindy noticed this, too.

"C'mon, Andrew," she said. "Time for bed now. Say goodnight to Pete and daddy." She got up from her rough-hewn chair.

Pete smiled when Andrew, looking wide awake now, looked at his mother and said, "Can't I stay up a little longer?"

"You have to get your sleep," Cindy said. "Think about the beach tomorrow."

Andrew looked at his father, and then back at his mother. He then looked at Pete. "Goodnight, Pete," he said.

"See you in the morning, Andrew." Pete smiled.

Andrew said goodnight to his father, and Pete watched Cindy put the boy to bed in a corner of the one room shelter and return to the adults. Darkness had deepened, and she lit a homemade candle and placed it on the table.

When the room became brighter, Pete saw that Cindy had tears in her eyes.

She stood by the table. "We almost lost Andrew," she said. "I just thought about that as I tucked him in. But we were the lucky ones."

Andy stood up.

"My best friend Donna—" Cindy started to cry.

Andy took her into his arms and held her. He looked at Pete. "Andrew had some bad bouts with diarrhea and was always dehydrated, but he's better now that he's been eating regularly."

Pete remained silent until Andy and Cindy sat down by the table again. He then talked with them for an hour about old and new friends, and lost friends. He shed a few tears of his own when he brought up Jenny's death, and he mentioned Linda's arrival.

When Andy and Cindy expressed interest in meeting Linda, Pete said, "Yeah, whenever you get to the Landings. I don't know if she'll get a chance to come to the quadrant. She's in charge of the main medical facility now, and I'm sure Lynn spoke about the outbreak of a mono-like illness in some areas."

"Lynn did mention an outbreak," Andy said, "but she didn't know a lot about it. Is there any danger?"

"Linda said it's just the poor diet weakening general immunity, mostly out on the plains," Pete said. "The danger of epidemic is very low since the people are so spread out." He yawned. "Sorry," he said. "It's been a long day."

Andy got up. "I'll prepare a sleeping area for you. We hadn't expected a guest, especially an important one. Lynn said you're a world hero."

Pete stood up. "I'm just doing my job—finally."

Andy smiled.

✳ ✳ ✳

In the early morning Pete walked with Andy, Cindy and Andrew the kilometer or so down the hill to the shore. They approached a group of about thirty people scattered on a small section of the twenty-five meter wide sandy beach. A few thin but boisterous children played at the water's edge.

The orange sun had just risen, and Pete felt its warmth on his face. It hovered low over the water and created a sparkling thread that led in to the beach. Waves splashed over groups of rocks both close to shore and tens of meters out. An old and almost forgotten smell of salt, fish and seaweed teased his nose. He briefly watched a couple of small birds run along the rough white sand and skillfully avoid the advancing and retreating water from the waves that broke just a few meters from shore. Their raucous cries contrasted sharply with the musical calls of the birds he had heard while walking down the hill.

"We used to have a larger group," Andy said. "We lost many when hunting got bad some months after the last ship."

Pete looked around. "I don't see any fat faces," he said. "I guess you didn't get anyone from the ship that just arrived." He recalled that the Council had directed that most newcomers be taken to areas farther from the farms.

"No one came here recently," Andy said.

Pete followed Andy around and met the members of the group. One of them, a man named Vernon, said to Pete when introduced, "I'm the only one left from the last ship." Vernon was thinner than any of the others, Pete thought.

When he and Pete were out of earshot of Vernon, Andy said, "Vern lost his wife and two children back at the hunting areas. The girl was four years old when we buried her. The boy only two. Donna died soon after the kids. She and Cindy had become close friends."

Pete walked alongside Andy across the sandy beach. "I don't know how Vern survived," Andy said. "He ate only enough to keep up some strength for hunting." He hesitated, and then added, "We haven't lost anyone since we came here to the shore, and we finally can stay in one place. That little house is the first shelter we've had in a long time."

"How'd you discover the fish?" Pete asked.

"Vern deserves the credit for that," Andy said. "After he lost his family, he just disappeared. We feared he had decided to go away and die alone, but he returned to the group a few weeks later and told us about the fish." He shrugged. "He brought us here, but didn't give any explanation."

Pete and Andy returned to the water's edge and rejoined Cindy, Andrew, and a number of others.

Four children, including Andrew, played a noisy game of tag. "The kids are excited," Pete said. He looked at Andy.

Andy smiled. "They've been getting noisier every day, but we don't mind. It shows they're getting stronger, even if they still look skinny."

"Yeah." Pete returned Andy's smile.

Pete sat down, took off his boots and socks and rolled up his trousers when he saw Andy do so. He stood up again.

He watched Andy pick up a sharpened stick, about two meters long, from a stack on the beach. "Take one," Andy said. "We've tried other methods, but spearing in the shallower areas has been the most successful."

Pete picked up a spear and tried to hold it the same way that Andy held his. He followed Andy to the water and waded toward a group of rocks. The water was just over knee deep. He watched Andy search the clear water, aim, strike, and pull out a fat wriggling fish about forty centimeters long.

He tried the technique himself. He missed his first five strikes, but managed to skewer a fish on his sixth.

"You learned quicker than I did," Andy said. He laughed. "You have to correct for refraction."

Pete extracted his prize from the spear and tossed it ashore next to where Andy had thrown his. He searched, and after only one miss caught another.

"We showed two other groups how to do this," Andy said. "I learned later that they found other good places along the shore."

Pete speared a third fish, and he watched Andy spear several more.

"You know, they do look like Earth fish," Pete said. "Generally fatter, but still similar. I couldn't tell from the small pieces last night."

"Let's go ashore," Andy said. "Looks we got all of them here."

"Only a few?" Pete asked.

"There'll be more tomorrow," Andy said. "They move in at night."

"So there must be a lot out there," Pete said as he and Andy reached the dry sand. He smiled.

"There seems to be a fish hierarchy," Andy said, "with the *alpha* fish taking the territories closer to shore. When we take the alphas, the remaining fish sort themselves out into new alphas." He shrugged. "We can't catch many in one day, but there's a reliable supply." He pointed to several small stacks of fish, a few hundred meters away on the beach, that others had speared. He then sat down on the beach and picked up his boots.

"Have you tried to go out farther from shore?" Pete asked. He pointed. "Looks like shallower water near those rocks. At least at this phase of the tide." He sat down and started to put his boots on without his socks. His feet were still wet, but the boots would make it easier to walk on the pebble-strewn sand. "You're surviving here, but maybe we can do better. We could build a floating device from fallen trees." He smiled. "Remember those old-time 'moving pictures' on Earth? Huckleberry Finn? They called it a 'raft.'"

"We've talked about that, but we've been too busy building the houses," Andy said. "We finished the last one just before I went to see Lynn." He hesitated, and then said, "Why don't we try it this afternoon? After we cook and eat what we have?"

*   *   *

Later in the day, Pete and the others gathered a number of dead trees, stripped away the branches and tied the logs together with vines. They built a crude and ugly raft, but it floated. Pete smiled when Andrew and another child, after searching the nearby woods, brought him a few pieces of strong bark for paddles.

Pete and Andy got aboard. Amidst good luck wishes they paddled out a hundred meters or so into the middle of a formation of large rocks that jutted up from the water. The waves bounced the crude raft, but it remained afloat. The two got busy with their spears.

When Pete and Andy returned to shore an hour later, the others let out a loud cheer. On the raft lay more fish than the whole group had speared in the morning.

Pete sat with Andy and watched while the others cleaned and pre-pared the fish and cooked them in a pit they had dug in the sand. He asked if he could help like he had in the morning, but they insisted that he had done his part and deserved the rest. He soon shared in the feast.

*   *   *

Just before nightfall, Pete helped Andy gather some wood and stack it near the shelter. He watched Andrew run among the trees and gather handfuls of twigs for kindling. After dark he helped Andy build a roaring fire. He smiled when he saw that Andrew had fallen asleep in the grass a few meters away. It had been quite a day for all, he thought.

After Cindy put the tired little boy to bed, Pete sat with her and Andy on the ground by the fire. "We seem to have had a successful day," he said.

"I can't remember the last time that Andrew wasn't hungry when he went to bed," Cindy said. "Even here by the sea. He didn't even wake up when I carried him in." She smiled.

Pete turned and looked into the fire. He wondered if people on Earth had, long ago, sat and talked by a fire. He glanced at the fat pink crescent moon high in the western sky.

"This celebration could use some wine," Andy said. "Too bad no one's had time to make any."

"Maybe we will soon." Pete looked at Cindy, and then at Andy. "This's been on my mind since yesterday," he said, "when Lynn told me about the fish. The ocean is big, and Pangaea has a huge shoreline." He hesitated and wrinkled his brow.

"Go on, Pete," Andy encouraged.

"It's simple," Pete said. "The fish could be similar around much of the shoreline. People need to look for the same shore features—the rock formations that must attract these same fish. Like the people you told. They can build more and bigger rafts. We just have to get the word out on the plains." He glanced at the fire, and then looked back at Andy. "Yeah, that's it. Harry Sigcrist has the new comm all set up."

"Sure, Pete," Andy said, "but listen to me. You know we can easily overhunt an area. Maybe we will overfish." He shrugged.

Pete turned and stared into the fire.

Andy continued. "In most areas, hunting lasted a few months at best." He hesitated, and then added, "But I understand about the large shoreline."

Pete stood up, and turned away from the fire. His shadow danced on the trees. "With six months of good fishing, we can get the farms going.

We have the beans and rice now. I'm working on other crops too, and you know how good this soil is." He looked up at the starry sky and the crescent moon, and then turned and looked at the fire again. "If we can get five or six good months with the pressure off the farms, five or six months with no raiding, we can feed everybody!"

*   *   *

Pete returned to the East Quadrant farms the next day. He sat with Lynn and Harry by the table in their shelter. The late afternoon sun beamed through a small window, illuminating scattered papers on the table.

Harry poured three cups of hot coffee, while Pete described the fish and the plan to spread the word.

Pete looked at Harry. "Andy will contact you about communications in a few days." He recalled that the new system could reach the hunters' wrist comms just over a thousand kilometers from the farms. "You can certainly get to the people closest to the farms," he said, "the ones most likely to raid."

"Yeah," Harry said, "I'm ready. I haven't yet sent that first broadcast, but it all works." He took a sip of coffee.

This could be the first broadcast, Pete thought. It would be a positive message rather than the negative Council decree. The councilmembers would have to agree, when Harry described the plan to them, that the fish message carried a higher priority than the raiding directive.

"This is all so wonderful," Lynn said. "I hope we can put the weapons away for good now."

"I know it'll work," Pete said.

The three talked over the details of the plan. Harry agreed to also ask the Council to arrange for a number of aircraft to transport plains people who were located at a distance from the shore.

After the discussion, Lynn looked at Pete and said, "Oh, I have a new story for you, too." She smiled. "You know we've established two small living areas here."

Pete had noticed some kind of organization. "I saw the grouped shelters," he said.

"Well, Pete," Lynn said, "all of us at the East Quadrant farms decided to name these 'villages' in honor of your discoveries." She looked at Harry. "Why don't you tell him? It was your idea. You started it as a joke. But we all took it seriously."

Harry grinned. "Pete, my friend," he said, "welcome to Beans, one of the twin villages of Beans and Rice."

Pete smiled. "Someday we'll have the twin cities of Beans and Rice."

Lynn said, "But I'm serious—" Her laughter stopped her in mid-sentence. Pete and Harry joined in.

Pete was the first to calm down enough to continue the conversation. "I guess I didn't tell either of you that the Council wanted to name the Landings after me. After all, it's a city and should have a city name."

"So is it MacDonald City?" Harry asked. "Or Petersburg?"

"I turned them down," Pete said, "but they gave me first choice on the new name." He hesitated, and looked at Lynn. "It's Brownsville," he said. "That'll be official in a few weeks."

Lynn looked at him and smiled, and he saw that she also had a tear in her eye. He nodded.

"By the way," Lynn asked, "what's happening between you and Linda? You seem to avoid talking about her."

"Linda's doing fine," Pete answered. "She's really adapted to this situation. I knew she was smart, and dedicated. But I had no idea she was so strong."

"Pete," Lynn said, "that's not what I asked you." She added, gently, "We've been helping each other. Maybe I can help now."

"I love Linda," Pete said. "Deep down I've always loved her, and I believe she still loves me. But things are turned around, and I don't know what to do about it."

"Maybe you should ask yourself," Lynn said, "what Jenny would have *wanted* you to do."

*　　　　　*　　　　　*

Pete returned to the Landings the next morning, and spent the afternoon catching up on his duties in the factories. In the evening he climbed to the top of the big hill near One and looked around. To the east lay the great spacecraft from Earth. Kilometers of gigantic wheels lay on their sides; their height blocked his view. He could see much of One, a little of Two and Three, less of Four and Five. Six, Seven and Eight were not visible from this hill. All this would soon be the new city of Brownsville.

He turned to the west. The red-orange sun floated just above the distant hills. Its peculiar squashed shape when it was so near the horizon, he thought, was due to atmospheric refraction.

Earth's sun used to look like that when setting, too. Under that sun, he told himself, Adam would receive the modified eighth hypersignal in a little over a year. He and Harry would send information about the cause in the ninth signal, even though they wouldn't know for sure for a long time. The Council insisted on "high gravity."

Pete realized that he could argue that point, and send something like "crop failure." He, after all, was a "world hero." He was sure to get his way. He sighed. Would it be better to just cooperate with the Council, with President Thackaray? he asked himself. *Maybe*, he thought, *there is a certain wisdom in their decision.*

What will help Adam the most? Pete had some time to work on that question.

He thought of his own more immediate problem, the reason he had come to the hill. He briefly mulled over his short discussion with Lynn, on the previous day, about Linda. Could Linda still love him after the way he had been neglecting her since her arrival? He and she were both very busy with the planet's problems, but he couldn't expect her to be patient with him much longer.

What would Jenny have wanted him to do? He looked up at the pink quarter moon, and then down at her metal sundial in the middle of the clearing.

In some low brush a cricket began its nightly song. The warm evening breeze carried the scent of roses, Pangaea's variety of roses. Pete stood quietly for a few moments, and he understood what Lynn had meant. He understood the message of the sundial. *Jenny just wants me to be happy.* He would never, he told himself, lose her; her memory would always be around to guide him.

He turned and started back down the hill, in the general direction of the closest terrie-parking area. Seven was a number of kilometers away, and he was in a hurry.

Chapter 25

It's Not An Option

Adam sat in his office in the early afternoon and wondered if he should continue his quest for more information on the "earlier setback." He had spent the better part of the past three weeks researching the full PANS records and had found nothing other than the one brief reference that had aroused his curiosity. He thought about the dozen people he had queried. All had claimed ignorance, but both Rob King and Brenda Avery had seemed elusive. Maybe, he told himself, he had just imagined that. He shook his head. He had better get on with his first priority, the total cancellation of the PANS plan. He could figure out the mystery later. It might not be important to him at this time; it might not have anything to do with the current problem.

He thought of Hugh Bruce and hit a couple of keys on his terminal. Bruce's face appeared. "Good afternoon, Adam."

"Hugh, can we get together now," Adam asked, "about why the plan is doomed to failure?"

Bruce smiled. "Be right over."

Adam hit a key and Bruce's face faded. He drank the last few drops of coffee in his cup, and looked up when Nola walked in and asked if he was busy. He invited her to sit down and wait for Bruce. "I can feed all my ideas to him," he added, "and hope he comes to the same conclusion. Help me out."

Adam just got those words out when Bruce arrived, greeted him and Nola and added, "I saw Rob on the way. He wants to be in on this. He's right behind me." Bruce sat down by Adam's desk.

Adam turned toward the door when King entered the office a few seconds later. "Mind if I join you?" King asked.

"Have a seat, Rob," Adam said. He pointed to the one remaining empty chair, and then looked at Nola and winked. Now, he thought, he could feed his information to two very well qualified individuals.

King sat down. "I like your explanation, Adam," King said. "I believe you are right, certainly about starvation. The oversight committee is skeptical, but I believe they will come around."

Bruce looked at Adam and smiled. "I don't think everyone's convinced," he said, "but everything you said fits."

"I hypered a message to the rescue ship this morning," King said. "I finally managed to get the government's permission. We can send more as we work this out."

Adam understood that this was the fastest way to inform the colonists about the team's deliberations. He offered Bruce and King empty coffee cups and his decanter. After they had filled their cups, he refilled his while Nola mixed her herb tea.

Adam took a sip of coffee, and then put the cup down. "I'll get started," he said. "I'll try to explain, but a lot of it'll be just thinking out loud. Help me if you can. I want to see if you come to the same conclusion. The PANS plan can never work."

"It looks like the four of us already agree on starvation," Nola said. She picked up her cup and took a sip of tea.

"Yes, I guess we do," Adam said. "Let's start with that, with Earth-Twin itself. When the explorers first left Earth long ago, I think the planners just envisioned some very small colonies for the foreseeable future. Could that be why they didn't perform more extensive farming tests on the planet?" He looked at King.

"I believe the early goal included only some small scale experimental stations," King said. "In those days, the great distance confounded most planners."

Yes, it's the distance. This was the critical point of Adam's argument, and he was glad that King had mentioned it first. The rush to handle Earth's growing population, he thought, led many to ignore that distance problem.

"Of course we must not send any more people to Earth-Twin," he said.

King nodded. "I am sure that no one will want to resume colonization. At least not on Earth-Twin. Even the government will have to concur—eventually."

"Maybe some diplomats in the future?" Adam asked without expecting an answer.

"We will certainly set up some kind of relations," King said.

If they're still willing to talk to us, Adam thought. "I know we all wish we could do something for them right now," he said, "but we can't help. The distance makes that impossible. By the time we can get any food there, nature or the colonists will surely have sorted it out."

Nola grimaced. "I'm afraid nature's way is to increase the death rate," she said.

Adam nodded, and took a drink of coffee.

"I agree," King said. "Sending food can only be a gesture, and we need that food right here on Earth."

"We can't help them, but we do have a consolation in this tragedy," Bruce commented. "If starvation's the problem, the colonists' numbers will eventually stabilize. I've always believed that the plan did more than just accommodate Earth's growth. It's also a first step in guaranteeing that the human race—the human mind—will continue in the event of a catastrophe in our own solar system."

"I hadn't thought of it that way," Adam said.

Bruce looked at him. "I've had that in mind from the beginning," he said. "It was my motivation for getting on the team. It wasn't the mission for PANS, so I kept it to myself."

"That may explain a few things." Adam smiled briefly, and then winked at Nola.

"I, too, agree that we can't send more people to Earth-Twin," she said, "and that we can't help them."

"We all agree that we cannot help Earth-Twin," King said. He looked at Adam. "But why does this mean that we must abandon the entire plan?"

"Why can't we continue on other earthlike planets?" Bruce asked. "If it turns out that Earth-Twin's gravity is the problem, we have it isolated."

"We can't isolate the real problem," Adam said. "I'll try to explain what I mean. Statistically, we can't expect to find another planet that's more like Earth than is Earth-Twin. Not closer than a few thousand limit-years."

He left as understood that even small numbers of people could not travel the thousand limit-year distances, at least not in the foreseeable future. Present and near-future telescope technology could not even tell which such planets, when they were detected, were the more earthlike. They would remain unreachable and unexplorable, he thought, for a long time to come.

He thought of another complication. At those distances, humans might have to compete with other intelligent beings for the more desirable planets. Although scientists had not yet detected such beings, statistical studies indicated that they might exist at the thousand-plus limit-year distances. The early PANS planners and the government had glossed over this possibility, he thought, when they had claimed that the plan was unlimited for far-future expansion. Such alien intelligent beings, most likely more advanced than humans, would have already learned the lesson Earth was learning now. They would jealously guard their territories.

"For the closer planets," Adam said, "like Earth-Twin, the physical differences will be major."

He took a sip of coffee. "Think of the possibilities," he said. "Year length, day length, seasonal variation and planetary orbits more elliptical than Earth's near circle. Different star colors, like Tau Ceti's orange. Planetary surface composition and atmospheric differences. Planet size. And that's just a short list." He need not, he thought, list everything for veterans like King and Bruce.

He looked at Bruce, and then at King. He nodded. "I guess my point is that we'll always have differences. I do believe we can colonize other planets, but only if we send relatively small numbers of people and allow them to adjust their own populations to the conditions of each particular planet. We cannot export unlimited millions—as required in a plan like PANS—over the increasing distances." He hesitated, and then added, "This is so even in those cases where we may plan to modify a planet. Remember, we haven't even been able to transform our own nearby Mars. That will just take too long—if it's possible at all." He sipped more coffee.

"I understand that we must settle for the closer but less-earthlike planets," Bruce said, "but you're making a good argument that we can't even do that, not for large migrations."

"Yes," King added, "for the closer planets, the different and inevitable problems will continue to inhibit us. And, yes, the distance itself, which will increase for each new planet, will add to the difficulty."

Thanks, Rob, Adam thought. *Thanks, Hugh.* "We must," he said, "for the less-earthlike planets, understand that Earth-Twin is the closest of these. Even if our scientists can find ways to solve the inevitable problems, it must be on a case-by-case basis and progressively farther away. They may gain expertise in solving new planetary problems, but will continually face new problems of distance."

Adam looked at Nola, at Bruce, and then at King. "I can't believe technology can keep up with this," he said. "Not ever. We can't even assist the closest such planet, not soon enough to be any help at all."

"I see your point, Adam," King said.

"I not only see your point," Bruce said. "I agree with you now."

King stood up. "I have to go," he said. "Let us bring this up with the full team tomorrow. I will schedule another early morning meeting."

*   *   *

That evening Adam stood with Nola on their balcony. He could not see Tau Ceti. It was just above the horizon and a light haze obscured the lower stars. He looked at Nola. "Would they even want our help if we could give it?" he asked. "After what we did to them, perhaps they'll just want to be rid of us forever."

Nola looked at him. "Adam," she said, "I'm sure it's not like that."

"What could I have done to avoid this tragedy?" Adam gazed in Tau Ceti's general direction.

"Could you have done anything?" Nola asked. "Why, even if you suspected that Bill's group erred on the gravity, would that have stopped the colonization?"

Adam shook his head. Could he have convinced anyone that the high gravity might be a problem, when the large-scale experiments couldn't, or wouldn't, be done?

"Even if you could've convinced Bill," Nola asked, "would that have stopped it?"

Adam looked at her. "You're right," he said. "Taking something like that to the political establishment would've been like beating my head against a brick wall." He hesitated, and then added, "But we now have some experimental results, so to speak, and we must use them."

"But not proof," Nola said.

Adam shook his head. "How can we prove anything?"

· 325 ·

He felt Nola take his hand in hers. "Let's go inside," she said. "You need some rest so you can talk to the team tomorrow."

He smiled and followed her inside. How could he have handled this situation without Nola at his side? he asked himself.

*   *   *

At the meeting, Adam found that only a few on the team accepted his conclusions about the fate of the PANS plan if his theories about starvation and about gravity were correct; a few were ready to recommend that the plan be terminated. He was unable to obtain such support from the majority.

A few weeks later he learned that the government leaders, after they had received King's report on the recent PANS team meetings, had agreed only to continue the indefinite suspension of the plan. The PANS oversight committee, and Chairman Bitterman, had refused to comment on its future.

*   *   *

At the arrival time for the eighth hypersignal, Adam sat with King in King's office and monitored the receiving equipment. The receiver, and its backup, remained silent. No beep announced signal reception, and no numbers appeared on the screens. Adam shook his head. The first seven counts, he thought, had all been received exactly at the time projected.

Thirty minutes later King described the situation to the team at the morning's team meeting. He asked for comments.

Hugh Bruce suggested that the signal might just be late, and for some good reason.

Adam looked at Bruce and nodded. Perhaps it was not a negative development, he thought. *Could the colonists be trying to tell us something?*

He relaxed when the team elected to meet daily to discuss the newest situation and examine the possibilities. He agreed with the team's decision to keep the public fully informed. He waited.

After just over a week, Adam arrived first when King convened an emergency team meeting early on Sunday morning. When all the others had gathered, King announced, "We received the signal shortly after midnight last night."

Adam shifted in his chair.

"It is not a population count," King said. "Instead of the number, we received a word—a single word."

Come on, Rob, Adam thought, *what is that word?*

King looked at Adam and answered his unspoken question. "'Starvation' is the word."

Adam glanced around at the other team members and saw that all were now looking at him. He wanted to jump up on the elliptical table and dance a jig. After all these years, he had proof!

King continued, "This is indeed confirmation of some of the basics of Adam's theory. Let us discuss what this means."

Adam picked up his cup and took a sip of coffee. He considered the real meaning behind the message in the hypersignal. His "proof" described a tragic failure in planning; doubters could no longer blame some unforeseeable natural disaster. He frowned. He had been correct, he told himself, but dancing on the table was not an appropriate response.

A long discussion ensued, but the team made no new decisions. Adam expected this, since all members had already favored the starvation scenario. He knew that, at this point, the team itself could only talk about it.

✳   ✳   ✳

Adam sat by the wooden table after the meeting had adjourned and the others had left. The government officials, he thought, must now accept at least part of his explanation of the crisis. They could no longer claim it was just a theory. He had been correct all along, even twenty-four years earlier when he had had only his vague misgivings at the time he joined the team.

He recalled a question he had asked back then: *How are we feeding them all?* Now he knew the answer. *We're not.*

There had been short-term reprieves. Advances in technology had handled particular symptoms of overcrowding, he thought, but civilization had relied primarily on voluntary growth control. Earth's population had continued to grow.

Voluntary control measures could never be enough; human nature was not so adaptable. With Earth's human population at twenty-five billion, he told himself, only involuntary methods would work in the long term.

Earth, he thought, did not have much time left. Even if other problems of overpopulation were solved, the increased energy usage itself would eventually lead to a heat catastrophe from which Earth's biosphere could not survive. Energy was never used up. However it was utilized, energy always turned to heat in the end; the immutable law of entropy could not be denied. In this way or another way, he told himself, nature would impose a more expedient solution to the human overpopulation problem. He grimaced. *Nature is doing just that on faraway Earth-Twin.*

The eighth hypersignal, he thought, had just added a dose of reality to his earlier notions. He got up from his chair and proceeded to his office. He sat down, contacted Nola by v-v and told her about the signal. He then got up, straightened his tunic, left his office and headed for Administrator King's office.

*   *   *

Later that day Adam sat with Nola in their eat-in kitchen. He lifted his glass of before-dinner wine, took a drink, looked at her and said, "I almost told you a story, a few years ago when we were riding bicycles in the park just after Bill died. I'd like to tell you that story now. It's about my father."

"I remember that," Nola said. "I've been waiting." She took a sip of wine, and then put her glass down on the table.

"We saw that young father teaching his little boy to ride," Adam said. "My father taught me to ride a two-wheeler when I was about the same age as that boy." He took a deep breath. "I lost him only a few years later, when I was fifteen. He was killed in an accidental explosion at the virtual mass drive research facility, when they were working on ways to increase the power. I've always distrusted technology after that."

Adam picked up his glass and took another drink. He looked into Nola's brown eyes. She wanted him to say more, he thought. *What would I do without her?* How many times, recently, had he wondered about that? He reached across the table and took her hands in his.

"I think about him a lot," he said. "We had so many good times together when I was a child. You and I took that ride just after Bill died. I tried to talk about it then, since Bill had become almost a substitute for my father—with his enthusiasm and all that. But I just couldn't get it out."

He squeezed Nola's hands and added, "I've never mentioned any of this to anyone."

Nola smiled.

"Senator John Bitterman headed the committee that investigated the accident," Adam said, "when he was just a first term senator. They messed up the whole thing, and I never did find out what really happened." He let go of Nola's hands and took another sip of wine. "I sent a letter of complaint to the committee," he said, "and the same letter to the news media. It was a scathing letter, and the media made it public."

He drank more wine. "I guess it was a pretty good letter," he said. "The media people invited me, then barely sixteen years old, to debate Bitterman on earth comm. I did. I was so excited. And so *naive*." He felt his heartbeat accelerate as he recalled the incident. "He tore me apart in front of the whole world. I was no match for him. I've been wary of politicians ever since."

Nola looked at him. "So that's why—"

Adam interrupted. "It was at a bad time in my life. Instead of investigating, he made a public fool out of me. I guess I've always hated him for that."

"I'm glad you're telling me about it," Nola said. She took a sip of wine.

"You've never pushed me," Adam said, "with questions about my father."

Nola smiled. "I knew you'd tell me when you were ready."

"And I'll tell you more later," Adam said. "We'll talk about him again." Adam took Nola's hands in his again, and they sat quietly for a moment.

Adam broke the silence. "This has gone far enough," he said. "The PANS debacle. I have the proof now. I'm going to speak to the government."

Nola looked at him. "Shouldn't Rob do that?"

"I talked to him after today's meeting," Adam said, "when I was debating it with myself. He said 'go ahead.' He even volunteered to go with me." He smiled. "But it's about time I faced this *myself*."

Chapter 26

The People

In the morning, two weeks after receipt of the modified eighth signal, Adam stood in front of the eleven PANS oversight committee members in their meeting chamber. He delivered a well-rehearsed explanation of planetary differences and distances. He described how Earth could not help Earth-Twin. He asked the committee to abandon the entire plan.

He sat down by the rectangular table, glanced at each of the seated senators, and then settled on Bitterman.

"That's all well and good," Bitterman said.

Adam noticed that, as in earlier encounters, the man did not look him in the eye.

"You scientists claim that other planets are formed by the same processes that formed Earth," Bitterman said. He nodded. "Shouldn't we be able to inhabit them the same? Could the Earth-Twin unpleasantness be just the exception that proves the rule?"

Adam gasped. *What a stupid comment!* Bitterman, he thought, hadn't listened to a word he had said. Or hadn't understood? He looked at the faces of the other senators. All except one smiled or nodded at Bitterman.

Adam looked at Senator James Warren when the man spoke. "John, we should at least talk over Dr. Hampton's concerns," Warren said to Bitterman. "I don't want to abandon the plan any more than you do, but in the light of this tragedy we must consider it."

Adam looked back at Bitterman, who glowered when he said to Warren, "Yes, Jim, let's do that."

Bitterman was a fat pig, Adam told himself. The man had been cordial at the meeting, but he was a fat pig just the same.

Modern medical science offered many ways to control one's weight, Adam thought, but all required will power. A few hundred years ago weight control had been difficult for many, even those with the will. Now control was easy for those who had the will, the perseverance. He determined that he himself would age more gracefully.

He listened and drank coffee while the committee discussed his ideas. Warren, a slim white haired man who had been on the committee since its beginning, appeared to understand. The rest of the committee, Adam thought, understood not at all.

Adam tried to interrupt a few times to explain some point. They mostly ignored him, he thought, although Warren seemed to go out of his way to be friendly. He wondered about Warren, and then shrugged it off. Not all politicians were like Bitterman.

At the end of the session, Adam found no counter argument when told that the committee members must spend a few weeks discussing his ideas among themselves in more detail. Bitterman made no commitments; he simply adjourned the meeting.

Adam thanked the committee for its time, left the chamber and walked out of the government building into the late morning sunshine. Bitterman had done it again, he told himself. The perfect politician had finessed him just like he had thirty-three years earlier.

This morning Bitterman had not been as insulting as he had been at that earlier encounter, Adam thought. *That's probably because this time he dealt with a man instead of a boy.*

Adam had another consolation. He had not looked the fool in front of the whole world; this meeting had not been on earth comm.

He shook his head. Now he could only wait. He decided to keep a low profile and hope for the best. He turned down the street and headed for his office.

*   *   *

Adam waited. A few weeks stretched into a few months, and he was not surprised when the oversight committee finally told the PANS team to wait for the next hypersignal for more information. Bitterman passed this directive only to Rob King. Adam received a preliminary voice-visual from Senator Warren, so he knew about it before King's announcement at a hastily scheduled PANS team meeting.

In the evening after the meeting, he sat at home with Nola at the dinner table and poured a cup of coffee while she mixed chamomile tea. "They hadn't understood a word of it," he said.

"Maybe that's too much to ask," Nola said.

Adam picked up his cup. "I didn't expect much from Bitterman," he said, "but I guess I didn't get through to the others, either. I told you about Jim Warren. I like him, but he doesn't support me on this, not on total cancellation." He sipped his coffee to test for temperature, and then took a big drink. "So they want to see the next signal," he said. "I think that's just a way to keep me off their backs for a while."

Nola nodded. She sipped some tea.

"Rob says that many of our scientists don't think that it's the gravity," Adam said. "They believe that the small-scale experimental results can be extrapolated." He shook his head. "Others—including Rob—tried to get the resources for a real test. The committee said it'd cost too much and take too long."

"It's such a nice night," Nola said. "Let's go out on the balcony."

Adam smiled. He and Nola got up, walked outside and stood by the railing.

"It's getting warmer out here," Nola said.

"Sounds like everyone else is outside, too," Adam said. He gazed at a random scattering of stars in the southwestern sky. Tau Ceti, he knew, rose above Earth City's horizon only during daylight hours in the spring. "I told you about my friends who volunteered. You remember. Pete. Linda. And Jenny."

"Yes, I remember."

"I got this strange feeling after we received that altered eighth signal," Adam said. "It was as if Pete had something to do with it, as if his 'signature' was on it." He hesitated, and then added, "I think that was just a flashback of my last in-person conversation with him. I said 'keep in touch.' Before I caught myself. He answered something like 'you never know.'"

He felt Nola take his hand in hers. She always listened, he thought, even when he talked nonsense. "Before Pete volunteered, I offered him a job here on the university teams," he said. "He was a talented researcher, and we could've used him. He said that he would instead be my 'Earth-Twin connection.' I know it's quite a stretch of my imagination, but I thought about all those things when we finally got that eighth signal." He looked at her.

Nola smiled. "Maybe that's not such a stretch, dear."

Adam returned Nola's smile. "Maybe. We'll see what he does with the next signal."

*   *   *

Like the eighth hypersignal, the ninth arrived a week late. Adam smiled when King announced the words "high gravity" at the PANS team meeting. He beamed when King congratulated him for his "educated guess" and the team followed with a round of applause.

The team discussed at length the meaning of the signal. Then, with some apologies to Adam, most team members voted against recommending that the plan be cancelled. Instead they would simply pass the new information to the oversight committee.

Two weeks later Adam stood in front of the senate committee and presented his arguments all over again. He then sat down, looked at Bitterman and waited for a response.

"No more will be sent to Earth-Twin," Bitterman said. "This committee decided yesterday that the indefinite suspension will be made permanent."

Adam smiled briefly. He picked up his coffee cup, took a sip and anticipated another discussion of his ideas.

"The plan will now concentrate on Earth-Mate," Bitterman added. "Since the problem has been isolated to Earth-Twin, it need not hinder the rest of the PANS plan."

Adam grimaced. He put his nearly full cup down on the table, and ignored the few drops of coffee he had spilled. Bitterman had planned it that way all along, he told himself. He stared across the table at Bitterman and imagined a smirk on the man's fat face, but he could not think of anything to say. The fat man had never looked him in the eye before, but this time their stares met. Bitterman, he thought, shook in his effort to hold that stare.

Adam started when Senator Warren broke the silence. "Relax, John," Warren said to Bitterman. "I haven't seen you so tense since you threatened to fire those engineers thirty-five years ago."

Thirty-five years ago? Adam thought. *Fire engineers?* He kept his gaze on Bitterman. The fat man turned away.

"I don't remember anything like that," Bitterman mumbled.

So Bitterman had pressured some engineers, Adam thought, thirty-five years ago. *What engineers? About what?* He stiffened in his chair.

"Come on, John," Warren said. "You know you pushed that big-engine vm project too hard."

"You fat pig!" Adam screamed. He jumped out of the chair and lunged across the table. Glasses, cups, water and coffee scattered in all directions.

Bitterman jerked backward in his chair, toppled over and flopped onto the floor. A glass of water hit him square in the face.

"You murdered him, you son of a bitch!" Adam heard himself yell. His hands might just about fit around that fat neck, he thought. He stretched toward Bitterman, but he couldn't move. He needed just a meter or so, but he couldn't get closer. He heard a whisper in his ear. "Calm down, Adam," Warren said softly. "He's not worth it."

Adam now knew why he couldn't move. Warren held his right shoulder and another senator his left. He was draped across the table and two other senators were on his back. He stretched his hands toward Bitterman again, and then gave it up. Warren was right. He had better get control.

Bitterman stumbled to his feet, and Adam remembered an old expression he hadn't heard since childhood. The fat man looked like a drowned rat.

"You'll be locked up for that," Bitterman mumbled.

Adam felt Warren let his shoulder go, and saw him look at the other senators. "Joe Hampton was the engineer who was killed when the big-engine prototype exploded," Warren said. Warren turned toward Bitterman, who was wiping his face with a handkerchief. "He didn't lay a hand on you, John. I'm sure everyone here will testify to that."

Adam saw Warren look at him, and then nod to the three senators who still held him down. He relaxed when they set him free.

"I'm still in charge here," Bitterman said as Adam got off the table. "The plan will continue. This meeting is over."

Adam looked at Warren. The man didn't say anything, but his expression read: "Sorry, you're on your own on that one."

Adam straightened his tunic, and noticed that the front dripped with coffee. He looked at the table. A pool of coffee, apparently from his own cup, covered the near side.

*   *   *

Adam sat at his desk and tried to drink some coffee. It had happened more than an hour ago, but his hands still shook. He put the cup down. For the first time in his life he had lost control. Would he have strangled the fat man? It would be better, he thought, if he did *not* ask himself *that* question.

He looked down at his coffee-stained tunic. *That* stain, he told himself, could be removed.

He had always believed that his father had been killed in some routine engineering experiment. Now he knew that it had been an early stage of the PANS plan, ten years before the government officially established the PANS team and seven years before the explorers returned to Earth. He had known of earlier projects, but not that far back.

It had also been an early part, he thought, of ambitious John Bitterman's quest for a legacy. He had been so naive when he had debated the man on earth comm. He complained then about the committee's incompetent investigation, but instead it had been that committee's chairman's cover-up of his own "mistake."

The cover-up was complete, he thought. Nothing appeared in the PANS records; he had thoroughly researched them nearly two years ago. *Nothing? No, two words.* "Earlier setback." He had spent the better part of three weeks, back then, trying to figure that out.

He tried again to pick up his cup with without spilling coffee on his desk. His hand still shook some, but he managed a sip.

He thought of the real meaning of today's discovery, and put the cup down again. His own father had been the first victim of the PANS debacle.

A beep from his terminal startled him. Senator Warren's face appeared above. "Got a minute, Adam?"

"Yes, I guess so," Adam said.

"I talked John out of filing charges," Warren said. "He knows that a trial, even on trivial charges, would make the whole story public."

The perfect politician wouldn't want that, Adam thought. "Thanks, Jim," he said. "I feel kind of ashamed of myself."

Warren smiled. "If it's any consolation, I've often felt like throttling him myself," he said. "Unfortunately, at least from your point of view, the plan must go on. We'll send Rob some new directives in the next few weeks."

Adam grimaced.

"By the way," Warren said, "I knew your father. He was a good friend."

Warren's face faded, and Adam leaned back in his chair. Warren, he thought, had served alongside Bitterman for many years and had worked up a strong dislike for the man. Warren, he told himself, must have grown very weary of that decades-long cover-up of the death of a friend.

What about Bill Avery? Avery must have known the whole story, Adam thought. He recalled how he had wondered about his being chosen for the PANS team from among many better-qualified applicants. Back then he had grudgingly accepted Avery's explanation about a "devil's advocate," but his old boss had almost always shrugged him off when he tried to play that role. He wondered if Avery had felt duty-bound to persuade the original team to hire him. Avery had probably not been at fault in the engineering rush that caused the accident, he thought, not like Bitterman. Perhaps the head of PANS had simply decided to "help" the surviving son. Avery had been a good friend, and the "father figure" in Adam's adult life, for nearly two decades.

What did his mother know? Back then, he thought, probably nothing. The cover-up was complete. Now she was Brenda Avery's best friend; she might know more. He smiled briefly, and looked forward to a long talk.

His hands had stopped shaking, so he picked up his cup and took a big drink of lukewarm coffee.

He thought about Earth-Mate. Things had happened so fast at the meeting that he had not had time then to consider that new target for mass colonization. An exploration team was on its way back to Earth, and Earth had already received much data by radio.

Earth-Mate was nearly twice as far away as Earth-Twin. *This madness*, he thought, *must be stopped.*

What was he to do now? How could he persuade the government to abandon the plan? How could he "topple" Bitterman without strangling the man?

He thought about the senator's fat face. All of modern medical science's weight control miracles required will power; he had thought about that before. *Yes, that's the key.* Will power and perseverance, he told himself, are part of the same character trait. The fat man was vulnerable; he could be forced to quit first. Adam must persevere.

He needed a strategy, but first he needed some rest. He got up from his desk, straightened his stained tunic and headed for home.

*   *   *

In the evening Adam sat with Nola on their living room couch while the autoprep prepared dinner. He told her of the day's events and concluded, "I've calmed down, but I'm still ashamed of myself."

Nola leaned over and kissed him on the cheek. "After what you just told me," she said, "I'd be disappointed if you hadn't lost control."

Adam nodded.

"About the rest of the meeting—apparently the committee was encouraged by the latest signal," he said. "They concluded that it was only an Earth-Twin problem." He hesitated, and then added, "But I think they made up their minds a year ago. The signal just made it easier."

"Sounds like it," Nola said.

"At last year's meeting they told me that the public would never be able to understand my explanation," he said. "The politicians think that people are dumb."

"Otherwise how could they get elected?" Nola smiled.

Adam chuckled, and then thought about the power of the voters. What better tribute could he give to his father than to beat Bitterman at the man's own game? His strategy would be politics. He looked at Nola. "We have to take the explanation to the public. People aren't dumb. We can and *must* make enough of them understand."

Then he thought about what he had just proposed. He thought about his public debate with Bitterman when he was sixteen years old. He grimaced.

He hesitated a moment and considered the two altered census signals. Those few words revealed that he had been correct all along, about everything, from the very beginning. He knew he was correct, but the officials weren't going to let go while they could still claim to be "doing something about the problem." It wasn't just Bitterman's committee, he thought; it was the whole Earth Government.

He looked into Nola's brown eyes. "The Earth-Twin tragedy created a climate for some real action right here on Earth," he said. "We can't let it slip by."

Nola nodded. "Yes, humanity is paying a terrible price for that opportunity."

"We can eat later," Adam said. "Let's go in the study right now and figure out how to handle it."

Adam and Nola got up and walked into the study. When they reached the desk, Adam said, "You and I'll set up an earth comm. We could afford to bide our time a little when the plan was on hold. But not now."

"Great! I like earth communications." Nola put her arms around Adam's neck and kissed him on the cheek.

At first her behavior puzzled him, but then he recalled the first time he met her. He sat down with her and hashed out a plan.

*   *   *

Adam and Nola worked on their plan for several weeks, but were unable to set up a comm. An earth comm could not be arranged by simply signing on to the supernet. The procedure required various authorizations; an agreement with one of the several commercial comm agencies was the most efficient method. Adam found that, although the government officials didn't control the agencies, they could exert a certain pressure.

*   *   *

About a month after he had decided to talk to the world, Adam sat at his desk in the afternoon and wondered what to do next. The government had announced the Earth-Mate colonization plan to the public a week ago, and the PANS team had begun preparations just that morning.

He heard his terminal beep, and King's face appeared. "Could you come to my office, Adam?" King asked.

Adam rode the jet lift to the top floor. When he entered the office, King pointed to a chair. "I have bad news," King said.

Adam sat down.

"I tried to talk the oversight committee out of it," King said, "and everyone on the team is also against it. But I must remove you from the team."

That fat pig! Adam thought. He pictured a smirk on Bitterman's face. He stood up. "So the government's kicking me out? Who was it that passed the directive on to you?"

"Committee Chair Bitterman," King said.

"Damn!" Adam spotted King's cleanup robot on the floor and wondered if he could kick the little silver and gray being through the window. He looked at King, and then decided he had better calm down. He must not lose control again, he told himself, and certainly not in Rob King's office. It wasn't King's fault.

He sat down again. "His job, I guess," he said.

"I believe they are afraid you will discourage volunteers," King said. He hesitated, and then added, "I also talked to Jim Warren. His was the only dissenting vote."

"I just want to get the voters to demand action," Adam said. "But—yes! I want to discourage volunteers." He nodded. "I have to stop this madness."

"Take it easy, Adam," King said. He smiled and pointed to the decanter on his desk. "Coffee?"

Adam picked up an empty cup and poured a half-cup of coffee. "It's all right, Rob," he said. "I won't do anything dumb." He looked at King. "Please don't feel bad about what you have to do," he said. "I know it isn't what you want."

King pointed to a document on his desk. "I have arranged for you to take a research post at the University," he said, "so that you will take some part in the work. I hope that you will accept this position." He added, "In spite of the government, we need you. We want you. The plan will continue, but, because of your theories, we believe that we will just run into more problems."

Adam looked at King. "We?" he asked. "Most of the team doesn't support me."

"Not officially," King said.

Adam stood up. "What do you mean, Rob? Only Hugh and two others."

"Everyone, Adam," King said. "It was a struggle for some of us. Old beliefs and old loyalties do not die easily. Most of us have nurtured the plan since its birth, so to speak."

"I don't understand." Adam looked at his half-full coffee cup on King's desk. He picked it up and took a drink while he stood in front of the desk.

"They are afraid that if they agree with you publicly," King said, "the government will disband the whole team. Then commission a new PANS team—carefully chosen." He added, "We are treading some very shaky ground."

So they know Bitterman almost as well as I do, Adam thought. He also thought about Senator Warren. Warren wouldn't support such a move, he told himself, but he was only one man. Although Warren could stand up to Bitterman, he didn't have as much power. He looked at King. "You mean they've been on my side all along?"

"Some more recently." King smiled. "Most for a long time."

Adam sat down again. "Why didn't they tell me that?" he asked.

King looked at him. "Did you ask anyone? Outside official meetings?"

"No, I guess I didn't." Adam chuckled at himself. He could have saved himself much anxiety. He glanced at the document on King's desk, and then picked it up. "What part will I play?" he asked. "At the university."

"The principal difference will be that you will no longer be able to vote," King said, "on the major decisions."

"I'll accept." Adam looked at King and smiled.

"Thanks, Adam," King said. "You made it easier for me. Feel free to call on me at any time. I will try to get you back on the team, but that could take a while."

"I'll do my best in the new job," Adam said, "but I intend to continue to try to talk to the people."

"People all over the solar system know that you alone correctly predicted both altered signals," King said. "You are in a unique position. You have the ear of the public."

The ear of the public? Adam asked himself. *Yes.* A few years back he had felt he needed to find the "exact" cause. Now he knew why. "And I'd better take advantage of that," he said, both to King and to himself. He drank the remaining coffee in his cup, got up and put the cup in King's *autoclean.*

"Good Luck, Adam," King said. "We are all counting on you."

"Thanks, Rob." Adam turned toward the door. "And thank you, Pete," he whispered as he exited King's office.

*   *   *

Adam and Nola spent nearly two months setting up a private earth communication system. At considerable personal expense, the two established a temporary agency. They received anonymous monetary donations, and Adam observed that the number of individual donations equaled the number of members who remained on the PANS team.

Bureaucratic hassles complicated the effort.

Senator Warren, late in the process, told him that Bitterman had tried to intervene in the beginning. The rest of the committee and other officials, Warren related, had not supported such interference with an individual right.

Eventually Adam spoke worldwide. In his evening earth comm, he explained why he believed that the PANS plan cannot work and must be abandoned. He emphasized that the conclusion would be the same even if a planetary difference other than gravity had been the cause of the Earth-Twin disaster.

He stood in front of the supernet crew and asked his worldwide audience to communicate with the decision makers. "If you can accept what I'm telling you, please make sure that the political leaders know about it. Tell them you'll use your voting power. If we're together on this, we can force them to act our way. Remember, *they* work for *us.*

Politicians often forget that." He thought of Bitterman, but did not mention the name.

Adam carefully explained that colonization of other planets was not itself the problem. If Earth had sent only a few million, he emphasized, the colonization of Earth-Twin could now be mankind's most successful endeavor as well as its most ambitious; celebration would have replaced grief. "I just hope to convince you," he added, "that we can't use space technology to solve a population problem that can only be solved right here on Earth.

"We all know that many of the advancements of the last few hundred years have been fortuitous. Even our attempt to migrate to the stars has depended on very lucky scientific breakthroughs like," he said without flinching, "virtual mass drive."

He concluded, "But now our leaders must make the tough decisions. They must impose an effective control. We can all individually affect population growth, of course. But to be effective in the long run, control must be the official policy of all humankind. It must become *Earth law*.

"We all know what happened on Earth-Twin. In a few years radio should tell us a lot more, but we can't wait. We can't let this happen again!"

✶   ✶   ✶

The next morning Adam, at home with Nola, tried to relax. "I wonder how well I got through to the people," he said as the two sat on the living room couch after breakfast. "I tried my best and I felt like I did a good job, but I don't know if I was convincing enough."

"I heard everything, dear." Nola smiled. "Why, you could've convinced me."

"Darling, you were my only live audience," Adam said, "other than the net crew. With a larger one, I could've—" A "beep" from the study interrupted him.

Adam got up, entered the study and waved his hand in front of the terminal.

Bright red letters in the space above the terminal told him that he had a message overload of ten million. He waved his hand again and the number started to grow—much faster than he could follow. He thought he saw ten million one hundred thousand flash by. He called Nola, and the two read a number of the messages. He had asked people to communicate directly with their elected officials, he thought, but apparently many also wanted to show him their support personally.

The next day Adam and Nola asked the entire PANS team and Nola's research group to help read the messages. All worked long days for a week, but could examine only a fraction. The messages came in faster than Adam and the others could possibly handle. The overwhelming majority of those read expressed support for him and included a promise to send a demanding message to the appropriate government officials.

*   *   *

Adam stood with Nola on their balcony at midnight. He looked at the stars and thought about the hectic week just past. They had saved all the messages, but exhaustion had forced the group to stop reading. He smiled. *I may just beat the fat man,* he told himself.

He looked at Nola. He noticed that she shivered a little, and put his arm around her. "It looks like we may be making some progress here," he said, "but what's happening over there? We haven't had a population count since the seventh." He felt her take his hand in hers, and saw her turn toward the western sky.

He looked in that direction, toward where Tau Ceti was now just out of sight below the horizon. "So far away," he whispered.

Chapter 27

Marigolds

Pete glanced back over his shoulder while he climbed the big hill near Brownsville's District One. His daughter had insisted that she could catch up after going back for her windblown hat, but she trailed a hundred meters behind. She looked all right, he told himself, but she would have struggled if he had allowed her to carry the can like she had asked. He reached the clearing at the top of the hill, put the watering can down and looked around.

He saw the edge of District Ten, the most recent arrival, far to the southeast. The Council had argued long and hard, he recalled, about that ship's hypersignal, and had finally decided that a normal population count would give peace of mind to relatives and friends on Earth. Eleven would arrive in a few weeks. The Council was still undecided on that one.

He glanced over his shoulder again and noted that he would have to wait a little longer. His thoughts drifted back a few years.

The shore fish had become scarce after only five months, but that had been long enough for the farms. The official records showed no starvation deaths in more than three Pangaean years. Such records might be just a little misleading, he thought briefly; communications with a few of the most remote areas remained poor.

Each new arrival of two million from Earth revived old fears, but so far the expanding farms had kept up with known demand. *How long will the ships keep coming? No one knows.* Until they stopped, he would continue his search for new native crops. Later he could begin his experiments with Earth crops. Adam and the rest of Earth, he thought, must believe that someone in Pangaea had already completed those gravity tests.

He looked to the west. More trees grew there now; his crews had transplanted several groves of fruit trees from more remote areas. One grove stretched almost to the hilly horizon.

He took a deep breath. The cheerful little flowers in the middle of the clearing, he thought, were more fragrant than similar varieties on Earth.

A few birds sang in the nearer trees.

He heard a small voice behind him. "Daddy! Jenny catch up."

He turned, looked down and smiled. "Daddy knew Jenny would," he said.

He watched his daughter turn away and look at the bed of small red, orange and yellow flowers a few meters away. She then looked at the watering can and pointed a tiny finger. "Water mary golds, daddy?" she asked.

"Yeah," he said. "That's Jenny's job now." He watched her pick up the can and carefully avoid wetting the sundial in the center while she watered the flowers.

"Someday, little one," Pete whispered, "your daddy will tell you the whole story." Someday she would be old enough to understand, he thought, and he would have to tell her. If luck held out, he told himself, she would never have to experience it firsthand.

When the ships stopped arriving, he thought, Linda and he could have the second child they wanted. The Council had put that into law a few years ago: one child per couple now, two after "cessation."

A certain number of newborns were necessary, councilmembers had claimed, to minimize future societal problems. This had been critical even while the starvation threat had remained; shipboard births could not be considered a dependable source. He agreed.

The Council had insisted that Earth would terminate the colonization after receiving the altered signals. That was surely correct, he told himself, but it meant new millions for a long time to come. That second child might not be possible.

He looked up at the cloudless sky, toward the orange sun high in the west, and felt the brisk wind on his face and neck. He then glanced down at his daughter. She was shaking the can, as if she wanted to make sure she used every drop of water.

He looked toward the orange sun again, and thought of Earth's yellow sun. *Earth has its problems, too.* He started to think about Adam and the hypersignals, but his thoughts were cut short.

"Daddy," his daughter said, "Jenny hungry. Go home now."

Chapter 28

Imperative

Adam leaned back in the chair and looked around at old familiar walls and a number of familiar, and some unfamiliar, faces. Nearly a year had passed since he last sat in this meeting room. The team meeting here today, he told himself, was not directly associated with the population administration; it just utilized parts of the building. He glanced down at the elliptical wooden table, picked up his coffee cup from its square pad and took a sip.

He shifted in his chair when he heard a commotion at the front, and watched team leader Hugh Bruce step up to the podium. Bruce glanced at the display on the viewing wall, and then turned to the seated group. "Welcome, members, to the twelfth weekly meeting of the planetary migration team," Bruce said. "Before we start, a few items." He smiled. "First, let's welcome our three distinguished visitors. Please hold your applause until they're all standing."

Adam watched Bruce turn toward Rob King. "Administrator Robert King," Bruce said. King stood up.

Bruce turned again. "The Secretary for Population Control—the officer responsible for overseeing implementations of the recent Earth Government imperative."

That's a mouthful, Adam thought. He smiled and got up.

"Most of you know him as Adam Hampton," Bruce added. He smiled.

"And the Coordinator for the new exotic-crop-environment research group at Earth University, Nola Hampton," Bruce continued. Nola, who had been sitting next to Adam, rose.

Applause filled the meeting room. When it subsided, Adam, Nola and King sat down.

Adam picked up his cup and took another sip of coffee.

"The other item," Bruce said, "you've seen displayed since you arrived this morning."

Adam glanced at the viewing wall, at the number that he had first viewed some ten minutes earlier. It read 11,928,447; thirty-centimeter-high numerals in bright orange stood out against the white background.

"As you know," Bruce said, "this is the tenth hypersignal from the old PANS plan. The administration received it earlier this morning. On time, of course."

More applause followed. When it died down, Adam watched Bruce glance at Nola, and then settle on him. "That's why I so rudely called you away from your work this morning," Bruce said. "Rob—and I— knew you'd want to be here for the first announcement of this encouraging news. The public will get it this afternoon."

Adam smiled and took another sip of coffee.

"Now let's start the meeting," Bruce said.

Adam took Nola's hand in his and squeezed it gently. He felt her squeeze back.

"We must finalize the initial population for Earth-Mate," Bruce said. "We've considered up to three or four million, but we may want to pare that down at first because of the distance."

Adam let go of Nola's hand and smiled at her. She smiled back.

"Let's look at a summary of our discussions of the last few meetings." Bruce brought up a visual, replacing the orange number.

Adam leaned back in his chair, and thought about that latest population count. The plaque, for the recently completed memorial sculpture just outside the building, could now be completed. The signal indicated that the number of dead reached just over eight million by the time the colonists wrested some control over their situation. The administration could use the old statistical predictions to get a closer approximation.

What about Jenny, Pete and Linda? Had they survived? Any of them? Had Pete really altered the eighth and ninth signals? Adam decided he didn't want to think about those questions right now.

He could only hope that the colonists' control was robust, that the arrival of the remaining ships would not upset the planet's new balance. Later hypersignals would tell that story.

He realized that the hypersignals, the eight population counts and the two modified signals, disclosed all that Earth knew about what had happened on Earth-Twin. The first radio was due in just over two years. Earlier details should then start to trickle in.

Someday he would know how they did it, he told himself, how the colonists triumphed. Now he could only speculate. *Was their solution complicated? Or simple, basic, fundamental?*

Earth's solution? Adam asked himself.

His first official act had been to boost worldwide production of SBE and several related compounds. The food factories had begun taking on additional help. King's administration was redirecting its efforts. The Earth Government was finally formulating new laws.

The new tax incentives and penalties law, he thought, while a boon to some and a burden to others, might just work well enough by itself. The government might not have to implement the well-publicized SBE contingency plan. He realized that he was speculating, probably unrealistically, but he allowed himself to hope.

He vaguely heard Bruce suggest two million as the initial Earth-Mate population and call for a discussion.

His thoughts drifted to Senior Senator John Bitterman, who had, more than six months ago, announced his retirement from public office. The fat man was still young enough for two or three more terms,

Adam thought, but unable to face the wrath of the voters. No one else, on the oversight committee or on the PANS team, had quit voluntarily. The government had later disbanded both groups.

He picked up his cup and took a drink.

Bitterman would have his legacy, Adam thought. The senator's untimely and lonely departure, and the ongoing government investigation of the early PANS planning, would write the number "eight million" into that legacy just as surely as the administration would write it on the memorial plaque. The real number, he told himself, would always be eight million and one.

He had publicized neither the senator's long-ago refusal to fund the gravity experiments nor the man's role in his father's death. Both would soon become public knowledge anyway, he told himself; he expected *this* investigation to be thorough.

On the positive side, Earth would avoid a near-term disaster. It could even be long-term, if the new political will endured. A precedent was being set.

Bruce's team was voting—by voice. Adam eavesdropped for a moment, heard the unanimous decision, and then returned to his thoughts.

He wondered what life would be like if something had been done, much earlier, about Earth's population. *What would Earth be like? Vast forests? Walks in the forest, without PIP? Wilderness? Wild animals?*

He had seen it via PIP. He had seen it on wall murals. He had seen it in the visos from Earth-Twin.

He glanced at the wall murals.

In the background he heard Bruce congratulate his team for its decision to limit Earth-Mate's initial population, sent from Earth, to two million.

He then looked at Nola, at the team members and at his own hands. If Earth's population had been limited to a number much smaller than twenty-five billion, he thought, only a fraction of the people on Earth would be here today. Would he be one of them? Would he be here? Would Nola?

He looked at the figures on the wall murals. *They*, he told himself, *would certainly be here.*

They had all died years before he was born. The farm elimination planners had called it an ecological side effect, and had been unable to save them from the countless trillions of dispossessed insects that lost their easy food supply.

The losses had begun slowly, he thought, and were first treated as isolated incidents. Only after a decade did scientists recognize the global nature of the problem and that only an unacceptable level of environmental poisoning could avoid total loss. A few years later only rotting hulks remained. The destruction was so complete that even heroic efforts by the genetic engineers had not been able to—and would never be able to—bring them back.

He thought of the "jungle" that Bill Avery had grown in his office. The architect of the farm elimination plan had surely needed that "elixir for his mind."

Trees. Living trees. Adam's father had explained such things.

THE END

About the Author

Gene Shiles is a scientist and professor, with many diverse interests. *Tribes of the Orange Sun* is his first work of fiction. He has a keen interest in Earth's natural environment, and the effects of the growing human population.